THE SITA'S FIRE TRILOGY: BOOK TWO

QUEEN OF THE ELEMENTS

AN ILLUSTRATED SERIES BASED ON THE RAMAYANA

VRINDA SHETH

ILLUSTRATED BY
ANNA JOHANSSON

FOREWORD BY
DR. ROBERT P. GOLDMAN

MANDALA
PUBLISHING

San Rafael, California

MANDALA
PUBLISHING

www.MandalaEarth.com

Find us on Facebook: www.facebook.com/MandalaEarth
Follow us on Twitter: @MandalaEarth

This book was made possible by a grant from Bhaktiland,
a non-profit supporting the expansion of quality bhakti art.
www.bhaktiland.com

Published by Mandala Publishing, San Rafael, California, in 2017. No part of this book
may be reproduced in any form without written permission from the publisher.

Library of Congress Cataloging-in-Publication Data available.

ISBN: 978-1-60887-660-0

Publisher: Raoul Goff
Co-publisher: Michael Madden
Art Director: Chrissy Kwasnik
Associate Publisher: Vanessa Lopez
Managing Editor: Alan Kaplan
Project Editor: Courtney Andersson
Production Editor: Rachel Anderson
Editorial Assistant: Tessa Murphy
Production Manager: Alix Nicholaeff

Book design by Mayapriya Long

ROOTS of PEACE   REPLANTED PAPER

Mandala Publishing, in association with Roots of Peace, will plant two trees for each tree used in the
manufacturing of this book. Roots of Peace is an internationally renowned humanitarian organization
dedicated to eradicating land mines worldwide and converting war-torn lands into productive farms and wildlife
habitats. Roots of Peace will plant two million fruit and nut trees in Afghanistan and provide
farmers there with the skills and support necessary for sustainable land use.

Manufactured in Hong Kong by Insight Editions

10 9 8 7 6 5 4 3 2 1

To the Princeton team of Sanskrit scholars who have translated Valmiki's *Ramayana* so beautifully—particularly Sheldon Pollock, whose careful deliberations made me once again see Rama as a hero.

To my daughter, Naimi Sharanya, who inspires me to be fearless.

Contents

Author's Note

I grew up with the Ramayana, though I was fonder of the Mahabharata, India's other famed epic. Things you grow up with tend to leave deep impressions, both positive and negative. This is true for me with this ancient story. I was in my late teens when my mother and I began the work of retelling the Ramayana, and now, more than ten years later (yes, publishing can take a lot of time!), my approach has evolved.

I discovered in my research that most people who know the Ramayana, including myself, often conflate several different version of the ancient tale. I have come to understand that the Ramayana represents a rich storytelling tradition; today there are more than two hundred versions, each variation tailored to its specific audience. All this was a total eye-opener for me (who was taught that there is only one authentic story!) and the beginning of forging a true relationship of my own with this ancient text.

First, I became increasingly aware of my influences: Where had I really learned "my version"? To my surprise, one of my biggest influences was devotional Bollywood films of the Ramayana; certain scenes played out in my mind as I'd seen them in any of the numerous Ramayana films I watched growing up. The images of these films took precedence over my own imagination. When I, for example, thought of Rama and Sita, a clear image of both appeared in my mind, a picture still taken directly from *Sita's Wedding / Seeta Kalyanam*, a 1976 Telugu movie starring a young Jaya Prada as Sita and Ravi Kumar as Rama. I came to realize that my imagination had been short-circuited and replaced by these movies. I was keen on reclaiming my own ability to imagine and see for myself. And to do this, I decided to immerse myself fully in Valmiki's Ramayana, considered by many scholars the ur-text, or the oldest existing version.

Second, I walked off an airplane and left my laptop behind, which contained the manuscript for this book, the second book of the Sita's Fire trilogy, which I'd recently finished. (Yes, Mom, I should've backed up my files.) I didn't have another copy and was devastated. Why did this happen? God, why did you do this to me? I cried. I had lost months and months of work. But then I suddenly knew why.

If I wanted to get this right, the attitude I had harbored in my heart was not going to work. If I really wanted to create something that I could stand by, I had to change my attitude toward Rama, who is the hero of the tale. You see, I'd been secretly holding a grudge against him. In my first draft, I avoided writing about Rama directly; I found it much easier to empathize with other personalities. In fact, I was downright suspicious of him. My main issue centered on Rama's treatment of his wife, the princess Sita, and I know I'm not alone in these thoughts. These toxic feelings colored my perception; I had already come to my conclusion. To me, he wasn't a trustworthy person. This judgment had thrown a monkey wrench into my ability to write anything inspiring or good about him.

Having lost my manuscript, I had an opportunity to approach Rama differently. And I did. Just the desire itself to understand Rama initiated a shift in my heart. I continued to think and pray hard about some of his actions that seemed incongruent not only with our modern social norms but also with the actions of a true hero. Not all of my questions have been resolved, but I'm choosing the mood of curiosity rather than judgment. I'm open to answers and fresh perspectives.

Since this is a book based on an existing story, my methodology has been to expand upon instances mentioned in Valmiki's text, often glossed over in a sentence or two. I have, however, taken many risks in this work by embellishing and creating narratives and events that are not found in Valmiki's text. I do maintain, however, that I've kept strictly within the realm of the plausible. Some may disagree, but this was my modus operandi. Take Manthara and Kaikeyi, for example, my villain and antihero from *Shadows of the Sun Dynasty*: What happened to these extraordinary women? Valmiki never says. They are not mentioned again. Like supporting actors in a performance, they play their small part and disappear. In such instances, I have taken the liberty to create endings and bring the arc of their storylines to completion. Every change has been made deliberately, with respect for the essence of each personality. If someone is interested in discerning what's in Valmiki's *Ramayana*, why not read a direct translation? Indeed, I highly recommend doing so; I came away from my immersion in Valmiki's text with a new admiration for Rama.

Finally, an astounding shift happened when I completed the entire trilogy. Only then did I discover who the central character really was for me. Certain powers Sita displays in *Sundara Kanda* (the fifth book of seven that compose the Ramayana) made me drastically reevaluate her character. In fact, I was staggered when I came face-to-face with my own unconscious assumption that this tale belonged to Rama, Lakshmana, Hanuman, or Dasharatha (in other words, the men). Yet that is how it's traditionally told, after all. Sita really does not get much stage time, to say nothing of the other female characters. I was stunned by the fact that I'd just assumed that Rama is the hero of the story, when really Sita is too! The chapters from Sita's point of view are evidence of this shift. They were my final additions to this book.

Foreword

The late poet, folklorist, and literary scholar A. K. Ramanujan noted with regard to those who grow up in India, that "no one ever hears the Mahabharata for the first time." The same can surely be said, and even more powerfully, about the Ramayana. Indian tradition has it that there are ten million Ramayanas, each one different for various reasons of region, language, and cosmic era. We must recall that even the oldest known version of the Rama story, the ancient monumental epic poem of the sage poet Valmiki, was not the first telling of the tale. The First Poet himself was told the story by the rishi Narada and then, with the divine inspiration of Lord Brahma, he rendered the story into a grand work of poetry and music.

The tale of Rama is universally regarded throughout South and Southeast Asia, not as a romance but as a history of real events that took place in a far distant past when the world was quite different from what it is today. But, then one might ask, how are we to account for the wide variety of versions in all the languages and cultures of the Hindu, Buddhist, Jain, and Islamic nations of the region, which span virtually all of southern Asia and extend into central and East Asia as well? Well, as noted above, one traditional Indian explanation for the multiplicity and variations of the tale is that the events of Rama's life recur over and over again with some differences throughout the cyclic eras of Hindu cosmology.

But perhaps the most convincing explanation was proposed by Professor Velcheru Narayana Rao, who noted that it is only fiction that remains the same from one edition to another, while events believed to be historical are reported differently by different observers and authors. This is what has been called the "Rashomon effect."

So, although tradition agrees that the tale of Rama is an episode of history, no two accounts of that history are the same. And so it has been from Valmiki's time down to our own, with the story rendered in every medium from poetry and prose to drama, dance, and modern TV and cinema, not to mention the innumerable painted, sculpted, and carved versions of the story that have dominated the visual cultures of Asia for millennia.

It is in this context and in this grand tradition that we now have before us the second volume of Vrinda Sheth's delightful and imaginative novelistic retelling of the immortal Ramakatha, exquisitely illustrated by Anna Johansson. In Vrinda's first volume, *Shadows of the Sun Dynasty*, she took us from the childhood of the epic hero through to the hatching of the intrigue to deprive him of his inauguration as king and send him into exile with his faithful wife, Sita, and devoted brother Lakshmana.

This second volume takes us through the banishment of Rama and his companions to the forest, through their life there up until the abduction of Sita, Rama's rage and despair, and the beginning of his search for his beloved. Like the first volume, the work is rich in psychological nuance and creative insights into the inner life of the epic characters, especially Sita. As in many renditions of the Ramayana, this tale includes creative variations on the received versions; for example, Vrinda has Lakshmana mutilate Shurpanakha, not in obedience to Rama's instructions but in self-defense. But her version does introduce an interesting insight into Lakshmana's disquiet over the teasing of the savage but pathetic creature.

Again in this second volume, the work is richly illustrated with Johansson's lovely, dramatic, and colorful illustrations. Especially noteworthy here are her charming renditions of natural scenes in the forest and the various fauna (and bloodthirsty monsters!) found there.

Once again, lovers of the Ramayana will find much to enjoy and also to debate in this lively, creative, and provocative retelling of the Rama story.

Dr. Robert P. Goldman
William and Catherine Magistretti Distinguished Professor of Sanskrit
The University of California at Berkeley
General Editor and Principal Translator of *The Rāmāyana of Vālmīki: An Epic of Ancient India*

Prologue by Someone

She feels the pain but cannot scream. Two of his twenty hands rest on her shoulders. His touch is light, almost tender. But Someone knows. If she moves even a little, his grip will tighten. His sharp nails will prick her skin like needles. Blood will well up, small drops, red like the rubies on the ceiling, the iris of the eye crafted onto the dome. High up, it looks down on Someone and the other consorts. At the top of the dome, the pupil of the eye opens to the sky. It represents his sight, from which nothing is hidden.

Someone has stopped hiding, for one cannot hide from the one who rules the elements. Sometimes a cloud is visible in the center of the eye, or a ray of sun; now it shows the stars in the dark night. Someone knows. She has stood under the eye at all hours, by his side. He sits on this throne here at the top of the ivory steps. On each of the thirty-two steps a maiden sits, gazing up at him as if hypnotized. They are his favorites, and Someone is foremost among them. She is exceptionally beautiful, she is told. This is why he took her, though she was just a short-lived human and a villager, having never stepped inside the indestructible capital in whose shadow her forgotten home had stood.

One of his hands holds her long hair, lifting it away from her back. The two hands on her shoulders hold her steady. With a fourth hand, he etches his name into her flesh, across her back. He needs no tools, for his nails are long and sharp. She has seen it done before, on other girls, but could not imagine this pain. Someone does not exist; there is only his nails piercing her flesh. She is only an *R*, then an *A*, then a *V* . . . the first three letters of his name. His names are many. He has lived longer than most. But his favorite is Ravana, the One Who Makes the Universe Wail.

She too has several names. She cannot recall the birth name she had before she became No One. Now she is Someone. Someone, who belongs to the king, the ruler of all that is. He controls the worlds from Lanka, the city made of pure gold. The golden towers of the palace are so high, they disappear into the clouds. She has seen this sight only twice, since she is kept inside. The first time she entered his quarters, she thought it was built for someone ten times his size. The eight pillars holding up the dome are each made of one hundred stacked elephants. Their bodies are marble, their eyes rubies, and their tusks authentic, taken from live elephants. She didn't know then that he can expand and grow at will and that he has destroyed many other palaces simply because they were too small to contain his greatness. Her home is cold, for gold is. The rest is marble and gems, even less warm; the palace so large it's empty, even with millions of residents. The marble gleams like a polished mirror. Every corner is decorated by a woman who herself is decorated meticulously, a detailed art piece, all for his pleasure. And Someone is part of the décor, earning many names of endearment. The grandeur of this gold, marble, and ruby kingdom is a small tribute to his vast glory.

It is an honor to be touched by him, to have one of his faces intent upon her. Those who say he has more than one face have never seen him. There is only one face at a time. He means to claim Someone completely. She will have his name written in every thought. He looks at Someone without blinking, holding her entranced. He is kind enough to spare her one pair of his eyes. He does this for her. She stands like a statue. Her tears do not dare flow. He begins to etch the next letter into her back.

A loud scream stops him.

Someone, who cannot move, feels a small jolt in her heart. His hands tighten on her shoulders. His eyes narrow. The hand around her hair tightens, jerking her head lightly back. His eyes leave her and he looks at the intruder, the screamer who dares scream at the One Who Makes the Universe Wail. Someone shivers while her eyes follow his. The consorts on the steps have stopped breathing. Standing on the thirty-second step, Someone sees only the outlines of the other women along the pillars and walls, small figures in the distance, as tiny and helpless as she is in this place of honor, her clothes stripped from her body.

The wine goblets in his hands smash against the ground, the shards shattering against her bare legs. Their king does not tolerate intrusions. Everyone in Lanka knows this. Every one of those three hundred and thirty-two women in the chamber is frozen. They will not awaken until he gives them a signal. His many arms claw through the air impatiently.

The next scream is louder, piercing and dissonant. Someone scrutinizes the intruder. She is the blood-drinker kind, with hair red as flames, like their king. Her face has been mutilated, and blood pours from her wounds.

"Sister?" he says.

Someone recognizes the screamer then: Shurpanakha, the long-lost sister. Her cruel eyes glow like embers. She stands on the white lotus, the centerpiece of the marble flooring, a place only his principal queen is allowed to stand. Golden tendrils spread out from the lotus, trailing up the elephant pillars all the way to the top of the dome, into the eye mosaic, like the spider web veins in a human eye. Shurpanakha flaunts her disregard for his rules by standing there, letting her blood drip onto the shiny, cold lotus. She is known for her schemes. Their king sent her away for this very reason, but now, without speaking, he opens his many arms to Shurpanakha, offering her solace in his embrace. Perhaps no being deserves to be mutilated like that.

Shurpanakha does not move. She has taken her place strategically. Someone understands now why only the principal queen may stand there. The golden veins spreading from the center of the lotus emanate from Shurpanakha's person, imbuing her hideous person with power. She opens her arms too and sticks out her face. She wants us to see the extent of the damage. Her face is flattened and piglike, with only two slits for a nose. Her skull has no ears. All three sites are bleeding and inflamed. She has done nothing to dress her wounds or heal them. Her eyes are angrier than Someone remembers.

Ravana whispers, as if to himself, "She wants revenge."

Only Someone hears him because she stands so close, as though one of his limbs. She often sees his heads speak in whispers to one another.

Shurpanakha speaks. "You sit here in Lanka like a fat pig!"

He never tolerates insults, but since she really is the piglike one, he sees the irony in her words. "Who has done this to you, sister?"

"You intoxicate yourself to stupidity," she answers, "while your enemies sharpen their weapons. See what they have done!"

Her flaming bronze hair is matted and caked with dirt. Her body is that of a hag, though blood-drinkers don't age as humans do. Shurpanakha looks like a monster now. She has returned to the right place; in Lanka she will be one among many. The consorts on the steps remain frozen; Someone sees only their chests moving with shallow breaths.

Shurpanakha speaks rapidly, almost incomprehensibly: "It was that brother! He did this! The brother of the other! Lakshmana. Rama. Those princes from Ayodhya."

"A short-lived human did this?" Several of his lips curve down. He is disappointed. He withdraws. Doesn't believe her.

Shurpanakha bursts into tears. Her whole face scrunches together. Her sobs are the only sound in the palace. Her voice echoes through the large chamber, bouncing off unyielding elephant tusks and walls that have no tolerance for any noise that he does not allow. Without emotion, the eye in the dome beholds Shurpanakha.

"Lakshmana, the brother, cut off my nose and ears, while Rama stood by watching with a cold heart. I will have their blood for this! I will suck it from their bones!"

Ravana's eyes turn to Someone. Terror runs down her spine. The carvings across her hip throb. But he isn't really seeing her. Someone has become No One again, his work on her back forgotten. She feels Ravana's thoughts become hers. He doesn't need to shield his thoughts from her, who is both nobody and his heart's beloved.

Someone no longer has thoughts of her own, so completely does his mind overpower her. He does not trust his sister. Ever since he killed her husband by accident, long ago, Shurpanakha has wanted revenge. He will never be fool enough to go near her traps. Is this one? Ravana wonders.

"You think Rama is just some ordinary short-lived human!" Shurpanakha shouts. "Do you really think a human could ever harm me? I underestimated him too. And his brother... But so did Khara and Dushana, your so-called mighty generals posted in Dandaka. They couldn't even avenge me!"

"Khara and Dushana?" His generals would not get embroiled in his sister's plots.

"Yes, they are dead," Shurpanakha says. "How do you not know this? You, who professes to know everything. You, who claims to control the world and all its elements. You really are nothing but a fat swine, happy in your tiny piece of muck."

Her nose starts bleeding forcefully. The blood seeps into her mouth. She seems not to notice. Ravana claps two hands together. Two maidservants rush forward with cloths to stop the blood flow. Shurpanakha flings both of them away, as if they themselves are the pieces of cloth.

She turns on her brother. "You pig! You misfit! You abomination! You coward!"

"Stop," he warns. "If you wish to keep my attention and your life, stop. Do not assume that our familial bond protects you."

Shurpanakha stops.

He softens. "Come, sit here with me. Hold this cloth to your nose. Tell me everything. Whoever has harmed you will be punished."

He does not believe his sister's report. While she has roamed the worlds at will, he has kept an eye on her. She has been sporting and playing her cruel games, displaying her usual recklessness for all life. Yet there is something different about her now. Something genuine that he cannot deny. Shurpanakha is frantic and hysterical, as expected of any other woman in the face of a crisis. And because of this, Ravana's heart responds, while his minds are repulsed.

This also, Someone knows. Though he has ten minds, he has only one heart. A guarded heart, certainly. A heart shriveled by too many immortal years. But Ravana's heart is not beyond yearning. It is not beyond responding to a woman's need. In this, Ravana's heart is no different than any other. That is why Someone stands by his side. That is why he needs her and all his kept women.

Shurpanakha remains standing. "Khara and Dushana are in the land of Yama," she insists. Drops of blood leaking from her nose splatter against the ivory marble. "They are dead. Their entire army is wiped out. I do *not* wish to sit. I want revenge! I tell you, Rama massacred every one of our fourteen thousand kin. Only I survive. I want you to stand."

Ravana rises slowly. Someone takes a step with him. Her hair is still in his hand.

"Liar," he says. "No king on Earth is a threat to me. If this Rama had gathered an army, I would know. There is no army. How can you claim that my men in Dandaka have been wiped out?"

"If you are so well informed, you knew Rama was in Dandaka. You knew he was exiled from Ayodhya."

Ravana is aware of it. Human politics matter as little to him as insect stool.

"That doesn't answer my question," he says.

"But it does." And now there is glee in her voice. "Rama alone killed our people. No one else. There was no army. Only him. He single-handedly slaughtered them, including the previously undefeated Khara and Dushana."

"One short-lived human cannot do this."

"I was on the sidelines of the battle *the entire time*. I thirsted for Rama's blood, for his flesh. I could smell it. But that moment never came. Don't you think I know what I saw?"

She stops her cries and stares at her brother. A sneaky look comes into her eyes. Ravana has become still. He is doing all sorts of things with his mind that Someone cannot fathom. He reaches out beyond the walls of the palace, searching for proof of Shurpanakha's tale. His energy fills the dome and he peers through the pupil of the eye. The starry night is obscured and in its place Someone sees nothing at all. He shakes several of his heads. Some of his heads whisper in unintelligible tongues.

A forgotten feeling rises in Ravana's heart. After living through thousands of cycles of the universe, he rarely comes across a thing he doesn't already know. How many girls has he branded before Someone?

She shrinks to less than No One, the excruciating wound on her back a speck of a speck of a speck on the universe's history of sacrifices. Though merely a flutter of surprise in his mind, she is hit by it like a tornado. She loses her footing. One of his hands catches her automatically. He has not forgotten her existence after all. Again, Someone's heart swells and she is safe in his. She places her feet steadily on the smooth surface, the chillness of the marble absorbing through the soles of her feet.

Ravana is titillated by Shurpanakha's report. Her tale is true. Khara and Dushana are gone. Their bodies are rotting near Panchavati. This was supposed to be an impossibility: his army destroyed by a single human man.

"There is more," Shurpanakha says. "A woman."

"I'm losing my patience." His voice is quiet, a whisper.

"I know you have many," she acknowledges. Her angry eyes sweep over Someone and then across the other women gathered in this cavernous chamber. To her, they are not individuals, just objects, like the marble elephant tusks: intact, holding the harem together. "I know you love to collect them. This one was special. I have never seen anything like her before. In fact, I tried to capture her for you. But the brothers intercepted me and, in the name of righteousness, mutilated me. I did this for you. And you just sit there, unmoved by my plea."

"Why would I care for a short-lived human woman?"

Without a word, Shurpanakha uses her skill as a *kama-rupini* and changes her form.

Someone gasps, and she feels something like devotion bloom in her heart. In place of

Ravana's mutilated and bleeding sister stands a woman who cannot be human. She is a goddess. The goddess gazes at Ravana with innocence and girlish sweetness. But her body is a woman's body, with lush curves and flawless skin. The goddess twirls around, letting Ravana see her from every angle. Ravana holds his breath, waiting to see her face once again. Someone's feelings are obliterated by the power of his concentration. He stares hungrily at the apparition.

The eye in the dome cannot stop staring at the goddess.

Ravana cannot turn away a single pair of his eyes. He has explored deep within the psyches of humans and demigods, but there is a depth in this woman that intrigues him. But then the divine woman smiles cruelly, and Ravana hisses, retracting himself completely from the momentary spell.

Shurpanakha stands before them again. She cannot hide how pleased she is with herself.

"Her name is Sita," Shurpanakha says. "She is the most beautiful woman I have ever seen, among the short-lived or immortal, I don't care."

Ravana stares at his sister. She has been gone so long he had almost forgotten her, even though he is not capable of forgetting anything; every word, deed, and vision of his life is imprinted in his psyche. No one has ever been able to understand how it feels to be Ravana. Maybe this woman will? It isn't just her flawless features. It is her delicate face, her eyes. Gentle, compassionate, and wild. If Shurpanakha can capture this sweetness in her imitation, Ravana knows the real woman will be a treasure, the kind of gem you stumble across once in a lifetime. And what a long lifetime it has been. Sita is a woman, Ravana can see, who gives her all to the one she loves. There is absolution in her eyes. A love that makes your soul immortal. Ravana wants this.

You will love me.

The command issues from all ten of his minds. Someone feels her insides heave. He commanded the same of her, and she succumbed. No one can deny Ravana what he wants. The stubborn ones are branded. And now he will find this woman and do the same to her. Soon Sita will stand in Someone's place, having his name written across her hips, an eternal wound.

Ravana whispers, "Sita will love me. On her own terms and by her own will. Sita will give me her love fiercely and completely."

Then suspicion rises again. He turns all his heads toward Shurpanakha.

"And what will *you* get out of this? You do nothing, my lovely sister, if not for your own gain."

"Oh, my sweet brother. I have learned this from you: Blood and murder are not the only forms of revenge. I do not long for Rama's death now. Not anymore. I long to see him suffer. I want him and his brother to be humiliated, to be torn from what they treasure. I saw the way Rama looks at Sita. He is the kind of weak-hearted man who cannot live without his wife. What kind of fool brings a fragile woman into the harsh jungle? He cannot live without her. Without his wife, Rama will wither away. He will be reduced to half a man. This is a fitting punishment for rejecting me."

Ravana nods. He agrees. "And an opportunity for you, sister. With Sita gone, you will return to Rama's side. You will turn his grief to your advantage, in a Sita-like form, perhaps."

"No. Rama is different. He sees me for what I am. I cannot take another form in his presence. Look at me. Will any man want me now? Rama is a prince, a godlike, strong man who shines like the sun. He would never choose an abomination like me. Like the true fool he is, he has bound up his heart and soul into this woman. He has vowed never to take any wife but Sita. So you see, my revenge is perfect."

Ravana smiles. He likes this revenge. It will last longer.

Shurpanakha speaks in a rush: "I have more. Those three—Rama, Sita, and Lakshmana— have gained a reputation among our kind. The brothers have been killing us off on the sly for more than ten human years. Marichi, our old friend, has managed to escape twice from Rama. Recall that he was a prisoner in Ayodhya for some time. Now a fit of terror overcomes him when you say Rama's name. He has given up our ways. He drinks blood no longer. He has become an ascetic. He knows Rama and Sita well. Get Marichi on your side. Persuade him to work with you. He is the best shape-shifter we know. Better than me. He will know what to do."

"How do I know that the Sita you showed me is real, and not an invention of yours?"

"Brother, I stole the image of her and locked it firmly into my mind. She is a gem of gems. I may have many flaws, but few have my skills as a *kama-rupini*."

This is true, Someone feels Ravana muse. Among females, she is the best. Better than most males too. Only Marichi is more skilled. Another truth from her mouth.

Someone feels his hunger and desire arise like never before. He does not want to ask; he knows it's an illusion. But he can't stop himself.

"Show me again," he commands.

The grimace on Shurpanakha's face is triumphant. She knows she has won. She will get her revenge. Ravana will steal this woman, Sita, away. Rama will rot in the hell of his love. Someone will fall into the merciless shadows as Ravana turns his attention to Sita. Someone feels intense relief, jealousy, and pity. She prays that Sita will be stronger. But she knows that not a single woman has ever stood against Ravana's will and lived.

Ravana is drinking in the view of this woman, this goddess in human form. She remains in the center of the white lotus. Her golden garment awakens the gold in the room, and the chamber glows. He knows it is his manipulative sister standing there, yet the vision does not absorb just one of his minds, but all ten. He sits down, spellbound and captivated by this human called Sita.

You will be mine. Forever.

The strangest thing happens to Someone. She too forgets that it is Shurpanakha. She sees before her the true goddess. Sita smiles at Someone.

Tears erupt from Someone's soul. Shurpanakha has brought them the greatest gift.

Sita is the one Someone has been praying to. Prayers she says only when she is absolutely alone.

Ravana's spell is broken and he turns his furious attention to Someone.

The claws of his hands grow gigantic. The eye in the dome pierces her. The elephants charge at her with their tusks swinging. The golden tendrils of the lotus wrap around her, suffocating her breath. Even inanimate objects serve Ravana's will. She falls to the floor, stone cold. Someone's last thought goes to Sita, and then she dies. He claws Sita out of Someone. Nothing remains. Someone rises obediently from the floor, standing ready, wanting nothing more than the last few letters of his name claiming her flesh and soul.

There is only one king, one lover, one ruler, one lord, one man, one god.

CHAPTER 1

Sita and the Exile

Perhaps this saga began when Ravana abducted his first innocent woman. She was to be the first of thousands. Every one of those women could have been the beginning of this story. Even though I am one of the women he abducted—the last, in fact—the story started long before I was born. And yet, I see now that every choice I made brought me closer to Ravana's trap. However, in speaking of Ravana I have brought you too far toward the end. Forgive me. I couldn't help but think of Ravana, for if there were no Ravana, there would be no Rama, like there would be no death without birth first. A tale without Rama would be no tale at all. Even Rama's story has many beginnings. Every story can start in endless ways, one thing a catalyst for the next. And so I look back across history, searching for the moment that determined the future.

It might have begun with two swans trumpeting and a king who laughed out loud. Who could have guessed such an innocent act would send a queen into exile? Kaikeyi's mother, Queen Chaya, was banished, and Manthara, the malicious hunchback, took her place. This allowed Manthara to gain undue influence over Kaikeyi, the princess of Kekaya, from the beginning. Even so, the defining moment may have been when Kaikeyi, a trained warrior, skillfully escaped from the battlefield, saving Emperor Dasharatha's life. Filled with gratitude, my valiant father-in-law gave Kaikeyi two unconditional boons. A dangerous gift indeed, considering that Dasharatha was the emperor of the world. Looking back even further, the story might have started when Dasharatha's ancestor, King Anaranya, made a prophecy with his last breath that a child of his line would kill Ravana, the ten-headed king of the blood-drinkers. Every son of the Sun dynasty since Anaranya felt the burden of those words: Would he be the one to do the unimaginable and slay Ravana?

No man—king or commoner—could expect to match forces with the greatest villain ever known in the universe, a being who had quelled the gods and defeated Yama, the lord of death. Anaranya himself had died brutally, crushed under Ravana's feet. Again I speak of Ravana without meaning to. He was that kind of creature, someone who preoccupied the minds of the holy ones who have existed since the beginning of creation.

And he lived in the minds of small children fearing sleep, fearing the darkness. For many of the first years of my life, I knew him only in the way a child does, from the tales, as a monster with ten heads. If you had asked me when I was sixteen, about to be catapulted into the world, Ravana would not have existed in my story. Rama, on the other hand, being the thirty-seventh son in Anaranya's line, must have thought about Ravana from time to time. Every father in the Sun dynasty whispered the prophecy into his newborn son's ear; Ravana's name may well have been one of the first words Rama heard. Even so, Ravana did not come into our life until many years later, and so this saga does not yet include him. He claimed enough space later. You are not welcome here, Ravana, even though I thank you for inadvertently calling Rama into existence.

Before I take you further, I must tell you more about Rama. He is, without question, the heart of this story. When I look at Rama, I think that Brahma, the creator, must have taken his best mold for a human and then meditated a long time on how to perfect it. Once Brahma awoke from his trance, he spent hours perfecting his mold and only then did he create Rama. That is how beyond perfect Rama is, no matter what angle you look at him from. His skin is smooth and light green; he glows like the morning sun. His chest and shoulders are broad and defined, his waist slender. His eyes are large, dark, and incredibly kind. Though his manner is often reserved, a gentle smile lives on his lips, and I don't think anyone can be in his company without feeling supremely at ease. That is why so many want to be around him at all times. Even when Rama was just seventeen, the elders in Ayodhya sought his advice. They chose him to be their future king.

In our personal quarters, Rama and I always had many friends and talented artists whose art found new heights in Rama's presence. I had Rama to myself only the last few minutes of the day, when we closed our doors and sought our resting place. You might guess by now what my favorite time of each day was. Since the moment I met Rama, he has been my anchor.

And oh, that first moment. It is unforgettable. Even though so much has happened since then, I can never forget how my entire existence changed when Rama and I beheld each other. I was fifteen, and it was the eve of the contest for my hand. I was standing on one of the balconies looking out at my father's city, Mithila. And suddenly Rama was there, looking up at me. Though he was a handsome stranger and unknown to me, the name "Rama" appeared in my mind. It was true that the emperor's son, Prince Rama, was known far and wide as the world's best archer, even though he was only sixteen. My father had come back from Ayodhya, telling me that Rama's skin was the color of an emerald when you hold it up to the light. The one looking up at me from below carried a bow and he glowed like an emerald.

Another mystical thing that happened was this: I felt a small golden key appear in my hand—a message from my own destiny. I had always dreamed about standing outside a massive black gate, with no way of gaining entrance. Rama held the key to my destiny, and I was one step closer to opening the gate. It would be many, many years until I found the location to that portentous place. Until I did, I thought it was simply a persistent dream. Yet, the moment I saw Rama, I knew so many things. More than I can ever put into words. My heart was no longer mine. I swore it, then and there, if anyone but Rama won my hand in that contest, I would withhold my garland and my consent. I would live out my life alone.

Rama and I have one unusual thing in common: We were both born in supernatural ways. Rama's father, King Dasharatha, had three queens but no children and finally conducted the most complex fire ritual known to man. It required detailed preparation and took more than one year to complete, and even then, there was no guarantee. The fire came alive, bringing the fertility nectar. Only when Kausalya drank this nectar did she get pregnant with Rama. Kaikeyi gave birth to Bharata, and Sumitra birthed the twins, Lakshmana and Shatrugna. I, on the other hand, was born from the Earth. The Earth cracked open at my father's feet, and there I was. That's why he named me Sita, which means "furrow."

Rama and I have both done things we shouldn't have been able to do. I lifted Shiva's bow, not knowing that it was impossible to lift. Rama became the undefeated archer of the realm at seven, even though he was not yet wielding a grown man's bow. Later, Rama also lifted Shiva's bow, an heirloom in my family that was so large it required five hundred strong men to pull it into the arena. My father had decreed that only the man who could lift this bow would win my hand. People thought my father cruel or crazy, for no one had been known to lift the bow. Except for me. And only the few who witnessed it would believe it. I still remember the look in my father's eyes when he saw me standing there with the bow in my hand. I understood that I must not do such a thing again. Most people are frightened when they see displays of supernatural strength. My father feared that human society would never accept me if I was too far from the norm. How right he was.

My life as Rama's wife was full that first year and a half, before he was exiled. I was intent on being a perfect princess and wife. I wanted nothing more than Rama's approval. But I was one among many who thrived on Rama's attention. His father, his three mothers and three brothers, his endless stream of friends—all of them laid a strong claim on him. I rarely got Rama to myself.

So I must admit what dawned on me as Rama's exile became a certainty: I would have

Rama all to myself. A selfish thought, yet I could not stop it. Rama and I were going to the forest alone. Just the two of us, Sita and Rama—if only I could persuade him to bring me along. For Rama of course did not want to subject me, a tender princess, to the harsh life of an ascetic. When Rama came to bid me farewell, he meant to leave me in Ayodhya for the entire fourteen years of exile. I became enraged, the way only a sixteen-year-old can be. My overpowering anger frightened us both. I momentarily severed my connection to my body, and when I returned, Rama assented. A miracle, truly. Rama, you will come to see, is strong-willed in the best possible way. Once his mind is fixed, nothing can dissuade him. When Rama set his mind on accepting the exile, it was as though it had been his own plan all along.

And therefore I must convey the magnitude of my small personal victory, even though I became an accomplice in my own bitter destiny. This choice of mine would shatter me completely, in all ways. I had no means of knowing that then, and so the first day of the exile felt like a personal triumph. While all of Ayodhya fell to pieces, devastated by a dynastic struggle, I was strong and whole, secure at Rama's side. As Rama reached for my hand, ready to leave the palace behind, I felt jubilant. Our sweet future together, just the two of us, unfolded before me. I was not afraid of living in the forest, bereft of comforts. Nature had always been my close friend.

As a child, I never was a typical princess. Before I met Rama, my favorite place was the gardens of the palace. For the first years of my life, my mother, Sunayana, could not persuade me to sleep on a bed. I wanted nothing between me and the Earth. I would lie with my cheek pressed against her surface and gurgle childish words. I was never as happy or content as when I had dust and dirt smeared across my face and hands. Unusual sensations often came to me when I was outside. The wind would whisper into my ear, the water swirling up to greet my fingertips. The Earth spoke to me in a language only I could understand. The elders around me told me I had an active imagination, and I understood that it wasn't humanly possible to communicate with Earth's elements. But if you dare to forget that you are a human, you might surprise yourself. There is an eternal spark deep within all of us. I learned the ways of humans and indeed forgot my connection to my true mother, the Earth goddess, Bhumi.

Still, as I walked with Rama into his exile, I was not afraid. I was eager to be Rama's sole companion. My hands tingled and I felt fearless, though my heart fluttered in my chest.

My secret joy lasted only a few minutes. Lakshmana, Rama's ever-faithful brother, threw himself at Rama's feet. Ignoring me by Rama's side, he spoke hurriedly and fiercely, begging Rama to allow him to overthrow the king and to imprison Kaikeyi. He wished to send her into exile, or better yet, kill her for treason. Lakshmana wanted to behead Kaikeyi without delay. He would do it if Rama allowed it. He wanted Rama to lead a rebellion against Ayodhya and take it back by force.

It certainly was not against the warriors' rules to do so. Rama had recently quelled an uprising by an evil man, the king of Kashi. That had been a violent combat; Rama had returned covered in blood. Ayodhya had celebrated that victory for months. Rama truly had all of Ayodhya on his side.

But Rama said nothing in response to Lakshmana's tirade, simply shaking his head once. Lakshmana continued, insisting on his violent plan. Rama's hand in mine tightened ever so slightly. Lakshmana had never disagreed with Rama before. Until this moment, Lakshmana had seemed like Rama's impassioned shadow, someone with a strong temper but never stepping away from the path Rama walked. Now he was trying to pull Rama with him to lift their weapons and destroy their enemy. Only, the enemy this time was his own father and mother.

Finally, when even my ears started ringing, Rama said, "Stand with me or against me."

Lakshmana fell quiet and bowed at Rama's feet again. "With you," he said. "I'm coming with you."

That's when the future I had envisioned dissolved. Lakshmana was coming with us. He would follow Rama anywhere, at any cost. Rama accepted Lakshmana's plea far quicker than he had mine. I understand why. Lakshmana is a warrior. He wasn't a weak and apparently defenseless girl like I was. I know how rare it is for a woman to walk away from civilization, giving up all comforts. In comparison to Lakshmana, I suddenly realized what an obstacle I would be to Rama. Every time Lakshmana glanced at me I could see the dismay in his eyes; he did not want me there by Rama's side. He saw me only as an encumbrance. I became all the more eager to leave Ayodhya quickly, before Lakshmana could voice his objection to my presence. I hid my feelings carefully out of respect for the others who were not as lucky as I. All of Ayodhya was in mourning over their imminent loss of Rama, their beloved king-to-be.

The Ayodhyans came to realize how impossible it is to change Rama's mind. He is not impulsive like Lakshmana, his loyal brother. Rama is not swayed by his emotions; he deliberates carefully and never strays from his decision. Kaikeyi required of him to renounce his right to the throne and live as an ascetic far from civilization for fourteen years. She wanted Bharata, the son of her womb, to take Rama's place. Rama agreed without a moment's hesitation. His father's word is his law, and Kaikeyi was using the king's authority to execute her will. It was complicated. And it remains so. Even now, many hold a grudge against Kaikeyi, calling her evil. Some argue, as Lakshmana did, that Rama surrendered his will too quickly. He could have opposed the exile. He could have overthrown his father's rule. This is how it will always be: one event and endless ways to see it. I had an inkling of this, despite being a young princess sheltered from the complexities of politics.

When we entered the chambers where our elders waited, I took in the scene with all my senses. The world's highest royalty had gathered to dissuade Kaikeyi from her scheme. Rama, Lakshmana, and I had come to bid them our final farewell.

As Rama stepped into the chamber, with Lakshmana and me in his wake, the whispers of the elders subsided. All conversation and persuasion stopped. Kausalya, the Great Queen, Rama's regal mother, was visibly shrunken, even if it shouldn't have been possible in a few hours. King Dasharatha, my noble father-in-law, looked like a very old man. Only Kaikeyi was apparently unchanged, standing tall and regal, glowing with immense beauty. Her black hair hung straight and silky past her slender waist. She was the youngest queen and the king's favorite, something Ayodhyans were not allowed to say openly though all knew it. I had learned this within days of my arrival in Ayodhya. Open secrets existed in Mithila as well, so I was not shocked by the whispers. Rama had in fact told me privately that his vow during our marriage—to never marry anyone but me—was a result of his father's favoritism. That was the closest Rama ever came to critiquing his father. Kaikeyi was without a doubt an uncommon beauty, even now when she was nearing forty years of age. However, a disturbing change had come over her, one not visible to the naked eye. Rama noted this too, for he looked at her more often than anyone else.

As we stood there beholding one another, all the attention focused on the two power centers in the room: Rama, the surrendered son, and Kaikeyi, the relentless queen. Both had the power to change the course of destiny. A word of resistance from Rama could escalate the tension, while a softening on Kaikeyi's part could dissolve the crisis instantly. Most situations are subject to the whims of human beings. Because I already knew what Rama would do, my eyes rested on Kaikeyi, who even under this immense pressure appeared calm. But her eyes were vacant; the vibrant Kaikeyi I had come to know was not there. The one before us was incapable of laughter, sorrow, or any emotions whatsoever. Later, Rama told me that is how a warrior must be when entering a battle zone, else he or she will break at once; violence is not natural to the soul.

Because Kaikeyi was so one-dimensional in her determination to follow through with her plan, I understood her state in a few seconds. My intuition then directed me onward. My father-in-law was crying pitifully, and I witnessed the burden of kingship and the promises that he must have made as king. One of hundreds, maybe thousands, of promises he had made now returned to haunt him. I could not even imagine what this felt like, I, who hadn't lived long enough to make many promises. My only real vow was to be faithful to Rama, and I did not need an oath for that: I belonged to him as completely as I belonged to myself.

Eight respected ministers stood in clusters near the Great Queen. No one seemed certain what to do. As I beheld my elders, I became sure that not a single person held the key to unraveling that web. Kaikeyi and Dasharatha were in the middle of it, trapped like flies, every move they made entangling them only further. I do include Kaikeyi as a victim, even though many still think of her as the spider. Rama never thought so.

Kaikeyi personally taught Rama many of his skills: how to ride a horse, how to drive a chariot drawn by four, how to wield a sword. She had always doted on Rama the way a mother would. Among the three queens, she was the most mysterious and compelling. She stood apart from the rest of them, having never fully adopted Ayodhya's customs. It was rare to see a woman with all these man skills. Kaikeyi laughed when my sister Urmila and I called them that. "Where I come from," she told us, "a skill belongs to the one who masters it. Not to a woman. Not to a man. And that is the way it should be." I couldn't help but agree.

Yet her very skills were used against her, turned into weaknesses, her intelligence undermined by her fear. She would die in the web that was cocooning her. She couldn't see it, but I did. Rama did. Although she spoke coldly and cruelly to him, casting him away, he looked at her with compassion.

Kaikeyi must have known this about Rama. She must have known he was incapable of going against his parents' wishes. She must have carefully considered how to manipulate everyone, getting them to comply with her timely plot. Still, Kaikeyi was not that kind of scheming person. Someone extremely manipulative stood behind this. Someone who knew Kaikeyi and all the people of Ayodhya very well. Someone who did not have Ayodhya's best interest in mind. Someone who could poison the minds of others. My eyes settled on just such a person, and a shiver ran up and down my spine.

Manthara was Kaikeyi's hunchbacked servant, a title she herself vehemently abhorred. She had always resented Ayodhya for not giving her the due respect as Kaikeyi's surrogate mother. I sought something redeeming in her features or her attitude but found none. Her back was terribly crooked, her face gaunt, her nose and chin jutting out like the sharp pieces of a broken pot. Manthara was known to be devious, but I don't think anyone in Ayodhya knew the strings she was pulling, the web she had created. Was this her personal vendetta against us all?

People's minds and motives are not easily discerned. Though I can beckon the fires from the center of the Earth and walk through fire unburned, the human mind is a mystery to me. Though I can speak to the Earth and her elements, the mind is a maze. When I think I know someone fully, they shock me. This happened to me even with Rama. Even now when I stand fully in my powers, I cannot fathom the skill and tenacity one needs in order to manipulate others. Manthara, the defiant hunchback, was an expert. And I have come to know that the Earth harbors many like her. It's simply incomprehensible to me. Rama says that I lack the brutality needed for such single-minded destruction of another being's spirit.

As we stood in the chamber, I became increasingly convinced that Manthara was the one behind it all. The evidence was there in her smile. The only person happy that day was Manthara. I had never even seen the trace of a smile flit across her eyes before. Rama had told me she had always been that way. I attributed it to her painful physical condition. But Rama said she had selectively hated him since the day he was born. She actively favored Bharata, Kaikeyi's son, who would now sit on the throne instead of Rama. Kaikeyi had always apologized and kissed Rama twice to make up for Manthara's malice. But not now. This day, they were one—the beautiful queen and her crooked servant.

The crooked servant who never smiled was grinning from ear to ear. I kept my eyes on her with horrified fascination. Manthara had frightened me from the beginning. I could not find her goodness. Now I wanted to understand her. I could see Manthara wasn't intimidated by the man's world that ruled the empire. She had made herself the master of how to bring down the empire. How could the whole kingdom—Rama's exceptional father, his eight wise ministers, and the ancient Vasishta—be controlled by this one woman?

The surprising thing was that no one seemed to notice Manthara. Everyone was supremely focused on Kaikeyi's handsome person. Manthara hid behind Kaikeyi, and Kaikeyi stood strong and beautiful, a carefully crafted weapon and shield. Manthara studied our devastated faces with unconcealed delight. I could not understand what true happiness

she garnered from it. If only someone could reach her heart, understand her reasoning, the exile could be averted. I was sure of it. I hold this conviction to this day. Can a crisis be averted by a true heart-to-heart? I think so. For, does not every contention live and breed in those hidden places in our heart, the ones we pretend are not there?

I assumed then that my father-in-law and all the elders had tried such an approach already. What I didn't know is that even the world's most skilled diplomat can be blinded by personal interest and emotion. Dasharatha was so afraid of losing Rama that he could see no way past it; his very resistance made it a certainty. The more he resisted, the more Kaikeyi demanded. Ironic, is it not?

Kaikeyi pressed the insurmountable facts upon us repeatedly. When she had saved Dasharatha's life, long before Rama was born, he had given her those two boons. Now she had stated her wishes. That was all. I could see why all Ayodhya's resources were focused on getting Kaikeyi to change her mind. Sumantra's appeal was the most powerful. He begged Kaikeyi not to continue her mother's legacy. For it was known that Kaikeyi's mother, Queen Chaya, had been exiled for her misdeed when Kaikeyi was an infant. Kaikeyi's skin tone did not change; she did not get angry or emotional. She was completely unmoved by Sumantra's words. Truly, it was like she was not a person at all. At this moment Rama intervened. He turned to Lakshmana and me.

"Our third mother has made up her mind, as have I. We will leave now."

This was a warning to Lakshmana. Even in his silence, Lakshmana's protest was loud. Having said this, Rama stepped forward. He did not want to delay anymore. He was Kaikeyi's foremost ally, conspiring in his own exile. She could have never done it without him, without Rama's sweet compliance. I call it sweet because it brought tears to all our eyes. He approached his father and Kaikeyi so gently, as if they were made of glass. Rama spoke softly, his every word resonating with a natural deference. He still cannot speak about his father without a warm glow shining in his eyes. Rama's softness gave Kaikeyi the courage to take her demand even further. With Manthara nodding vigorously behind her, the queen called for bark cloth, the dress of the forest dwellers, and demanded that Rama and Lakshmana strip off their royal garb, including every piece of jewelry they wore.

Kaikeyi continued orchestrating the exile with a competent hand. She acted as though King Dasharatha was nothing but a decrepit fool. She smirked or laughed dismissively whenever he spoke. That was the strangest thing I noticed about that day. Previously she always gazed at his face, clung to his words, and went out of her way to touch him often. Now the barrier between them was as solid as a real wall, and I found myself silently praying that such a wall would never, ever stand between Rama and me. I couldn't bear it. I would break, as my father-in-law was breaking in front of our eyes.

With a quick movement, Kaikeyi turned on me. I wish I could say I faced her bravely, but I was not accustomed to hostility, confrontations, or punishments then. Her demeanor toward me was like a physical blow. I was nothing to her, but she wanted to show the world the extent of her power. She demanded that I follow Rama's example by removing my jewels and the silk dress I was wearing. She handed me a strip of rough bark cloth to wear. The assembly hissed in rage at Kaikeyi.

Rama raised his hand in warning. It was his first and only act of defiance. Rama defended me, pointing out that the exile was his alone, and I was a princess, free to dress as one. And so it was that Rama and Lakshmana left Ayodhya wearing bark cloth and little else, while I was adorned grandly for Rama's coronation. Rama also did not hand over his signet ring, which I was happy about. I loved to press the ring into my skin and watch Rama's name imprinted there for a few moments. The only thing Kaikeyi deigned to grant her stepsons were a handful of heavy weapons in place of the responsibilities of a king.

As the moment of parting came close, anxiety seized my heart. Where was my little sister? Urmila had not come to bid us farewell, as I had expected. I looked around but I did not see her anywhere. Certainly she would come to see Lakshmana, her husband, one last time. She had to come. We would not see each other for fourteen years. My heart ached as I began to understand what I would miss. My closest maidservant, Padmini, was crying in a corner, and my fierce head maid, Rani, gazed at me with solemn eyes. I couldn't imagine what Lakshmana felt. But I did not see his eyes search the premises for his wife. Perhaps Lakshmana already knew that Urmila would not come.

Her absence was the only thing that made my feet lethargic as I stepped onto the chariot after Rama. My eyes remained hopeful until the chariot began moving. That was when Dasharatha ran into the street, ordering the chariot to stop . . . only, his voice was broken and his order came out like a croak. Rama's composure cracked for the first time, and all my attention went to him. I firmly turned his body forward, saving him from seeing his father stumble and fall, sprawling on the ground. That moment was symbolic to me. The dynasty was crumbling and falling apart. There was nothing we could do now. We had another life ahead of us. Even though we were exiled for fourteen years, we left with the knowledge that we might never return. That, I think, was the wisest notion we possessed. Perhaps it prepared us in some small measure for the trials to come.

CHAPTER 2

The Border

The four horses snorted angrily as the chariot flew across the fields. The grass hissed, the wind jeered. Even the blooming fields were screaming in fury, or so it seemed to Lakshmana. Everything was enraged like he was. Except for Rama. Though Sumantra, Father's loyal minister, held the reins to the chariot, Rama's self-control was the only thing moving them forward. If only Rama could see that his sense of dharma was nothing but folly! Since when was it righteous to heed the wishes of a demented servant? Lakshmana envisioned Manthara's ugly face, then Kaikeyi's beautiful one. In his mind, they were one person. If Rama had allowed it, Lakshmana would have killed that poisonous, two-faced creature.

Next to him, Sita sighed lightly, a whisper in the wind. Lakshmana looked at her from the corner of his eye. Why was she here? This was *not* a fitting place for a princess. He stood as far from Sita as he could. She was only sixteen years old, neither strong nor mature enough to withstand the harsh life ahead of them. Though he was only a year older, Lakshmana knew that his experiences on the battlefield had prepared him. Despite this, Sita appeared serene and unfazed. Lakshmana was not. It took all his concentration not to do something rash, like force the chariot to turn around, or to scream at the top of his lungs. Looking sideways at his brother, Lakshmana clenched his jaw and took steady gulps of the wind that flew by too fast.

The moment Father had turned on Rama, heeding the evil queen's wishes, Lakshmana had severed all his previous loyalties and made Rama the king of his world. That meant he had to put a leash on his fury; Lakshmana's new king did not condone this anger. Lakshmana had offered to subdue the uprising, but Rama would have none of it. "Father's promise is my promise," Rama kept saying. Because of their father, Rama was barred from civilization, cast out like a filthy criminal. Even now, Rama repeated those words often. Hot air escaped from Lakshmana's mouth as he sighed.

The chariot rushed from Ayodhya, the indestructible city. They thundered through the land of Koshala, as if pursued. Lakshmana's king was set on living as an ascetic, executing Father's promise to perfection. How could Rama do this? When was a warrior's dharma *ever* to run away? Why was Rama choosing to submit meekly? Their departure from Ayodhya was the coward's way. Lakshmana could not understand it. This was the first time in his life that Lakshmana disagreed with Rama. It sat like a stone in his gut. Yet here he was, at his brother's side, voluntarily. This was his duty, as clearly as Rama's duty was to do what Rama did.

To subdue his temper, Lakshmana focused on his sensations: the thundering sound of the horses' hooves, the swaying motion of the chariot, the sight of flowering fields, the sun and the wind against his skin, and the fragrance of the sandalwood paste melting on his forehead. This morning he, along with every citizen of Ayodhya, had decorated himself elaborately, eager to celebrate Rama's coronation as crown prince. Lakshmana drew the back of his hand across his brow, wiping the sandalwood paste off. The fresh smell was an insult to the acrimony of the day.

The chariot lurched, running across a rock. Rama moved with the sudden jerk, holding Sita to him. Lakshmana stumbled, his hipbone slamming into the side of the chariot. Rama turned to him.

"I'm fine, I'm fine," Lakshmana said, rubbing the side of his hip.

He saw the care and concern in Rama's eyes. An outsider might think they were on a casual outing, set to go hunting in Ayodhya's woodlands. A more astute observer would notice their lack of entourage, their ascetic dress, and their frantic pace. But looking at Rama, no one would guess that Rama was being exiled by those he loved the most.

Rama's demeanor left a deep imprint on Lakshmana. He was staggered by Rama's compliance. Lakshmana concentrated intensely on following his brother's example. He studied Rama, carefully mirroring Rama's behavior, as he had done since childhood. With the wind in his hair, Rama was calm personified; his movements and words were deliberate, not a word or gesture unnecessary. The economy of Rama's bearing made his presence potent and significant. This was always the case, today being no different. That was the astonishing fact. Despite the intensity of what Rama was facing, he did not act out.

Like his brother, Lakshmana stood braced in the chariot, watching the scenery of their land fly by. He too looked ahead, never looking back. But Lakshmana knew he didn't fool anyone; his eyes and feet were restless; his sighs were frequent; his true feelings were clear to everyone. He had even threatened to lift his sword against their father, meaning to kill the king if it meant victory for Rama. Remembering that moment, Lakshmana covered his eyes, pressing his fingers into his eyelids until all he could see was darkness.

"Bharata will be a good king," Rama said, and Lakshmana dropped his hand from his eyes.

Lakshmana clenched his jaw. He wished Rama would stop saying that. "Are you sure that it's wise," he ventured, "to consider Bharata our ally under these circumstances?"

"He is our brother, Lakshmana."

"Yes, but he is also next in line to the throne. He could not have been completely oblivious to his mother's scheme."

"Do you really believe that?"

"At this point, I don't hold anyone above suspicion, Rama."

It was true that Bharata had always been a kind, brave, and virtuous brother. But hadn't Kaikeyi been sweet, supportive, and loving too, until this day?

Rama looked at Lakshmana appraisingly. Lakshmana felt his eyes narrow.

"The act of consecrating you as crown prince was a mere formality," he insisted. "Everyone knows you are meant to be king after Father. Only Manthara opposed it. But who is she, really, but a malicious hunchback? How could it be that *she* got her way?"

"Manthara is complicit in this scheme, yes. Bharata is innocent. You know how he always insisted on giving the kingdom to me, even when we were young boys. Remember when we were just ten years old, and Ayodhya's oldest prisoner, Marichi, was freed by his accomplice? Bharata felt he had failed when I recognized the impersonator as a blood-drinker while he didn't. Of his own accord, Bharata declared me king and renounced his claim to the throne. He thought of this before any of us did, Lakshmana. We know where Bharata stands on this."

"And yet a few days ago, you also thought you knew where Kaikeyi stood. Maybe Manthara is the only honest one among the lot! We always knew she hated us."

Rama sighed. "I trust Bharata," he said, and turned forward.

Lakshmana clenched both his fists. He did *not* trust Bharata one bit. He didn't care what Bharata had said when they were ten. They had been children then. Now they were grown men with wives of their own and the ambitions that came along with adulthood. Lakshmana gritted his teeth. He had to stop thinking about Bharata on Rama's throne!

The tricky part was that beside Bharata, in his mind's eye Lakshmana could see Shatrugna, his twin. Father had used to call them Drip and Drop because he could never tell them apart. That had seemed funny. Now it felt sick. Shatrugna had always been Bharata's shadow and was clearly on the enemy's side. Lakshmana could trust no one now. If Rama refused to see Bharata as his enemy, it only meant that Lakshmana had to be extra vigilant. This was a dynastic struggle that no one had seen coming. Or maybe Father had. Was

that why he had planned to crown Rama in a hurry while Bharata was absent? If Father had waited for Bharata to be present, all this confusion would be clear. They would all know for sure where Bharata stood, instead of going on faith, like Rama did.

Lakshmana beat his fist against his thigh. Rama's docility was embarrassing. Where was the unstoppable fighter who killed the demoness Tataka and her two revolting sons, Marichi and Subahu? Where was the fighter who had led the charge against Kashi and invoked divine missiles to slay the enemy?

Rama's power to destroy and fight had not awakened, not even twitched. He simply accepted the exile, showing no hesitation. He made it look easy, as if it were every day he was excommunicated from his family, kingdom, and community. He didn't allow his personal feelings to stand in the way. Lakshmana knew the truth, however: Rama was hurt. It wasn't anything Rama said or did. It was a feeling between brothers, the way Rama looked into Lakshmana's eyes a moment too long, revealing for a split second the frozen avalanche that would at some point unfreeze and cascade past his measured actions.

"That's why I'm here," Lakshmana said, speaking to himself as he always did when he was upset. "No one knows Rama the way I do."

Sita turned to him. "What did you say, Lakshmana?"

Lakshmana shrugged. Thankfully, the wind had blown away his words. The last thing he wanted was to contest Sita's closeness to Rama. The princess stood with her hand on Rama's back, as if her slender arms could support Rama's weight. A month shy of eighteen years, Rama had grown into his manhood and was as tall and strong as a man could be. Lakshmana wondered how aware Sita was of Rama's turbulence. Surely, she had seen sides of Rama no one else had. If Rama's words were sparse, Sita's were even more so. She had only said a handful of words all day. Lakshmana could not look at Sita for more than a moment at a time. And yet his eyes sought her. She was decked elaborately from head to toe. Her small crown, an oval crest-jewel, caught the sun whenever she moved. It was a family heirloom, a gift from her father. Lakshmana had never seen her without it. There would be no use for jewelry in the forest. There was no use for Sita in the forest! Lakshmana could see no justification for her presence. Why had Rama allowed it?

Just then, Sita gazed up at Rama, as if in reply to Lakshmana's doubt. Rama and Sita looked into each other's eyes, saying nothing but communicating so clearly that Lakshmana had to look away.

Lakshmana did not want to think of Urmila, his own wife. Yet he had little control of his thoughts. The parting from Urmila had gone all wrong. Lakshmana's passion had clouded his speech and butchered his words. He had done his best to explain, stumbling over words like *brotherhood* and *loyalty*. Urmila had stared at him as if he were a lunatic. With her every word and gesture, she undermined his decision to leave, calling it ridiculous and crazy. Her inability to instantly understand him had incensed him, as he was already aggravated. He could say none of the words he had planned. All Urmila could see was his choice to leave her and follow Rama. His responsibility, she cried, was toward her, not his brother. Lakshmana had been unable to bear her tears or her accusation. He had hurried away, leaving so many things unsaid. "I will never forgive you for this!" she had called after him. Now it would take fourteen years before they would reconcile. There was no room to doubt his decision, no room at all for his feelings. Discovering that Sita was accompanying Rama had been a blow. Sita's presence highlighted Urmila's absence. But Lakshmana would *never* have allowed Urmila to come. Never. It was akin to asking for blood on your hands. Sita was bait to a million dangers. Lakshmana would protect her with his life, but she was Rama's responsibility. Her blood would be on Rama's hands. Lakshmana shivered in the heat.

The sun was high in the sky now, with unrelenting rays that blazed down on them. Drops of sweat trickled down Lakshmana's ribs. Since their stepmother had revealed her scheme, none of them had eaten or even sipped water. Sita's cream-colored skin was already turning rosy in the heat. How would she withstand the onslaught of the elements and seasons?

One of the horses snorted, and Sumantra, holding the reins, murmured something in a low voice. Though he was a minister of highest rank, he had always been an excellent hand with horses. Sumantra had been present on the day Dasharatha and Kaikeyi first met, in the land of Kekaya, famed for their equestrians. The emperor had immediately fallen in love with Kaikeyi and asked for her hand in marriage. Lakshmana and every Ayodhyan child heard of this love story, but only in whispers. Why had no one put a stop to Father's favoritism of Kaikeyi? Ayodhya had not been the same after Kaikeyi arrived. That's what the whisperers said. Now it *certainly* would never be the same.

The four horses pulling the chariot had been galloping at their maximum speed for several hours. The thunderous noise of their hooves clattering against the ground softened; the chariot left the road and began driving through fields. Koshala's cultivated lands, with its neat fields and orchards, stood in striking contrast to the wilderness growing around them. The jungle spread itself out before them, mountain peaks swelling in the distance. They were approaching Koshala's farthest limit. Lakshmana could see it up ahead.

Rama leaned over the chariot's railing, toward Sumantra. "The border approaches."

Sumantra reined in the horses, and the chariot slowed. While the chariot was still rolling, Rama jumped off, stretching his arms and legs as soon as he landed on his feet. They had been standing for hours. When the chariot came to a halt, the blustering horses neighed and snorted. Their large bodies twitched from the exertion of the journey.

Lakshmana remained on the chariot, his legs full of lead. It wasn't too late. They could easily turn around and return to Ayodhya. Sita began to hand Rama his weapons, and this made Lakshmana get off the chariot. Silently he took over and accepted whatever Sita handed him, putting his weapons in one pile on the ground and Rama's in another. Rama went to the border of the land, turning to face the kingdom he was about to leave.

Lakshmana couldn't stop himself. "Don't do this, Rama," Lakshmana said. "Can't you feel the millions of heartstrings that hold you back? No one wants you to cross this border. No one. Please don't heed Kaikeyi and the hunchback. Please."

Behind him, Sumantra reinforced the plea with words of his own.

As if Rama had not heard them, he gave Sita his hand and guided her down from the chariot. Together, Sita and Rama walked to the borderline. Without looking at Lakshmana, he offered his free hand to him. Lakshmana understood. This was his final moment of choice. He had to shut up and take Rama's hand, or rage on and return to Ayodhya.

Lakshmana did not hesitate. The city was no longer his home. To go back there now would be like returning to a cave infested by venomous snakes. Lakshmana swallowed and stepped forward. He took Rama's hand. Warmth, energy, and power radiated from Rama's palm into his. Lakshmana's breathing grew calmer.

Rama raised his gaze toward the sky and spoke. "Koshala, land of my birth, caretaker of all I hold precious, guard my father, King Dasharatha. Guard my mother, Kausalya, and my younger brothers, Bharata and Shatrugna. I leave you in peace and prosperity. May you remain this way until I return. Keep those within your boundaries safe, and bless those who depart so they may return to you."

Rama's face was neutral, but tears ran down his cheeks, dropping to the Earth. There was no guarantee they would return, no guarantee that the great city would flourish. They left Ayodhya to its fate and walked toward their own. Rama remained facing Ayodhya for some minutes. Lakshmana gripped his brother's hand tightly. He felt the strength of their hands pulsate back and forth. This reminder of their physical prowess made him feel confident in their mental fortitude. He affirmed his position as Rama's shadow, someone who would execute Rama's will. Just like Father's word was final for Rama, Lakshmana surrendered to Rama's will. He just couldn't yet believe where Rama's will was leading them. The wild, dense jungle spread out for miles and miles behind them, a severe, untamed realm.

"Return to Ayodhya now," Rama told Sumantra. "Tell my father that his will is being done. Inform the king that you saw us cross the border. Ensure that my third mother hears this. Kaikeyi's mind must be at ease. We will continue on foot from here."

Dismissed by Rama, Sumantra, who had been at their side since the day they were born, broke into tears. Sumantra had not believed that Rama would truly leave Ayodhya.

Rama began to strap on his weapons. Lakshmana followed suit, feeling the weight of each weapon on his body. He tightened his belt around his hips and lodged his sword and knife securely into their scabbards. He donned light chain mail and wore protective armlets that covered his wrists and upper arms, before putting on finger guards. He slung his shield across his back, feeling the cold metal press into it. Above that, he placed his arrow-packed quiver. Unlike foot soldiers, the princes were not trained to wear all their weapons on their person. Fighting from chariots, they kept their weapons within arm's reach, only a choice few on the body itself. Fighting on foot was an extreme measure, a true indication of a life-and-death battle.

They had brought two bows each: a wooden longbow for distance shooting and a smaller one for close combat. Rama pressed the tip of his longbow into the ground, securing it there with his foot, and proceeded to tie the string at the other end. As Lakshmana carefully tightened the strings on his bows, he saw Sita touching her fingertips to the ground.

She spoke to the elements. "Earth beneath our feet, protect our steps and guide our way.

Sky above us, protect our minds and keep us calm. Trees and plants around us, allow us to walk among you safely. Water and wind, protect us from all sides."

Her eyes were closed but her hands moved through the air. Every movement she made was intentional, like a priestess invoking the gods. Lakshmana's heart began to race. Rama had prayed for Ayodhya's safety. Sita prayed for the elements to protect them. What was Lakshmana's prayer? He was there to serve Rama. That was as natural as breathing itself. But now he was Sita's servant too, and in this area he had no experience. He did not know her. She was connected to him through his other relationships: firstly, as Rama's wife, and secondly, as his wife's sister. The wife he had left, the wife he would not see for fourteen years. He who had just begun his life as a man had to return to boyhood and restrain all thoughts of what it meant to be a husband. And so Lakshmana did more than pray. He swore to chastity.

Weighed down by his weapons, Lakshmana felt like he was the last man standing on the battlefield. His anger began churning again. No army was there to back them up, no bodyguards, no men-at-arms. He locked eyes with his brother, steeling himself to do whatever necessary in the journey ahead. Did Rama see how taut his jaw was, how vigilant every muscle in his body?

Rama offered his hand again to Lakshmana. With his companions, Rama stepped over the border, renouncing his claim to Ayodhya. As he crossed over, Rama visibly shuddered, but his tears had dried in the wind.

"We must go as far from Ayodhya as possible," he said.

On this, Lakshmana agreed. They were not safe in a kingdom where Kaikeyi ruled.

"Bharata will be a just king," Rama said, "but we will give them no reason to seek us."

The fact that Rama was alive was reason enough.

"They will hunt us down," Lakshmana said, and then bit his tongue. He had made his choice and had to keep quiet. Without looking back or acknowledging Sumantra, who was still standing by the chariot, they walked into the jungle.

CHAPTER 3

One of Us

The trees opened their gates and let Rama in. He was welcome there, he felt this, as low-hanging branches brushed against his back, the leaves caressing his skin. A band of pink-faced monkeys lounged in the nooks of the trees; they glanced at Rama and his companions as they passed but continued grooming one another. With every step Rama took, he felt the energies binding him weaken. Father's love, which had sustained him since his birth, was disappearing, like a final piece of clothing slipping off, leaving him naked, exposed. Yet what did he need clothing for when he was banished to the jungle like an animal? The monkeys did not hide their nakedness. After nearly eighteen years in civilization, Rama was leaving it—which civilized parts of himself must he abandon to survive? He did not know. So he resisted the urge to reach for what was falling away. He did not hold on to the weakening threads, the relationships that had created his personality, just as muscles and sinews made his body.

Birds called to one another, announcing the arrival of newcomers. Full of trust, the birds were not alarmed by the weapons Rama and his brother carried. Bees buzzed about, searching

for nectar. The flowering season had not yet come, but flower buds peeked out, the first signs of spring. The season of Rama's birthday. When passing flowers and trees that Rama knew, he named them: soap nut, pomegranate, sandalwood, palm, banana, bamboo. When they walked by a ripe and pungent pepper plant, Sita sneezed, and Rama's eyes watered from the spicy scent. This kept his mind attentive and present, for the mind's favorite pastime was revisiting painful moments.

"Look, Sita," Rama said, pointing to a champak tree. The white blossoms were as large as her hand, the citrus fragrance hidden inside the pod.

"Your mother's favorite," Sita said.

Exactly Rama's thought. Mother used to place bowls of water with floating champak flowers in every possible corner, filling her quarters with the fresh scent. Rama sighed. He felt Sita's hand caress his back, like the soft touch of the leaves. Mother's sorrow had roots that were older than Rama. Had he done the right thing, leaving his mother defenseless in Ayodhya?

As if in answer to his thought, Rama caught sight of the small white stars of the night-blooming jasmine. He did not point out this flower to Sita, for it was Kaikeyi's favorite. Rama could not think of his third mother with ease. Kaikeyi had transformed into a stranger.

Sita examined with care everything he pointed out. She even smiled once. Sita had shown an unknown side of herself when Rama meant to leave her in Ayodhya. A volcanic anger had taken hold of her; she had turned lifeless in his arms, her consciousness leaving her body. Rama had felt her heart stop beating and thought, for an instant, she was dead. For that long moment, he knew life without Sita. It was the most bewildering moment, like having a body but no soul. He understood then that he could not leave Sita in Ayodhya, for his own sake as much as hers. Since then, Sita was like an expansive sky, holding him effortlessly while he searched for direction in this directionless state.

Lakshmana walked ahead, slashing at the vines in their way. Rama did not have the heart to point out that it would be easier to wind their way through the dense forestry. The forest yielded to them, if only they allowed it. Rama saw his brother's effort as the desire to demonstrate his compliance. But anger burned in Lakshmana's heart, for the first time directed toward Rama. Lakshmana continued to hack a way through, creating a tunnel in the thick foliage that suffered silently.

Despite the dense terrain, they kept a steady and unrelenting pace. The sounds of the forest created a symphony around them. They stopped often to slake their thirst but walked past fruit trees. Rama had no appetite, and his companions declined as well. From the bluff of a river, Rama observed playful dolphins and lazy crocodiles. A herd of animals with long, pointed horns looked like enemy ranks. A flock of birds crooned above their heads. When Rama looked up to see the birds, they were barely visible through the dense leaves and branches. A few steps later the trees parted, displaying a vast blue sky. There were no discernible patterns. The disorder around Rama resonated with his inner state.

Again he noticed that Sita was the eye of the storm, the peaceful vortex of the chaos, calm personified. Her hands spontaneously caressed the flowers within reach, and butterflies fluttered around her. Rama wondered how long she could go on before she tired. But his princess was totally focused, intent on matching his purposeful steps.

Many miles into the jungle, they decided to take a few moments of rest at a waterfall. The flood of water crashed down on the rocks below. The sound was forceful; Rama's head was the rocks, the pounding waterfall his exile.

Motioning to Lakshmana to stand guard, Rama put his bow down and turned to Sita. "How do you feel, my princess?"

Beads of sweat rolled down Sita's temples and her hands were shivering, but she only smiled. Seeing her determination, Rama brought her to the shade of a tree and sat her down.

Lakshmana remained close to them, scanning the area. Every few seconds his head snapped in the direction of a sudden sound.

Rama took one of Sita's feet in his hands and examined it.

"No, no," Sita protested, pulling away her foot. "I'm fine. We can keep walking soon."

"Sita, give me your foot." Rama held out his hands, looking sternly at her.

As he had suspected, the tender flesh of her foot was raw and bright pink. It pulsated with heat and energy in his hand. Unlike Rama and Lakshmana, who had plenty of calluses and scars, Sita was not used to physical exertion or hardship. Her feet were not used to walking like this. When he found a thorn in her right foot and two in her left, he became sterner yet.

"This is not a game for you to prove your tolerance! If you don't tell me when you are in pain, or when you are tired or hungry, then I will be forced to carry you and feed you, like a child."

Frowning at her, Rama used the tip of his smallest knife to carefully dig out the thorns. Drops of blood welled out from her foot. Then he easily lifted her in his arms to show her he really could carry her from then on. Rama carried her to the waterfall, placing her feet into the pond of cool water. Sita said nothing during Rama's doctoring.

Splashing her feet gently in the water, she said, "I know we've been here only a few hours. But it is different than I expected. Truly, I was not aware of those thorns. The Earth feels so soothing beneath my feet."

"You were born from the Earth, after all, my princess."

Sita's eyes glowed, and Rama noted that Sita seemed more in her element in the jungle. How was that possible, when they were homeless and exiled?

"My father loved to call me Daughter of the Earth," Sita said. "I never tired of hearing him tell how I simply appeared from the freshly plowed furrow. If the Earth really is my mother, I feel her presence here. It feels like reuniting with someone I used to know but have forgotten."

Sita rested against his arm and pointed to a curious turtle peeking up at them from the rippling pond. Rama was present for her easy banter but far off at the same time. The fish were dancing in and out of the water, while frogs and turtles sat on lotus leaves, soaking up the last hours of sunshine. It was almost peaceful.

Rama had journeyed on foot through forests like these once before. That had been two years prior, when he was fifteen, his first time leaving Ayodhya without his family. That time

the holy Vishvamitra had been his guide, Lakshmana had been by his side, and nothing had seemed impossible. Rama had slain his first blood-drinker, the ferocious demoness Tataka; he had lifted Shiva's mighty bow and won Sita's hand. He had slept on the ground with only his arm for a pillow. At that time, he had seen the beauty of the wilderness.

Now, trees with gnarled trunks resembled Manthara's crooked form. The snarl of a wild beast in the distance made him reach for his bow. Sharp rocks pierced the soles of their feet. Shrubs with thorns scratched at their ankles, drawing blood, and Sita's feet were already bleeding. Where was the path leading them? Sita and Lakshmana were loyally following him; he was their Vishvamitra, with none of that holy one's mystical prowess or foresight.

Rama bent his face to the pond and drank deeply and then splashed his face with the refreshing water. The next second an arrow whistled through the air. Rama whipped around, waterdrops flying in the air and sprinkling Sita's cheeks. Lakshmana stood akimbo, his bow held high. Lakshmana's arrow hit its target, piercing a large buck with a shiny black pelt. The buck fell to the ground with Lakshmana's arrow lodged in its heart. Already the light of its soul was growing dim. Sita gasped, pulling her feet out of the water. Lakshmana drew another arrow to his ear. The buck bleated and thrashed its horns. Sita stood and ran to the dying animal.

"Sita!" Rama cried out.

She ran straight toward the dying buck. With Sita approaching the target, Lakshmana could not release his final arrow. The buck's horns thrashed with unpredictable jerks. As Sita knelt by its side, one of the horns scratched her forehead. Lakshmana, who was nearest, ran forward, trying to pull her away.

"Do not touch me," she warned, placing her hands on the dying animal.

The animal grew calmer instantly. Rama watched intently, knowing that something invisible to the human eye was happening. He sensed the communion between Sita and the animal. She whispered soft words to the buck, gently patting its muzzle. Despite the fatal arrow, the buck was no longer in pain. Lakshmana drew close to Rama, astonished by Sita's behavior. The buck stopped moving, its unseeing eyes staring darkly.

Sita looked up at Lakshmana. "You killed him."

Lakshmana blinked rapidly and looked at Rama for support. Rama walked closer to Sita, considering the best response. He understood that Sita was not accustomed to hunting, to seeing a living creature die.

"You have never seen an animal killed before," Rama stated gently, reaching out to put his hand on Sita's shoulder. This time she did not move away but instead looked up at Rama.

"No," she acknowledged, tears rolling down her cheeks.

He should have known; he should have anticipated this. Sita had been carefully sheltered. She was not trained in warfare, like Kaikeyi. Rama and Lakshmana, on the other hand, would be unable to count how many animals and humans they had killed.

Rama sat down at Sita's side. Her hands still rested on the buck. A light trickle of blood seeped from the scratch on her forehead.

"The first time we saw Father shoot a deer, we were in tears. All my brothers and I," Rama said, rubbing away the blood with his thumb. "Remember, Lakshmana?"

Lakshmana nodded. "But it could have attacked us," Lakshmana said, pointing to the buck and its long, sharp horns.

Sita hid her face in her veil, drying her tears. She made no response to Rama's words; he sensed the topic was far from resolved. Rama took a deep breath and stood up, offering Sita his hand. Her display of emotion threatened to unravel him.

"We need to keep moving," he said.

Lakshmana stepped forward to retrieve his arrow from the corpse. They could not afford to leave even one behind. Their supply was limited; Rama did not know when they would have the opportunity to craft new ones. As Lakshmana ripped out the arrow, a stream of blood gushed out, splattering against his chest. Rama looked at the dead buck, knowing that if winter had been upon them, they would have skinned it. Tanning a hide was not a skill they had learned as princes, but they would eventually need pelts to protect them from the cold. Now, the season was warm enough that drops of sweat rolled down Rama's back. Sita would be spared that sight, for now.

Rama quickly led them away from the waterfall. He glanced back once, silently offering the black buck up to the forest animals. Soon they fell into a fast, rhythmic pace. As they walked, Rama felt a prickling at the back of his neck. Lakshmana had an arrow ready in his hand. Sita's eyes darted back and forth. While she might not have a warrior's second sense, she noticed their heightened vigilance. Rama saw nothing out of the ordinary. Another group of pink-faced monkeys watched them with yellow, unblinking eyes. Lakshmana was staring them down. One might think that Lakshmana took the monkeys for Ayodhyans in disguise, there to assassinate them. The trio continued walking, though Rama could not shake off the feeling that they were being watched.

If they were being followed, who could it be? Rama could not believe Lakshmana's theory. Rama was quite certain there would be no blood-drinkers in this region, so close to Ayodhya's borders. Blood-drinkers were by nature cowards, feeding on the most defenseless. For centuries, Ayodhya had fiercely protected its borders and beyond. The Sun dynasty had even kept the blood-drinker Marichi a prisoner for hundreds of years, to remind the kings what the true enemy looked like. As a boy, Rama had met Marichi imprisoned in the sun-cell. That was the first time he had ever seen a blood-drinker. Marichi had insisted that Ravana would free him from the prison, and perhaps it was true. An impersonator had managed to breach all of Ayodhya's security and free Marichi. Those were the only blood-drinkers Rama and his brothers had encountered in their youth. The blood-drinkers who lived on Earth had long since retreated to places like Dandaka, the borderland, a place where man had no dominion.

Wherever Rama looked, he saw only the expected creatures of the forest. Two squirrels froze mid-chase, one of them upside down on a tree trunk. A bird stopped pecking its feathers, preparing to take flight as they approached. As soon as they passed, the squirrels continued their chase; the bird rested its beak in its wing. The feeling of being followed, however, pressed in upon them until it became unbearable. Lakshmana could not take the tension.

"Run!" he whispered fiercely.

Rama grabbed Sita's hand and began to sprint. The wind rushed at them as they ran, ducking under tree branches. What were they running from? They clambered up a slope and hid behind a boulder. Sita pressed her back into the rock wall, while Rama and Lakshmana drew arrows to their ears.

A clear voice called their names: "Rama! Lakshmana!"

The voice was familiar. Rama looked at his brother.

"I told you they would come for us," Lakshmana whispered in a hiss.

"Rama!" the voice called again.

Sita pressed her hands against her heart.

"Do you recognize that voice?" Rama asked them.

"No," Lakshmana said, and Sita echoed him.

"I do," Rama said, putting down his bow.

"Trust no one," Lakshmana insisted.

"Guha?" Rama called out.

"Yes!" the voice responded.

"Of course," Rama said. "How foolish of me to give in to flight."

Quickly, he told Sita of Guha, the man he had befriended at the Summit of Fifty Kings. He was the leader of the Nishadas, a large forest tribe that swore fealty to Ayodhya. Rama rested his bow against his shoulder, offering Sita his hand. Rather unwillingly, Lakshmana followed suit. The three of them made their way down the slope, with less haste this time. At the bottom of the hill, Guha waited. Dressed in tiger skins and striped with white clay, he looked feral and untamed, kin to the animals of the forest. Rama's heart grew warm. Guha dropped to one knee. The claw necklace around his neck rattled, and his spear thudded against the ground.

"Guha, my friend," Rama said.

All the shadows around them came alive, turning into a tribe of men. Guha's people, the Nishadas, had an uncanny ability of blending into the forest. Rama had heard of it, but never seen it. Guha rose with the unexpected grace Rama remembered. Guha was a skilled wrestler, and no matter how many times Rama tried to beat him at the summit, they had always ended up in a tie. Guha's matted hair reached down to his knees, though much of it was tied into a massive topknot on his head. His skin was dark as night. His matted locks were decorated with feathers and precious stones. Rama pulled Guha into his arms, and the two stood for a moment, heart-to-heart.

"I couldn't believe what my scouts told me of two warriors and a princess," Guha said, his white teeth bright against his dark skin. "I had to come and see for myself. And it's you!"

Rama felt relief release the last tension in his belly. They had been watched after all, but the eyes had been well-wishers, not enemies. The crowd of Nishadas surrounding them were kneeling and exchanging words rapidly. The only word that Rama could pick out from their excited banter was his name. They gazed up at him with a look that Rama recognized. Ayodhya's people looked at him this way. Rama's throat tightened. Everyone but his own father loved him.

Guha knelt again, this time in front of Sita. Before he lowered his gaze, awe shone in his eyes. "My queen," he said, his head bowed.

No one had called Sita that before. She would have become queen. Now that future was uncertain. Sita glanced up at Rama. How should she respond? Rama knew that she easily felt self-conscious when someone's eyes lingered on her. Here, the city codes and etiquette did not hold, and no response was required of her. It was not necessary to point out that Sita was a princess, not a queen. Guha's devotion was clear. That was what mattered.

Guha stood and faced Rama again. "You honored us," Guha said, "by crossing into our lands several hours ago, my king."

Rama's manner instantly became grave. He didn't mind Sita being called queen, but he was no king. "Guha, my friend, I'm not your king, nor even the heir to Ayodhya. I stand before you alone, with no possessions, no kingship, nor land."

Guha's eyes widened. He froze in place.

"On the order of my father," Rama said, "I have been exiled from Ayodhya for fourteen years. By the emperor's decree, I'm banned from setting foot within any city."

Rama took a deep breath. Guha was speechless, his dark eyes filling with questions.

Rama could feel Lakshmana's rage roiling, strong as a hot wind.

"To me you are the king of Ayodhya," Guha said. "It's to you that I swore fealty. It's you I follow. I have not seen Emperor Dasharatha for many years now. You are my connection to the higher kingship beyond the forest where I rule."

His eyes left Rama's face for a moment to take in Sita and Lakshmana.

"My faithful Sita," Rama said, "and my brother have accompanied me of their own will."

"This is an injustice!" Guha exclaimed.

His hands were trembling before he clenched them into fists.

Seeing Guha's impassioned response, Rama's heart started beating faster. He thought of Lakshmana's words, that all the men in authority favored Rama. He saw in Guha a friend who would stand with him and fight. If Rama desired, his allies would unite and rebel against this exile. Rama clenched his jaw. Rama and Guha measured each other.

"No matter what your official status may be," Guha then said, "you are *my* king. You must come with me and allow us to honor you as our revered guest."

"I'm sworn to lead the life of an ascetic."

"Even holy ones pass through our dwelling for a night or two. Rama, my friend, you're feet are already in my kingdom. Our city is nothing but the forest itself."

Rama considered this truth. "Very well. We will stay with you this night," he said. "Then we must cross the river Ganga and continue away from Ayodhya's lands."

Guha barely waited for Rama to finish before he held Rama's shoulder, leading him away. Rama took hold of Sita's hand, and the three of them were carried away by the eagerness of the Nishadas. The men who had surrounded them disappeared with a rush into the greenness, but not before Rama saw a black buck slung across one's shoulders.

As they approached Guha's village, Guha pointed out the settlement. Though footpaths had been made by regular walking, there was no clear demarcation from the forest itself. This relieved Rama, for he was determined to execute his father's will to perfection.

When they got closer to the village, flowers rained down upon them, sticking to their hair and fluttering against their skin. Surprised, Rama looked up and saw dozens of children dangling in the treetops. When their hands were empty, the children slid down the branches with glee.

The children huddled around Rama, touching his bows and weapons. The reverence of the children heightened Rama's awareness of himself and his companions. He understood how remarkable they appeared, even in their stark attire. Sita was dressed like a true Ayodhyan princess, decorated with all her jewelry, which was like a second skin to her. The children stared at each of them without a trace of shyness. A group of young girls looked up at Sita, their eyes round like the full moon.

"I have three sisters," Sita told them, referring to Urmila and her two cousin-sisters. She touched the top of their heads with her fingertips. "May you always remain the closest of friends throughout your life."

Guha immediately translated Sita's words and her blessing. The girls giggled and shyly reached out to touch Sita, as if to make sure she was real. The crowd of children grew.

"This is a dream come true for them," Guha said, and laughed. "You are the hero of our realm, Rama. We sing songs about your accomplishments. Many of the boys train in archery every day. Since we are hunters by trade, we don't discourage their enthusiasm. They all want to be like you, the king in Ayodhya."

When they continued into the village, the children followed, a lively shadow. Rama took in the forest dwelling. Unfamiliar smells prickled his nostrils: smoke from cooking fires and the scent of freshly caught fish. The Nishadas put everything aside to greet their guests. They began singing in exultation. Their clapping hands and stomping feet created rhythmical patterns that accompanied their jubilant song. Moving together as one, the Nishadas looked like undulating ocean waves. Hundreds of men and women danced in a circle around the visitors, stomping their feet, clapping, sweating, smiling, and singing with joy.

As the song began to subside, Guha announced the reason for Rama's visit, telling them in few words about the exile. The singing ended abruptly, and the crowd became somber.

"All is well in the kingdom," Rama assured them. "Have no fear. My brother Bharata will rule. He is very dear to me and I trust him. I thank you for your warm welcome. You have given me great joy."

Rama knew that under any other circumstance, they would have been fed and showered with gifts. Yet this was no ordinary visit. "Please tell them of my restrictions," he said to Guha. "We cannot accept gifts, nor offerings of food. Please understand."

"This is a great restriction you place upon us," Guha said. "It will be easier to agree to your terms if we can serve you in some way while you are here."

Lakshmana stepped forward. "I would like to learn how to build a dwelling and any other skills that would be useful for us as we grow accustomed to living in the forest."

Guha clapped his hands together and called over two of his men. "They will assist you."

The women claimed Sita, pulling her with them. Rama let go of her hand only then. Guha made a gesture and the children scattered unwillingly, watching Rama from a distance before they began to follow Lakshmana.

Rama and Guha faced each other. Guha crossed his arms over his chest, standing with feet firmly planted on the ground. Like Lakshmana, Guha wanted Rama to rebel. Rama could feel it in his friend's demeanor. Instead of pressing Rama, however, Guha was quiet, allowing Rama to simply be.

His eyes sought Sita, surrounded by tribal women whose language she did not speak. The women gathered around her, humming like bees around a honeyflower. Many of them carried a child on the hip and whispered to one another. Most had a big red hibiscus flower behind an ear. Their hair, pulled up high on their heads, was bound tightly into a big bundle. Like the men, they wore skins from different animals around their hips and sharp claws and teeth in their ears and around their necks.

Rama had noticed early in their marriage that Sita, a rare beauty, shied away when she was the center of attention. Rama had helped Sita remain open when people gazed at her, sharing his father's advice: *Connect to your heart. Be still. Take a deep breath. Welcome their attention.* Father had taught him that openness garnered trust. It was impossible to trust someone you could not see. Sita was effortlessly employing those skills now. She and the tribal women were holding hands and examining one another's hair and dress.

Guha broke the silence. "How can I serve you, Rama?"

"There is one thing . . ."

Seeing the tribal women's curiosity over Sita's hair had given Rama an idea.

"I would like to mat my hair like yours," Rama said.

Guha's face split into a grin. That was not what he had expected. "At your service," he said. "Please be seated while I collect sap from the banyan tree."

Lakshmana returned to Rama's side. He too would mat his hair. The Nishadas gathered to witness the hair ceremony. Guha returned with a clay pot full of sap.

"We do this ritual for our little ones when their hair grows past their shoulders," he said.

"When it comes to forest living, I am a young boy, really," Rama said.

"Please sit here," Guha said, leading the two princes to a large slab of wood in the center of the village.

The women brought Sita back with a log for her to sit on. She shone like a jewel in their midst. The rest of the Nishadas squatted on their haunches and watched.

Guha dug his fingers into Rama's scalp and started slowly making circular motions, tangling the strands of Rama's hair together. The Nishadas began a gentle hum. The birds in the trees added their voices to the melody. Taking a large chunk of Rama's hair in his hand, Guha rubbed the hair and the sap together, making a thick, compact dreadlock. He continued like this until all of Rama's glossy locks had transformed into chunks of matted hair.

Rama watched Lakshmana's hair similarly transform. With the bark cloth across their hips and matted locks, they belonged to the forest. There was no going back. Rama looked at Sita and saw tears shining in her eyes. She too saw the finality.

"You are one of us now," Guha said. He repeated the words to his people, and they cheered loudly.

Rama looked at Sita's thick black braid and noticed the question playing on her face. In Ayodhya, a woman's hair was one of her distinct attributes. Even the men of the palace took care to comb, wash, oil, and trim their hair. But that would not be their life for the next fourteen years. Rama went to Sita's side, bowing his head, so she could feel his sticky locks, heavy with tree sap. Sita did not request to have her hair matted. Rama was glad. He loved her silky hair, the way it flowed like water through his fingers. And yet, a part of him wondered if she accepted the exile as her own . . . Maybe she longed to return to Ayodhya.

The sun began to set, and the long day was finally over. Honoring the terms of the exile, Rama and his companions left the parameters of the village, seeking shelter under a large fig tree. From there they could hear the fast-paced waters of the Ganga, swirling and full of life. Lakshmana gathered leaves, hoping to cushion Rama and Sita from the hard ground. He had a pained look on his face, and Rama noticed his lips were dry and cracked. When he touched his own lips, he felt roughness there. Lakshmana brought water from the Ganga, and they offered it up to the twilight before they sipped the water in silence. Rama had been moved by the generous warmth of the Nishadas, but he knew there was no respite from their journey. Tomorrow they had to cross the Ganga. With Sita by his side, Rama fell asleep.

CHAPTER 4

The All-Seeing Bharadvaja

Lakshmana was deeply exhausted, but he could not sleep. Looking at his brother, he felt a churning in his stomach and had to avert his eyes. There was nothing he could do about them sleeping on the ground like the poorest of the poor. With aching eyes, he stared into the dark night, finding some minute solace in the sound of the restless Ganga River.

More than once he dozed off for a moment, only to jump up, instantly awake, with an arrow drawn to his ear, aiming at a threatening sound. One time it was only a rabbit hopping out of the bushes. The little creature looked at Lakshmana with shiny eyes, twitching its nose. Unmindful of the arrow pointed at it, the fluffy rabbit hopped over to the sleeping couple, sniffing Sita's ear. Sita smiled in her sleep but didn't move. From the bushes, another two rabbits appeared, and soon all three of them were resting next to the princess. Lakshmana sighed and put away his arrow.

At the break of dawn, Rama stirred and Lakshmana fetched fresh water from the Ganga again. Quietly, the three of them drank the water, sipping it carefully now that their stomachs were so empty. Since stepping across the border on the previous day, none of them had eaten. Guha was soon there, carrying a jar of honey.

"This will give you energy for your journey," he said.

But Rama refused, handing it to Sita. But Sita would not eat unless Rama did. Lakshmana barely noticed the ache in his belly. Then Guha negotiated what he really wanted.

"Then you must allow me to ferry you across the Ganga. We have more than five hundred boats. You must allow us to serve you in this way."

"You are cunning, my friend," Rama said. "You brought the offering of honey, knowing I would refuse, so that I would have to accept your other services."

Guha bowed with his hands to his heart. Together they strode to the bank of the river. Crocodiles lounged nearby, and every so often a dolphin or a fish jumped up, greeting the morning. Lakshmana looked at the Ganga's rapid current and realized how difficult it would have been for them to cross her waters on their own. Unless Rama used one of his celestial missiles, of course. He could do all sorts of things with those weapons. But his brother would not use them for his own gain.

Lakshmana stepped into the boat first and, on Rama's command, gave his hand to Sita. When Sita's hand touched his, he realized it was the first time he had ever touched her. He held her hand firmly, determined to convey his complete loyalty to her.

With Guha's skillful guidance, they reached the opposite shore in a matter of minutes.

Guha held Rama's hand for a long moment. "No one will cross the Ganga without my permission," he promised.

He touched Rama's feet and jumped swiftly into his boat, pushing it away from the bank.

They were on their own again. They turned from the Ganga and began to walk. The sun rose steadily and the forest was full of light. Lakshmana felt anything but. The growling sounds of tigers in the distance felt like a real threat.

"Do we have any idea where we are going?" he asked. Every tree looked the same.

Rama paused, looking around at the dense greenery. He rubbed his forehead for a moment, shading his eyes with his palm. His brow furrowed, his eyes closed, the stress visible on his face. Sita's hand flew up toward Rama but hovered only for a moment before it wilted.

"I think I know the way," Rama said, pulling out a tightly rolled scroll from his quiver.

Lakshmana had no prior knowledge of the scroll, though he recognized the handwriting as Vasishta's, their old teacher. Vasishta was thousands of years old and had served the Sun dynasty from the beginning, more than thirty generations. The holy ones lived for many thousands of years. It was almost impossible to imagine what they had seen and acquired over all those millennia, treasures of unimaginable wisdom. Yet, they were humans. All humans had the potential to be like the holy ones, for whom years would certainly feel like minutes.

Lakshmana had not witnessed Vasishta handing the scroll to Rama. Even if he had seen it, his suspicion would have remained. The preceptor's script was more flowing than usual, suggesting that he had written it in haste. Lakshmana leaned close to Rama, reading the scroll together:

Rama, blessed boy,

Do not lose sense of your purpose. You have always known what to do, even as a young boy. Do not lose faith in yourself, with your father removed as your guide.

There are enlightened beings living in the forest. Seek them out. They will shed new light on your path. The first one of these is Bharadvaja, who lives beyond the Ganga. After you cross the holy river, keep following the sun and walk south. You will surely come across the holy one's sanctuary. Go there without delay. He will send you onward.

I know your path must seem dark and hopeless. I can only direct you to others of my kind who know far more than any one of us. Find Sharabhanga. Find Sutikshna. Find Agastya. If I know anything at all, they will be expecting you. They will greet you with utmost happiness. You will find answers with them.

The forest is not as empty as you think, Rama. You are not alone.

Your ever well-wisher,

Vasishta

"'The forest is not as empty as you think,'" Rama said aloud as he slowly rolled the scroll and put it back in his quiver. He said the names of each holy one again. "We must do as Vasishta says. Bharadvaja's ashram will be our next destination."

"We could be walking into a trap," Lakshmana said.

"But I got this directly from Vasishta's hands," Rama countered. "Unless you question his loyalty."

Lakshmana shrugged, choosing not to say what was written on his face. He had no alternate solution to offer, so he followed Rama's lead, as he always did. He could not, however, adopt Rama's trusting ways. Lakshmana knew that a real threat hung over them.

Who was to say that Vasishta was not part of Kaikeyi's plot? Had he really put his best effort forward to stop the exile? Despite his misgivings, Lakshmana felt his spirits lift a little; it felt good to have a clear destination. As he contemplated meeting Bharadvaja, a long-living sage like Vasishta, his mood plummeted again.

Vasishta's eyes were penetrating and saw way too much. One couldn't hide from such wise men. That was the problem. Unlike Rama, Lakshmana felt gloomy at the prospect of meeting the holy ones who lived hidden in remote corners of the jungle. As long as they kept their eyes on Rama, it was fine, but as Rama's brother, Lakshmana got his fair share of attention. Vasishta had always directed wise words to Lakshmana. Wise words were a bitter medicine, Lakshmana knew. The holy always advised against anger and hate. This holy Bharadvaja would surely see Lakshmana's anger and tell him to forgive. No matter what Bharadvaja would say, Lakshmana was *not* prepared to expel what he felt. It was the truth. Rama had been betrayed. He had been unfairly punished and banished from his own kingdom. Not everyone could be as generous as Rama. Someone had to stand up for what was right.

"Maybe Vasishta gave us all those directives," Lakshmana quietly muttered so that Rama wouldn't hear, "so he could keep track of us. So they could hunt us down."

His older brother would not take well to any elders being maligned. Even if it was true! And so the cycle of suspicion revolved in Lakshmana's mind as he trudged along. He barely saw the green jungle around him, barely felt the twigs and creepers scratching at his shins and knees, but his eyes seldom wavered from Rama and Sita a few paces ahead of him. Of course, his ears were alert, his hand tight on his bow, the taut string cutting into his upper arm every time his arms moved in rhythm with his feet. Ideally, a bow would be strung only before battle, when it was needed. Here, there was no way of knowing when the bow might be needed, so Lakshmana didn't mind the tug of pain in his left arm.

They covered many miles before they reached another river, the Kalindi. Her waters were less rapid and less wide than the Ganga. They didn't see any crocodiles either, but that didn't mean there weren't any. Sita still wore her long, flowing dress, the one she would have worn for Rama's coronation. The heavy silk would absorb water in no time and pull Sita under.

After a few moments of deliberation, the brothers decided to make a raft. Lakshmana was actually impressed with how their theoretical knowledge translated into a floating raft. The sun was well past its zenith by the time they made their crossing. The makeshift raft held them nicely, and they used long branches to navigate toward the other side of the river. Crickets chirred and beasts growled in the distance. When they reached the other side, Lakshmana felt a small sense of accomplishment. He glanced at their handiwork one last time before walking away from the river in search of their next goal. As they pressed forward, they searched carefully for signs of a habitat.

Evidently, Vasishta's scroll told no lies. Not that Rama would have ever expected it to. Soon they saw signs of human life. Columns of smoke rose in the distance, and the closer they came, they saw tattered bark cloth spread out to dry. A milking cow watched them walk by, while a tame herd of deer ignored them. Lakshmana felt a stitch of guilt when he saw a herd of antelopes, a black buck standing in the center, with his long horns pointed to the sky. The animals' ears twitched, but otherwise they paid no heed to the humans walking by them.

By this time, the exiles had come upon a path, and Rama hesitated. He seemed unsure how to proceed. For a moment, Lakshmana wondered if they would be welcome after all.

A few seconds passed and then an old man appeared on the path up ahead. He possessed a bright white beard, but his aged body did nothing to obscure the grace radiating from within, lending him youth and vigor. Seeing them, he lifted both hands high in the air.

"Rama! You are here!" he exclaimed, hastening his steps. "You and your companions are here! How could I have kept you waiting?"

The old sage muttered a string of admonishments under his breath as he hurried toward them. "Been waiting all this time for them. Kept them waiting, old fool!"

A number of other ashram residents gathered around the newcomers. They were all aged men, set on offering their last years on Earth to asceticism and *tapasya*, or austerity.

Bharadvaja enveloped them with a warm welcome, which preceded his physical nearness. Bharadvaja's joy in greeting them was such that Lakshmana felt the cloud of darkness held at bay. Nothing could truly dispel it. Not until blood flowed and the wound was cleansed. But thoughts of vengeance were whisked away, as if Bharadvaja was personally cleaning away unwanted thoughts. He clasped their hands and allowed them to touch his feet, though only briefly. He embraced them repeatedly. He greeted them so effusively, Lakshmana felt the holy one had been anticipating this moment for a long time.

Bharadvaja said as much, moments later. "I have been waiting for this day. I've counted the days since I saw the vision of your appearance here. I'm blessed and humbled."

"We are the ones humbled," Rama said. "Your kindness and warmth are a soothing balm to me. Our hearts sorely need a welcome like yours."

The sage turned sober, hearing Rama's reminder of why they were there. "The exile," he said. "Yes."

"You know already?" Rama looked surprised.

"Yes, certainly. Let me not forget. For me, this moment in time is the culmination of my good karma, but for you it is a heartbreaking time. Before we lodge ourselves firmly in the here and now, there is something I must do."

The sage turned to Sita, his face splitting into a grin that Lakshmana could describe only as blissful. The sage had a pink blossom in his hand.

"I understand you love flowers," he said to Sita.

Instead of just giving Sita the flower, Bharadvaja traced circles in the air around her, worshipping her, offering it to her in the most respectful way. Sita cast a startled glance at Rama before she smiled. Why was the revered sage worshipping her when it was to be the other way around?

"Your mother sends her greetings and her love," Bharadvaja said to her as he placed the flower into Sita's hand.

"My mother?"

"Your mother, the Great Mother, the Goddess Bhumi."

Sita's face showed her utter surprise. None of them had met someone who claimed to commune with the Earth goddess directly. Sita had a thousand questions written on her face, but simply asked, "What else did my mother say?"

"She is happy that you are here in the forest, closer to her. She understands the complexity of your destiny, where every moment cannot be celebrated."

Hearing this unexpected revelation, Sita was lost for words.

"She walks with you in your dreams," Bharadvaja said kindly. "You can find her there. Now, come with me. All three of you."

His earlier eagerness washed over them again as he led them into his ashram and beckoned them to sit. Everything was prepared for them: three seats, three clay cups filled with fresh water and fresh banana leaves piled with fragrant fruits. Other sages residing with Bharadvaja gathered at a respectful distance.

"As you can see, we've anticipated your arrival. It's all very simple, but the best we can offer. Please relax and eat to your heart's content. You can abandon your inhibitions here. Unlike Guha's territory, my ashram is not a kingdom, nor within the parameters of any civilization. You are welcome to stay here as long as you like. It will not violate the terms of your promise."

Lakshmana sipped the water; it was sweetened with honey and lime. Was there anything they could say that Bharadvaja did not already know? Lakshmana pondered this while eating the fruits with gusto. Sita really was the Daughter of the Earth, a title that had been lightly thrown around within the palace. It had to be so, when Bharadvaja himself had communed with Bhumi. It was all so hard to imagine. And yet, Lakshmana enjoyed the reprieve from his inner turmoil. If the escape from himself was a permanent side effect of living with Bharadvaja, Lakshmana would consider it. But he knew they were too close to Ayodhya's border, hardly two days away from home. They could easily be found.

Once his guests had finished their meal, Bharadvaja said, "I have a good grasp already of the events as they transpired, but I would like to hear from you. It never ceases to amaze me the richness of detail and emotion that each person contains. Oh, yes. If I asked Sita to describe the events that brought you here, you would hear a completely different story than the one Lakshmana would tell. Is it not, Lakshmana?"

Bharadvaja turned his all-seeing eyes upon Lakshmana, a moment Lakshmana had been dreading. He had never mastered the openness Rama talked about, which Father had taught them. When anyone looked at him too closely, Lakshmana felt his walls and defenses come up, as real to him as any other part of his self. Maybe that was his way of being truly seen, by saying, "You can never truly see me." That's who he was. It was extremely uncomfortable now, to have Bharadvaja seeing through his carefully constructed walls. It felt like the sage saw to the core of Lakshmana's soul. Lakshmana wanted to get up and run. Instead, he shuddered and closed his eyes.

"You will be known forever as the most loyal brother," Bharadvaja said kindly. "There will never be a brother like you. You have crowned your brother as your king, and I salute you."

Lakshmana looked up, shocked. He hadn't told anyone that. Bharadvaja's words were affirmations to his strained nerves, telling Lakshmana he had made the right choice. A feeling of gratitude rushed up from nowhere, and Lakshmana wanted to say something in return to the sage, but Bharadvaja had already turned back to Rama.

"Tell me what happened from beginning to end."

Rama had not spoken to either Sita or Lakshmana about the actual event. They both leaned forward as Rama revealed the exile as he had experienced it. Lakshmana had not been in the room when Kaikeyi revealed her true self. Now that he saw the scene through Rama's words, not even Bharadvaja's calming presence could quell the churning in his stomach.

"I am not just a son, but my father's servant," Rama said. "I would do anything to dispel the darkness that surrounded us and restore Father to his former vigor. As soon as Father refused to look me in the eyes, life took on the elements of a dream. All I knew for certain was that I had been sent into exile by the people I love the most. And here we are."

Rama spoke of their third mother, how she singlehandedly orchestrated Rama's exile. The silence was thick with Rama's words. Bharadvaja's eyes never strayed from Rama.

Rama ended by asking, "Should I have acted differently?"

The question was in the air for a while. It wasn't Lakshmana's place to give the obvious answer.

Bharadvaja spoke, his voice too loud in the silence. "Allow me to offer another perspective," he said. "May I do that?"

Lakshmana's wrath broke. He began to take long and deep breaths.

Bharadvaja waited until Rama nodded.

"I applaud your restraint, Rama. Your humility and your loyalty. For a human being, it's nearly impossible to do what you've done. We are built to lash back, as your brother here longs to do. You, Rama, are not built that way, and I bless you to continue on that path. From your words, we have received a clear insight into the here and now, the happenings on Earth. Now let me bring you to another, more timeless perspective."

All three of them nodded seriously.

"Imagine a universe where darkness has begun to usurp the light. That is the universe we live in right now. The usurper of light may not seem real to you, but he is a person and his name is Ravana. That name, I know, has some meaning to you. From the beginning of creation till now, the worlds have never known a being like Ravana. We know that soon enough, Ravana will order the planets to orbit backward in his experiment to reverse time. That is one small example of his selfish plans. Ravana cannot be allowed to live until the time of dissolution. All higher beings agree on this. Let me say that the extent of his brutal power is evident in what the cosmic powers have been forced to do.

"Having tried every other method to end Ravana, the pure-hearted ones journeyed to the Ocean of Milk and petitioned for Vishnu's help. He was now their only hope. Hearing their distressed call, Vishnu, the one who upholds the world, acknowledged that Ravana had roamed freely too long. The cosmic balance was in peril. Vishnu agreed. He would put an end to Ravana's destructive presence, subduing the blood-drinkers yet again, as he had done to Ravana's ancestor."

While Bharadvaja spoke, they listened attentively. Lakshmana felt his curiosity awaken. What did Vishnu's descent and these old legends have to do with Rama and his exile? There had to be a connection. Maybe Rama understood more. Though Bharadvaja's words seemed arbitrary to Lakshmana, he knew they were not. When Lakshmana was a youngster, he had made the mistake of dismissing Vasishta's words, considering them irrelevant or unfathomable. He had learned over the years how portentous and deeply relevant they always were. Rama was better at unraveling the messages behind the enigmatic stories. For now, all Lakshmana could do was listen as the sage spoke. He would ask Rama later.

"Although Vishnu agreed to subdue Ravana, it could not be done by sending the Sudarshan Chakra, his brilliant discus, to sever Ravana's head. He had already tried that, another evidence of Ravana's unheralded power. Ravana now sports the scars from Vishnu's lethal discus across his chest. Even Vishnu is bound to honor the complex web of protection that Ravana has woven around himself. You see, no divine being can kill Ravana. Vishnu cannot kill him. The only weakness in his armor is the fact that he is not immune to a human being. The irony is, of course, that an ordinary human has no chance against Ravana. Therefore, Vishnu accepted the limitations of a human mind and body. Vishnu, who is perfectly capable of being in many places at the same time, stayed where he was in the middle of the Ocean of Milk, in repose on his giant serpent, Ananta-Sesha. Like Shiva, Vishnu's stillness and meditation are uninterrupted, no matter what he does. He experiences the existence of the entire cosmos as the pause between his inhalations. Yet Vishnu's energy descended, a glowing presence too large and too bright for human eyes. The Earth goddess Bhumi trembled, feeling the descent of Vishnu's fathomless essence. It was so expansive, she feared being swallowed by it. How could she hope to contain it within her limited sphere? How could it be contained within a human frame? Yet Vishnu's energy was so subtle that only Bhumi and a few other enlightened beings were aware of its presence. Would Ravana feel it? the ancient ones wondered fearfully. Would Ravana notice the shift of energy on Earth and retaliate? But Vishnu gently wrapped his consciousness around the circular orb that is Earth and became a natural part of it. All of a sudden, everyone felt calm and happy, as if everything had become perfect. For that moment in time, it had."

Bharadvaja closed his eyes, as if relishing that perfect moment, before he continued. "All this had to be done in extreme secrecy, without so much as a cosmic whisper. The thirty gods prayed, and we prayed that Ravana, with his ten heads and vast mind, would not guess the

stealthy scheme of his destruction. The fear of discovery sent a tremor, like an earthquake, through the higher beings. We have tried and failed before, and we have all paid the price. The sun does not rise without Ravana's consent, and the ocean does not move. From the highest to the lowest beings of creation, we are all at Ravana's mercy, slaves to him. Our wives and daughters are kept women in Ravana's palace. Every child who is born could be Ravana's choice morsel. It's up to him, not the laws of nature."

Bharadvaja's anger was palpable now. Lakshmana had not failed to notice when the sage said *we*, he included himself in the band of rebels who had conspired against the king of the blood-drinkers. Lakshmana wondered what Bharadvaja had lost in their failed attempts to end Ravana.

"Ravana *must* be stopped," Bharadvaja said more forcefully. "He *will* be stopped. Vishnu's consciousness embraced the Earth and waited for the right time to take birth in a human form. All of us are aware what it means to accept a human body. A soul entering a human form is the most fragile and the most lost of all beings, losing its awareness of its eternal soul, bound by the veils and the laws of nature. Thus, Vishnu offered up his complete omniscience to become one of the creatures Ravana dismisses as pathetic, helpless, and worthless. Yet this human man is the only hope for our world. Our only hope."

Bharadvaja smiled, the kind of smile Lakshmana would expect on a warrior thirsty for revenge. "Ravana did not take note of the birth of yet another human being. After slaughtering and devouring millions of humans, Ravana has left Earth mostly alone. His blood-thirsty minions have been driven out from civilization. In many places, Ravana is even forgotten. Earth's people have forgotten the menace that perpetually hovers over them. The name *Ravana* and the fear it once incited have gradually disappeared. People believe what they see and experience. We are called the short-lived ones for a reason. Our memory, I fear, is as short as our lives. Now, other mythical monsters are invoked to chasten naughty children. Are they not?"

They nodded. They had certainly been raised on tales of Ravana. Ravana was real; Lakshmana and his brothers had learned this when they were eight years old and introduced to Ayodhya's oldest prisoner, a blood-drinker named Marichi. It was Marichi who convinced them that blood-drinkers existed and that Ravana was their king. Lakshmana believed him but maintained some question about the ten-headed blood-drinker king. All creatures idolized their ruler.

Bharadvaja continued. "Even though this human was born for a very specific purpose, his path toward Ravana is not a missile-like straight shot. Instead, it is full of unexpected events and tragedies. He is, after all, human."

"Do you know who he is? This avatar of Vishnu?"

It was Rama who had asked the question.

"Certainly," Bharadvaja said, with a twinkle in his eye. "I have never taken my eyes off him since the day he was born."

His eyes rested on Rama. Lakshmana held his breath. It couldn't be! Yet, who could outsmart Rama? Or outrun him, or outshine him? No one. Unless Rama chose to hold back, wanting to remain equal to his peers and brothers. It wasn't until Rama killed Tataka, the giant demoness, and broke Shiva's bow that Lakshmana had understood for sure what he had known for years: Rama could do things that no one else could. And now Lakshmana knew why.

"It's you, Rama," Lakshmana said, closing his gaping mouth. "You are the avatar!"

Rama burst into laughter and shook his head vigorously. "Impossible."

Now that the words were said, they sounded strange to Lakshmana too, though it had seemed perfectly clear in his mind. Vishnu was someone who slept on a giant black snake with unlimited heads, far away, in the Ocean of Milk. Rama was his brother, so familiar and close, sitting right there. Lakshmana began shaking his head too, acknowledging the flight of his imagination. He glanced at Sita to see her reaction, but her serene countenance gave little away. Lakshmana turned his eyes on Bharadvaja to see his take on what Lakshmana had said.

Bharadvaja smiled brightly and said, "If I revealed his identity now, Ravana might hear us. Then all our secrecy would be for naught."

There was a twinkle in Bharadvaja's dark eyes. Was he jesting or serious?

"Also," Bharadvaja added, "this man does not know who he is. I don't think he would believe me if I told him. It's really not that different from approaching any human and telling them that they are eternal souls, not mortal bodies. It's something most of us know deep within, but it's knowledge very few can truly understand. Human life is a process of discovery. Each of us is born on Earth for a specific purpose. We simply do not know destiny's plan for us until she has us tight in her grip."

Bharadvaja turned to Lakshmana, and it seemed to Lakshmana that Bharadvaja was purposefully less enigmatic toward him. Indeed, Lakshmana wished he could obscure or ignore the sage's next words. They were about Kaikeyi, the witch, who was a false, vindictive mother.

"Do not blame Kaikeyi," Bharadvaja said. "It's hard to see her goodness now, I concede that. But she has set a plan in motion that no one else could have done. You'll see. This exile will turn out to be a blessing."

"What is the purpose of this exile?" Rama asked, a new eagerness in his tone.

He really longed to understand where Father's betrayal was taking them. *Betrayal* was Lakshmana's word. Rama kept calling it *Father's promise*, but what kind of virtue lay in a promise that punished the innocent and rewarded the scheming?

"If humans were meant to know what was ahead," Bharadvaja said loudly, as if trying to overpower Lakshmana's inner monologue, "the Lord above would have gifted them with foresight. If you are set on knowing, then look within. Though I caution you, don't expect quick answers. After all, I have been looking within for more than eighty thousand years, and I'm only at the beginning of what you would call omniscience."

Rama bowed his head at Bharadvaja's feet. Lakshmana did too. Eighty thousand years! That's how old the all-seeing sage was, though he hardly looked older than Father. Lakshmana knew that the inward-gazing path was not for him. He barely had the patience to withstand each hour—let alone a hundred years or a thousand!

"But I will ask you to ponder something," Bharadvaja said. "If you were to meet this man who is Vishnu, and he was confounded and heartbroken, what advice would you offer him? Think on that. There may be some answers there for you."

Rama and Lakshmana looked at each other. Wise beings like Vasishta and Bharadvaja always found ways to nudge others into deep thinking. And it was something to ponder: If the omniscient Lord placed himself within a human form, how would he experience the world?

"Now, shall we speak about more practical matters?" Bharadvaja asked, taking charge yet again. "Vasishta sent you to me for that reason alone. I'm afraid I've taken liberties in my interactions with you."

"We are deeply grateful for all your illuminating words and for your assistance," Rama assured Bharadvaja.

"I would be most pleased if you decided to stay here at my ashram," Bharadvaja said. "You could peacefully live out the term of your exile here. It's a simple life, but you will lack no food or shelter. I would be most delighted if you decided to stay here with us."

"We thank you for your hospitality and warm welcome," Rama said. "Somehow I think you know what our answer must be. We cannot stay here. It's too close to Ayodhya. The kingdom has been torn asunder. Men—especially warriors—have been known to act rashly under such circumstances. It's my duty to lead my wife and my brother to a safe place, farther from Ayodhya."

"Yes, you speak the truth, though I couldn't resist offering. There is a place called Chitrakuta, a mountain peak, which will suit you. You will find ample fruits, honey, and fresh water there. From the peak of that mountain, you will be able to see far and wide. You will have time to run from any intruders, if that's what you choose to do. It's a few days' journey from here. I will give you clear directions. But please honor me by resting here one night. The sun is far past its zenith."

Rama nodded, folding his hands at his chest. There was no reason to resist the invitation to stay the night.

Bharadvaja called to his disciples, who had remained at a respectful distance. "Show our guests the beds we have prepared for them."

Lakshmana knew that by the standards of the palace, the ashram beds would not even count as such. They could hardly, however, be more austere than the beds from the night before, the plain Earth. Lakshmana, who had slept only few hours in the past two days, felt the heaviness of his eyelids. He could hardly persuade himself to get up and follow Bharadvaja's disciple. He certainly did not get a chance to examine the ashram beds; he fell asleep before his head was on the cushion, all his weapons still decorating his body.

CHAPTER 5

Brotherhood

Lakshmana's eyes opened at dawn. He had slept the entire night without a single dream. His thoughts pounced on him: Had Urmila finally succumbed to exhaustion as well? How did she fare in the palace without him? Without a husband, would she be mistreated? What kind of place would Ayodhya be, under Kaikeyi's rule? Would Urmila still love him after the long fourteen years? Her large eyes had been narrow with anger, her red mouth a tight line. *I will never forgive you.* Lakshmana threw an arm across his eyes. He thumped his forehead with his fist. Stop! This was not a good way to start the day.

One of the disciples brought him warm milk with honey to drink. It was flavorful in the cool spring morning. Outside the thatched hut, jugs of water waited. Rama was awake. The brothers took turns helping each other bathe. In the moments of scrubbing himself clean with the refreshing water, Lakshmana could forget. While pouring the water onto his brother, Lakshmana could forget. But the moment Sita peeked out from the hut, Lakshmana's mind returned to reality. Sita could not bathe out in the open as the brothers did. She had to hide inside the hut. This was no life for a princess!

Before they left, Bharadvaja's disciples fed them sumptuously. Bharadvaja remained silent, emanating contentment and joy. After receiving clear directions, they bid Bharadvaja farewell, who said these words in parting: "The closer you get to a mountain, the less you are able to recognize it as such." He asked them to instead keep an eye out for a gigantic banyan tree that lived at the base of Mount Chitrakuta.

They spent the day walking, becoming more adept at avoiding the thorny underbrush and rocky areas. They stopped only once, when the sweet aroma of ripe mangoes filled the air. The branches of the mango tree hung low, heavy with fruit. The mangoes were so ripe, they fell into Lakshmana's hands at the lightest touch. Lakshmana plucked fruits for Sita and Rama before devouring his first mango. Hunger took over, and they ate in silence, filling their empty bellies. They threw the pits of the mangoes into the forest, the sticky juice running down their arms. Sita's cheeks were smeared with mango pulp; she had devoured the juicy fruits with abandon.

When night prevented them from walking farther, they found a level area under an oak tree. The grass was soft under Lakshmana's feet. This was to be their first night on their own in the forest. The brothers began gathering branches to build a fire. There was still a light chill in the nighttime spring air. After the fire had been kindled, Lakshmana broke the silence.

"Both of you rest. Let me stand guard."

He was sure he had a sleepless night ahead anyway.

"We are not yet in a terrain where blood-drinkers roam," Rama assured Sita. "The only danger here is from wild beasts. The fire will keep us warm and ward off predators."

Rama and Lakshmana unstrapped their weapons and kept them within arm's reach. Sita sat close to Rama and gazed with sleepy eyes at him. Rama's mood with her was light, as if they were here for the pleasure of it. After some time, Sita curled up in the grass next to the fire. With the warmth of the orange flames glowing on her skin, Sita fell asleep on the ground, evidently unperturbed by the unfamiliar setting and the hard Earth beneath her. Lakshmana wished he could surrender to the experience as she did. But every muscle in his body felt tense. He could not escape the bitterness of the situation.

The brothers sat together in silence, leaning against the oak tree. As stillness came upon them, Rama's heaviness became pronounced. Lakshmana silently waited. What would his brother say? Rama remained in his reverie. Lakshmana stared at the fire and its wild, blazing flames, a reflection of the turmoil he felt within.

Even though Rama looked grim, Lakshmana held back, wary of the vehemence he felt. What could he say that Rama didn't already know? Lakshmana didn't agree with Rama's decision to honor Father's promise. Kaikeyi deserved death or imprisonment for the rest of her days. Lakshmana began to make a list in his mind of the various punishments that could be meted out to Kaikeyi. Rama's voice interrupted Lakshmana's internal rampage.

"Keeping Sita safe is our first priority," he said. His voice grew thick as he continued. "I shouldn't have brought her with me. It's madness."

Rama pressed his hands against his temples, but like a dam bursting, his emotions pushed forward and he spoke. "No matter what angle I look at it from, I *cannot* understand Father. How did he allow this to happen? I see that Kaikeyi trapped Father in his promises. I see that Father was pushed into a corner. A promise is unbreakable. If Father taught me anything, it's that. But still . . . I expected Father to find a solution, to do something, to be a man of action, to find a way out. Unless . . . unless Father didn't want a way out."

Lakshmana held still. He had been waiting for this moment, his anxiety building in the face of his brother's unnatural calm. Rama was always levelheaded, coming up with innovative solutions when everyone else was stumped. This situation was different. Few things mattered to Rama the way Father did. Kaikeyi had also been one of Rama's favorite people, someone he spent much of his free time with.

"Until this day," Rama said, "I felt safe under Father's protection. I felt protected by his righteousness and his knowledge. I felt I knew every part of his thought process, often better than he did himself. Now I feel like I never understood him, that there were things he kept from me. When Father did *nothing*, the strangest feeling hit my heart. Even when he finally begged me to overthrow him, his words came too late. It was an empty request. He knew I would never do that to him."

In Lakshmana's opinion, Rama had been overly dutiful, sacrificing his own future for their father. It wasn't right. But if Lakshmana said a word now, Rama would withdraw again to his controlled frame of mind, to his public position, and put on the face that he showed the world and even to Sita. So Lakshmana put aside his own convictions and remained quiet. It was Rama's turn to share.

"I can only conclude," Rama said, "that Father wanted me to be exiled. He chose Kaikeyi over me. Father chose to draw borders around every city in the world and exclude me from them. Why?" Lakshmana sighed heavily, and Rama continued. "Father was always my foremost ally, my best friend and advisor. He taught me to be calm and just, not to make hasty decisions. Now I don't know him anymore. He is powerless, completely under the sway of Kaikeyi's will."

Rama spoke with a keen eye for every detail at the scene, remembering that their father's eyes had been closed and his body motionless, as if he could avoid the situation by feigning sleep. Kaikeyi had hovered over the king like a ruthless master whipping a dying horse.

Lakshmana felt his breathing go shallow, reliving those moments. But Rama had not cracked under pressure; he had only become calmer and sharper, a better warrior than Lakshmana. When Rama began to speak about Kaikeyi, it took an enormous amount of Lakshmana's willpower to quell his tongue.

"Why did Mother turn on me this way?" Rama asked. "Her welcoming embrace, quick laughter, and playful presence are vivid in my mind. I don't know who this other Kaikeyi is. She stood by Father's side like Death's crone. She pretended like she didn't know me or care for me. She was like a hard, ruthless diamond, Lakshmana."

A venomous snake, Lakshmana thought. He did not speak.

"She had no compassion for Father's suffering," Rama said. "Father looked like he was dying...pale and sweating. She who doted on Father, who adored his every word, was indifferent. Why did Mother suddenly hate us?"

Lakshmana wanted to punch the ground and shout, "You are faultless, my brother! Kaikeyi waited to show her true self until the question of the throne came up."

Lakshmana bit his teeth together, locking his jaw. He was sure his lips were compressed in anger, his eyes bloodshot. He couldn't help that, but at least he was silent, and Rama's eyes were full of tears anyway. He wouldn't see how Lakshmana struggled to simply listen. It was a listener Rama needed, not advice or a call to arms.

"Father...," Rama said, his voice cracking. "I've never seen him like that. Defenseless, like an old, broken man. I wanted to do everything in my capacity to bring him back to his power, to make him see that his word counts. No matter how long ago he gave our third mother those boons, they are still potent. His promise is powerful. It must be respected. You understand, Lakshmana, don't you?"

For the first time, Rama turned to Lakshmana for some assurance. It was a moment that Lakshmana had dreaded. He didn't want to lie; truly, he did not agree with his brother's decision to leave the kingdom without a fight—a fight that they would win! But the remembrance of Father as a broken man left Lakshmana more vulnerable than he had expected. Next to Rama, Father had been Lakshmana's foremost role model too. The king's fall from grace, as Lakshmana saw it, hurt in many different ways. Lakshmana's lips began to quiver as he remembered how quick he had been to wish death upon Father. If Rama hadn't intervened, Lakshmana could have easily killed Father then and there. Lakshmana shuddered and reached for his brother.

"I do understand," he whispered. "I feel ashamed that I turned on Father in those moments."

"No one acts perfectly under duress."

"Except for you, Rama."

And that made Rama's shoulders finally collapse; silent sobs shook his body. Lakshmana's unshed tears also welled up, and the brothers held each other for comfort, crying for each other as they had done as boys. Supported in this way by Lakshmana, Rama voiced every feeling he had, shedding an old way of being and coming into a new one. Lakshmana could see the transformation occurring in his brother. As Rama confided in his brother, days of tension melted away from him until finally he felt silent.

"We have fourteen years in this forest ahead of us," Rama stated. He leaned back against the tree, resting his head against its rough trunk.

Lakshmana stood up to feed the dying fire. Sita slept deeply, breathing evenly. When Lakshmana returned, Rama's face was clear. Lakshmana took his place by his brother's side again. Feeling the uneven bark dig into his back, Lakshmana pushed his feet into the ground, feeling the tree's resistance and support. He dug his toes into the Earth, and a surge of power shot up into his feet, very much like a blessing. It filled his legs, back, and chest. He flexed his arms, experiencing the strength of his fingers, as if he could grab hold of the air and make a weapon out of thin air. He looked at Rama. There was a light smile on Rama's shadowed face.

"The most important thing is that we are alive and together," Rama said. "You are full of vigor, and so is Sita. Your presence reassures me. Thank you for coming with me."

Lakshmana's tight nerves had already softened by Rama's openhearted revelations. Now his brother's gratitude invigorated him.

"And think about this, my brother," Rama said, nudging him, "we can do anything we want. We can go anywhere. I can't remember when I've had this luxury before."

In a few seconds of reflection, Lakshmana leaned forward and imagined the endless tasks and responsibilities of the kingship lining up before Rama: the people he needed to talk to, the citizens he must see, the uprisings he must quell, the moods of the palace he must tune into, and more. Ruling a kingdom was intricate and complex, and moments of peace were fleeting. Rama had never shirked those responsibilities. Now they had fourteen years ahead with no one to be accountable to, no routines, and no decisions that affected millions of people. It was possible, for a moment, to see the blessing in this . . . to see it as an adventure. He nodded to Rama.

"It's just you, me, and Sita now," Rama affirmed. "With you by my side, I'm more worried for whatever is out there."

Lakshmana found his voice. "Your optimism is frightening, my brother." He was smiling too. It was true; he was grateful to be there next to Rama. There was nowhere else he could be.

Rama closed his eyes and leaned back against the giant oak tree, peace evident on his face. Without opening his eyes, Rama said, "I refuse to live with anguish for the next fourteen years."

Rama looked lighter, a great burden lifted from his shoulders.

But Lakshmana could not forgive and forget, as Rama was intent on doing. Kaikeyi slithered through his bloodstream like toxic venom, and Bharata, their brother, was right there next to her, with hungry eyes. Lakshmana did not for a minute trust Bharata. As if Kaikeyi had come up with all this on her own! Her scheme was inspired by the fact that Bharata wanted the kingdom for himself. The best way would be to annihilate Rama forever. Was Bharata willing to kill Rama to secure his claim to the throne? Lakshmana was capable of killing anyone who stood between Rama and the throne; he thought no less of Bharata's capability.

"As soon as dawn is here to shed light on our steps, we *must* continue to walk," Lakshmana said. "We will not be safe until we have disappeared completely into the jungle."

While Rama kept his eyes closed, Lakshmana's thoughts continued. Would the people of Ayodhya forgive Bharata if he killed Rama? What choice did they have? The citizens of a kingdom were at the mercy and whim of the king. That's why the people loved Rama so passionately; he didn't treat them that way. He listened to them; he really heard their desires

and suggestions, honoring their wishes above his own. Because of his popularity, Rama was a dangerous opponent. If Bharata was in on his mother's scheme, they would certainly find an opportunity to completely eliminate Rama. It would be foolish to think otherwise.

CHAPTER 6

Sita and the Fire

My eyes were half closed, but the fire dancing on my eyelids kept me awake. My dreams had been more vivid and disturbing the few nights since the exile. Always I found myself standing at the entrance of a black gate, shut out. I didn't look forward to sleeping and finding myself trapped in that dream-scene again.

I peeked over my shoulder at my beloved, sitting with his brother. He was not just putting on a brave front. He is the most courageous person I know. But I felt that because of me, he was a frozen river. The surface was still, yet the water coursed rapidly below. At any other time, I would have pressed him to confide in me. In this situation, I could not be that person. I was part of the problem. He had brought me into the exile against his better judgement. My small triumph swelled in me again. At this moment I could be one of many grieving in Ayodhya. Instead I was there, right where I should be, close to my beloved.

I felt the fire flicker warmly across the front of my body. I had never slept next to a live fire before. My back, facing the dark, sleeping forest, felt cool in the spring breeze. I was neither warm nor cold. Half-half. A fitting description of how I felt. I had not slept on the bare ground since I was a small child. With my head resting on my elbow and my body curled up in the grass, I could feel the dampness of the Earth seep into my skin. The grass had tickled me when I first sought shelter on the ground. It was soft and prickly all at once and so foreign from our beds at home. But now, this was to be home.

Giving up the thought of actually falling into the dreamlands, I gazed into the fire, its heat flushing my cheeks. I could hear the steady murmur of my beloved talking behind me. For once, Lakshmana was silent. For a brief moment I let myself contemplate what it would be like living alongside Lakshmana during the coming years. The fourteen years stretched ahead of me, long as an eternity. They stretched not before me but into me, tearing out what I held precious. The most precious was here with me: Rama. My choice was made. This knowing increased the force of the brutal cleanse of my mind. It surged through me, shouting, "Out! Out!" to every object, attachment, and person I had left behind in Ayodhya. I saw some logic to it. None of those people or things would serve me in this exile. So I silently let my mind go on this brutal rampage until it turned its cleansing force on *her*. My sister Urmila.

I brought my mind to a complete halt. It was as if I caught Urmila's hand and begged, "Stay!"

"I don't want her to leave me," I whispered to the fire, beseeching its support.

"You left her," the fire replied fiercely.

A jolt ran through my body. The fire had just spoken to me. I perceived it as clearly as a real voice. *You left her.* The fire within me awoke in recognition of the kindred element outside of me. I felt its keen attunement to my thoughts and I opened my heart to its gaze.

I kept my murmurs soft, not wanting to interrupt the discussion behind me, which was becoming heated like the fire. But I too had a need to speak.

"I did not leave her," I insisted. "My fate was decided when I walked around the sacred fire, holding Rama's hand."

The fire crackled, saying, "I was there, remember."

I smiled ever so slightly. Fire had been present at countless marriages and funerals, the eternal witness and purifier of human cycles. Perhaps it had been there before and after the worlds were destroyed and re-manifested. I was conversing with someone far wiser than I. I knew that. And so I said, "My decision to go with Rama was no choice at all, but destiny itself."

"But do you think," the flames prodded, "that Urmila would see it this way? You chose Rama over her. Exile over her."

I felt tears rise to my eyes. "You are right. I'm not going to see her for fourteen years. I don't know who I will be when I return."

"*If* you return," the fire offered—a possibility I truly had not imagined.

My beloved's voice cut through my thoughts. My heart jumped. I focused on *not* hearing what he said. Instinctively I knew . . . those words were not for me. He hadn't hidden himself from me, only for me to spy on him now. Resolutely I turned my eyes to the fire. I truly had no experience conversing with one of nature's elements. The palace was full of people and

activities. My sister was always close at hand. We had considered ourselves lucky that we had married into the same family; we could share our daily lives with each other. Not anymore.

"What solace can you offer me, Fire, in face of this loss?"

"I live within each of you," the fire whispered to me, dancing slowly, then rapidly, turning black at its tips, blending with the night.

"Are you burning within *him* now?" I asked.

I could not fully ignore the power of Rama's outpouring behind me. I had to force myself to keep still and stay to myself; I wanted to run to his side. Feeling my need to be distracted and pulled in, the dancing flames spoke again about my sister.

"If you feel you had no choice but walk with Rama into this exile, what then of Lakshmana?"

I startled. I had not been able to get to know Lakshmana well; he was so opposite to Rama. I couldn't understand his words or thoughts. Especially not now. I remembered how terribly and unspeakably angry I had become when Rama had faced me with his resolve to go without me into exile. I had seen him as the cruelest, most hardhearted person I had ever met; having tied me to him with the deepest bonds of love, how could he entertain the thought of abandoning me for even a second? My anger had been so forceful, it pushed my consciousness from my body and I fled. Something had happened while I was unconscious, but I could not clearly recall it. Only that it had felt like being in the arms of my mother. Later, I learned that my mother, the Earth goddess, had warned me about my future. In that vision, I had seen the enemy. At this time, however, I had only the vaguest perception of my mother as a real sentient being. What I did know beyond a doubt was that no words, no tragedy, no turn of events, could ever dissuade me from following Rama wherever he had to go. I was his, forever. But my sister had been abandoned. She was forced to live without her beloved.

"How could Lakshmana leave my sister?" I demanded, feeling outraged on her behalf.

The fire was not silent but responded in a language I could not understand, speaking as fires do, devouring the branches and leaves, turning everything within reach to ashes.

"Are you just going to leave me with this terrible question?" I pressed. I let my distress show. "How could Lakshmana leave her behind for fourteen years? How could he choose anything but her? How could he desert his own wife? Oh, she will *never* forgive him for this!"

"Do you mean that *you* will never forgive him for this?"

Another challenge, putting me in my place.

Who was I to judge the love Lakshmana had for my sister? What did I truly know of her reaction to his announcement that he would leave? I had not even said farewell to her myself. I had not seen her one last time. And that memory unlocked my tears.

"I didn't have time to say good-bye," I whispered, the tears rolling hotly down my face. "What if"—I pressed my eyes against my arm—"what if I never see her again?"

Despite its earlier challenge to my mortality, the fire neither confirmed nor denied our future reunion. My sister's beautiful face appeared before me. I had always thought her more striking than I was, more vibrant and joyous. She was less than a year younger than me. Our mother Sunayana had always called us her double miracles. She had not expected to have any children. Later, I came to know I was not her daughter the way Urmila was. Urmila was not my sister the way our cousins, Shrutakirti and Mandavi, were sisters. I was a foundling, adopted. Yet, learning the story of my birth had only made me feel more tender and protective over my sister, my belonging to her and to them tenuous.

"Aside from Rama," I confessed to the fire, "there is no one I love as much as my little sister. She is like my other half. She grew up watching me, following me, doing as I did. In turn, I watched her, aware of how much she depended on me. I had to be grave and wise, so she could be carefree. But when we married on the same day, to these brothers behind me—"

"I was there, remember," the fire chided ever so gently, reminding me again who I was talking to, if not just myself.

"Yes, you were there," I conceded, "but can you know what I felt on that day? Can you know what my sister felt? Do you know how marriage changed us?"

My challenge seemed to make the fire sparkle more vividly, as if it enjoyed my defiance.

"I may not know," it responded, "but you do. Not only your own feelings, but your sister's too."

"Yes," I whispered fervently.

My beloved's murmurs behind me had grown quieter. I hoped they would not catch me there awake and demand to know what I was up to. Surely Rama would rethink his decision to bring me along. I recalled how sternly he had treated me when he found the thorns in my feet. If he caught me conversing with the fire, what would he say? On the eve of my wedding, my father had cautioned me not to diverge from normal behaviors of other humans. Yet this conversation with the fire felt natural, as if I had done it often. So I continued.

"Why didn't Lakshmana insist on Urmila coming too? Rama allowed me to come. And he allowed Lakshmana to come. Is it not reasonable and fair that Urmila could come along?" My grief flared into anger again. It was too easy to take on the mood of my fiery friend.

The flames were unyielding, almost teasing. "Some things, sweet princess, you must discover on your own."

The words *on your own* echoed in my soul like a warning. "On your own, on your own . . ."

I shivered, noticing the fire dying down and the night wind engulfing me. Just then Lakshmana came to stir the fire and feed the flames. I felt him glance down on me, and I kept my eyes carefully shut, my breathing long and even. Whatever reasons he had for choosing to come to the forest without Urmila would not be easily discovered. I knew that. Once Lakshmana returned to our beloved's side, I sighed and pulled my veil more tightly around me. I gave the fire one last look, grateful for the warmth it shared.

Anna

CHAPTER 7

Surviving in the Wild

When Rama woke up, a blanket of dew covered him from head to toe. Everything around them was damp with moisture. Sleeping on the bare Earth, Rama was reminded again of his first mentor, Vishvamitra, the fierce warrior-sage who had whisked Rama out of Ayodhya. That had been the adventure that brought Rama to Sita. He glanced at her, his heart swelling. She was asleep, one of her cheeks resting against the ground. A light film of dew covered her. A smudge of soot from the fire darkened her cheek. Her firm decision to embrace the exile as her own had changed everything for Rama. If he hadn't secretly wanted it, perhaps he would have managed a stronger resistance. Lakshmana certainly thought so—yet another area where Rama was not being the strong man his brother expected. Still, Lakshmana had listened in the night to Rama's torment, and Rama was grateful for his brother's presence.

They had no fresh clothes to change into and no food to eat, so they began the day's journey by searching for water. The pond they found was shallow yet sufficed for washing their faces and mouths. The morning sun began to dry up the night's

dampness. Rama walked with lithe feet as they journeyed toward Chitrakuta, the mountain crest they could see in the far distance. A dense length of forest stood between them and their destination, and the closer they got to Chitrakuta, the easier it would be to lose sight of the destination. *The closer you get to a mountain, the less you are able to recognize it as such.* Those were Bharadvaja's parting words. They seemed, as always, to resonate with meaning. Just like the legend of Vishnu had been. It was interwoven with clear undercurrents that had tugged at Rama's heart. There was so much to contemplate, but for now their primary concern was to find the largest banyan tree they had ever seen. This was the landmark that stood at the base of the mountain.

Chitrakuta would be their first home in the forest. If all went well, they might even live out the term of the exile there. If they settled now, they could prepare for the winter. When the land was covered in frost and the fruits on the trees were gone, they would need shelter and food. Bharadvaja had thoughtfully given them advice on how to make clay pots and almond cakes and instructed them how to roast wild roots in the night fire.

As they pushed ahead, the Earth was soft and the grass tickled Rama's feet. A few lengths later, it turned dry and sandy, wafting up at their ankles. Deep breaths here prickled his nostrils. On their way they passed many enchanting sights, such as bodies of crystal-clear water teeming with aquatic life. Demoiselle cranes flew overhead, and they spotted a sloth bear with two cubs on her back.

When evening approached, they found the banyan tree that was as massive as a small mountain.

"There it is," Rama said, pointing at it. "Impossible to miss, as Bharadvaja promised. He called it Shyam, and now we can see why."

As the name implied, the bark of the tree was dark blue, like lotuses, with patches of gray.

"That is the biggest tree we've ever seen," Lakshmana said, speaking for them all.

The shock of aerial roots extended high into the sky, only to finally arch and reach toward the ground, in many cases forming new tree trunks. Close to it, Rama espied a river with muddy banks. The blue lotuses hugging the banks were in full bloom. Right behind Shyam, the ground began to slope upward.

Chitrakuta was before them. Assured that their destination was near, Rama led them to the shade of the banyan to rest for a few minutes. The bow-like branches created a hollow space that felt like a cave. Under the shelter of the tree, there was a damp, musty smell. Rama touched its trunk, feeling the patient soul infusing the tree with life.

"This tree reminds me of Father," Rama said. He couldn't stop the wave of sadness that reached his eyes.

"I can feel its ancient and wise presence," Sita said.

"Father would *never* allow anyone to cause us harm," Rama said, turning to Lakshmana, who was convinced that assassins were on their heels.

Lakshmana answered, "The way he would never exile you for no crime at all?"

Before Rama could defend Father, in one breath Lakshmana said, "Even if Father wouldn't allow it, how do we know if he has any power? With free rein, who knows what other schemes Kaikeyi and that hunchback will invent!"

Lakshmana was right.

"I'm afraid your words ring true, my brother," Rama said. "Bharata is not there yet. Long as it seems to us, only three nights have passed. It will take at least two weeks, even on the swiftest horses, for Bharata to return from Kekaya to Ayodhya."

"I do *not* understand the wisdom in seeing Bharata as our ally."

"Lakshmana, imagine how you would feel if I distrusted you and your intentions. Is Bharata, our beloved brother, really a stranger to us now? Don't we know everything about one another? Haven't we spent all our lives together? Bharata is like my second self—as you are."

Lakshmana clenched his jaw, and his fists had a life of their own.

Rama took a deep breath and said, "I take your caution seriously, Lakshmana. And I've been thinking. . . . I do fear for Father's life, and for my mother, Kausalya. I think we always knew that while Kaikeyi was loving toward us, she did not treat our other mothers with the same concern. In her transformed state, I don't know what Kaikeyi is capable of and this worries me a great deal. Lakshmana, you could make your way back to Ayodhya in three or four days. Sita and I will complete this exile together. I would feel greatly eased if I knew that Mother and Father were protected from Kaikeyi and Manthara. Until Bharata gets there, you are the only one I fully trust now. Lakshmana, you must return to the city."

Lakshmana looked utterly stricken. If Rama gave him an order, he would have no choice.

"You speak truly, Rama," Lakshmana said, his words again rushed, the words tumbling over one another. "But I renounced Ayodhya when it renounced you. I have no loyalty to that place or its people now. Please. Please don't order me to go back there."

Sita stirred and Rama felt it. Rama heard her say, "Urmila—" But Lakshmana quelled her with one look and then threw himself at Rama's feet, the way he'd done when the exile was a fact. Lakshmana's anguish immediately replaced his anger. He leaned his forehead on Rama's knee. His words were muffled, but it sounded like he simply repeated, "Please, please."

Rama glanced at Sita, who was looking at Lakshmana with an unusually stern expression. She agreed with Rama that Lakshmana should return. Rama knew all too well what it

felt like to be cast away; he couldn't do this to Lakshmana. Not against his will. He would let Lakshmana think on it before he brought it up again.

He gently placed his hand on Lakshmana's head. But the worry for Father and Mother persisted. Rama would feel appeased if he knew that Lakshmana was there to protect them, especially from Manthara. The hunchback had hated him since the day he was born, probably because he was born before Bharata. This was clear to Rama now. Suddenly he thought of Sita's father. Would he blame Rama for bringing his daughter to this dangerous place?

"Your father will no doubt curse the day he gave your hand to me," Rama said.

"Don't," Sita said. "I asked your mother to inform him that it was *my* choice."

This was news to Rama. Sita had thought ahead of him in this regard. Yet it was like Lakshmana said. Those people and those places did not belong to them any longer. For fourteen years they would have no connection, no familiarity. It was better not to think of them at all.

Bless us with endurance, Rama prayed to the ancient banyan. *Protect my father.*

Without another word, they began their ascent to Chitrakuta. The higher they climbed, the more of a view they gained of the vast forest. Bharadvaja had described Chitrakuta well. The threesome came upon waterfalls, gurgling streams, flowering trees, and dancing peacocks. Cuckoo birds sang above them. Rama kept his gaze on Sita, intent on easing her progress up the steep mountain. He took one step and turned to help her. Lakshmana carefully hovered in the background. Once they had an arching view of the forest, they sought a level part of the mountain terrain and found a natural clearing where the ground was even. It was perfect. Twilight began to cast shadows, and Rama knew they had to claim the land for themselves.

"I think we have found what we are seeking," Rama said. He put his hand on his bow and when he did, pent-up fury that he hadn't known rose into his fingers.

Lakshmana's bow gave a light twang as he brought it forth. They would claim the land together. Rama wouldn't let anything jeopardize their safety there. Sita stood frozen behind them, as Rama turned one direction and Lakshmana the other. Rama's arrows yearned to fulfill their lethal purpose, and the next moment one of them shot through the air toward its target. Lakshmana's arrow was only a split second behind Rama's.

One part of Rama felt Sita's reaction behind them. She flinched with every arrow. The other part was intent on the hunt. He had not voiced aggression toward his elders; he had not agitated for a rebellion. There was no trace of hesitation in his being. He acted automatically, drawing arrows to his ear and releasing them. His arrows found several hidden targets, but the animals were fleeing much before they usually would have. Rama paused, looking at Lakshmana. The animals had cleared out, as if someone had told them to run.

"Sita, stay close to me," Rama commanded, moving into the clearing.

Sita neither heeded nor heard Rama's command.

Rama returned to her side. "Sita?"

She made no response, not even with her eyes, which looked straight ahead, like the dead buck's unseeing stare.

Set on the hunt, Lakshmana moved forward swiftly.

Rama stood by Sita's side, saying her name. There was no indication that she had heard him. The moment his fingertips made contact with her skin, Sita collapsed to the ground, released from her terror. She covered her face and cried into her hands. Rama clenched his jaw. This was the scene with the black buck happening all over again.

When Lakshmana returned with a handful of bloody arrows, Sita was still unreachable. Nothing he or Rama said could console her.

"May I speak frankly?" Lakshmana asked of Rama.

"Don't you always?" Rama answered. His tone was short, distraught over Sita's reaction.

"Sita is not meant for this life," Lakshmana said in a rushed whisper. "If she is so affected by this, how will she endure fourteen years with us?"

"Just say I agree with you—what are our choices? We can't go back to Ayodhya now and return her."

As Lakshmana spoke, Rama looked down at his arms. Blood trickled from one of the scars on his bow arm. He hadn't ripped open any of his scars in years. He had been handling his bow carelessly.

"We could return to Bharadvaja's ashram," Lakshmana said. "I'm sure he would find a way to contact Vasishta. They could send someone from Ayodhya to escort her home."

"A few minutes ago, you did not trust anyone in Ayodhya."

"I don't. But Sita is not their target. They would never hurt her. She won't be able to cope here. All the comforts she needs are there. Her sister and her cousins are in Ayodhya. She will not have to see these unbearable sights. This isn't the life for a princess. Think, if we encounter blood-drinkers. Her life will be endangered, and who knows what other horrors this forest harbors!"

"I said all this to her before we left, Lakshmana. She would not listen. Her home is where I am."

"But—" Lakshmana said, but stopped.

Sita stood and, without a glance at them, walked away. In a trancelike state, she moved straight ahead and disappeared behind the trees.

Rama followed Sita at once. He found her standing over a dead doe. When Rama saw what Sita really was looking at, his heart grew cold: A little fawn was by its mother side, despondently nudging her mother's nose.

When Sita reached out and put her hand on the fawn, the little one did not flinch. With gentle hands, Sita lifted it into her lap. She smiled through her tears. "I'm naming her Mila, after Urmila."

Lakshmana came up behind Rama in time to hear this. Even if they could not comprehend Sita's reaction, this was something they understood. It had happened to them during their first hunting expedition as young boys. It had been even more dramatic, the dying doe expelling her fetus in her fright. Father had allowed them to take the orphaned newborn home. Since then, Rama had never felt entirely comfortable hunting deer. Father had insisted it was a perfect lesson. Sometimes a warrior was forced to kill even those he had affection for.

Watching Sita caressing this little fawn, Rama didn't have the heart to protest, though the facts were clear: They didn't have a shelter, food, or resources even for themselves. But Sita had already adopted the fawn; it was clear in the tender strokes of her hand on its tiny neck.

"Come then, Sita," Rama said. "Bring the little one with you. Let us settle for the night."

They had less than an hour's worth of light left. They were living on air at the moment, their stomachs empty of food. Soon they located the closest fresh water source, a small waterfall with a sandy bank full of rocks. They sat at the base of the waterfall, chewing on licorice roots they had dug up. It wasn't much, but it was something. None of them had ever had to think about food before, but it would be their primary concern from now on. Mila lapped water from the waterfall and quickly returned to Sita's side. This night they would sleep with the starry sky as their roof, though Lakshmana promised to mimic the cottages he had seen at the other two dwellings. They needed a shelter from wind, rain, and cold, and the feeling of home that a structure could provide.

The next morning, Rama and Lakshmana skinned the animals they had killed and stretched the hides from tree to tree. At least their deaths were not in vain. After Sita awoke and noticed the skins, she stood in contemplation for a long time.

Rama came to her side and then Lakshmana did too.

"I don't know what happened to me yesterday," Sita said, her voice husky. "Your arrows hit *me*. I felt every one of them. It was *I* who died. I wanted to rush forward and stand between the animals and your lethal arrows. I wanted to protect them. Save them. And I felt my warning rush ahead of your arrows and send them fleeing. I couldn't save them all, but I sent a few of them to safety. That's the only way I can describe it."

She turned to Lakshmana. "One part of me accepts and understands what you were doing. Seeing your mastery with your bows, I knew you were born to this. That you were trained to do this. You must have learned to hunt before you came of age. Your compassion has been hardened to make you better warriors. I understand this. I do not hold your actions against you."

"We wanted to ensure the safety of this place we will inhabit," Lakshmana said.

Rama added, "Hunting and killing are not sins for a warrior."

Sita took a deep breath. "And yet . . . I felt their terror as if it was mine."

There was no facile response to Sita's heartfelt revelation. Had they done wrong in claiming the forest in this way? From a warrior's standpoint, certainly not. But Rama had felt disconnected from Sita then, like she was unreachable. Since the first moment they met, the bond between them had been vibrant and resonant. It frightened Rama to feel Sita beyond reach.

"I don't like seeing you like that, Sita," Rama said.

Sita looked at Rama and said, "Please . . . don't send me back to Ayodhya."

Lakshmana frowned and averted his face. Rama felt the corners of his mouth lift. Both of his companions wanted to send the other back.

The sounds of the forest filled the silence. A bird chirped and its mate answered. A few monkeys chattered loudly. The three of them sighed deeply all at the same time, and then turned to their assigned tasks. Rama and Sita collected mud and began their experiment with crafting clay pots. Lakshmana gathered materials for the cottage and began to set up the structure.

When the clay pots were drying in the sun, Sita explored nearby, seeking fruit trees and berry bushes, all the while singing so they could hear where she was. The adopted fawn was of course Sita's constant shadow, like a child clinging to its mother's skirts.

Suddenly, Sita cried out, and Rama immediately paused his work and looked up.

"Come quickly!" Sita called, with laughter in her voice.

The strangest sight greeted Rama. Sita was covered in bumblebees. Above her, a honeycomb dripped its golden liquid. The bees had left their home to investigate Sita, as if she was a flower. With the bees tickling her skin, Sita started twirling around, and the bees swirled with her like a golden whirlwind. Mila kept her distance, eyeing the buzzing bees suspiciously.

Rama quickly found large leaves to catch the honey in. When his hands were full, he called to Lakshmana to do the same. The opportunity was not to be missed. Lakshmana filled as many large leaf cups with honey as he could hold. When Sita came to a standstill, the bees lingered for a few moments and then returned to their honeycomb.

His mouth watering, Rama handed a leaf cup to Sita and drank the honey as if it was water. The golden honey was nectar, and they drank and drank till they could stomach no more. Drunk on honey, the three of them burst into uncontrollable laughter. Lakshmana hooted so loudly, he started rolling on the ground in fits of laughter. Sita bent double, tears squirting from her eyes. Rama had never seen either of them laugh like this. The forest echoed with their mirth. Mila was busy licking and chewing the honey-drenched leaves.

From then onward, they had a sure way of collecting honey. For whenever Sita approached the hive, the bees left their honeycomb and started buzzing around her. Rama or Lakshmana would carefully extract one or two layers of beeswax and let the honey drip into their clay pot. It became a dance they did together whenever they needed honey. Though Lakshmana didn't say it openly, it was impossible to ignore Sita's golden touch with the forest and its creatures.

In this way, weeks passed by, bringing them into the month of Chaitra. Spring blossomed all around them, exploding with colors and life. They got closer and closer to a day Rama wanted to avoid, the ninth day of the moon. His eighteenth birthday.

When the day came, Rama did not want to celebrate.

"I don't want to celebrate mine either," Lakshmana said. His was two weeks later.

"Why?" Sita asked. "I know we can't imitate the grand ways of Ayodhya. But will we live without celebration for fourteen years?"

"I have never turned a year older without Father," Rama said.

With that, he felt an enormous need to be alone. He was grateful that neither Sita nor Lakshmana pursued him as he turned away from them. It was still difficult for Rama to reconcile the father he knew with the father who had sent him away.

If there was one source of light for Rama in those first months of exile, it was Sita. She not only accepted this new life but actually thrived. Often, she woke up humming sweet melodies. She adorned their simple cottage with clay pots painted with minerals. She tended the creeper of flowers that had appeared by itself and was blooming close to the ceiling. When she rose in the mornings, the first thing she did was commune with the wildlife. It was like she was determined to show them there was a harmonious way to coexist with the forest's animals.

Whenever Sita strode out of the cottage, her friends—as she called them—gathered around her. All the creatures wanted was to sit in her hand or lap or on her shoulder and feel her gentle hands upon them. Sometimes she kissed them on the crown of their feathered heads. Rama sat on the steps of the cottage, watching her. She was especially fond of Mila, of course, and the birds had grown used to her, often perching on her back when she lay on the ground.

Rama pulled Sita into his lap, and one of the birds hopped over and nestled on his shoulder, cocking its head and looking at him.

"Remember the morning of your coronation?" Sita asked, playing with one of the locks by his ear. "We were speaking about how many children we would have."

"Hundreds," Rama said with a large smile, but then quickly became serious.

The bird on his shoulder flew away. Rama remembered. Sitting together bedecked in jewels and fine silks, waiting to be summoned for the crowning, they had spoken of the children they would have. Rama had asserted that he would train all his children to become warriors, even the girls. He had used Kaikeyi as an example, saying that her skill proved the warrior ability every woman had. This was mere seconds before he had been summoned to Kaikeyi's palace and summarily banished from his home.

Rama looked at Sita in his lap. Her loyal little Mila was by her side. Rama knew why Sita had brought this topic up. They had not lived as man and wife since the exile began. He had waited for her to ask. He had thought about what they had to do.

"We cannot risk having a child while we are in exile," Rama said.

Quietly they joined hands, Rama intertwining his fingers with hers. Sita looked up at him; she understood him perfectly. They would truly be embracing the ascetic life in all its aspects. Unbidden, images of the Nishada children of all ages flooded Rama's mind. They had been so joyful to see Rama and his companions, displaying agility, strength, and vivacity. It was possible to raise children, even in the jungle.

As if reading Rama's mind, Sita said, "If we truly belonged to here, if we ourselves had been raised here, we would assume that it was natural. We would welcome children of our own. But we belong to Ayodhya. Our roots draw us home. Only then will we feel safe enough to expand our family."

"I'm sorry," Rama said.

"Don't be!" Sita's exclamation startled Mila and the birds flew up for a moment before settling back down around them. The morning sun was growing brighter. "In no way whatsoever are you at fault in this situation, Rama."

"Do you agree with this decision?" he asked.

"Your affection is all that I need," she answered.

Rama prayed that his heart would stay soft and open. He knew that even holy ones found celibacy a challenge. Those who restrained their senses sometimes became sharp as swords, cutting away anything that would sway them from their vow. Rama was not one of them. He had not foresworn his wife, his future, his children, his kingship. It was all simply on a temporary hold. But he would hold on to Sita and give her his full affection. Anything else would be unfair. Anything else would be contrary to his nature.

"Sita, do you remember what you said, right before Sumantra summoned me that day?" Sita cocked her head, trying to recall, looking from one side to the other, just as the birds did. "You said that you wanted to invite many animals to live in the gardens until the day you were blessed with children."

Sita's face split into a radiant smile. Together they looked at the small gathering of birds, squirrels, and of course, little Mila. At least this wish had been fulfilled. The animals of the forest swarmed around the princess at every turn.

"Let's go for out for a morning bath, Rama," Sita said.

Lakshmana was already at the base of the mountain, bathing in the river. This had become their routine, the hike up and down the mountain a daily sojourn.

Sita started twisting her thick hair into a coil on top of her head as she walked with Rama down the path that had appeared by the trampling of their feet. Mila scampered next to Sita, licking her fingers every now and then. As they bathed, they saw Lakshmana on the opposite shore of the river, doing a routine with his sword. Seeing Lakshmana's accomplished yet aggressive movements, Rama stretched his limbs in yogic postures and then sat down to meditate.

Swimming toward them, Lakshmana called out, "I'm ready."

Rama opened his eyes. Lakshmana climbed onto the shore. Dripping with water, he got on his feet and cut his sword through the air. The drops of water flying from the sword looked like blood. Rama, who did not entertain such thoughts, felt his insides grow cold.

"If they come after us, I will be ready for them," Lakshmana said.

"Who precisely do you mean to kill?" Rama asked.

"All of them! Every single one of them who actively or passively participated in exiling you. The witch, her hunchback, Bharata, Shatrugna, Father . . ."

And the list went on. Rama remained silent for a long time after Lakshmana had finished talking. Lakshmana fidgeted against the stillness.

The questions came at Rama with renewed force: How could one woman move a whole kingdom to expel their future king? Was anyone in Ayodhya truly safe? What was happening in their hometown now?

And so Rama said, "Your words make me feel strongly that you must return and safeguard Ayodhya."

Lakshmana shook his head. "I have to be here to join forces with you when they come after you."

"If they wanted to have me killed, Lakshmana, they would have done it while I was in Ayodhya."

"I'm sure Manthara wanted to. Don't forget that she has threatened your life before. She will convince someone to seek you out and finish her work."

Rama sighed. "The thoughts you harbor are futile. You have to let it go. Leave Ayodhya and its people behind. We will not see any of them for fourteen years."

"I wouldn't be so sure," Lakshmana said, and turned away.

He often took rounds beyond their settlement to look for signs of intruders. So far, he had found nothing to report. Rama could not bring himself to believe that Bharata would ever . . . Yet it was a regular point of contention between the brothers.

The oppressive mood lifted toward the evening when they absorbed themselves in making new arrows. Lakshmana sharpened the arrowheads against a rock. Rama whittled branches to create the bodies. Sita fastened peacock feathers to the tail of each arrow.

Lakshmana lifted the tip, examining it against the last light, and commented on how perfect the arrow was, how very sharp to the touch. Rama agreed, continuing to create the shaft of the arrows from branches. United in this task, harmony was restored between them and they entered a silent agreement not to speak about the exile anymore.

One month later, when Sita turned seventeen, Rama insisted on decorating her hair with flowers he had picked. They foraged for delicacies, finding jujubes, the small, sweet fruits that became sweeter the longer they were left to dry up and wrinkle. In the evening, Lakshmana held forward a basket that he had fashioned by twining twigs together.

"It's not much," he said.

"It's beautifully crafted," Sita answered, admiring the gift.

When she accepted the basket from him, she saw that it was full of almonds. Rama and Sita looked at the treasure.

"I only had to lean against the tree and the almonds rained down on me," Lakshmana said. "It must have known it was your birthday."

They pounded the almonds against a rock, collecting the coarse meal on a banana leaf. Sita squeezed the syrupy juice from the jujubes into the almond meal, forming them into small cakes. The cakes needed only a few minutes over the fire to bake. That night, the three of them enjoyed almond cakes and roasted pumpkins. After subsisting on fruit and roots, it was a real feast, and almond cakes became one of their staple foods.

"My first birthday in exile," Sita said.

She didn't need to add that they had thirteen more to go.

CHAPTER 8

Unwelcome Guests

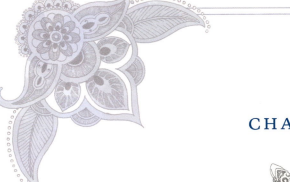

Aside from occasional discord between them, their life in Chitrakuta was surprisingly peaceful. Lakshmana dreamed of Urmila often. They were not comforting dreams, for she always repeated her parting words, insisting she would never forgive him. Lakshmana found himself pondering those last words during daytime hours. Depending on his mood, the tone of Urmila's voice changed. One day he was sure her voice had been sorrowful. Another day it was full of only reproach.

Weeks turned into months; their bodies grew lean and their muscles defined and taut around their sunburned skin. Even Sita's soft feet hardened, growing calluses. She could walk for hours now without getting tired. Four months went by.

"I'm beginning to think," Lakshmana said one morning, "that no one is in pursuit of us."

"You sound disappointed," Rama said.

"Not disappointed. Surprised."

"You were absolutely convinced someone would pursue us?"

"Yes."

"Such an act would be expected only if the force usurping the throne was inimical and acting only in their self-interest."

"How is that not the case?"

"Lakshmana, you know I don't see Bharata in that way."

The brothers left it at that.

They had discussed and disagreed on this several times already. Though Rama defended Bharata, he didn't like when they talked about their home in Ayodhya. He always told Lakshmana to keep his mind there in the forest. Lakshmana hadn't meant to bring up the disagreement again. He swallowed down his words and concentrated on the fact that, as far as he could tell, no one was pursuing them.

Lately, Rama had been expressing feelings of joy. Roaming freely, he was becoming the king of the jungle, with no obligations. Lakshmana knew that Rama could take on any opponent, a raging beast or a supernatural creature. So far they had not encountered anything of the sort. Even the tigers in the area kept their distance. Now that they knew the forest better, the brothers left most of their fighting gear in their small cottage. All they really needed was one of their bows and their quivers. Sometimes they roamed around the forest to see its delights, but they never went too far from their base on Chitrakuta. This was the ideal place for them. Living in a clearing near the very peak of the mountain, they were hidden from view, but they could see for miles. If anyone was coming for them, they had a good vantage point.

On this particular day, they trekked down the steep mountain to bathe in the river. Although they went down together, each one of them claimed their own spot on the bank of the river; it was an unspoken arrangement, giving one another privacy. A few birdcalls punctuated the air, and a small herd of deer was already at the water, lapping the clear, fresh liquid.

That day, as every day, they dipped into the water fully clothed, cleansing their bodies and garments. The rising sun was quick to dry the bark cloth. After bathing, they sat in meditation, turning inward. When they were dry and content from the sun's rays, they filled the clay pots with water and began the ascent back to their home.

"Let me carry yours," Rama said, snatching Sita's pot out of her hand before she could protest.

When they reached their dwelling, Sita went to the bilva tree to pick some of its fruit.

"Sing, Sita," Rama said in a gentle voice.

The brothers faced the rising sun, preparing to worship Surya, the sun god. If they could hear Sita, they did not need to keep an eye on her as she skirted the surroundings at Chitrakuta. Every day, the brothers prayed to the sun through doing the full-bodied salutation to the sun. Sita picked fresh fruit for their breakfast.

The sound of the brothers' rhythmical breathing and Sita's song filled the quiet morning. When Sita stopped singing for a moment, Rama froze in the warrior's pose.

He immediately called out, "Sita?"

With a small laugh, she resumed her song, just where she'd left off.

Because this was a daily ritual by now, Sita had exhausted her wealth of songs and often made up her own songs and words. Today she was singing about a little deer that was lost in the forest and couldn't find its way back home. Sita came back humming, her baskets loaded with fruits and berries. Her fingers were smeared with berry juice, staining her palms in an almost decorative way.

"I stopped singing," she told them, "because I was imagining what should happen next to the little deer in my song. And then out of nowhere, I thought maybe it got shot by one of your arrows."

Rama and Lakshmana looked at each other, shaking their heads. Sita had never stopped dropping hints that she didn't like them directing their arrows at animals she considered harmless, like deer, birds, and waterfowl. Even mighty antelopes and gazelles with sharp horns were harmless in her book.

"But that seemed like a tragic fate." Here she looked at both of them in a less-than-subtle way. "So I had to pause and imagine another fate for my little friend."

Sita lifted her hands to the sky and sang a happy ending to the song.

When Sita stopped singing, a silence descended on the forest. Lakshmana noticed at once that the forest was unusually quiet. Sita cooed to her friends, coaxing them from the shadows, expecting the family of rabbits to hop out, or the busy squirrels, or at least the fawn she called Mila. Even larger animals would sometimes peek out at her, though more reticent and shy. Getting no response whatsoever, Sita turned to Rama.

"Strange," she said, voicing what they all felt.

Sita went to the edges of the clearing, calling out to her animals, calling them by the names she had given them. There was no response.

With tension filling the air, the three of them stood in silence, barely breathing . . . just listening. Lakshmana was dismayed that he had not noticed anything earlier. The animals knew the forest better than anyone and, with their sixth sense, they were the best measure of what was happening in the forest. Something was surely amiss.

Now that his senses were alert, Lakshmana couldn't miss how off-balance the harmony of the forest was. The animals had gone into hiding, taking shelter in their caves and cubbyholes. When Rama and Lakshmana turned toward the expansive view of the forest that Chitrakuta offered, they saw it immediately—a cloud of dust moving slowly but surely in their direction.

"A terrible storm?" Sita asked.

"No, Sita. The way the dust is wafting in the air, creating a cloud, doesn't look natural. It's a stampede of some sort. Something is moving directly toward us."

Rama didn't have to speak further. Lakshmana strode toward the largest tree in their clearing. The sala tree was in bloom. Rama and Sita followed him and stood at the trunk of the tree. As he climbed the large tree, Lakshmana disappeared behind its bloodred flowers.

Lakshmana concentrated first on grabbing the branches with his hands and finding footholds on the bark. When his footing was firm, he reached for a higher branch, climbing easily, like a cat. When he got to the highest branch that would carry his weight, he found his balance and tiptoed out to its tip. Clearing away the abundance of leaves, he focused on the disturbance on the horizon.

"Definitely man-made, my brother," Lakshmana called, without looking down. "I see a caravan of people extending for miles. They are moving ahead steadily, which indicates a clear goal and direction. Unless they change direction soon, they are headed straight toward Chitrakuta."

"What else do you see?" Rama asked, calling up through the thick branches. "Look at the very front of the caravan, if you can. Any indicator of who these people might be? Any flags?"

"Yes, my brother, there are flags. Several flags . . ."

Steadying his gaze, Lakshmana looked unblinkingly at the flags in the distance, willing his eyes to see. Slowly an image emerged from the blurry cloth waving in the wind. It was a tree. Lakshmana's heart started thundering, but he didn't want to tell Rama until he was sure. Focusing on the flag and its emblem, Lakshmana made sure it was a pomegranate tree after all. Bharata's emblem.

"Son of Kaikeyi!" Lakshmana shouted, as if it was an oath.

Seeing that familiar flag, Lakshmana was instantly flooded by emotions he had kept buried. He had seen enough. He dropped down from the height above, the leaves whistling past him and branches whipping his body. He hardly felt them. Landing with a soft thud on the ground, Lakshmana straightened out and ripped his bow from his chest, feeling the taut string razor his back.

"I cannot believe this!" Lakshmana spit out through clenched teeth.

The feeling was all the more jarring to him because he had expected something like this. Their departure from the kingdom had been too smooth; not a single emissary from Ayodhya had been sent to spy on them to assure they were honoring their agreement. Lakshmana had been very vigilant, expecting someone to pursue them, to keep an eye on them. But he had not expected this. Ayodhya made their move in such an obvious manner! It was a huge army.

The enemy had to be really afraid of what Rama and Lakshmana were capable of doing, and rightly so. Lakshmana began pacing around the clearing quickly, making assessments in his mind. His back was stinging lightly where his bowstring had grazed across his skin. This was war. He had no time to wield his weapons with care, as long as they did their job. He wasn't, after all, like Rama, who was deliberate and concise even under immense stress and pressure. Lakshmana was instantly hit by a wave of anxiety. Had he made new arrows? Were the quivers full? Were they as well prepared for this as they could be?

"We should put out the fire at once," he said.

The smoke from the fire billowed into the air like a flag of their own.

Rama held up his hand. "Lakshmana, please calm down and tell me what you saw."

Lakshmana stopped abruptly, swaying in place, looking at Rama with eyes hot with anger.

"Isn't it obvious, my brother? Bharata has come, bringing his whole army! He means to destroy us completely! We are such fools! No, *I'm* a fool. You're too good to think the worst of

people. I'm the fool! Here I was, expecting a spy or two, or a few assassins. But Bharata certainly is the son of Kaikeyi. Set on destruction, he has brought an entire army and means to surround us and finalize his claim to the throne. There is an army with horses and elephants marching toward us. Obviously, Ayodhya will not accept another king while you are alive. Bharata has come to obliterate you and claim the throne once and for all."

Rama did not move a finger. Indeed, he leaned into the tree, letting Lakshmana finish his rant. Sita looked up toward the top of the tree as if she longed to climb it and see for herself. The decision to run or stay was not hers to make anyway.

They had two options. Either they could take their few belongings and run with the spirits of the forest, or they had to stay and face what was coming. Lakshmana was clearly in favor of the latter. Yet his intention in staying was very different from Rama's.

"I will kill that traitor myself, Rama! I swear it. I don't care that he is my brother. I can't stand by in silence and let that scheming and manipulating witch win. I will kill Bharata and destroy his entire army and end this once and for all!"

Rama's silence and steady gaze finally got to Lakshmana and he went quiet, if only externally. He continued to seethe. But what could he do without Rama's consent?

Judging by his brother's calm silence, Lakshmana already had a feeling what was to come, and he didn't like it one bit.

"Lakshmana, my brother," Rama said slowly, as if to penetrate through Lakshmana's fury. "I see your loyalty to me. I've felt it again and again. It means more to me than the kingdom itself. But your anger is blinding you. Your clarity of judgment is clouded by your emotions. I've heard your description of what you've seen, but my conclusion is different than yours. Will you hear me out?"

As if he had a choice. Lakshmana kept silent. After all, Rama had heard him out, more or less. Lakshmana did have a lot more to say, but Rama was not the right target for his volatile emotions. Lakshmana took a few seething breaths and nodded.

"I see my brother Bharata coming toward us with a great entourage," Rama said. "He is traveling in a way befitting a king, the way we would have traveled before we were exiled. Indeed, the council would not have allowed Bharata, the heir to the throne, to travel alone."

Lakshmana's teeth clenched and his lips turned down without his knowing. Rama was candidly outlining the division between them and their brothers, Bharata and Shatrugna, who were still in favor with the kingdom. Rama and Lakshmana had been protected princes too, but who had cared to protect them when they were mercilessly banished? Bharata, meanwhile, was still protected and privileged.

"Knowing Bharata's true and gentle character," Rama said, "I consider it impossible that he would come here with the aim to kill us."

Knowing Lakshmana was going to interrupt, Rama lifted his hand to say, "Hear me out. Even if Bharata turns out to be in on his mother's plan, even if he has turned on us, this would not be the way to find us and kill us. Think it through, Lakshmana. Bharata knows warfare as well as we do. How would you seek out your enemy hidden in the forest? What would be the best way? Tell me."

"I would send a handful of my most trusted assassins to finish it quickly, quietly, and competently," Lakshmana grudgingly admitted.

"Exactly! The fact that Bharata is coming with such a huge following strongly suggests he has another agenda."

"But what is it? What could he possibly want? Is he coming to gloat at our misery?"

"In that case, he won't find us so miserable. But no, I don't imagine that is his purpose. My only thought is that they have come to bring Sita back, to save her from this harsh life. But there is no point in guessing, now that they are so near to us. Have patience, my brother. We will find out soon enough."

"Are you saying we should sit here and wait?"

Rama lifted his eyebrows in answer and pushed away from the tree, uncrossing his arms. Taking Sita's hand, he walked over to sit in their usual place, on the black buckskin. As he lowered himself, he invited Sita to sit with him. He put an arm around her to assure her. Lakshmana picked up Rama's bow and quiver and took it to him. Rama frowned slightly, looking at the bow.

"Please, Rama. If only to assuage my anxiety, keep your weapons close by you and allow me to wear mine."

"You can keep yours. I will leave mine by the cottage, where we keep our weapons."

Lakshmana was not happy about this but carried the bow and quiver and hung them next to the swords and shields.

Rama had made his choice to wholeheartedly trust Bharata, whatever his intentions might be. Lakshmana would not. Lakshmana stood armed, ready to intercede within a second's notice. Even if Rama didn't acknowledge it, Lakshmana knew this was his duty to his king.

After this, all that was left for him to do was wait.

CHAPTER 9

Sita and the Deer

After so many months of peace, I felt the air charged with a sickening tension. It was time for blood to flow. The threat in the air now was worse because it was directed at other humans. And not just any, but our own family. Since the animosity came all from Lakshmana, I stayed close to Rama even though his recent words left me torn: *My only thought is that they have come to bring Sita back, to save her from this harsh life.* The pronouncement sat like a barb in my heart. Would he send me away?

So I found no solace in the actions of my protectors; Rama sat still, like a panther. Lakshmana—even in his attempt to be collected—paced about in agitation. We had chosen not to run, but every second was an eternity . . . waiting for our visitors to declare themselves. Having trudged up and down the mountain countless times, we knew exactly how long it took. The first time we made the trek, it had taken us hours. Now that we had established a path, it took us less than one. But our visitors didn't know about our path, and quite possibly it would take them hours to find us.

I sensed a feeling of anticipation from Rama. He had been cut off from the land he loved and the people he knew, and now they were so close. But Rama thought they had come to fetch me back to Ayodhya, and he had said nothing about resisting them! My victory on the day of the exile was running into sand, and I realized how dependent I was on Rama's decision. His casual words threw me into turmoil and I needed a few moments to myself. Another very real worry pressed at me: Where was Mila? Were the animals safe with so many humans approaching?

"I have to find Mila," I told Rama.

"Go, then," Rama said, "but not out of sight."

With my heart on Mila, I stood up. I knew what Rama meant when he cautioned me to stay within sight. Today my protectors had other things on their minds. Otherwise, they made it their first task to guard me. At all times I felt Rama or Lakshmana watch me; one of them was always keeping an eye on me. I couldn't always tell which one of them was on duty, and I didn't know how they divided the task. Sometimes it was discussed out loud, especially if I made a request to go somewhere and one of them accompanied me. Other times, if I was just roaming around, seemingly free, I knew one of them had their eyes casually trained on me, ready to intervene at a moment's notice. I didn't truly understand the need for this vigilance, for the forest seemed like a wondrous place to me. Their protection only made me feel fragile, like a small child one must protect from herself.

"If you see Mila, call for me," I told Lakshmana.

He eyed me with disbelief, staggered by my ill-formed priorities, no doubt. I didn't care.

"Don't do anything rash," I whispered.

I saw a storm brewing within Lakshmana. It was just like the first days of the exile, when both of my protectors had sought an outlet for their fury by hunting the forest's creatures.

"Remember that they are dear to me," I added, to make sure he understood me.

I hoped that my affection for the animals would add a layer of protection. Lakshmana looked ready to burn down the entire forest, if only he could get his hands on Rama's betrayers.

"Stay close," was all my brother-in-law said.

I understood his anxiety today. Though I did not always understand their vigilance, I knew I had no concept of danger. I had never been attacked; I had never been afraid for my life. I treated every creature in the forest as a friend. What did I know of our enemy? Nothing, truly. I turned away from Lakshmana.

"Mila," I called out softly.

I picked some sweet-smelling clover that was her favorite. I waved it in the air, hopefully wafting the fragrance to her. "Mila, my sweet friend, where are you?"

Sometimes Mila would appear from nowhere, squeezing her shiny little nose through my elbow as I was meditating. The fierce love I felt for her surprised me. I could only compare it to what I had heard of a mother's love. I who had no children, who had not yet started dreaming of my children, felt a motherly affection blossom in my heart. I could watch Mila for hours, admire her antics, kiss her, and play with her. While Rama and Lakshmana did their weapon routines or talked politics, I played with Mila. She loved me in return.

Along with all the animals, she had disappeared. I was struck with a vision of Mila and my other friends being killed. The animals had found me, the way one finds a kindred spirit. I could always count on them to soothe me. Today, none of them answered my call and I was worried—especially for Mila, my little one.

I stayed within sight even though for once neither Rama nor Lakshmana took note of me. If only I dared ask one of them to accompany me to find Mila. Neither of them cared about a silly little deer. Another day, they would humor me, I knew it. But not today.

"Mila, Mila, Mila," I chanted, turning here and there.

She always came within a call or two. She never strayed far from me. My heart was growing sick with worry.

"Oh, Mila, run far from these warriors," I said out loud, meaning the ones at the base of the mountain. I prayed that she had the sense to stay far, far away from the humans invading the forest. It seemed like most of the animals had been warned by the dust storm caused by the approaching army. I only hoped that Mila hadn't run in the wrong direction.

While I worried about Mila and plucked some more grass, I tried to avoid the barb in my heart, the fear that Rama would soon send me back. The very ease with which he had suggested it made me certain that he had contemplated it often. He wished to send me away.

Even though Rama had beckoned me to sit with him, I had not been able to reveal my mind. I saw how preoccupied he was with the arrival of our unexpected guests. Rama so often made me the center of his attention, so I refused to claim it now that his mind was clearly elsewhere. I was not that kind of wife.

Kaikeyi had been that kind of woman. When Rama's father's attention strayed, Kaikeyi resolutely pulled it back. She did it as skillfully and obviously as she reined in her favorite stallions. I had never judged her for it—until she misused the power she had cultivated over the years. Now I consciously avoided falling into her footsteps. I would not be that kind of woman.

Ironically, though, it was precisely the reason I was afraid of what Rama might do. I didn't feel I had cultivated the power to truly stand against him. When he had granted me leave to accompany him here, I had almost fainted again with relief. It was a privilege, not my right. If Rama decided to send me back to Ayodhya, I would have no recourse. Perhaps Rama and Lakshmana spoke about this when I was not within hearing, as they had done on our first day in Chitrakuta. Perhaps they planned all along to send me back to Ayodhya; they desired to live here alone without me.

Tears prickled my eyelids and I pressed my nose into the grass I had collected. Mila would make me all better, if only I could find her. This thought made my eyelids prickle more, for I suddenly felt sure I would never see her again. Either she had been ruthlessly killed or I would be sent back to a place that no longer was my home. The fresh grass in my nostrils reminded me of countless times when I had fed Mila with my own hands.

"Mila, Mila," I crooned, throwing the grass about, as if creating a trail for her.

That's when I stumbled upon a small flock of five deer hiding behind the trees. They watched me cautiously, ready to bolt.

"Have you seen Mila?" I asked. "A fawn of your kind, about this big?"

I showed them Mila's size with my hands. I didn't feel at all silly speaking with them, though if my protectors had been present, I wouldn't have done it. In answer, Mila's little

face peeked from the underbrush. I fell to my knees and held out my arms. She came to me at once, as eager for my affection as I was for hers. The others, full-grown deer, kept their distance. I hugged Mila close with both my hands. I loved to press my nose into her neck, inhaling her earthy animal smell. Her velvety fur was soft and silky, more soothing than any fabric in the palace. With Mila pressed to my heart, I had a moment of strong intuition, a communication that rose through my feet, becoming full-body knowledge: We were not in danger. That was what I knew.

So, I counted Mila's white spots—as I had done many times—kissed her nuzzle, and hummed a lullaby to her. She was not afraid of what was happening below, and I looked into her deep black eyes to see what made her so calm. Deer, I knew, had that inner sense that most animals have. They were also, however, easily fooled, and therefore prey to hunters. A deer in distress would first of all freeze, pointing her ears to locate her target, and then she would sprint, fast as the wind. By then it would often be too late. I knew this now, for I had witnessed it firsthand.

"No one will harm you," I assured her, knowing that she understood my words. "I love you, my little Mila."

I gazed deep into her beautiful doe eyes. Her long lashes shaded her dark and fathomless eyes. I could feel that she returned my love fiercely. If I had to leave Chitrakuta, it would feel like leaving my own child. Mila licked my chin, reassuring me. How could I have known that this innocent and pure affection would later become my weakness and make me blind?

Then I heard Rama's voice call me in the distance. Mila's ears perked up, and the deer in her new herd became still. I realized I had strayed out of sight. I could not see Rama, which meant he could not see me. Quickly I began to retrace my step, eager to show how obedient I was, how they didn't have to worry about me. When I turned to see if Mila was with me, I saw her standing by the others of her kind, patiently beholding me. She would stay with them for now. Perhaps it was the beginning of a farewell between us.

Rama sat cross-legged where I had left him, glowing with his emerald luminesce. He was more beautiful than anyone was allowed to be. He needed me by his side; I could see that. Was he merely holding me close for a last few minutes? When bidding me farewell in Ayodhya, he had done this, crushing me to his chest, only to let go.

I approached cautiously, reminding myself that I should not make Rama's decisions harder for him. But sometimes I flared up with unexpected power, as I'd done that day. I could not promise that I was capable of leaving in a subdued manner.

"They are approaching," Rama said, and I heard that he was right.

The murmur of voices, the sounds of footsteps. Rama's family was near. Or our enemy, if Lakshmana was right. Lakshmana's mood, which had only grown more erratic, could not touch me anymore. We were not in danger. Mila was safe. She had found a herd. This gave me solace, in case my fear became reality and I had to leave Chitrakuta.

Four Brothers

As the minutes dragged into hours, Rama felt how impossibly still he had become, taking in the chaotic sounds at the base of the mountain. He could clearly hear the ascent of those who were coming. Rama wondered whom Bharata would send up . . . a messenger, a minister, a soldier? Was Father there among them? Which beloved face would Rama behold today?

Lakshmana shifted his weight from foot to foot, emitting hot sighs. It seemed that their future was unfolding once again, as the visitors approached.

Rama's heart lurched as he saw who was approaching. There was no mistaking him: dark and handsome, striking in his resemblance to Rama. Bharata, his beloved brother Bharata.

Right behind Bharata, Shatrugna followed like a shadow. Not even their mothers could tell Lakshmana and Shatrugna apart. Behind Shatrugna, Rama saw Sumantra, Father's trusted advisor, and to Rama's surprise, Guha, the king of the Nishadas. These were all people Rama had chosen to trust. But he had not expected to see them like this, a united front. For a brief moment, Lakshmana's suspicions took hold of Rama: Had they all turned against him?

Lakshmana tightened his grip on his bow. It was as if Rama could hear Lakshmana think, "Bharata might resemble Rama, but he is nothing like Rama." Kaikeyi too had been famed for her beauty, and she had been poison in a dashing vial.

When Bharata saw them, he stopped in his tracks. Intense emotion shone in his eyes, and he called out, "Rama! Lakshmana!"

Bharata broke into a run toward them.

Lakshmana took one step forward. If he were an animal, he would be growling.

Bharata froze. Behind Bharata, Shatrugna faced Lakshmana with a plea in his eyes. Shatrugna was Lakshmana's mirror image, exuding an anger of his own. Lakshmana refused to engage and kept his fury trained on Bharata.

The four brothers faced one another for a moment that seemed to go on forever.

No one moved. They hardly breathed. They who had shared their childhoods, who had learned everything together, stood apart like strangers, fearing that at any moment something would happen to destroy their brotherhood. How could they begin to find one another again?

This was chiefly between Rama and Bharata. The claim to the kingdom was between them. There was so much Rama wanted to say and do, but he kept his eyes on Bharata. Rama allowed absolutely nothing to show on his face. Bharata would have to reveal himself first.

Facing Rama, Bharata inhaled sharply as if assaulted and took a step back. Under different circumstances, at a different time, Rama would have greeted his brothers much differently. Had it only been a few months since they had seen one another?

As the silence lengthened, Bharata's face became increasingly strained. Rama remained seated where he was. He felt Sita's solid presence. His mind sought answers to the unexpected visit. Unlike Lakshmana, Rama had not expected this. Bharata and Shatrugna were unarmed. Bharata, in fact, was dressed like an ascetic and even had matted his hair. It had to be Guha's handiwork. Rama's eyes did not leave Bharata, though he sensed that Guha and Sumantra both wanted to speak. Bharata was in distress; that was clear. Yet he had brought an entire army.

"I almost can't believe that I'm seeing you with my own eyes, Rama," Bharata finally said, with a tremor in his voice. "I had almost lost hope of actually finding you. My prayers have been answered."

The sincerity in Bharata's voice was genuine. Rama felt a shield disappear from his eyes. That was enough for Bharata. His demeanor broke and he resumed his run, falling at Rama's feet. Lakshmana hissed, but Bharata was not deterred this time.

As Rama reached out to Bharata, he saw his own hands. His fingernails were black with dirt and his hands stained from manual labor. They were not the hands of a prince. Rama was not the royalty he had been a few months ago. How had he and Bharata been separated like this, one anointed for kingship, the other thrown into exile? How was it that he, Rama, now lived in poverty, digging the Earth for roots to feed his family?

He pulled Bharata close. The two brothers held each other tightly. Rama felt Bharata's hot tears drop onto his shoulder. Rama's heart opened easily, for it had never truly been closed.

It pained him to see the distance Lakshmana was enforcing against Shatrugna. Shatrugna took a step toward Lakshmana, but Lakshmana stood still. Shatrugna hesitated, and then turned to Rama. If they had been politicians alone, Rama would never have welcomed the intruders before knowing their intentions. Lakshmana's position was not only hotheaded. Rama still knew too little about this surprise visit or what his brothers wanted. But Rama could not stop himself from welcoming Bharata. He beckoned to Shatrugna, including him in the embrace. The three brothers held one another, while Lakshmana stood apart with cold eyes.

Bharata pulled himself away and stood staring at Rama. "I still can't believe it," he said. "I fear that I will awaken any moment and find myself once again in the nightmare of my life. Every night I've dreamed of you, my brother. And every day I've longed to see you."

"I have thought of you often, as well," Rama said, looking into Bharata's eyes. *Why are you here?* he longed to ask. But the words felt premature. Bharata seemed lost for words, and so Rama spoke, in the way a royal elder would.

"I trust that the kingdom is safe in your hands and that you are working closely with the ministers and counselors to restore peace to Ayodhya. I trust that you take Father's counsel seriously and defer to his wisdom in all matters. Most foolish is the young who dismiss the words of elders. Father is the most seasoned and righteous politician. He will always guide you in the right direction."

Speaking of Father, whom he thought of every day, Rama felt his chin quiver. He often imagined the moment when he would reunite with him. "I've assured Lakshmana many times," Rama said, "that you will be a just king, a worthy successor to Father, who has ruled with outstanding statecraft and affection for his people. I—"

"Rama," Bharata said, interrupting. He frowned so fiercely his brows had become one. "Every word you say pains me deeply. You assume I have stepped onto the throne in your absence."

"Don't look so aggrieved, my brother," Rama answered, placing his hand on Bharata's shoulder. "That was the agreement when I left Ayodhya. This was Father's decree. The king's word must be upheld. Who else would take over the crown, if not you? You are fair and brave, fit to rule."

"Stop, Rama, please stop," Bharata pleaded.

Shatrugna put a calming hand on Bharata's shoulder. Lakshmana's eyes narrowed. Rama felt his confusion grow. Just then, Rama beheld the last thing he expected: the queen mothers.

Rama's confusion turned to alarm. Kausalya was gaunt, her cheeks hollow, grief lining her face. Seeing his mother's sweet face, a flood of emotions rose, but Rama contained them immediately. His eyes went to Sumitra, the mother of the twins, who was standing behind Kausalya. And then Kaikeyi, Bharata's mother, the instigator of this dynastic clash.

Lakshmana hissed when he saw Kaikeyi. She seemed not to notice. Her eyes never moved from the ground. She didn't even look up once to see Rama.

A foreboding feeling gripped Rama. Part of him understood at once what this meant.

There could be only one reason why the queen mothers were here and Father was not. To ward himself from this truth, his mind flooded with questions. What were the queens doing here? They were too old and respected to be undertaking this kind of excursion. They must have been traveling for months, tracking Rama down in this isolated region. And for what?

Sita had none of Rama's reservation and went forward to embrace Kausalya, holding the older woman close to her heart. Rama reluctantly followed Sita, touching his mother's feet; he allowed her to touch his cheek once before he moved away.

Rama and Lakshmana exchanged a long look as Lakshmana went forward to greet his mother, Sumitra. Their mothers should not have been there. None of them should have come there. Lakshmana did as Rama did and kept his greeting brief. More and more of Ayodhya's preeminent citizens began to fill up the clearing, until it seemed like all of Ayodhya was there.

Rama's eyes swept across the influx of people, taking a moment to acknowledge each of them. All he could think of was Father, Father, Father. With Rama's eyes sweeping across them, the soft murmur of the people's voices ceased.

"Father?" Rama asked, a tremor running through his body.

"Rama . . . ," was all Bharata could manage.

There was a great sorrow in his eyes, a plea in his voice. Rama's heart ripped apart with the dreadful knowledge of the truth. *No.*

"It can't be," he whispered, his voice choking up. His other concerns melted away, as trivial as a brief illness.

Bharata's voice took on the formal tone as he relayed the news. "Father has left us, Rama. When I was still in the land of my grandfather and you were walking into the wild, our father, the esteemed king, left us and went to the heavens. His last word was your name."

Rama turned his eyes slowly to Lakshmana, as if he needed him to verify what he'd heard. Lakshmana's face was frozen, his eyes staring ahead. Whatever they had prepared for, it was not this. Never in their thoughts had they even once expected this news. Father had not been on the verge of death or even in ill health. His weakness on the day of the exile had not seemed fatal. The shock was so great to Rama, his eyes rolled back into his skull and he staggered where he stood. Sita called his name, and then he started crumbling to the ground.

Lakshmana threw his weapons down and ran forward. All three brothers ran forward to Rama's aid. Catching him in midair, they cushioned Rama's fall and sank to the Earth with him. Rama felt all his brothers come to his aid. Lakshmana held Rama to his chest, Shatrugna and Bharata close by. He heard his brothers' silent sobs. Sita was near and she sprinkled water gently on his face, calling his name.

With those waterdrops and his brothers' tears on his skin, Rama opened his eyes. Tears ran from his eyes as he looked to the sky. "Father! This was not part of the agreement. I have longed every day to see you again. Your presence on this Earth gave me great comfort and security. What is the use of returning to Ayodhya after fourteen years, if you will not be there to greet me?"

The brothers huddled together, receiving permission from one another's tears to grieve openly. The terrible wound that had stood between them—their father's last act of exiling Rama—became inconsequential. Throughout their lives their father had loved them unconditionally; he had trained them in all matters and had always been there to guide them at every milestone. How would the rest of their lives mean as much without their father's approving presence? They grieved not only for the loss of their father but for the future they would never have with him. He was their hero and mentor. And now he was gone.

Full of sorrow and condolences, Sita returned to Kausalya's arms.

"It has been four months since his death," the Great Queen said. "He could not even live three days without Rama. I thought I had grieved enough"—she wiped away her tears—"but seeing my son so undone . . ." She rested her head on Sita's shoulder.

"We cremated Father's body," Bharata said.

Rama stood, wiping his tears. "I am his eldest son. I must perform the funeral rites in his honor."

Bereft of the palace's resources, it would be a humble ritual. Following his heart, Rama knew what to do. Together, the brothers walked down from Chitrakuta, followed by Sita. As they reached the base of the mountain, a large crowd of soldiers on horses and elephants greeted Rama. No wonder there had been a veritable dust storm in their wake. It looked like Ayodhya's entire army was there. As the princes continued toward the river, the king's guards formed a protective line around them. A solemn mood spread throughout the large gathering.

The brothers dipped into the crystal-clear water of the river, offering the water back unto itself, praying for their father's soul to continue its journey in peace.

"Father, let this be for you," they said, one by one, as the water, sparkling like diamonds, dripped from their palms. They submerged themselves under the water three times to cleanse away any karmic residues that bound their father to them. They prayed for his soul to journey on without fetters, releasing him from any grievances.

As they trudged back up the slope of the mountain, Rama felt weary with grief. He leaned on Sita, finding her surprisingly strong. When they sat together, there was only room for thoughts of their departed father.

"Though Father was a busy man, with heavy decisions on his hand, he always made time for me," Rama said. "I never felt that I intruded on him. He always put away everything, making himself available to me, even when I was a boy with childish complaints."

"He trained us himself," Lakshmana remembered aloud, "leading by his example. 'Don't give in to anger,' he told me. And I never saw him overcome by such emotions. He was relentless in battle and a righteous politician, wise in the ways of the world."

"Whenever I did anything good, however small," Shatrugna said, "he acknowledged me with fitting words that warmed my heart."

"Father knew me better than I knew myself," Bharata said. "He would help me see solutions I couldn't imagine on my own."

"How lucky I am," Rama said, through fresh tears, "and you, my brothers, that we had a father like King Dasharatha."

Through their words, the brothers' deep affection for their departed father filled the air. The princes continued reminiscing in this way, with arms slung around one another.

Sumantra approached them and said, "Rama, I see no change in your love and respect for your father. It's truly commendable. Your palace is now a cottage with a thatched roof, ornamented only on one side by gleaming weapons sheathed in gold. Your fingernails are blackened by manual labor. Your body is lean, every muscle outlined, from the austere diet and life you lead here. Yet I have not heard you say one word of reproach against the king's last act."

Sumantra was speaking boldly, reminding them that Dasharatha was indeed responsible for exiling Rama. Rama didn't mind. He wanted everyone assembled to know that more than ever, his father's last decree was his torch.

"Father led an exemplary life," Rama said. "He raised four sons who miss him intensely now that he is gone. My brothers, we have a lifetime of memories full with Father. It's time now to say farewell. The longer you stay, the more difficult our parting will be."

They would have to continue their mourning individually. Rama knew he would never lose the desire to see Father once again. But now it was time to honor Father's final promise.

Turning to Bharata, who had stayed close to his side, Rama said, "Bharata, I thank you for your determination to find me. I'm grateful I didn't have to spend fourteen years yearning for Father, only to find later that a reunion was impossible. But you should not have come here. Our mothers should not have come. You could have sent a messenger to find me and convey this tragic news to me."

"That's not why I'm here, Rama," Bharata answered.

"Then why?"

Finally the question stood between them.

"I want to return the kingdom to you. Come home with us."

Although Bharata was the only one who said "Come home with us," every person at Chitrakuta, including Lakshmana, turned their eyes on Rama. If Rama agreed, they could all return home and Ayodhya would return to its normal state of affairs. All of this could be a forgotten chapter. The surge of hope was so strong, Rama stood and took a step away.

"Ever since you were exiled, Rama," Bharata pleaded, standing in turn, "everyone has pushed the kingdom on me. But it's not mine. I don't want it! I have been accused of plotting with my mother to get the throne for myself. That is a lie! Your opinion is the most important to me, Rama. I can't bear to think that you or Lakshmana would suspect me."

Rama felt Bharata's anguish. Perhaps he was enduring the most difficult position of all.

"Will you hear me out?" Bharata asked.

Rama nodded, and the two brothers sat again. Seeing Bharata's need to make his side of the story known, the assembled group of people settled down to listen. As if every detail was imprinted clearly in his mind, Bharata began from the beginning. He spoke as if he was piecing it together for himself. No one said a word as Bharata began his tale, full of emotional charge . . . like a confession.

Bharata Speaks

When Bharata began to speak, Lakshmana went to stand by the cottage he had built. He leaned against the side of it, in the shade. While Lakshmana felt united with his brother in their shared grief, he did not fully trust him. He was not eager to sit and listen to him. Lakshmana gripped his bow; he observed the assembled gathering, who had segregated into smaller groups under shade-giving trees.

"I know that each of you looks at me," Bharata said, "and has a preconceived notion of who I am; Prince Rama's brother, Queen Kaikeyi's son, second in line to Ayodhya's throne."

Bharata alone was sitting in the glaring sun. "You will argue that mother and son contested Rama's ascension to power. We were so close to it. Our claim was strong. How could we resist the opportunity to fight for the throne?"

Bharata paused, looking straight at Lakshmana—who immediately averted his eyes—and said, "Those are your thoughts. Not mine." It was as though Bharata tailored his confession to Lakshmana. But Lakshmana was not interested. He crossed his arms, hugging his bow into his chest. Bharata continued.

"You look at recent events and think you know what role I played. You believe I was a pivotal figure in securing the throne for myself, that I stood behind my mother in her schemes. You see no other way this dynastic crisis could have occurred without my active participation, or at least my consent. You think me a puppet in my mother's hands, or she in mine. I beg you today to suspend your judgments. Please hear me out. I beg you."

"Go on," Rama said in an even voice. A soft breeze blew threw the trees.

"The truth is that I knew *nothing* about my mother's scheme. Nothing. But again my dissenters feel certain that she alone could not cause such destruction. But she was not alone. She had help. But I was not by her side, and I refuse to speak for her. I refuse to have anything to do with her. I can only tell you my story. I can only insist that I knew nothing about her scheme."

Bharata laughed. He seemed oblivious to the sun, burning into his back. "My story begins with an admission of complete ignorance. While my entire family was facing tragedy, I was at my grandfather's, occupied with simple pleasures, oblivious of my family's downfall. My absence, some say, was a calculated move, a ploy to appear innocent."

He stood up, but didn't seek the shade, as Lakshmana had expected. Instead, Bharata paced as he explained. "I ask you to hear me out with difficulty. I almost want you to hate me. I have been cast into darkness and shame. But I cannot surrender to it.

"Before all this occurred, I believed I was connected to my father in such a way that I would immediately know if something was wrong. Wouldn't I somehow sense the personal and collective unrest in Ayodhya? I have looked back again and again, searching for some signs of a deeper knowing within myself." Bharata shook his head and grew silent.

"You did have one premonition," Shatrugna responded. "The dream. Remember?"

"Yes, Shatrugna. I had a dream. I had seen Father falling from the top of a high mountain into a lake of cow dung. Father's hair was disheveled and he laughed hysterically, like a madman. It was terrible to see my noble father this way, and that's when I struggled to wake up. But the dream didn't stop. I saw Father submerged in thick yellow oil, his dead face floating above the surface. A hideous female demon with the face of Manthara dragged him on the ground by his hair. Her laughter reverberated in my dream world, as the ocean dried up. The moon fell to the ground and the sun was extinguished. All of Ayodhya and the world beyond were covered in darkness.

"That's when I woke up with a palpitating heart. Moments later, I was summoned to my grandfather's court. A messenger from Ayodhya had come: 'Return to Ayodhya.' That was all. The messenger would tell us no more. Still polluted by the dream images, I wondered if I was awake or in a nightmare. I traveled day and night and cut the journey in half, arriving in seven days. I crossed thirteen rivers and pushed my stallion beyond its limits. My horse was wild-eyed and foaming at the mouth by the time we arrived. I didn't feel much saner myself. My pounding heart had been my steady companion. The feeling of doom had not left me since the nightmare.

"I approached the city gate with trepidation. Finally I was home. Perhaps all was well. I hoped my fear was mere foolishness, the dream having no bearing on reality.

"The new day was starting as I burst into Ayodhya, but I was greeted by a heavy silence. There was no sign of life from the millions of people who inhabit our large city. Even the birds, elephants, and cows were quiet. The despondent eyes of Ayodhya's people brought me to a halt. They just stared at me. I felt deeply ashamed. But why?

"I could not act as I usually do and greet them in a friendly manner. I stayed on my horse. I kept silent. I had never seen the people so hostile.

"I urged the tired horse forward to my father's palace. He was the one I was most eager to see. He would open his arms and say, 'My son!' I felt like a small boy, impatient for my father's love."

Tears ran down Rama's face. Lakshmana sniffed and swallowed his down.

Bharata continued. "My call for Father echoed through the empty palace. I urged my exhausted stallion to my mother's palace. There, the soothing sounds of flute and sitar sounded softly in the air. Birds were cooing and peacocks pranced. Seeing this, I began to feel at ease.

"Then I saw my mother on her throne, motionless like a statue, bedecked in sparkling diamonds. She looked neither cruel nor ruthless. She was her usual dazzling self, but she sat erect, her back straight like an arrow. There was something formal in her demeanor. I had never seen her look so majestic, so powerful. But it was all wrong, like the overextended strings of an instrument, ready to snap at any moment.

"When she saw me, she sprang up at once. She became so animated, another person entirely. As if I was a small boy, she kissed me again and again on my forehead and cheeks. I was surprised by her eager demonstration of affection.

"After touching her feet, I immediately asked, 'Where is Father?'

"She ignored my question. She urged me to sit down next to her on the throne and give her news about Kekaya and her father, my grandfather Ashvapati. Stifling my impatience, I sat down. I answered her questions dutifully, but again asked about Father. Impatiently, she answered, 'The king died eighteen days ago.'

"There was no trace of lamentation in her being. As if extending good news, Mother started going on about how now *I* would be king. Because her demeanor was so strange, I didn't quite understand her words at first. A string of questions appeared in my mind. If Father was dead, why wasn't she sad? If he had died eighteen days ago, why didn't they send for me at once? Why did everything about my mother scream of victory . . . her countenance, her dress, her entire palace? Why was she glowing and squeezing my trembling hands in joy?

"I pulled my hands away and cried into them. Overwhelmed by exhaustion, pain, and sadness, I sank to the floor, sobbing. 'What message did Father leave for me before he departed?' I asked.

"His last words were for Rama, she said. He had been exiled for fourteen years."

Bharata stopped and glared at his mother. Kaikeyi sat with her face downcast, showing no sign of having heard a word of Bharata's tale. Lakshmana was surprised that she was even allowed to keep company with the other queens, after all she had done. No one else looked at the queen, however. She was clearly shunned. A small punishment for her enormous crime, in Lakshmana's mind.

"I was so shocked by her words that my tears ceased at once. The only other prince in our dynasty that had ever been exiled was Asamanja—infamous for drowning his playmates in the river Sarayu, while standing by and laughing. The thought of Rama committing a comparable crime is impossible.

"I searched my mother's face to see if she would burst into laughter and reveal that it was all a bad joke. She got up from her throne. The sun glowed behind her. She was a large black shadow towering above me. Then she revealed to me the entirety of her scheme, starting with the two boons and the reasons for her actions.

"She had done all this for me so I could be king.

"The words that had come out from her mouth revealed a poisoned perception, a way of thinking that I had never known. The words she spoke came from a place of delusion so deep I felt like I was going to sink in and drown. She continued to speak of the glorious future ahead, when I, her son, would be the king of the entire Earth.

" 'Stop!' I finally managed to cry. 'Stop at once! I cannot bear to hear another word.'

"She abruptly closed her mouth and looked at me with astonishment. I could see she had not expected this response. What did she think of me? Did she really think I would dance on Father's dead body in glee or that I would be happy that my innocent brother and his princess were homeless and banished?!

"Yes, she truly did think I was going to celebrate with her, thank her, and even congratulate her. But she saw something in my eyes that warned her. She stopped talking and lifted her hands up, shielding herself, shaking her head imploringly. She began to move away from me instinctively, but again she resumed her words. Now there was a plea in her tone. I must not have understood, she insisted. She was offering me the throne, giving me the most amazing gift. Suddenly, I understood why people had been avoiding me and looking at me with contempt.

"The king was dead because of me! Rama was exiled because of me!

"The wave of self-hate was so intense, I pushed it down at once. If I allowed the full weight of it to hit me, I would run out and fling myself off my mother's balcony. Instead I felt a massive rage overcome me. I knew for the first time what it was to be completely controlled by anger. The rage gave me power and it raised my heavy body from the floor.

"Her composure and attitude began to change. I could almost see a dark veil in her consciousness slither away. Her eyes filled with fear. She was mortally afraid to see reality as I saw it. She pleaded with me more desperately to accept the kingdom. She extolled my supposed virtues. She pointed toward the amazing future we would have. The king was dead. Rama was far away. No one stood in our way.

"'Have you no heart?' I asked, interrupting her. 'Don't you feel *anything* when you talk of Father's death?'

"Without my knowledge, my right hand found the sword resting at my hip. With that immense anger raging within me, I unsheathed the sword and charged toward her. Grabbing her throat with my left hand, I raised the sword high in the air, ready to strike. My mother cried out, and I woke up from my violent thought. I stood paralyzed with my hand on my sword, but my eyes had warned her what my rage was capable of. My hand longed to follow the vision I had seen. Realizing how close I myself was to committing an unforgivable crime, I backed away.

"'You heartless creature!' I screamed. 'Rama and Father loved you. *Worshipped* you. They adored you beyond words. And you have cast them both away! My heart burns to think that I came from you, who conceived and carried out this wicked, heartless scheme. I cannot bear to be near you any longer!'

"Bile rose in my throat and my whole body was in a state of revolt. I was afraid I might faint and be stuck in her presence. I began to run out from her palace as fast as my legs could carry me. As distraught as I was, the pain had just begun."

Bharata stopped in the center of the clearing, shielding his eyes from the sun, as he looked around at the listening clusters of people. "I don't hold it against you . . . but for the first time in my life I was treated as a traitor. Wherever I sought relief, I was first rejected and rebuked. You assumed immediately that I had known about my mother's actions, that I had prompted them somehow. Feeling the constant presence of your suspicion and hostility has been the most humbling pain in my life. Being innocent is not enough. Doubt and enmity follow me wherever I go. I've been climbing a wall of thorns, never getting to the other side. Lakshmana, my own brother, would kill me, if Rama allowed it. What Lakshmana doesn't know is that I would welcome his arrows. I long to be free of this shame I carry day and night."

Bharata closed his eyes. Lakshmana felt a slight shift in his own emotions.

Bharata sighed. "Eventually I came to know that, actually, Father did have a few last words for me. He had stipulated that if I had any part in my mother's scheme, I was not to come near his body or light the pyre. He conditionally cast me off and denounced me as his son. Shatrugna, the youngest, would light the fire and ensure Father's descent to heaven. Vasishta swore to my innocence, and I was allowed to fulfill my role as the eldest son present. Then I saw Father's body submerged in a vat of oil, just like in my dream. It was horrible to see. Father was so clearly not there. At least I got to do this last thing for him.

"Then—strangest of all—the ministers wanted to crown me king! The kingdom was in too much turmoil, they said. Rama was already lost to us. Who knew where he was in the vast jungle. The only way forward was to put me on the throne. I was shocked and sickened. Did they really think I would take the throne? I had proclaimed myself innocent of my mother's scheme so many times, only to take the throne anyway? Wouldn't this inadvertently show, through my behavior, that I was condoning her actions?

"Father wanted Rama to be king. I wanted Rama to be king. That was the only way to peace and prosperity that I could see.

"Only in my darkest moments did I blame Father. Why had he not called me back for the coronation? If I had been in Ayodhya, none of this would have happened. I would have stopped my mother at once. Father's lack of faith in me, his fear that I might want the throne, this was the worst pain of all. So many people suspected me for wanting the throne, but they, after all, didn't know me. Father knew me! He knew me better than I knew myself. Or so I'd always thought. I didn't know whether to rage against Father for his faulty judgment or search deeper into my soul for a part of me I couldn't see."

Bharata turned to Rama, facing him squarely. "We have followed your tracks for months, Rama, but we were always a step behind. The three of you moved a lot faster than we did, with our large entourage. With so many of us, we were able to spread out and locate more quickly what direction you must have taken. Alone I might never have found you. Finally Guha and Bharadvaja told us you had made your settlement here in Chitrakuta. Here, we finally found you. I cannot describe the feelings that collided within me when I saw you again, my brother. Relief. Joy. Fear. Bliss. I cannot express how complete I feel now, being in your presence. The only thing I can compare it to is the contentment I used to feel in Father's presence. Rama, please, come home with us."

Bharata reached for Rama's hand, gripping it tightly. "That is the *only* reason we came here. If you are intent on honoring Father's final words, I will take your place. I will stay here in the forest for fourteen years and atone for the sin of having a mother like Kaikeyi. It seems only fair to me that I should switch places with you, Rama. I beg you. Bring the happiness back to our lives by returning to Ayodhya. Become our king. Only this could minutely assuage Father's absence. Ayodhya needs you. We need you. Come home."

Lakshmana whispered his estranged brother's words: "Come home."

Rama's Resolve

Rama's eyes never strayed from his tortured brother. Even after Bharata fell into silence, Rama kept his eyes intently on him. He wanted to make sure that Bharata had said everything he wanted to say. Silence descended on Chitrakuta. Bharata had spoken in earnest. The anticipation of the assembled Ayodhyans was high. They all wanted what Bharata wanted. Rama was thoughtful, but he knew what he must do.

"I trust you completely," he assured Bharata. "There was never a doubt in my mind that you were blameless in all of this. Ask Lakshmana."

Lakshmana nodded. He had not yet said a word directly to Bharata. His hands *had* relaxed around his weapons. Bharata's plight was heartfelt.

"I've listened to you and felt your pain," Rama said. "I'm deeply aggrieved that we have been pitted against each other. You have been unfairly targeted and accused. I hope that will end today. I commend your determination and the struggles you have undertaken to be here with me. Let everyone here absorb your complete innocence and bring your story to their homes and hearts. Don't blame yourself anymore, Bharata. I'm proud to say you are a brother of mine."

Bharata hung his head and closed his eyes. His breaths struggled through him in great heaves. Rama turned his gaze on the assembly, fixing his eyes on the queen mothers. There was something important in Bharata's story that Rama wanted to address. Rama would not speak to them as a friend but as their king. He would speak the way Father had done when addressing his people. Rama looked at his mother. Kausalya was thin and frail, but in her eyes, Rama saw acceptance. She knew what he would do. Next to his mother, Sumitra stood like a shadow. The one Rama was really looking for was not as easily found, for she did not want to be seen.

Kaikeyi stood apart from the rest of the people, as though she didn't belong. It was as Rama had suspected; Kaikeyi was treated as a pariah, a convenient scapegoat for all Ayodhya's fears and anxieties. Rama saw clearly now that Lakshmana was not alone in his hatred of Kaikeyi. Like an unwelcome disease, she was barely tolerated. Although still walking among them, Kaikeyi was scorned. She was blamed for everything—the king's death, Rama's exile, and the chaos in the kingdom. All of it was placed squarely on the queen's shoulders. The queen, who had been regal and exquisite, had shriveled. With hunched shoulders and a downcast face, she resembled Manthara, her crooked servant.

In a flash, Rama considered Kaikeyi's three avatars. First, the lively mother and rosy lady whom Father had adored. Second, the harsh and ruthless queen powerfully setting a vast chain reaction in motion. And now, a diffident, inconspicuous woman taking up as little space as possible, a dim shadow of her former self.

Rama was aware of the many eyes scrutinizing him. They were eager for him to break the silence, to respond to Bharata's final plea. Rama drew his thoughts in, piecing them together.

"Each of you knows the power of karma and destiny," he said in a strong voice. "The circumstances we find ourselves in are not a coincidence. I have been exiled from my kingdom for a reason. It's not arbitrary. Once we accept this fact, we dispel our tendency to cast blame. Let me say it plainly. I'm requesting you to forgive Kaikeyi."

Somewhere in the crowd Rama heard a loud "No!"

Kaikeyi looked up abruptly and into Rama's eyes.

Rama's eyes swept across the crowd while he said, "As individuals, we must treat others with compassion and forgiveness. When they are aggressors, as Kaikeyi was, it's a challenge. Your anger toward her was not wrong. Your passion for justice makes you worthy citizens of Ayodhya. Until now, each of you has done your duty by opposing her, by disagreeing with her scheme. You've shown commendable loyalty to me and to King Dasharatha. Since the time of the initial crisis, however, the issue has changed. We must look at it differently. Look at Queen Kaikeyi now. Is she the cruel queen you think her to be?"

Everyone turned to look at Kaikeyi, as if realizing for the first time that she was present among them. Kaikeyi straightened and wrapped her white sari tighter around her shoulders.

Undeterred, Rama continued. "From a political perspective, it was a master move. In one stroke she forced us all to follow her will. After hearing Bharata's tale, however, we know for certain that none of this was preplanned. She had no allies, except for Manthara. It all simply aligned: Bharata's absence, Father's urgency, and those fateful, long-forgotten boons.

When a person acts so contrary to their usual nature, I see the handiwork of immovable, inscrutable, indestructible destiny. Before my exile, none of us suspected Kaikeyi would do anything like this. Father did not expect it. No one did. Isn't it so?"

Rama turned to his mother, Kausalya, the Great Queen.

"Mother, you have always been the acknowledged queen of Ayodhya. The example you set is followed by thousands. I must speak openly about something that ever was kept in the shadows in Ayodhya."

Rama looked into her large, soulful eyes and saw what he had always seen, the currents of sadness that ran there. His voice grew apologetic. "Mother, I know your heart. I know the grief you harbored even before Father died. As a child, I did not understand why. As I grew, I began to understand more. You and Kaikeyi have been rivals all my life. You, of all people, have reason to resent Kaikeyi. And so I ask you: Do you think Kaikeyi meticulously planned this? In your heart, did you ever suspect that she had anything but the deepest love for me?"

Rama's throat grew dry and a dull ache rose in his heart. The memory of Kaikeyi's rejection was painful. Kausalya's eyes were as hard as steel, but then she did something that Rama had not anticipated.

She put an arm around Kaikeyi. "I thank you for this opportunity, my son. I have longed to speak publicly about this."

She turned to the citizens of Ayodhya, gathering her breath to speak, although her arm around her rival already spoke volumes. "For twenty-two years, I witnessed Kaikeyi gathering the king's love to herself. I warned them both that it was not auspicious, that it would cause destruction. I could see that much. But I did not know that *she* would destroy him. No. I did not suspect it. Like my son, I see other powers at work here." She turned to Rama. "Kaikeyi's affection for you, Rama, struck me always as pure and clear. I did not expect her to turn on you, or I would have protected you from her with all my power. Her love for our husband, the king, was possessive and selfish, but I did not anticipate either that she would turn on him. I can see now that the shadows of her past grew so large they suffocated the light. She did not see that her actions would lead to her self-destruction. And so I agree with you, my son. Kaikeyi deserves forgiveness."

Gently, the Great Queen pushed Kaikeyi forward. "This woman, the third queen of Ayodhya, former wife of the emperor, deserves more than our forgiveness. She has won my admiration and respect, something I never imagined I would feel for her, my bitter rival."

Rama did not understand. He felt the swell of questions grow in the crowd, most notably in Bharata. Kaikeyi had been in their midst for months, but only now were they actually seeing her. Kaikeyi lifted her gaze and looked at the people around her. The pure strength in her being was unmistakable. She was not broken. But she was not proud. Rama saw that what he had taken as timidity was in fact humility. Kaikeyi was not diminished; she was transformed.

"I am grateful to be here among you," she said. "I thank the Great Queen for allowing me to speak. I thank each of you for listening to me, I who do not deserve your attention after the ruin I have caused in our kingdom. I do not expect you to forgive me."

She clasped her hands together. "Because of the Great Queen's kindness, I ask you only to see me now for what I truly am." She lifted off her veil and revealed her hair, shorn of its long, bountiful locks. "I am a soul," she said. "Above all else, I am a soul. Everything I knew myself as, those are all temporal coverings. Once I was stripped of my attachments, I could finally see this. Everything that I identified with, which made me the proud and selfish queen I was—every one of those identities—they have been taken from me. I am the proud favorite wife of Emperor Dasharatha no more. He cast me off before his death. I am a wife no more. I am the mother of my son Bharata no more. He too has rejected me. I am Manthara's child no more. She abandoned me when our scheme fell apart. I can take shelter in my physical beauty no more; it too fades each day. I am no longer the identities that bound me to my ego."

She turned to Rama, though she did not look into his eyes. "You, who would now be our king if it wasn't for me, you must decide my fate, as I unfairly decided yours. I accept whatever you think is best. If you would like to exile me to these forests, I will stay here. If you would like me to return to Ayodhya, I will comply. Whatever the people of Ayodhya think is best, I am ready to do."

She took a step back and hid again behind her veil. Rama saw the two queens exchange a soft smile before Kaikeyi almost disappeared in the crowd again. Rama was astonished. He looked back and forth between his two mothers, who were now no longer in a feud. The death of the king had dissolved their reason for rivalry. But there was more. Kaikeyi could have continued her quest to become the most powerful queen in the kingdom, but she had not. She had completely changed course. She had shorn her hair and, along with it, her previous identity.

"Thank you, Mother." Rama's voice was soft.

Kausalya, who had the strongest personal reason to shun Kaikeyi, had led the way and forgiven Kaikeyi before anyone else.

Rama walked closer to his third mother. The crowd parted to let him through. Kaikeyi sank to the Earth and did not look at Rama. "I mean what I said, Rama. I don't deserve your forgiveness."

"But I want to forgive you," he said, because he had not fully done so. "If not for your own sake, then for mine."

When she did not respond, Rama's pain surfaced. "Am I still only the insignificant person standing in your way to the throne?"

Kaikeyi looked up and into his eyes. Despite her wise words and her new realizations, there was the inescapable human pain. "I never knew," she whispered, "I never suspected that your father would die. I-I didn't want him to die. He was your father, but he was everything to me. Losing him, I lost myself. I am all alone now."

Her words were so quiet, only Rama could hear them.

"Where is Manthara?" Rama had to ask.

Kaikeyi had never been alone; Manthara was ever at her side.

Kaikeyi bit her lip, and then a great sigh escaped. "As good as dead. When she realized it was all falling apart, she poisoned herself. But she never was as skilled with poisons as she imagined. She survived. Now she is paralyzed and blind. Whether she can hear or not, I do not know, for she repeats only the words *It's mine*. She is completely dependent on Ayodhya's servants for all her needs. A position she would have utterly despised were she conscious, but she is not. She recognizes no one."

Lakshmana stepped forward. "Manthara deserves no sympathy from us. Even her current condition is self-inflicted. I cannot forgive her, Rama. And Kaikeyi is no child. She knew what she did."

A murmur of assent ran through the crowd.

Lakshmana's words somehow resonated with Kaikeyi. She squared her shoulders and lifted her chin. She smiled up at Rama, a semblance of her old, fierce smile.

Rama saw in her a desire to give up all deceit, and then she spoke.

"If Manthara was here, I would not shun her. She was the only mother I knew. People accused me of being a replica of my exiled mother in body and soul. But Manthara raised me. She is the only mother I have known. She had the power to sway me into believing that you and your father meant me harm. I was determined to never be like my true mother. This was my deepest fear. To be discarded, to be exiled, to become nobody, like she was. She who once was a queen, disappeared, torn from her children as if she had never existed. I would not allow anything to separate me from Bharata. Manthara knew this. She used it against me. I see that now. Before she died, she revealed that she had orchestrated my mother's exile too. With her last words, she wanted to prove to me what a fool I was to have loved her. But I knew in that moment that only love could have healed her. Manthara was never in favor in Ayodhya, and this pained her greatly. What she did, she did out of love for me. What I did, I did out of love for Bharata."

Kaikeyi paused and looked around, realizing how many ears were tuned to her words. "I make no excuses. I am revealing this only for you, Rama. You deserve answers for your peace of mind. I know how wrong I was. I know how wrong she was. Manthara knew it too. She said your name, Rama, many times before she lost her sanity. Her eyes were haunted, her features twisted with fear. She couldn't bear to see me in ruin. I accept it. I was not strong enough to see that she played upon my weaknesses. I allowed her to manipulate me. I see it now. But I was complicit in my own poisoning. Manthara is *not* the sole culprit. I deserve every ounce of Ayodhya's blame, for I cannot in truth promise you that I could act differently than I did. I could not shun Manthara. I should be shunned, in turn."

Rama took her hands. Mother and son looked into each other's eyes, a battle of will. She began to breathe laboriously, tears rising to her eyes. She wasn't as strong as she pretended to be. Rama recalled the countless times that Kaikeyi had held him and soothed him during his childhood. As if she was a stubborn child, Rama pulled her into a tight embrace. Slowly her resistance melted and then she clung to him. Absorbing his kindness and understanding, she cried softly. Rama stroked her back gently.

No one spoke or interrupted the reconciliation. Rama released Kaikeyi from his embrace. She took a step away on shaky feet, rubbing away her tears. Rama could see the glow of her soul peek through her weary eyes.

"I know it's far too late," she said, "but I hereby retract my two boons. You alone can bring prosperity back to Ayodhya, Rama. Reverse this tragedy. I only came here to say this to you myself. I take back my wishes. No part of me wants those boons to come true. I know it's terribly late. But it's not too late for you to come home with us. Come home!"

This was a plea no one could disagree with. The anger of the assembly was replaced by agreement. The people called out, "Yes! Come home!"

As Rama had with his own mother, he concluded his exchange with Kaikeyi by saying a heartfelt "Thank you."

It had not been easy for Kaikeyi to publicly reveal her innermost workings.

Rama had to face his people again.

"My exile was preordained," Rama said. "After hearing Queen Kaikeyi's words, I know it beyond a doubt. She does not stand before us defending her actions. How can we continue to condemn her with a clean conscience? I plead with each of you to find forgiveness in your heart. I ask you to withdraw the blame that is enveloping Kaikeyi and to set her free."

Rama glanced at Lakshmana but settled his gaze on Bharata. By his own admission, Bharata had spent the past few months distancing himself completely from his mother, ashamed of his own birth. "I request this especially of you, Bharata. As long as you bear this grudge against your mother, you will lead a poisoned life."

Rama addressed the citizens of Ayodhya. Speaking to his people, he was Rama, their king. "Let this be a lesson for all of us. Kaikeyi took counsel from someone whose intentions were malicious. We know there will always be people like Manthara in this world. Not everyone is honest and pure. Not everyone lives in a prosperous, abundant Ayodhya. Manthara chose to live in a hateful Ayodhya, clinging to poisonous thoughts, making that her reality. Kaikeyi's biggest mistake was to allow a person like that so close to her. She allowed Manthara to whisper twisted truths into her ear. Kaikeyi chose to accept Manthara as her confidant; she chose to trust Manthara instead of trusting the king or trusting me or any of the wise ones of the kingdom. Choose your associates wisely."

Rama was silent for some moments. He sensed a general softening toward Kaikeyi. A final caution came to Rama and he proclaimed it: "The mind longs to indulge in its fears. It seeks every opportunity to amplify its worries and to find them in reality. In one part of her heart, Kaikeyi feared that I would turn against her, that the king would cast her out, that Bharata, her own son, would become a pauper. That fear became her reality, and she turned it around on us, her family. Our hidden fears are our worst enemies."

Against his will, Rama's eyes flickered over to Sita. Her graceful presence was the backbone of his existence. What would he do if anything happened to her? Was she really safe here in the jungle? Wouldn't it be wiser to send her back to Ayodhya?

Rama quickly retreated from his private concerns and returned to his public persona. "We must be vigilant against our fears, which long to possess us and force us into desperate actions. See them for what they are. Seek counsel with those who are wise. Let us close our ears and hearts to words motivated by distrust and fear. Let us all live in a prosperous Ayodhya."

Everyone cheered loudly. They took his last sentence literally. They heard an admission that he meant to return to Ayodhya with them. Rama felt heavyhearted but he refused to make his father's death pointless. He refused to unravel the intricate web that had been cast. He had been propelled out beyond Ayodhya, and he meant to explore why. He walked to the center of the clearing to command the people's full attention.

"Hear me now, once and for all. I've listened carefully to Bharata's plea. I'm touched by his purity of heart and determination to see me on Ayodhya's throne. I'm aware of Queen Kaikeyi's official request that the boons be discarded. My heart feels fulfilled, having seen you once again. You also have seen that I am well. Sita and Lakshmana are well. Both of them are free to return with you."

Rama turned to his two faithful companions. He had to offer them this escape.

"Sita, the people of Ayodhya love you. You will be safe there. Return with them. The same goes for you, Lakshmana. I cannot bear to see you separated from your wife because of me. Please return, both of you. I am prepared to endure this exile on my own."

Sita and Lakshmana looked at each other, two flames of one fire.

"Never," they said simultaneously.

Rama inclined his head in agreement. He could not force them to leave.

"My dear people of Ayodhya," Rama said, turning to them. "I will not come back to Ayodhya. My father's word is my word. He sent me to the forest unwillingly, and he paid the price with his life. There is nowhere else I can be but here. This exile is my destiny. I do not claim to know the answers, and neither can I shed light on the future. Only when I return to Ayodhya in fourteen years can I hope to answer your questions. All I know now is that I must stay here and continue my journey. And all of you must return to Ayodhya and continue your individual work there."

A collective moan arose, but Rama silenced them with his hands and motioned for Bharata to come to his side. "Here is Bharata. Accept him as your king. I can think of no one more fit to take my place than him. He has proven himself free from selfish motives. He is a worthy successor to King Dasharatha's mighty empire."

Rama offered the kingdom back to Bharata, fully and wholeheartedly.

Bharata pushed away Rama's hands. "I. Don't. Want. It!"

Bharata had emphasized each word, his handsome face streaked with tears.

"But you must take it," Rama replied. "It is yours now. Those above you have decided these things."

If Bharata wanted the kingdom even a little bit, in the smallest recess of his heart, despite what he had said, this was his chance to let that desire be shown; Rama was returning the kingdom to him with open hands.

"It's yours," Rama repeated, affirming Bharata's right to the throne and allowing him to take on the burden and glory of the crown. "Truly, the land of Ayodhya and the world she rules are yours, my brother. When I return in fourteen years, you can return the kingdom to me. But for now, you are worthy. The people have agreed." With a sweeping motion of his hands, Rama indicated the people of Ayodhya who were there.

"They are not here for me," Bharata said, shaking his head. "They are here for you!"

King Dasharatha's eldest sons locked eyes, communicating wordlessly, seeing as if with one vision what the future would look like if Bharata agreed and stepped onto the throne.

They both knew kingship was never simple. Rama could not come back after fourteen years to have the throne easily transferred back to him. Bharata was so much Rama's brother in every sense of the word, from physical likeness to character; Rama was confident that people would come to accept and love Bharata the way they loved him. Rama experienced for a moment what it felt like being replaceable. In fourteen years, loyalties would be shifted. Rama's return would not be a joyful homecoming but a cause of tension. If he returned to reclaim the throne, his people, who would then be Bharata's people, would be in turmoil again. Bharata could have borne a son of his own. This story could be repeated in the next generation. Bharata too was a powerful warrior.

Rama could see all this in Bharata's eyes and knew that Bharata would not back down. He would not prolong this dynastic struggle. He had given the kingdom back to Rama already. That was it.

Deeply touched by his brother's strength of vision, Rama closed the distance between them and held Bharata to his heart. The brothers stood like this for moments, arms tightly around each other. Affectionately, they exchanged endearments only the two of them could hear. After a few moments, they embraced again, clasping each other's hands.

Bharata declared, "I will serve my brother by being the guardian of Ayodhya until he returns. As my brother's servant, I cannot go where he is forbidden to go. I will stay outside the city gate while attending to all matters of state. Like my virtuous brother, I will sleep on the ground, lead the life of an ascetic, and will not enter any city."

The simplicity and humility of Bharata's decision touched the hearts of everyone who knew the rules of the kingdom. The ministers present sent out words of blessing. To finalize this pact, Rama stepped onto a pair of golden shoes. These shoes would be on the throne in Rama's place, symbolizing that Bharata was merely following Rama's footsteps.

"But know this," Bharata said, close to tears, again facing Rama. "If you do not return when the fourteen years are up, I will end my life. I will light a fire and walk into it. This is my solemn vow. Do not tarry, my brother. Without you, my existence is bleak and unbearable."

Rama embraced Bharata again. Bharata's desperation was difficult to behold.

"When the term of my exile is complete," Rama announced to all, "I will return without delay."

Having come to this agreement, Rama had said all there was to say. The longer they remained together, the more intense the desire to stay together would grow. The arguments could easily be renewed, the cycle of questions reinitiated. So Rama turned away, taking Sita's and Lakshmana's hands. He did not say farewell to his mothers or to anyone else. There had already been too many good-byes. Without looking back, the exiled prince withdrew into the cottage with Sita and Lakshmana.

The Borderland

The harmony they had experienced at Chitrakuta was over. Lakshmana could not stop thinking about Urmila's absence; she had not been present in the large entourage from Ayodhya. The pathway down to the river reminded him of this, for he had expected to see her waiting at the bottom of the path. The base of the mountain was trampled and muddy, reeking of horse and elephant dung. A fair reflection of how Lakshmana felt. A heavy feeling clung to him, no matter how he tried to cast it off. Lakshmana could not stand to be in this place any longer. Despite the amicable parting between Rama and Bharata, it would be unwise to abandon caution. Rama too agreed that politics were fickle. Bharata had in essence built a highway from Ayodhya straight to Chitrakuta. If that was not enough reason to leave, Chitrakuta was no longer their haven; the illusion had been shattered. In its place, Rama admitted he could see only his mother's sad eyes, Kaikeyi's torment, and Bharata's plea.

They agreed to abandon the dwelling. Taking only their weapons and a few animal skins, they left the home they had created at Chitrakuta and wandered again into the unknown.

On their way out, they stopped under Shyam, the magnificent tree, and communed with the ancient banyan one last time. Lakshmana felt Rama's roiling grief over their deceased father; he had always been closest to Father. Sita stood quietly in her tattered garments. This observation was another leftover from Ayodhya's visit. Lakshmana had been reminded how an Ayodhyan saw the world. By that standard, Sita looked poor and unkempt, with her callused hands and feet. Lakshmana dismissed his usual thinking, wherein he wished her back in the city. He felt closer to Sita now. Her resolve to stay had united so fiercely with his. It had been a moment of true camaraderie. Neither of them would ever agree to return to Ayodhya without Rama. He respected her for this. Sita's hand rested gently on Shyam and she turned her gaze to Lakshmana. He stiffened, afraid she would mention Urmila and see his pain. He left the banyan tree and waited in the sun for his brother and the too-perceptive Sita.

The spring in Chitrakuta had been pleasant, even magical. Lakshmana saw this in retrospect. As he stood in the shade and waited, the heat of summer wrapped itself around him. Within minutes, he was dripping with sweat and longing for the musty smell and shade under Shyam. Sita and Rama soon joined him and, as they began to walk, it was impossible to stride fast; the sun sent rays of lethargy into their minds. Their departure was further slowed when Sita's pet deer, Mila, began trailing them. Sita repeatedly stopped to embrace the fawn.

"She has a flock," Sita said. "She is content with them."

Still, neither Sita nor Mila was able to say a final farewell. At last, Rama intervened and turned the deer toward Chitrakuta and would not let her follow them any longer. He told Sita and Lakshmana to walk ahead, while he soothed the restless deer. Lakshmana noted Sita's distress and wanted to say something. But again the shields around his heart asserted themselves. If he began a heartfelt discussion with Sita, it would not take long for her to bring Urmila into it. Lakshmana gripped a few branches in their way, holding them aside for Sita to pass. When he let the branch go, his clenched fingers came away with a handful of leaves.

When Rama caught up with them, Sita asked no questions about her pet deer. She walked ahead without looking back. The intensity of the heat claimed their full attention. They had no place to retreat to, no way of escaping it now. The blazing sun flushed their skins red, and water became their best friend. A languid laziness overtook them, an inability to think past the pressing heat. Each hour came and went, like a slow, torturous dance.

Their need for water brought them to every water source they could find. They were seldom the only ones at the waterhole. All the forest creatures were parched. The smaller ones fled when Rama and Lakshmana approached. Elephants paid them no mind, but other beasts were not as carefree. This Lakshmana learned when they encountered a tiger.

It was a small pond, obscured by low-hanging vines. Lakshmana did not see the beast until they were face-to-face with it. The large tiger paused its drinking, looking up at them with big yellow eyes. Lakshmana inhaled quickly and then did not breathe at all. Sita had never been so close to an animal that was truly dangerous. The tiger faced them eye to eye, as vigilant and wary as they were. His tail swished behind him lightly. His yellow eyes never

blinked, never strayed from them. Lakshmana felt the heightened danger in the air. The cat could spring from stillness to action before his breath returned. Automatically, Lakshmana reached for his arrows. Within the blink of an eye, both brothers had their arrows nocked and drawn to their ears.

"No," Sita said quietly but firmly. So they stood frozen, arrows pointed at the large cat.

"Rama?" Lakshmana asked.

Rama had always been good at the languages of the five-clawed beasts, one of the subjects of their schooling. The tiger fixed his stare on Sita, his tail moving rapidly. Rama emitted a low growl, barely parting his lips. The tiger's ears shifted and his tail became still. Rama roared formidably. The tiger turned his eyes on Rama.

Lakshmana recalled the lion that had nearly been killed by the kings at the Summit of Fifty Kings; Rama had miraculously saved it.

The tiger before them made one small sound and then, without breaking eye contact, began lapping up water.

"He will not harm us," Rama said, "but I think it's better if we leave him alone."

Carefully, they backed away, arrows still aimed at the tiger. Sita did not retreat with them and stood smiling at the tiger, who was looking up at her with his yellow eyes.

"Sita," Lakshmana called, as loud as he dared. "Come at once!"

She did as he said, backing away with them. When they lost sight of the beast, they put their bows down and turned away.

"What were you thinking?" Lakshmana demanded, turning to Sita, his voice sounding harsher than he meant. His hands were tingling and he was angry at her recklessness.

Sita's shoulders slumped. In a subdued voice, she said, "He would have let us drink there."

Lakshmana turned to Rama. "Sita may be right," Rama said.

Lakshmana waited. Sita's lips were dry and chapped. She was so thirsty she wasn't thinking. Wouldn't Rama admonish Sita or warn her?

Lakshmana could not be silent—even if he was overstepping his boundaries. "Never do that again, Sita, please. You don't know how unpredictable a beast is. One wrong step and he could have pounced on you. You could be dead. We can only protect you if you accept our discernment and rely on us."

Sita nodded, accepting his words.

Less than a mile ahead, they found a spring and gratefully drank. They continued in silence. Survival was their prime concern; there was no space for complex contemplations. After walking for miles and scavenging for food—sometimes finding none—they were exhausted. Without thought, they curled up on the ground and slept.

The heat of the summer became hotter, heavier, and more humid each day. The moist air clung to their skin, making them perspire within minutes of the dawn. Whenever they came across a body of water, they gratefully sought relief in its coolness. Sita's hair curled around her face, escaping from her long braid. Lakshmana's matted hair hung heavy down his back, attracting moisture. Even at night, the air was balmy and hot.

Despite the discomfort, Lakshmana felt the growing ease with which they moved through the forest. He felt less and less like an intruder. All three of them felt in harmony with the simple rhythms of forest life. Because of this, the brothers incurred fewer reasons to kill any animals crossing their path. Sita commented on it several times. She blessed their newfound restraint. After bonding with the animals at Chitrakuta, her compassion for them had only grown.

Lakshmana observed his two companions, finding them to be extraordinary creatures, the likes of which the forest had never sheltered. Watching Rama, Lakshmana knew that the forest had a new king. Rama had accepted the forest as his domain. Whether he knew it or not, Rama was creating a symbiosis with the forest; he was becoming an elemental part of it. To ask the forest now to be without Rama would be like reliving Ayodhya's great loss. Rama was majestic as he strode ahead purposefully, a warrior's attitude of certainty. Sita, as usual, was harder to describe. She was not like a princess anymore. There was something wildish about her, like a wildflower in full bloom. But it was hard for Lakshmana to look at Sita for any extended period of time, the way he gazed at Rama. For one, he didn't want her to feel discomfited. And there was another reason. One Lakshmana could not even look at. The only time Lakshmana did not feel withheld with Sita was when she sat next to Rama, hand in his, gazing up at that face they both loved. At such times, Lakshmana felt free. He could tell stories, laugh at their words, and feel as though Sita was his close friend.

As they walked, they talked about what they would do. They never said, "For the next

fourteen years," but it hung over them, a constant shadow. They had no real plan, only the sense that they had to disappear.

"Bharata found us," Rama said, "because we were settled in one place. We should not be so easily found again."

"I agree," Lakshmana said, relieved that he wasn't the only one of that mind.

Still, he felt a pang in his heart. There was no reason on Earth for anyone in Ayodhya to seek them out again. Yet they might. The implied distrust, the precaution against their own people, felt heavy. Being with them so recently, Lakshmana had felt relief from constantly emanating caution. It was unpleasant to distrust his own family. Yet Lakshmana had to keep doing so. They did not want to be found again.

"Walking seems to be the only solution," Rama said. "We cannot settle down."

For solace, Rama brought out Vasishta's scroll. Perhaps some of the teacher's old words would lend them guidance again. There were many holy ones to seek out.

"Look!" Rama looked over the scroll with round eyes.

Lakshmana and Sita hurried to his side.

The scroll was blank.

"How is this possible?" Lakshmana asked.

At once, he sought solutions. Had someone exchanged the old scroll for a new one while they weren't looking? A myriad of faces flashed in his mind. It would have been Sumantra or any of the ministers. But why would one of them do such a thing?

"It's the same scroll," Rama said. "Look, it has been crushed by my arrows, after months in my quiver. Oh wait, there is something here. One sentence."

Rama read it out loud:

Go to the forest of Dandaka.

"That's it." Rama turned the scroll over, examining it carefully. "How did Vasishta do this? Yet we know he has unimaginable powers."

"Dandaka?" Lakshmana couldn't keep the question contained. "That forest is reputed to be the most dangerous one."

"Yes," Rama said, putting an arm around Sita, who remained silent.

Lakshmana said, "But of course you will heed this advice because it comes from Vasishta."

"Of course." Rama shrugged apologetically as he rolled up the scroll.

With the preceptor's new directive in mind, they set out toward the south.

"Some say Dandaka is forbidden to mortals," Lakshmana said.

"Humans do not go there," Rama agreed. "Only holy ones live here."

"And the opposite of holy ones," Lakshmana added.

Sita looked over her shoulder at him. "Do you mean blood-drinkers?" she asked.

She had not yet encountered a single blood-drinker. How would she react?

"From what we've learned, yes," Lakshmana confirmed. "That's why I wouldn't have chosen this as our destination."

"Dandaka is a territory," Rama said, "that departs from the human realm. It's a borderland."

Lakshmana thought of what he knew of borders and lands. Of course, every kingdom had borders. Crossing Ayodhya's borders four months back had been a heavy moment in their early trials. The tears that streamed down Rama's cheeks had told Lakshmana how much it cost him to turn away from his birthright. In the jungle, though, what distinguished one forest from the other?

"A borderland?" he said, giving voice to his thoughts. "What makes Dandaka different from any other part of the forest?"

"Remember the king of Kashi? He was desperate to fight blood-drinkers and came straight to Dandaka. It is known for harboring the mystical and magical. Let's not forget that blood-drinkers are supernatural too, living far longer than humans."

"Sita, did you know they call us 'the short-lived ones'?" Lakshmana asked.

"Yes. My sister and I especially loved the children's stories that described the time difference between our realm and theirs. One day in Indra's realm is half a year on Earth. And the night of the gods spans another six months. The authors of the tales have ever used this to their advantage. By their accounts, our exile is merely fourteen days!"

"Dandaka is full of mysteries unknown to man," Rama said. "Those who seek to transcend this world find their way there. Strangely, Dandaka is home to the most enlightened and the most degraded, those who seek light and those who want to extinguish it."

"There is no telling which type of being we will encounter," Lakshmana cautioned.

After many days of walking, Chitrakuta became one of many mountain peaks swelling behind them. They were reaching Dandaka, a vast jungle that promised to swallow them up. Shrouded in sunshine, protected by his bloodline, which connected him directly to the sun god, Rama walked into Dandaka the way a king walks into his empire. Lakshmana felt the confidence exude from his brother. Despite his earlier questions, Lakshmana immediately recognized that they were entering a new realm.

"Look at the flowers and the trees," he said to his companions. The wildlife was noticeably larger, one leaf now the size of Lakshmana's palm. "It's like we have shrunk to half our size."

"The soil is richer here," Sita said. "Do you smell how fragrant the Earth is?"

Lakshmana could not discern the difference in smell but continued marveling at the large tree trunks. "Blood-drinkers lurk here, that is sure. I long to see some of the magical things we've heard of. Kinnaras, beings who are half human, half animal. Apsaras from heaven, who are born to sing and dance, and do it so well you fall into their spell."

As if Dandaka heard Lakshmana's longing, the leaves began to shiver and an eerie melody drifted through the trees, dancing on the leaves to reach them.

"Singing Kinnaras," Lakshmana promised, leading them eagerly in that direction.

Rama took hold of him at once and gave him a look. "I will not let you fall into their spell."

Only then did Lakshmana recognize that he was pulled by the song, as if by unnatural compulsion. They walked on, enchanted by the sweet melody and the mystique that filled the air. Every time they were close enough to clearly hear the melody, it abruptly stopped. The unusual birdsong, a distant roar, and the rustle of leaves filled their ears. The persistent song melted into the background, losing its initial power. Then it began again, pulling the wanderers closer.

Within minutes, they came upon a flock of Kinnaras. Lakshmana was fascinated by the sight of the half-human, half-animal creatures. They were not nearly as clearly half-half as portrayed in pictures back in Ayodhya. They had four limbs and walked upright as humans did, but some were covered in fur while others had feathers. Lakshmana saw tails, beaks, and claws. It was impossible to say what animal any of them resembled. Their feathers and plumages were as bright and bold as gems. The tales proclaimed that Kinnaras never had children, for they did not want anything to come between their love; it had to be so, for Lakshmana saw that they roamed about in pairs and had eyes only for each other. When Sita and Rama drew near, the songs only grew louder and more enchancting. That all changed when the Kinnaras caught sight of Lakshmana. They grew visibly alarmed, taking hold of each other, ushering each other away and disappearing within seconds, taking their love-songs with them. Strange, Lakshmana thought. The trio continued undaunted but then came upon the Kinnara flock again. Even this time, the Kinnaras scattered when sighting Lakshmana. The third time this occured, Lakshmana stumbled slightly, his sword scraping a strip of bark from a sandalwood tree, the fresh scent wafting up. The thirty gods were to be thanked for this, for when the same occurrence happened the fourth time, Lakshmana stopped and pointed to the tree.

"Look! We have already been here. This is the fourth time we are passing this sandalwood tree. What is happening?"

Rama examined the mark.

"Time is acting strangely," Sita said. "We keep coming upon the lovemaking Kinnaras in the same exact moment."

"You noticed this?" Lakshmana asked.

"Yes, I thought they were enacting some dance where the patterns are repeated. But now I realize that we have reached them continuously at the same moment in time."

"And they always grow agitated at the sight of me," Lakshmana said. "Am I so despicable?"

Rama leaned against the tree, fingering the tree bark. "What do we do to break the spell?"

The three of them regarded one another. Lakshmana looked around for some clue. "I'm the one that disturbs them. Why don't you go ahead without me?"

"No," Rama said. "What if you get stuck here and we are released? I cannot risk that. I will invoke Bala and Atibala."

"The sister-shields?"

Rama had a whole arsenal of celestial arrows. Bali and Atibala protected him from fatigue and injury. How would that help now? The Kinnaras were not causing them bodily harm.

"They will keep us together invisibly," Rama said. He placed an arrow on his bow and instructed Lakshmana to do the same. Together, they said the mantra that would call the sister-shields to them. The very first time Rama had invoked Bala and Atibala, they had appeared in a dazzling yet ephemeral form, visible only for a few seconds, acknowledging their new master. They were incredibly beautiful, like sunbeams, with golden hair and glowing skin. This time, Lakshmana did not see the celestial sisters at all but immediately felt their warm energy wrap around his every limb, like a second skin.

"Let us go," Rama said, and strode toward the Kinnaras holding Sita's hand. "We will not let the Kinnaras disappear from us this time."

Lakshmana followed uncertainly. He wished he could stay behind, hidden in a tree perhaps. That way Rama and Sita could inquire about the way out. But what if his brother and Sita were whisked away and he alone got stuck in this maze forever?

The three of them walked rapidly, intent on breaking the spell that held them trapped. This time, the Kinnaras appraised Lakshmana and did not shy away. In fact, he felt immediately accepted by them. What had changed? Why did they accept him now?

As these questions formed in his mind, he felt the sister-shields blaze up on his skin, growing more solid and palpable, almost like they were two real women clinging to his arms. The Kinnaras meowed in approval. He heard clucks and purrs, saw tails swishing. A few of them covered their beaks with their wings and looked at him with faces hidden. It seemed to be a gesture of appreciation. The Kinnaras, with their supernatural vision, were not impervious to Bala and Atibala. They could see them! They deduced that the sister-shields were Lakshmana's mates. Now he was no longer a threat to them.

The Kinnaras eagerly surrounded them, and though they had no language in common, flashes of information rushed through Lakshmana's mind. It seemed that his thoughts were as visible to this flock as the celestial sisters were. Within seconds the Kinnarasa pointed toward a place to their left. The exit. As the trio turned to leave, the love-songs grew louder and louder, beckoning them to stay, just an hour, just a minute, just one second. In return, unimaginable pleasure was guaranteed. Lakshmana grew dizzy from all the impressions but kept his eyes on his brother. Rama had folded his hands at his chest in the gesture of thanks and was already headed towards the exit-point.

"The Kinnaras have created an enchanted space where time stops," Sita marveled, putting some of the information they were receiving into words. How she could formulate thoughts or speak through the onslaught of enchantment, Lakshmana could not guess. "It allows them to extend their pleasures beyond the reach of time," she concluded.

Soon they came upon two trees whose branches had intertwined to create an archway. Flowering vines hung like a curtain, reaching toward the ground. When they parted the vines and stepped out, the maddening song ended abruptly. A fresh wind blew across their faces. The maze had released them.

Rama chanted the mantra to release Bala and Atibala. Lakshmana's skin grew cold in the absence of their warm touch. The coldness spread to his heart, for he knew one thing now: As a lone man, he was a threat to any couple. It went beyond personal feelings or loyalty, for it was ingrained in the psyche of all creatures who mated and protected their chosen mate. Even if Rama or Sita did not feel this way, it was still an undeniable fact. The Kinnaras' reaction to him had demonstrated a universal truth, one that Rama and Sita would be too gracious to ever express.

Lakshmana looked at his companions, seeing them as the couple they were, absorbed in jesting and laughing, speaking of the flamboyant Kinnaras. They didn't notice him or his heavy heart. Determined to stave off any self-pity, Lakshmana brought his attention to the external.

Lakshmana began to notice an increase in predatory creatures. Crocodiles lounged on the riverbanks, occasionally exposing their sharp teeth with the yawn of a jagged snout. Lakshmana had learned that crocodiles were lazy creatures, rarely motivated to give up their spots in the sun. And yet in their vacant, motionless eyes he saw the cold malice. One wrong step and the crocodiles would be upon them.

A harsh harrowing noise disrupted the forest. Instinctively, Sita covered her ears.

It was a hideous gurgling and slurping, like a mad elephant drinking down a waterfall. There was no reprieve from the terrible noise ahead, the sounds of a death struggle. About twenty trees ahead of them, Lakshmana saw the elephant on the ground, its trunk thrashing through the air, emitting shrieking honks of pain. A blood-drinker twice the size of its prey held the elephant's half-severed head away from its body. Horror made the hair on Lakshmana's body stand on end. Rivers of bright blood flowed from the ghastly wound. The blood-drinker's tongue darted out of his mouth, slurping the blood greedily, the source of the chilling drinking sound.

"No, no, no," Sita cried, shielding her face from the sight.

The giant grabbed the elephant's swaying trunk, wrapped it around his arm, and twisted the head off completely. The elephant stopped struggling. With a grunt, the blood-drinker lifted the elephant's head and impaled it on his spear.

Lakshmana gaped in shock at the blood-drinker. This forest was truly sized for the vicious demon before them. His skin was scaly like a crocodile's and the color of tree bark. He had the features of a human, except for the fangs at his mouth. Everything Sita had been warned about was embodied in the monster before them. Gigantic as he was, the blood-drinker held a spear twice his size. On it, he had impaled the heads of tigers, deer, and now that of the elephant. Fresh blood oozed from their tattered necks.

The next second he stood in front of Rama, Lakshmana, and Sita, as if he had known they were watching.

"Short-lived creatures!" he bellowed. "If you treasure your pathetic lives, why have you come to my forest?"

The blood-drinker lunged forward and snatched Sita, plucking her away like a ripe fruit. Sita screamed, but the blood-drinker was louder: "Run back to where you came from!"

Rama was motionless, paralyzed by what was happening.

Sita was like a little doll in the blood-drinker's hand.

Lakshmana pulled an arrow to his ear, and roared, "Wake up, Rama!"

He released his arrow and then another. Rama snapped into action, and his anger visibly surged. Holding his bow at arm's length, Rama released a shower of arrows onto the blood-drinker. Any other demon would have been dead, but not this one. Their arrows flew through the demon like a knife through melted butter. The blood-drinker laughed, his large belly shaking. Sita wobbled like a rag doll. Her skin was ashen, her eyes terrified. The clouds began to gather into a dark storm, the sun deserting them.

"No weapons can kill me," the blood-drinker boasted. "Brahma, the creator, blessed me with this boon. Now this sweet-smelling woman is mine."

He sniffed at Sita. "Run away from here, both of you, before I decorate my spear with your useless little knobs for heads."

Laughing loudly, the grotesque one flung a bloody tiger head at them and bared his fangs.

Rama roared, ripped out his sword, and ran toward the demon.

"My name is Viradha," the demon cried, "but today I will be your death!"

Rama sank his sword into Viradha's belly, and Lakshmana's sword cut into him a second later. Blood squirted from the gashes, splashing onto Sita. Viradha tucked Sita under an armpit and grabbed Rama and Lakshmana with his hands. With unnatural speed, he began running deeper into Dandaka.

Sita bashed her fists against the demon. The clouds began rumbling, and rain pelted down on them. Rama and Lakshmana struggled to free themselves.

Sita screamed, "Just take me! Leave them both!" She stopped her fists from moving and hung limp to show her surrender.

Rama roared in a fury more terrible than the thunder above them. He twisted his sword into the socket of one of Viradha's arm and pulled free, severing the arm entirely. Lakshmana plunged his sword into the other arm socket, crushing bones as he did. Viradha's scream exploded, joining the booms of thunder. Sita fell from Viradha's tight grip and was flung toward the ground. Lakshmana gained his footing and, along with his brother, sprinted alongside the demon, who was still running but had lost his equilibrium. Armless and bleeding, Viradha crashed onto the ground and lost consciousness.

Showing no mercy, Lakshmana beat Viradha's unconscious body with clenched fists. Rama ran over to Sita and helped her up, moving her away from the blood-drinker.

However, Viradha soon regained consciousness and tried to get to his feet, his fangs showing with every snarl. Rama ran to Lakshmana's aid. No matter how harsh their blows, how well-aimed at his vital organs, destroying the bones of his face, the demon remained alive, kicking and snarling, baring his fangs at the brothers.

"He spoke truly," Rama cried. "He can't be killed by any weapon, not even our bare fists. We must bury him alive. Lakshmana, dig a pit."

Rama put his foot firmly on Viradha's neck and, strangely, the demon stopped thrashing. Lakshmana dug his sword into the ground, loosening the dirt, and began using his hands to dig the grave. He saw Sita trembling with her whole body as she watched anxiously. The Earth began to yield . . . but it would take hours to dig a pit large enough to hold Viradha.

"Use a divine missile," Rama directed. "The one invoking Vayu, the wind. It can tunnel into the Earth."

As he spoke he never broke eye contact with Viradha. The blood-drinker was in some kind of trance. Lakshmana pulled an arrow to his forehead and recited the mantra to invoke the wind god. When he shot the arrow into the meager pit, a harrowing wind blew up from the pit and spit out dirt. Lakshmana ran forward, looking into the concave space. It was quite a bit deeper. No doubt Rama could have done it with one arrow, but Lakshmana kept at it, releasing many arrows into the hole until it grew deep enough.

When the grave was ready, Lakshmana helped haul the giant into the pit. As soon as Rama's foot left Viradha's neck, the demon let out an earsplitting scream and thrashed wildly again, trying to get back on his feet. When he hit the bottom of the pit, Lakshmana threw heavy rocks onto his body, crushing him to the ground. Rama lifted a massive boulder, the muscles in his shoulders straining against the weight, and hurled it into the pit. All of Viradha's bones broke, popping like firecrackers. Still Viradha's screams persisted, until the stones and dirt finally covered his face and the pit was closed up.

Sita stood by, shivering in fright. This was nothing like seeing arrows shot at a distant target, hitting their mark. There was elegance in that. Here, there was none. Sita had never before witnessed such brutality—no mercy, no dignity, nothing majestic in the way Viradha was being crushed and suffocated to death. The princess slumped to the ground, her limbs trembling.

Rain continued to whip down on them relentlessly. Standing over the freshly turned Earth, Lakshmana felt like he had been snatched out of an elusive dream; the beauty of Chitrakuta was a fleeting memory. There Sita sat, smeared in blood. Hopefully most of it was Viradha's. Her hair and clothes were in disarray and she looked at them with fright in her eyes.

Kneeling at her side, Rama had to shout to be heard. "It's over now!"

Sita disappeared into Rama's embrace. He closed his eyes as he held her tight. Lakshmana turned his face up to the storm, letting the rain pelt against him. The raindrops grew soft. The thunder quieted. The storm was passing.

Rama released Sita, and the three of them stood looking at the grave they had made.

Just as the sun peeked from behind a cloud, an almost imperceptible energy floated up from the Earth and into the sky.

"Viradha's spirit," Sita whispered.

As Viradha's celestial body hovered around them for a few seconds before disappearing, the atmosphere changed. It had been dark and hideous. Now it was light and glorious. Lakshmana allowed the transformation to envelop him, stunned by the nature of this forest, where the ugly and the glorious coexisted. When the celestial being that once was trapped in the blood-drinker's body ascended to the heavens, Lakshmana's spirit was elevated with it. Together the three of them stood at the grave of the dead, smeared in his blood. Yet they were purified, for they had witnessed a soul being freed.

"Come," Rama said. "Let us not linger here any longer."

Rama unwillingly let Sita go as they began walking. Sita fell into her place in the middle, and Lakshmana led the way. Lakshmana was shaky on his feet, the sudden adrenaline and viciousness of the fight still lingering in his body.

They had not walked long when Lakshmana came to a sudden halt. Ahead of them, they saw the rotting corpse of a mutilated ascetic, doubtless one of Viradha's victims. Rama's hand went to Sita's face, covering her eyes, but not fast enough. The dead ascetic's eyes were gouged out, half of the skin ripped from his face, and a round, gaping hole was where the stomach had been—clearly the handiwork of something malicious. Rama's attempt to protect Sita from the vile sight was futile. No matter what route they took, they came upon decomposing bodies, until finally they started walking on bones. The leaves on the large trees were brown and shriveled, as if the evil here sucked the nutrients from the Earth. The skeletons crunched under their feet, mountains made of human bones.

Lakshmana could hear Rama's breathing grow laborious; he was angry. Dandaka was not only unsafe for Sita, but for the holy ones as well, who had come here to practice transcendence. The holy ones practiced asceticism and *tapasya* to withdraw from the world, to leave their mortal bodies and fly up to the heavens. Violated by the likes of Viradha, the holy ones were defeated, and nothing infuriated Rama like injustice toward the vulnerable. The most enlightened and respectable of their kind were being devoured in gulps, their ascent to the higher regions interrupted by the fangs of man-eaters. Rama took the lead, firmly grasping Sita's hand. Dandaka had turned into the land of death. Despite this discovery, they had no way to go but forward.

CHAPTER 14

Sita and Anasuya's Gift

Although Dandaka gave us a terrible shock, I was gaining my grounding again through the movement of my body as it walked through the new terrain. The Earth was always there, soothing under my feet, no matter what the parts above her looked like. The greatest reprieve, however, was when the forest opened up and displayed another dwelling. The promise to meet other human beings was very welcome, and I could feel my need to interact with others of our kind. It was as strong as hunger. And in those days, hunger was real.

Indeed, I have never been as hungry as I was during those first months of the exile. It was a dull ache in the pit of my stomach. Even small hunger pains can feel like the beginning of starvation. I would discover only years later what true starvation felt like, and I think the first months in Chitrakuta prepared me for it. On our mountain peak all three of us were hungry and constantly thinking of food. We were just now developing the survival skills to meet our body's needs. We had the bodies of pampered royalty used to foods like fragrant saffron lemon rice with roasted cashews. We were not trained for this life, and for me that was the main irony of our

situation. We had found that we could store some fruits, like bananas, mangoes, and coconuts for a few days, but most other fruits and berries went rotten too fast and attracted flies and insects. And after we abandoned Chitrakuta, we had no option but to scavenge every day for our nourishment.

Finally we came upon the signs of habitation in Dandaka. The ashram gleamed like a jewel up ahead, and we quickened our steps, eager to learn of its inhabitants. Their simply crafted cottages clumped close together. It was more intimate than Bharadvaja's ashram, where fires had blazed, milking cows had walked about, and countless yogis had been rapt in meditation. I looked forward to escaping the death valley behind us and to entering the sacred realms of the holy ones.

The sage who came to greet us was indeed ancient. Bharadvaja, with his bright white beard, had looked like a youngster in comparison. When my valiant husband heard the name of the holy one before us, he fell at the sage's feet, as did Lakshmana and I. His name was Atri, and like Vasishta, he was one of Brahma's mind-born children, one of the original authors of the holy scriptures. Atri immediately brought refreshments for us, pouring fresh water from clay pots for us and offering us fruits, which we gratefully accepted. Yet the greatest surprise for me was when I saw an old woman, bent and trembling, coming up behind him.

"This is my esteemed wife," Atri said. "Anasuya."

I took a deep breath. Aside from the Nishada tribe, I had not met another woman in these forests. My surprise must have been clear, because Anasuya looked up at me and said, "Yes, it is unusual. Very few women have the endurance and determination to live under these conditions. Like you, Sita, I chose to walk with my husband, following his path of asceticism."

Anasuya's skin was more weathered and wrinkled than any I'd ever seen. Her eyelids drooped over her eyes, yet they were the eyes of a young girl's, bright and alert, and so I could not stop myself from feeling that I was meeting a friend. As if there was no age difference between us, we began to talk eagerly. I, who usually was not verbose, must have flooded Anasuya's ears with my mindless talk. I told her of my last encounter with a group of women, the charming Nishada women:

"Maybe because we could not understand one another, they touched my hair, my hands, my face, and my dress. I felt as though I was standing in the middle of a soft, caressing breeze. I accepted their curious affection. In turn, I reached out to the woman closest to me and felt the mountain of hair piled on top of her head.

"In one swift move, the woman pulled out the long, sinewy root that secured her bun. Her thick locks cascaded down her back. She swung them over her shoulders and held her hair forward for me to examine. All the other women did the same, standing around me with their hair free. I saw that their hair separated into matted coils, like the roots of a banyan tree. The texture was like lamb's wool. Laughing, the women wound their roots around their hair in a practiced motion and pulled them back up into large buns on top of their heads. That was the most efficient hairdo I had ever seen, even quicker than a plain braid.

"With lots of gestures, they told me about dancing nymphs that played in the forest, especially near the Ganga River. Then they pointed at me, indicating that I was more enchanting than those Apsaras, that I was like the goddess from the tales they told at night around the big fire. They were very kind to me. I've thought about matting my hair ever since then, as my husband and brother-in-law have done."

Anasuya listened patiently. I realized only then how much I missed talking to my sister, my cousins, and the other women of the palace.

Anasuya took my hand. Arm in arm, we strolled into the sanctuary of their ashram. The thatched roofs of their cottages were dry. The recent storm we had encountered had not reached here. The tattered cloths around my body had quickly dried in the air, but I could still smell Viradha's blood in my hair. I wanted to forget all about the demon and the brutality of my protectors. Anasuya stopped in the center of the cottages and squatted by the fire pit that blazed there. She poured a ladle of ghee into the fire. The fire pit was decorated with flowers and leaves arranged in careful patterns. Before she straightened, Anasuya adjusted one of the petals, so I knew this was her handiwork.

"It's so beautiful," I said.

"It's my meditation," she answered, and reached for my arm again.

I gratefully received her affection. "I cannot tell you how starved I am for another woman's company."

"You get used to it, after a while."

"How long did it take you?"

"Oh, a few hundred years."

I slowed down. The flow of words stuck to my lips. I was in the presence of an ancient and wise soul; I was merely a child. Anasuya hooted and pulled me along with her. We locked ourselves in her cottage, forgetting time as we talked. She asked me first about my birth, for she sensed that there was something different about me.

Through Anasuya's presence, I was able to access the memory of my birth, a tale always told to me, and now I was telling it, as the true witness that I was:

"Goddess Bhumi lifted me from the center of the Earth and pushed my body through her soil and out into a freshly plowed field, to face the sun for the first time. I saw through the eyes of a newborn infant. The bright light of the day made me close my eyes and cry. I was not sad or afraid. I cried because that's what my body needed to do to embrace this new embodied experience. Until I faced the daylight and felt my mother's warm hands withdraw behind me, I had not known what it felt like to be alone. After I was pushed out from my mother's dark and safe womb, my father, King Janaka, was there to embrace me. 'This will be my daughter,' he said, for they were childless at the time. I do not recall those words. But I experienced his energy and his hands, just as warm and assuring as my mother's had been. I was safe with my father. He has told me this story countless times."

"A proud father," Anasuya said.

I smiled. I did not tell her of my father's warnings to me, his observations of me as a child: "When you cried, it rained," he told me. "When you were angry, the fires crackled. When you screamed, the Earth trembled. No one could imagine that these occurrences were tied to a little child. But I observed it, many a time." At the age of three, when I had mastered speech, all this stopped, my father had told me. His words had forced me to remember the painful farewell from the Earth and the Sky, a denial of the elements that I am made of. He worried that I would not be accepted if I was too different. This exchange occurred on the eve of my wedding night. I carefully heeded my father's advice, even now.

Anasuya sat cross-legged on her straw mat, her thin arms trembling steadily. She told me of her birth to the legendary Kardama Muni and Devahuti, who had nine daughters and one son, conceived only after Devahuti embraced her husband's asceticism. As a reward, Kardama Muni had created a flying mansion and many other extravagant pleasures for his wife. Like her mother, Anasuya had many illustrious children and embraced her husband's way of life.

Although Anasuya was focused on spiritual goals and uninterested in her mortal body, she hadn't always been that way. It was with girlish delight that we began talking about things that were trivial to Rama and Lakshmana, such as the realities of a woman's body, which responds to the moon each month. Anasuya gave me much valuable advice, from praying to the goddess to making teas with coriander seeds, licorice root, and cinnamon.

"Though it's hard to believe," Anasuya said, "I was young once. And I was very stylish."

To prove her point, she opened a cupboard and brought out several baskets that over-flowed with women's paraphernalia. I looked into the baskets, seeing precious objects I had not expected to see until the exile was over: bundles of colorful silk cloths, makeup, fra-grances, creams, oils, and jewelry, all packaged in exquisite bottles and vials. It was as if I was seeing a piece of my former life within this basket—a life I had told myself I didn't miss, but the way my fingers longingly caressed these items revealed a different story. Every item there was a priceless treasure.

"You are prepared to go without any of these, I know," Anasuya said, "or you wouldn't be here. It's not sinful to wish for small comforts. I used these for many, many years, until finally my desire dwindled. Aging will do this to you. Now my pleasure is no longer tied to my body. But, Sita, you are a young girl, hardly a woman yet, by my reckoning. How old are you, precisely?"

"Seventeen," I answered.

Anasuya chuckled. "I'm afraid I cannot recall what it feels like to be seventeen. But your vitality and vivaciousness remind me of myself as a young woman, and I took pleasure in all these objects. I thought you might too. Some of the potions will, for example, keep your hair silky and smooth. Take whatever you want."

But I couldn't bring myself to touch anything, afraid that my composure might crack.

"Don't be shy about embracing your feminine beauty," Anasuya said. "You have a hus-band who loves you and protects you. That is heaven for a woman. I will speak frankly, for that is the luxury of old age: A big part of your husband's love is tied to your body, his pride in possessing it, thinking it belongs to him. There is joy in that feeling, though it certainly does not belong to him. Neither does it belong to you. It belongs to the elements it was made of, to which it returns once your soul journeys on. These truths will be revealed to you over time. Now the truth in your life is that you are a young woman in love. Your duty—let's call it that to make it more official—is to celebrate your body's beauty by decorating it and enhancing its natural charm. That's what all these items are for. And so I say again, take anything you want. I certainly do not use them anymore. And to tempt you further, I must reveal that they originate in heaven. They will last longer than Earth itself."

"You are so kind to me," I said.

She was saying everything I needed to hear, answering questions I did not know how to articulate. I said, "To survive in exile, I was sure I had to forget being a woman. I thought I had to become tough and unfeeling."

"Like a man?"

"Yes, I suppose so. I don't mean to say . . ."

"That men are unfeeling? No, they are not. They have the same softness we have, but it is evoked by different things altogether. Often, it awakens unwillingly. And so it must be, for the sun and Earth have ever had their places and functions."

I saw then the natural way of being who I was. I couldn't be Lakshmana or an ascetic, though I'd been trying. With this knowing, I reached and touched one of the bundles of cloth. It was pure white and shimmered with all the colors of the rainbow. When I touched it, it lit up, ablaze with colors. When I removed my hand, the cloth turned white again. Puzzled, I looked at Anasuya.

"I told you they were imbued with magic," she answered. "That material in particular is called the Essence. When you wear it, it takes on the color of your deepest essence."

I was hesitant to touch the bundle again, yet I was drawn to it. I didn't know what I might find out and was wary. Now I smile at such hesitation, since the only true way to live is with full acceptance of your nature. Until you do, life will remain confused, half lived. At that young age, I was living as fearlessly as I knew how to. I just didn't know that self-discovery would lead me to greater self-fulfillment. I know most people are courageous at heart. I also know, however, that the irresistible human tendency is self-criticism. There is a voice that lives within us, whispering the very words that create fear in our hearts. Looking back, I can see it was that voice, the voice of fear that whispered into my ear, "Don't touch it." The shimmering had stopped and the cloth was pure white again, the rainbow tones a mere hint of its potential.

I felt Anasuya's eyes on me. She had no doubt noticed how I was drawn to the Cloth of Essence and also fearful of it. But she did not say anything right away, and so I turned over other objects in my hand, mindful of how little I could truly carry with me as we walked away.

Although Anasuya had professed her lack of interest in these matters, she was swept up in helping decide which objects would be best suited to me. If she had been less interested, I surely would have snatched a thing or two, eager to seem as detached and wise as she. Now I aspire to be like she is, a woman of such wisdom and knowledge that she can allow herself to respond to the playful desires of a young heart. Above all, she delighted in my delight, and that was a gift. As I had suspected, she encouraged me to pick up the Cloth of Essence again. In fact, she was so persuasive that before I knew what I was doing, we were discarding

my worn bark cloth and draping me in the magical cloth. There seemed to be an unlimited supply in the bundle. Like two artists, we danced together, decorating me in the pure white cloth. I have to admit that I kept my eyes mostly closed or averted, the rainbow tones shimmering in the periphery of my vision. I was fearful what color it would turn, afraid of knowing my essence. But I trusted Anasuya wholeheartedly and so I danced with her.

Once I was fully draped, Anasuya was very pleased with her creation. "Astounding," she said, and sighed. "It was meant for you."

I opened my eyes and, to this day, it remains a key moment in my self-understanding. I could not believe my eyes. The pure white cloth had turned golden, as if woven with golden strands. It shone and danced, the rainbow undertones still there. I carefully turned this way and that, waiting for the cloth to take on a more subdued color, something less vivid and shocking. I could not believe that I was such a golden shining soul in my essence.

"Not what you expected?"

My hands went to my face. "Will it always be such a stunning color?"

"As long as you are who you are. It responds to you."

"If I'm angry, will it turn red, or dark, perhaps?"

"I think your anger is the color of fire, my dear. But no. It only responds to changes in your essence. I suppose if something changed you on the deepest level, the cloth will respond to that. But I have never heard of this happening."

"What color was it when you wore it?"

"As pure white as it was before you wore it." She smiled with self-satisfaction.

I nodded. I could see the pure white light emanating around her. Her aged body could not fully contain the brightness of her soul. I wondered suddenly, if I could see myself, was I actually shining golden, like the garment I was wearing?

"It will never get stained or dirty. It renews itself."

The jewels I usually wore sparkled with new zest against my heavenly attire. I was overwhelmed by this magical gift, but Anasuya's generosity had not reached its end. She instructed me to sit down, and though her hands trembled too much to apply any cosmetics herself, she oversaw my work, telling me what to do. I lined my eyes with *kajal* and massaged a fragrant cream into my skin.

I adorned myself as I would have done in the palace, but my thoughts strayed to the years ahead. Our first year had not yet come to completion. Anasuya had lived in asceticism for far longer than our term of exile. How had she done it?

I abandoned decorating myself and asked her.

"You must not think of yourself as separate," Anasuya answered. "You must not keep yourself apart. Think instead that you belong here, and then you will. Acceptance makes life easy. It's when you question and resist that it becomes hard."

I let her words sink in. I felt healed by her acceptance of me, her trust that I could thrive here. I felt a subtle acceptance of who I was transform me under her gentle guidance. She had offered me the right amount of introspection and advice. I was a little closer to accepting I was the glowing being that the Essence Cloth revealed.

As she combed my hair, which I had brushed only with my fingers in the past four months, I closed my eyes and enjoyed the feeling. I contemplated what she had said about the body being made of the elements. That resonated greatly with me. I had always felt a great pull to nature. I decided then and there to be open to the connections I felt in the fire, the wind, the Earth, and the sky. Perhaps nothing would come of it. But I would know for sure. I would no longer question or resist my affinity to them.

"There," she said, giving my head a tender pat.

She had braided my long hair into its usual simple braid. This felt perfect, as I was already adorned beyond comfort.

When I stepped out of Anasuya's cottage, with her holding my arm, Rama's jaw actually dropped. I felt like I was the only person in the whole wide universe. But then I felt Anasuya's weight on my arm and saw Lakshmana standing next to his brother. I blushed fiercely and could not look at anyone.

"Rama, your wife is a goddess," Atri said, and there was an amicable feeling in the air.

There was no way to discern whether Atri's words were spoken as a jest or the words of the all-seeing sage he was. Neither did it matter to me, for I was discovering what it was to be a wholehearted human being. A goddess was far beyond my conception then.

For no reason, Rama reached for my hand and electricity jumped between us, like we were both glowing with the sun. Atri and Anasuya excused themselves, saying they had their prayers and rituals to attend to. Lakshmana also had some urgent business. Rama saw nothing but me and it was heaven, like Anasuya, the wise one, had said.

The next day, we continued our journey. I never saw Anasuya again, but that one meeting with her touched me so deeply, I felt ready to walk into the next years of the exile fully embracing my true nature. If I had not, if I had continued resisting and questioning, I would not have survived what was to come.

CHAPTER 15

Masters of Magic

Every day in Dandaka had been unpredictable, and Rama wondered if he had made the right choice bringing his companions there. After leaving Atri and Anasuya's dwelling, the travelers spent the night under a tree that leaned against a rock, a natural shelter. It was close to a pond of clear water surrounded by fruit trees. Despite Vasishta's scroll, uncertainty crept into Rama. Where to go next? How to spend the exile usefully? Contemplating such questions, they spent yet another night by the pond. As it turned out, Rama did not have to search for the next sage named in Vasishta's scroll. One of them came seeking him out.

Rama was sitting on the ground cross-legged but sprang to his feet when he saw a group of sages approach. The holy ones were thin and wiry, glowing with the cleanliness of their *tapas*. Sita and Lakshmana stood up behind him. Lakshmana's hands were on his weapons. One could never be too careful in this borderland. When the emaciated ascetics reached Rama, they fell at his feet and grasped his hands.

"Tiger among men," one of them said, bending his head so low his white beard touched the ground. "We have been praying for your arrival. Every day we have been waiting for you."

"You are here now," another one said.

Though they spoke in the language of the people, their enunciation was so refined, Rama heard the wisdom of their minds.

"I am your servant," Rama replied, gently touching their shoulders and receiving their hands in his.

They all spoke, one after the other, as if they were of one mind.

"We are devoted to peace and simplicity."

"But we live in constant fear."

"We don't need much . . . a quiet tree to sit under."

"Some leaves and roots."

"A fruit once in a while."

"But the blood-drinkers pursue us."

"They have taken over Dandaka."

"Preying on our blood and flesh."

"Protect us, strong-armed one."

"Protect us."

Rama noticed Sita's eyes filling with tears. The memory of Viradha was fresh in her system. These gentle souls had to face such terrors every day.

Rama hugged the sages even closer and said, "It's my duty to protect you. I vow that as long as I am here in Dandaka, I will protect you. My brother Lakshmana and I will do everything in our power to seek out and destroy your tormentors."

Rama swore it, and then Lakshmana swore it. The assembled sages clasped their hands and raised them to the sky in great relief. Their faces were wet with tears. Many of them were old and feeble, yet they looked innocent, like little children.

"From now on, you are safe," Rama promised, gazing at each one of them intently. "You have nothing to fear anymore."

Jubilantly, the old men fell at Rama's feet before he could stop them. Rama's heart filled with warmth. Perhaps this was the purpose of the exile. He would protect the holy ones and rid Dandaka of blood-drinkers.

"I am Sharabhanga," the white-bearded one said. "Stay with us at our ashram. It is presently under my care."

It was Rama's turn to fall at Sharabhanga's feet. "Vasishta, my blessed preceptor, instructed me to find you." He explained about the scroll and their quest to meet the holy ones.

"Instead, you have sought me out," Rama said. "We are blessed and will gladly stay with you."

A new vigor infused the holy ones. They lightened up, as if the blood-drinkers were already gone. Rama felt lighter too. Since the beginning of the exile, Rama had searched

for clues like this, seeking to understand the reason for it. Now he would be in the service of the most vulnerable and valuable of human beings. The holy ones, along with women and children, deserved protection. Rama could do what he was best at: fight. With his brother, he could keep the holy ones safe.

They walked less than an hour, and the ashram came into view. It was an ancient dwelling, the largest Rama had so far seen in the forest. It had many cottages, blazing fireplaces, and cows being milked. There was an intense energy surrounding the hermitage; the hair on Rama's arms stood up in awe. These grounds were as sacred as a temple.

Though the ashram was beautifully maintained, Rama noticed at once how vulnerable it was to an attack at any time. There were no walls, no moats, no gates, not even a protective fence encircling the ashram. He did not doubt that mantras enforced the parameters, but he also knew that it took intense concentration and effort to keep such a ward in place. Of course, the hermits were not thinking about protecting their land or their lives. Quite the opposite; they lived austerely, striving to transcend all mortal boundaries, beginning with the fear of death. As Rama surveyed the neat grounds of the ashram, he saw many ascetics standing or sitting with their eyes closed, as immobile as statues.

"Forgive those of us who do not greet you appropriately," Sharabhanga said. "They are observing vows and are not fully aware of their surroundings."

Rama touched the ground in reverence, looking up at those souls barely clinging to temporal existence. He remembered how the three of them had suffered from lack of sleep in the first days of the exile. Even now they had grown lean, living on fruits and roots. Yet the ascetics were deprived in every way, their ribs straining against translucent skin. It was awe-inspiring. Sita's hands had been joined at her heart ever since they stepped into the ashram. The holy ones showed them around and then assembled a feast for their guests: fresh milk, honey, and ripe fruits, including luscious roots and edible leaves. The ascetics did not share the food with them, explaining that they had already consumed their weekly quota.

Rama thought his life had been stripped to its bare minimum, but these ascetics lived as if they were made of spirit alone, no matter at all.

When they finished the meal, Sita retreated to the cottage they had been given. Rama noted to himself that she had been unusually silent.

Rama and his brother settled down with the holy ones. Sharabhanga was a disciple of Agastya, one of the most reputed holy ones.

"For a long time," Sharabhanga said, "we truly didn't mind the blood-drinkers. They were almost like a gift sent from above. We naturally strive to transcend our fear of death and mortality. With a constant and real threat upon us, we felt that we would quickly give up the innate fear of death."

Rama shook his head. One did not come to Dandaka to die in a blood-drinker's claws.

"Then we began to understand," Sharabhanga said, shaking his head too. "If our mortal frame is snatched away from us before we reach the perfected state, our penance is in vain."

"We have to start all over again," another sage named Muni said. "Then we are forced to begin the cycle again, take a new birth, be a child, become entangled in the world and its relationships . . . Only the most determined might find their way back here to Dandaka to continue their meditation where it was interrupted. We who are here count ourselves lucky. The human body is not designed to tolerate the *tapasya* we undertake."

"Indeed it is not," Sharabhanga said, becoming suddenly grave. "What we do here is not child's play. A creature of creation will rarely find ways to transcend it. Every single soul is bound to the laws of nature. A determined soul might learn to bend those laws and develop powers that are mystical. From the beginnings of time, empowered mystics have walked among us, on the same journey as the rest of humankind yet on their own trajectory. Over time, these yogis can develop many unique abilities, or *siddhis*. Only if their *tapas* is uninterrupted."

"What kind of unique abilities?" Lakshmana asked.

Sharabhanga smiled, seeing the fascination in Lakshmana's eyes. "Read minds, for example," he answered. "Manipulate matter, including their own bodies. Assume any shape or size. Withstand the most horrific physical hardships. Be in two places at the same time—anything that is usually impossible. Some mystics manage to live thousands, even millions of years, until the worlds come to their inevitable apocalypse. Yet, the end is always there. Simultaneously, the end and the beginning of the cycle, a course more certain even than the journey of the Earth around the sun. Most cannot dream of, in plain words, breaking the cycle of Samsara."

Rama was not expecting Sharabhanga's next words.

"At this time, there is one being alone that is close to breaking the cycle: Ravana, king of the blood-drinkers, also known as Dashamukha or Dashagriva, meaning 'Ten Heads' or 'Ten Necks.' He has mastered the laws of nature. When other mystics were content to travel at the speed of mind, Ravana was not. He wanted more and didn't care what the price might be. He fears neither light nor darkness and has achieved a level of power that rivals every other being within the known realm of creation. Not even Yama, the lord of death, can summon Ravana to his presence. While every other soul is under Yama's dominion, Yama is under Ravana's, like all the gods are."

Rama and Lakshmana looked at each other. They had not known this about the legendary blood-drinker king.

"Even Ravana's physical body is better equipped than most others to contain the multi-layered knowledge he has acquired over thousands of years. Your esteemed father, my dear princes, received his name, Dasharatha, 'Ten Chariots,' because he appeared to be in ten places at once, wielding his bow. In Ravana's case, however, his name, Dashagriva, 'Ten Necks,' is perfectly descriptive. He has ten necks, ten heads. Each of his ten heads is capable of thinking many thoughts at once. His mind is constantly active, aware of countless things. His twenty arms are restless, living a life of their own, moving like tentacles around him. I know, for I have personally seen him. Spoken to him. In his conscious mind, Ravana can effortlessly behold every second of his long life. He can slow his senses down and look at a memory from every angle, a frozen moment in time. He forgets no one, remembers every small incident, feels every occurrence keenly, and processes it through his ten separate yet collective minds. He is, in other words, the bane of the universe. Hence his name, Ravana, the One Who Makes the Universe Wail."

Ever since they had come to the forest, it seemed to Rama that he was becoming more aware of Ravana as a real person. Bharadvaja's words had been clear. Now Sharabhanga was describing his firsthand account of the demon king. If Rama saw a two-headed creature, he would look twice. What to speak of one with ten? Ravana was as remote as he was indestructible.

"Why does a being with such power and knowledge take pleasure in drinking blood?" Rama asked. He had asked much the same question when he was eight and sitting at the feet of Marichi, Ayodhya's former prisoner.

"A tiger takes the blood of a deer and thinks nothing of it," Sharabhanga said. "Ravana is half blood to the gods, but his mother was a blood-drinker. He could have chosen either path. Coming into his power, Ravana and the following he attracted destroyed the boundaries that create order and harmony among people and the worlds. Like a plague of poisonous wasps, they swept across the worlds and still do whenever they please. No one is safe. He cares only to feed his senses and his people. I cannot say why he has the taste for human blood."

"I once asked one of their kind this question," Rama revealed. "He would have me believe that they were created that way. Just as a tiger preys on a deer."

Sharabhanga thoughtfully stroked his beard. "Who is responsible for creating a creature like Ravana? This is your question."

"Or who created blood-drinkers in the first place?" Lakshmana added.

"You know I do not have the answer to these questions. But I do know this: Once the world is created and set in motion, it gains a life of its own. The laws are set in place, and the planets begin their numbered revolutions around the sun. Within this time and space, all souls are set free to explore. A soul's imagination is born from the Source and is in some sense as endless and deep as the Source itself. Thus, the interplay between species and ideas breeds many strange things. Perhaps at the beginning of time, even the tiger and the deer were not natural enemies."

"Were you not there at the beginning of time?" Rama inquired, for Sharabhanga seemed enlightened beyond Rama's conception.

"I am old, dear boy, but not that old," Sharabhanga chuckled. "Only Brahma, the creator, could tell you. Or one of his sons."

Vasishta. Their old preceptor was one of Brahma's mind-born children, created without a mate or mother, something that was unheard of later. Since childhood, Rama had engaged in long conversations with Vasishta and Father, while his brothers preferred to play or fight. But he had not known what questions to ask.

"Ravana may be beyond our reach," Rama said. "But when we entered Dandaka we killed Viradha, and we will continue the work of protecting you, by destroying Ravana's followers."

"Twilight is here," Sharabhanga said. "The favorite time of blood-drinkers. Soon you will hear them crawling out of their holes."

"We will stand guard," Rama promised.

Sharabhanga lifted his palm in blessing, and the gathering dispersed.

That night and every night that followed, Rama and Lakshmana took turns guarding the parameters of the ashram. As weeks went by, the brothers slew many blood-drinkers, but there was no end to it. For every one killed, two new appeared. At this rate, Rama would have to stay in the ashram for the rest of his life to honor his promise.

Basking in the sunlight, Rama and Lakshmana sat on the steps to their cottage, discussing the dilemma. A group of ascetics sat at their feet, listening to them going around in circles. Sita, true to her newfound passion, was on the other side of the ashram, nursing a baby fawn that had been hurt. Rama had been waiting for an opportunity to speak without her hearing.

"The problem is that we are merely on the defense," Lakshmana said. "We stand and wait for them to come to us. What we need is to attack."

Rama sighed. "We've talked about this already."

"Yes, but what's the solution?"

The facts were plain: They were concerned for Sita's safety. One of them needed to stay close to Sita. The encounter with Viradha had cemented this fact; Rama could not afford to let down his guard even for a moment. Yet he had vowed to protect the holy ones. To do this, they needed to pursue the drinkers.

"One of us circling around the ashram at night isn't enough," Lakshmana insisted, and Rama agreed. "We've already destroyed the ones lurking around here. Now that we are here, they have only become stealthier."

"In the last few days, there have been no sightings," Rama said. "But they are out there, keeping their distance."

"If only you and I could join forces and go out there together!" Lakshmana exclaimed.

One of the ascetics chimed in for the first time. "It seems like both of you are very eager to kill the blood-drinkers!"

Rama turned to the holy one. It was true they both yearned to fight. But how could he explain this to the ascetics without seeming bloodthirsty?

Rama's weapons longed to be wielded and used. Rama felt purposeful when he killed a blood-drinker, for they were clearly the enemy. When Rama made his promise, he had come alive and his bow had come alive. Rama also had seen the spark in Lakshmana's eyes, the excitement of being on the hunt. Rama was only beginning to flex his skills as a warrior. This gave him and Lakshmana undeniable pleasure and purpose. It was what they were trained to do. But how to explain it to those whose lives were given to *ahimsa*, a life of complete nonviolence?

"When you were young," he said to them, "you know, before you became ascetics?"

He waited to see some nodding heads before he continued. "There must have been something that made your blood boil with passion and purpose."

A few heads nodded in assent.

"You see, before Lakshmana and I could even talk properly, we had bows and arrows in our hands."

"My brother never let go of his," Lakshmana said, "not even in his sleep. Before Rama came of age, he surpassed every other archer in the kingdom. Believe me, they lined up to try. They challenged him. Every warrior likes a good fight, a good opponent. Rama defeated every single one of them when he was only seven."

Rama was smiling. "My mother used to joke that I had better put the bow down for a minute or else it would fuse to my hand. Little did she know her words made me grip my bow tighter."

Lakshmana laughed and several others did too.

"Lakshmana thought like a warrior from a young age too," Rama said. "Once, we had a huge mud fight in the royal gardens. We were four or five years of age."

Lakshmana groaned. The ears of the hermits perked up. Seeing Lakshmana's reaction, their backs straightened, eyes alert.

"Lakshmana and my brothers, Bharata and Shatrugna, teamed up against our mother, Kaikeyi, who was a fierce warrior. We showed her no mercy and were proud to see her covered in mud. But then my mother, the Great Queen, arrived, and we were fearful of her admonishment, and hid behind a tree. My other brothers and I were content to wait and see what would happen, but not Lakshmana. He rallied us together to make mud balls while we waited. Whosoever approached our fort would be the enemy and we would launch all our mud balls at them. This was his plan. We didn't think twice before following his leadership, and Manthara, Kaikeyi's confidant, was bombarded with mud by us."

"She did not see the game in it," Lakshmana said. "But she blamed Rama, thinking him to be the instigator. She held a grudge against Rama after that."

"Without our knowledge, our father had watched our marksmanship, and Father treated us differently after that. We were sent to begin our official training."

"You started wielding weapons at age four?" a sage asked.

"Weapons with blunt edges," Lakshmana assured them.

"This is to explain," Rama concluded, "that Lakshmana and I were raised from the beginning to wield weapons. We had to learn to see death differently. We were trained to not just tolerate killing but to find some measure of satisfaction in it—unsavory as it may sound. I certainly feel humbled revealing this to you who are peace personified."

"You have your dharma," Sharabhanga said, "and we have ours."

"Thank you for that kindness." Rama smiled broadly at all of them.

"But our initial problem hasn't been solved," Lakshmana pointed out.

Rama disliked referring to it as a problem, since Sita was at its center point. He looked past the group of hermits to see Sita sitting under the shade of a tree. One of the milking cows was at her side. The princess, fawn, and cow seemed to be deep in conversation. Rama

would give anything to preserve Sita's peace. He had felt the loss in her heart when they walked away from Chitrakuta and from Mila, her first pet deer. Sita never mentioned the deer by name again, so Rama knew she kept it hidden in her heart.

"The solution is simple," Sharabhanga said, bringing Rama's attention back. "Leave her with us. We will protect her."

Rama carefully hid his reaction and so did Lakshmana; they did not want to offend their hosts by ridiculing the offer. But how would the sages protect Sita when they were sorely in need of protection themselves? Most of them were stooped and slow-moving. Some were constantly trembling. There was no one younger than a hundred there. Some of them were closer to a thousand or, like Sharabhanga, many thousands. The holy ones were prey to the blood-drinkers. Rama could not entrust Sita to them. Respecting Sharabhanga thoroughly, Rama was shocked by the contradiction of his offer.

"We can keep Sita safe," Muni assured them when the brothers were silent.

"How?" Lakshmana ventured.

Answering Lakshmana's unspoken challenge, each one of the unassuming hermits morphed. As frail as the ascetics appeared, their years of penance had given them power. Sharabhanga's list of unique abilities exploded in the daylight. Suddenly, Rama and Lakshmana were surrounded by shocking sights: Two sages levitated, one shrank to the size of a pea, two disappeared altogether. Sharabhanga shot up into the sky, easily lifting his friend with him. A tree caught on fire, only to appear the next moment unharmed, neither charred nor burned.

All this happened in a moment, and then everything went back to normal. Again the hermits were at Rama's feet, looking up at him with innocent eyes. Lakshmana snapped his head toward one of them and then the other. The unassuming holy ones were filled with *siddhis*.

"Magical powers!" Lakshmana exclaimed. "Why, then . . . why do you need us?"

Rama was as awestruck as Lakshmana. Bharadvaja had anticipated their arrival and known their minds; Vasishta had the ability to see past the physical body. But this was blatant magic, something they had heard about but never seen.

"Why don't you simply band together and put an end to the blood-drinkers?" Rama asked. "Our deadly arrows seem like a child's toys compared to your immense powers."

"With one word or glance," Lakshmana said, "you could wipe them all out!"

The wise ones turned wiser yet and looked at them patiently. A few of the hermits looked sly, excited to have stumped Rama and Lakshmana. Rama and Lakshmana waited for answers, full of curiosity.

Sita's attention had been caught; she kept throwing glances at them, while the fawn draped over her legs lapped honey from her hand, its pink tongue darting across Sita's fingers.

The sages waited for Rama and Lakshmana to find the answer to their own question. Why did they need protection when they were full of *siddhis*? It was a riddle. If they had all these powers, why had they let themselves be at the mercy of the blood-drinkers? Weren't there mountains of bones in Dandaka? Why had they allowed this?

"It might be hard for you to understand," Sharabhanga finally said, "but like you, we have certain vows. We cannot—we choose not to—use our powers for our own good."

"We ascetics have learned this rule the hard way," Muni said. "Some of the vilest creatures who have toppled the balance of the universe started out simply like us. Ravana, whom we spoke of on your first night here, was an awe-inspiring ascetic, tolerating unimaginable austerities. Of course, he had his own aim from day one."

The rest of the hermits shuddered at these words. Rama felt intrigued to hear yet another reference to Ravana. To him, Ravana was the enemy who had killed his ancestor, Anaranya, thirty generations back. To the ascetics, Ravana had once been one of them.

"Ravana was not so different from any one of us," Sharabhanga said. "Like us, he chose *tapasya*. He stood, frozen on his toes, controlling every muscle for millennia, without eating or drinking. When he received no response from the universe, he cut off one of his ten heads, offering it into a blazing fire, calling out to Brahma, the creator. After ten thousand years, Ravana cut off another one of his heads, but Brahma refused to give in to his call, knowing his darkness and hoping he would desist from his austerities. When Ravana was poised to cut off his final and tenth head, Brahma could no longer ignore the nearly headless ten-necked one. For such is the power of *tapas*. It has to be acknowledged, or the worlds fall into chaos. Ravana had made himself suffer more than humanly possible, proving himself superhuman. When Brahma appeared, poised on his white swan, Ravana had only one wish: immortality.

"The creator is himself doomed to face the end of the worlds, along with all other souls. He does not have the power to grant what he does not have. But Brahma restored Ravana's ten heads to him. This of course placed Ravana back to where he had started nine thousand years earlier. Hardly pacified, Ravana's ten heads made their demand, hoping to find their way to immortality after all. He demanded this:

" 'No weapon, whether a curse or a manifested one, will have the power to kill me. No supernatural being, whether in the higher worlds or the nether regions, will be able to give me a fatal wound. No sage, mystic, angel, or beast will be able to send me to the land of Yama.'

" 'So be it,' Brahma said, and disappeared on his white swan.

"Brahma cannot deny the desires of a soul who undergoes penance. Through his *tapas*, Ravana acquired many powers: He can change his form, fly, and read minds. Brahma's boon made him, to all purposes, deathless. Any being that might have had a small chance of destroying Ravana in a fair fight has been eliminated by Brahma's boon. Ravana began to experience that there were no limits to his prowess. His sense of time has changed. He outlives countless generations of humans who live and die in one of his days. He dictates the movements of all the elements—wind, rain, sun, the orbiting planets. He is the god of the thirty gods, second only to Shiva and Vishnu.

"And yet the final death awaits him. When the entire universe is absorbed back into Vishnu and regenerated anew, Ravana *will* meet the end, like everyone else. For he is not immortal. Ravana knows this. Even the ancients who live from the beginning of creation until its final end, even their bodies will be annihilated then.

"Ravana's soul, like all souls, is eternal and timeless. Yet he wants to live in his ten-headed form forever. He refuses to face the end of the world and transform with it. In plain words, his powers have turned him from the truth and the light. For all that he sees, he cannot see."

The story of Ravana's ascent to power cast a dark shadow upon the bright day. It seemed like the leaves were shivering and that the wind had slowed down. An ominous feeling clung to the air. Rama recalled Bharadvaja jesting that Ravana might hear them. Sharabhanga's words made this seem plausible.

"You have told us this," Rama said, "to illustrate why you chose not to use your magic powers. But I am afraid that I still do not fully understand. Surely you, a pure-hearted and enlightened being, is beyond comparison with Ravana."

"But not beyond temptation," Sharabhanga fired back, and Rama understood.

Sharabhanga also felt the darkness in the air. Perhaps he himself had conjured it. "We use our bodies to interact with the natural elements, and we are not subservient to them. We are the masters of magic. As you might imagine, such powers can easily be misused, no matter how enlightened."

His face turned dark, his eyes becoming slits. "You cannot truly imagine how intoxicating it is to bend the natural laws, to know how to manipulate nature and matter. When you can travel at the speed of light or take any form you please, you start feeling all-powerful. Yes, I know the path that Ravana took. I can see it as a fork in my path, always beckoning me. So it is for all masters of magic, and for this reason the use of magic has been clearly divided into black and white, as it's often referred to in the civilized world. It is no exaggeration. There is no middle ground. If we allow ourselves to play with our magic, especially for our own motives, over time we would turn into blood-drinkers. Every one of them started out the way we did. Many of them have magical powers. They change their form at will, they read your fears, they stalk your dreams. They have acquired these powers through penance. Siddhis don't come cheap. But they use their powers for their own selfish pleasure, self-absorbed and dark. When you decide that you are above the laws of nature, only because you have mastered its elements, your heart turns. You can imagine its color."

Yes, Rama could. It wasn't a choice between black or white. It was far more complex—a color that could not be described but felt—a transformation that called for total surrender. There was no middle ground.

"The balance you accomplish is truly commendable," Rama said. "I do not know if I could achieve it."

Sharabhanga laughed then, and the chill in the air was gone.

"You are too modest, Rama," the holy one said. "I have seen the color of your heart. It shines like an emerald in the sun. The darkness you resonate with is just the shadow of dark green within you."

Rama wasn't sure what all that meant, and Lakshmana looked quite puzzled as well. Sita was standing nearby now; she smiled knowingly at Rama. How much had she heard?

Although Rama had deeply respected the wise ones before, his perspective had broadened. He had gotten a small insight onto their path and its temptations. He felt a completely new awe toward them, especially because they were so unassuming. Mastering even one *siddhi* was akin to owning large quantities of wealth or being unusually beautiful, both of which led to pride. Rama had wrongly viewed them as feeble. Now he saw that they were anything but. They chose to be helpless and to withhold their powers, and Rama felt all the more determined to protect them. He knew they were capable of protecting Sita better than he himself was. Sita would be completely safe in their hands.

"Sita?" Rama said. "Our hosts have demonstrated their ability to protect you. Lakshmana and I have proposed to launch a more aggressive attack on the enemy that lurks in the shadows. If we leave you here with them during the nights, will you feel safe?"

Sita hesitated for a moment. The hermits looked perched to launch into another demonstration for her benefit.

"No. I mean yes," she said, smiling at them, lifting both her hands. "No, you need not do that again. I'm deeply touched by your willingness to use your magic for my sake. And yes, I feel safe here."

After Viradha's attack, Sita was no longer a naive girl; she knew she needed protection.

"It's decided, then," Rama said, folding his hands at his heart. "The masters of magic will protect Sita while we protect you and this forest. I am grateful to you."

They all folded their hands to their heart, returning Rama's gratitude.

When twilight, red as blood, was upon them, Rama and Lakshmana were ready. They hurried to strap on their weapons and prepared their attack.

CHAPTER 16

Sita and Ganga's Blessing

As my protectors came alive with their appointed task, I had to find other ways to occupy my time. I felt little interest in their nightly adventures, how many blood-drinkers they had killed, or how. They, on the other hand, had a need to speak about it, much as they would have relived glorious battles were we in Ayodhya. Even though they were rarely wounded, I knew what they were doing was dangerous. I had seen them up against Viradha and knew now how violent it was, how close death could be. I understood their need to recount those tense moments, savoring their victory, in order to be fresh and free for the next night's attack. When Rama and Lakshmana were not speaking of previous killings, I found them planning future ones. So I withdrew to my own sphere, turning my attention to the many wonders of Sharabhanga's ashram. I was upset with my husband but did not know how to articulate my feelings.

Though I often thought of Mila with her shiny nose and dark eyes, I had made new friends in Dandaka. Even Sharabhanga's milking cow followed me, the bell around her neck jingling. Sometimes she mooed in my ear until I massaged her neck with firm strokes. She always returned the favor by licking my cheeks with her raspy tongue, which tickled so frightfully it was hard to bear. Other creatures found me too—parrots, sparrows, squirrels, monkeys—so I was never alone.

Even here, however, the doors to my affection were flung wide-open by a deer, a fawn that I nursed back to health. I named her Lali, "Little Girl." Something about her doe eyes evoked my tenderness, like a child does to its mother, a love that is not rational but abundant. Most of the holy ones kept to themselves, intent on their penance. But as I walked through the ashram with my flock following me, I felt their eyes trail me with affection. Like me, they saw little difference between animals and humans. We were of one mind in this.

We had stayed nearly a month in Sharabhanga's ashram, and I understood that we would leave soon. Though I stayed away from my protectors' talks, I overheard them say that they had uprooted blood-drinkers for several miles around. Soon it would be time to venture onward, to say farewell to Lali and bid farewell to the friends I'd made here. Lali, the sages had promised, would be welcome to continue living with them. She had become too tame to return to the wild. It might have been wiser to distance myself from the friends I'd made, but our imminent departure had the opposite effect on me.

With Lali close to my side, I explored the ancient forest dwelling with more fervor. Anasuya's advice had unlocked my heart. Every day all my senses were flooded with perceptions of the Earth and all that she contained. It is still this way for me. I don't quite belong to myself anymore. I feel the Earth's movements, how she accommodates a spectrum of colors within her sphere. That was the hardest thing to get used to—the strong currents of darkness that are right there next to the light. In the forest, I began to understand how easy it was for any given human being to choose darkness over light. They truly are side by side, equal options afforded to the souls living here.

I took in the wealth of impressions and at the same time I ran from them. A human body and mind are not equipped to handle what was coming to me. It's no wonder Ravana needed ten heads to do what he did. In my attempt to shield myself from the dazzling impressions my heart naturally absorbed, I sought refuge in the ashram. Every day I discovered something new: an altar or a pathway. Before Sharabhanga's time, there had been another sage with greater powers, who had built the ashram; there were things here that Sharabhanga professed he did not know.

One place I stumbled upon like a secret was a *kund*, a sacred pond encircled by a man-made enclosure of stones, built like an altar, a place one could go to cleanse one's mind or body. Sharabhanga told me it was Ganga's *kund*, filled with her holy water.

"We who live at this ashram never go anywhere else," the holy one said, "but men such as us cannot live without the Ganga. So we built this *kund* and invoked the goddess here. Being full of mercy, she agreed to pervade the water with her purifying presence."

He told me to sprinkle the water on my head and one drop in my mouth, prostrate before the goddess, and then enter the water. I recalled the second day of the exile when we had crossed the actual Ganga River. Riding in Guha's boat across her swirling waters, it had been easy to imagine that *exile* was only a word: The Earth belonged to everyone and no one. That truth had touched my fingers as they played with the current. At this *kund*, I felt the same expansive and distinct wisdom. I thought of it as Ganga's nature; she would never exclude a supplicant from her grace. I imagined her wise eyes, the color of the water, full of compassion. I imagined her in a white garment, something like the foam on the crest of a wave. And suddenly I knew that if I kept imagining her like this, she might actually take form before my eyes.

So I walked down the steps of the *kund* and sprinkled the holy water on my head. I stepped into the water fully clothed, venturing to the last step of the staircase, submerged up to my neck. This confounded my friends, who loved to sip the water but not bathe in it. Lali, who followed me everywhere, would not follow me into the water. She settled on the steps, watching me. Two little birds perched on top of my head. The flock of birds that had trailed me settled on the stones around the *kund*. I stood like that for a long time, feeling the water with my hands. I did it for pleasure, though I knew some of the holy ones undertook it as a *tapasya*. The *kund* was quiet, filled with an atmosphere I found soothing. It felt like magic could happen here, and it did.

The serene waters began to ripple against my feet. First, I thought it was a swarm of fish, but the current became stronger and moved up my body, until I saw the whole *kund* swirling like a river. The birds flew up, startled by the sudden commotion. The water parted and revealed the face of a huge crocodile. Its snout and black eyes emerged first, and I quickly moved up the stairs and out of the water. Like the birds, I was more astonished than frightened. White foam splashed up as the crocodile emerged fully, but my eyes no longer saw it. Instead, I was spellbound by the rider of the crocodile, a goddess draped in white and holding a golden pot in her hand. Because I had seen the vision of her in my mind first, I was not shocked. Without words I knew who she was, for who could it be but Ganga herself emerging from the *kund* of her name?

I was astounded at seeing the words of the scriptures come alive. She was the mistress of crocodiles, draped in white, and her appearance alone granted the beholder peace and prosperity. My mind became calm, yet flowing and alive.

Ganga sat perfectly motionless on the titanic crocodile, looking at me with her deep blue stormy eyes. Her flowing dress was no different from the white swirls of water. Her hair flowed around her body all the way to her feet, no different than flowing waves. Her large eyes, the color of the deep waters, looked at me with endless benevolence.

"You must not be afraid to speak your feelings," Ganga said. "For your words are wise, and a woman's words are like liquid honey to a man's heart. He needs them to live. If he rejects them, he will dry up and become rigid. Too many hard hearts have sought my waters for absolution. I who am a woman, I who whisper into their hearts, I give them the words of love they need and make them whole again."

Unknowingly, I put my hand over my heart to protect it.

"No, princess of the Earth," she said, "do not ever fear to speak your heart. Your words are good and true. Your wisdom is golden. The truth you see is not innate to man, for he rules the world with a sword and does not like his hand to be stayed. Trust your heart and share your wisdom."

Ganga touched me lightly on the top of my head and gave me the golden pot. "This vessel is ever full of my water, which grants liberation. You will need it, and when you do, simply call upon it and it will appear in your hands, for it is yours."

The golden pot was heavy with water in my hand.

Then she disappeared into the *kund* as swiftly as she had come, the golden pot with her. But I knew that a gentle thought would bring it to me, for I felt it hover in my mind, ready to appear in my hand. I stood for many long minutes looking at the still surface, not a ripple revealing the presence of the goddess. A small pool of water trickled down my forehead from her blessing. I was more astonished at her blessing than at her appearance itself. How had she known when I had not?

Lately my heart had felt troubled. I couldn't have said why, but now I knew. I was withholding a part of it from Rama. Words I longed to say but couldn't, fearful of his response. I knew that confronting a man about his actions was a perilous thing to do. Rama had never, not even once, turned his anger on me or spoken to me in a harsh manner. Then why was I afraid?

I was afraid because I had seen Rama's anger when he shot down the forest animals, and it frightened me. Because I loved him so completely, I couldn't bear his displeasure. Even in its restrained form, Rama's anger burned ice-cold. I feared my words might push him away, and he might turn that anger on me. I relied on his love to sustain me, to make sense of my existence in this world. Without it, I would perish.

Fortified by Ganga's encouragement, however, I resolved to open my heart to my beloved. I sat at the top of the *kund*'s stairs for a while, allowing the sun's rays to dry me. Lali chewed on some clover a few feet away. Now that my feelings were no longer hidden from me, it would be deception to hide them from Rama. I had to gather my courage.

When I returned to the ashram I saw Rama at a distance, sharpening arrows, as he and his brother often did these days. I knew why it had to be done, yet the stone remained in my heart. Here was the cause of my withheld anger. As I approached, Rama looked up and our eyes met. The coldness in my heart disappeared. I blushed from his attentive gaze but was also aware of the frightened throbbing within my heart.

If Ganga had not blessed me, I would not have found the courage. Rama and Lakshmana called me brave, praising my adjustment to the forest and the way I handled dangers, even Viradha's attempt to abduct me. In all those instances, however, I had been seamlessly united with Rama. The place I was about to venture to, I would no longer be by his side but in front of him, confronting him. I wanted to find my long-forgotten veil and hide myself in it.

"What is it, Sita?" Rama asked, perceptive as always.

I could dissemble no longer. When I spoke, my words were deliberate. Unknowingly, I had labored on them for some time.

"Rama, no one knows the path of dharma better than you. Your valor is exemplary and your vow to protect the holy ones befits you."

I paused. The easy words had been said.

"Go on, my love."

"When I see you like this," I motioned to the pile of arrows, "I feel uneasy at heart. You and Lakshmana speak of little else than slaying blood-drinkers. Holding a weapon provokes violence. Any person, whether a king or a common man, will feel an increased urge to kill, having weapons at hand. But violence breeds only violence. There is no end to it. It is not my place to instruct you, who are not only a trained warrior but whose knowledge of dharma is far greater than mine. And yet, I have witnessed your actions, Rama, and my heart is not at peace. I do not feel the rightness of your actions now. Whose thirst for blood will be slaked first, theirs or ours?"

I pressed my hand to my lips. Rama did not respond immediately; I carefully looked at my beloved's face to gauge his temperament. He looked at the ground, deep in thought, his features grave.

"I didn't realize that my actions troubled you," Rama said. "Though you are pointing out a fault in me, I accept your words. Because I know you love me, I don't take your caution as criticism. Your concern is well founded. I cannot, however, put my weapons away and lead the life of a true ascetic, for I have made a promise to the holy ones. I can only assure you that I will not turn my arrows on harmless animals that are innocent. My vow to the holy ones has given me a purpose. It gives me a reason for the exile, to use my skills as a warrior to defend them. My bow must be my constant companion. But I will keep your words close to my heart and examine my motives as I place my arrows against my bow."

Rama clasped my hand. Together we sat side by side in silence. The demands life made on us, and every human being, destroyed perfect choices. Even Rama had to compromise his values. This would become all too clear as later events unfolded.

Kill or Be Killed

As night came, Rama's weapons did come alive. His bow glowed with anticipation and the arrows jumped into his hands upon the lightest touch. It was time.
Like mighty predators, Rama and Lakshmana slipped into the dark forest. The moon
was half full yet shone brightly that night. Lakshmana's weapons gleamed golden,
and he smiled at Rama. Knowing the area around Sharabhanga's ashram as safe territory, they sprinted deeper into the forest, falling into an effortless pace, their bows
and minds alert. Yet, miles into the forest, they did not encounter the enemy. Not a
single blood-drinker was in sight. The brothers slowed to a walk . . . silent shadows
in the night. Once the blood-drinkers became the hunted, they had become stealthier, hiding when night came. But it was their feeding time and they could not hide
for long.

"Did you notice how many bucks are about tonight?" Lakshmana asked.

This was unusual. Rama followed his hunch and fixed an arrow
on his bow. He thought of Sita's caution, her call to reduce their
violence. But out here, there was only one choice: to kill or be
killed. Without warning, Rama swiveled and fired his arrow.

The arrow zoomed through the night and pierced a black buck with long, deadly antlers. A humanlike scream emanated from the animal's throat. Struggling for his life, the blood-drinker's real shape returned. His fangs were nearly the size of antlers. His eyes crossed in pain as he fell dead to the ground.

Discovering their enemy's new trick meant only one thing: No one was safe from their arrows. Taking Sita's advice to heart, Rama unleashed his arrows only when he was sure. One black buck rested in the middle of its female herd. The brothers left that one alone; the female bucks would not be fooled by a blood-drinker. Animals seldom were.

The half-moon rested in the sky, throwing partial beams across their path. Daylight would find many dead creatures in their wake. With Sita safe in the hands of the holy ones, Rama and Lakshmana hurled hundreds of unsuspecting blood-drinkers to the land of Yama.

After several hours of combat, the brothers sank down under a tree, steadying their hearts.

"I only have a few arrows left," Rama whispered. There was satisfaction in that, for Rama never wasted an arrow. Sharabhanga's ashram would be safe now.

Lakshmana pulled out a handful of arrows, handing them to his brother. Rama shot a quick glance at Lakshmana's quiver, noticing it was nearly empty.

"I prefer my sword anyway," Lakshmana explained.

"Keep them," Rama said. "My bowstring is going to snap soon. It needs to be replaced."

"On our way back, we can recover some of the entrails from the animals. Make sturdy new strings for our bows. Their deaths will not be in vain."

"Pray Sita sees it that way."

A sudden noise warned them that their rest was over.

"We stay together," Rama ordered. He could feel the blood-drinkers were up to something. He had an arrow nocked on his bow. He wouldn't hesitate to shoot one in the back. He no longer considered them worthy of a warrior's death. Just then, what he absolutely least expected to see appeared from behind a tree: Sita.

Rama gasped. "Sita?"

Sita smiled and twisted her braid as she did when nervous or thoughtful. Her other hand rested on the head of a small fawn, one of her pets. Rama dropped his bow and moved toward her, as if compelled.

"Rama, no!" Lakshmana shouted. "It's not her! It's a trick!"

Sita's eyelashes fluttered anxiously at Lakshmana's voice. So like the real Sita. But Rama was close enough to see that "Sita" did not quite look herself. It was a very close imitation, but the eyes were truly amiss. He had learned this lesson when a blood-drinker breached Ayodhya's walls in a perfection impersonation of Vasishta. Only Rama had seen through the disguise, as he did now. No magic could dispel the cruel coldness he saw in those eyes.

With a shout of dismay, he lifted his bow again. "For this, you deserve to die a thousand deaths!"

Despite the anger in his voice and the blood pumping in his heart, his arrow didn't leave his bow. He couldn't do it. The image of an arrow bursting into Sita's heart stopped him cold. Even though it was an imitation Sita, he couldn't do it.

"You can't fool *me*!" Lakshmana shouted.

Even *his* arrow narrowly missed "Sita" as she laughed and flew away. Within a heartbeat, they were surrounded by Sitas. In a grotesque imitation of Sita's love, they called to Rama in mockingly alluring ways. One leaned against a tree, the other opened her arms. Small deer scampered about, licking Sita's fingers.

"Don't let Lakshmana hurt me," an imitation Sita cried. "He wants to kill me!"

"He never wanted me to be here," the next Sita said.

"Come to me, Rama," another coyly called.

"Rama, don't let them get to you," Lakshmana admonished, steadying his brother's shoulder. "You know they are not her."

Rama's heart was chilled, but he nodded. Yet, however many Sitas he pointed his arrows toward, his arrow stayed stubbornly on its bow. He broke out in a sweat. All the Sitas laughed, soft and sweet. A sound that was sickening, it was both so like Sita and unlike her. The many Sitas appeared and disappeared behind trees and bushes, beckoning Rama.

"Lakshmana, I just can't," Rama whispered. "What if one of them is real? What if they really caught her somehow?"

Lakshmana stared at Rama like he couldn't believe Rama's weakness. The blood-drinkers had successfully located Rama's weak spot. They must have spied on them for days, absorbing the details of Sita's appearance and her mannerisms. Lakshmana wasn't fooled; he knew they were not Sita. Seeing the brothers' hesitation, the Sitas started slowly coming closer. Like a magnet, Rama drew closer too, but Lakshmana clamped his hand on Rama and tugged him back.

"Rama, trust me," Lakshmana cautioned. "I will do it. Whatever you do, don't stop me. Stay close to me. Keep your arrow on your bow. Don't let them see how well their trick is working."

Lakshmana said no more and turned to the Sitas, showering them with arrows. Sita screamed loudly, and Rama flinched. It sounded so much like her. Shot by Lakshmana's arrow, the blood-drinker was forced to resume his real body. Rama recognized Lakshmana's words as true. Whichever Sita he looked carefully at, he could tell it wasn't his wife. But there were so many of them! Rama pointed his sharp arrow at each of them, staying slightly behind Lakshmana.

The Sitas ran in all directions, crying, "No, Rama, please!"

"It's me, your wife!"

"Don't kill me!"

"Please!"

Fat tears rolled from their desperate eyes. If he wasn't so furious, Rama might have admired their stubborn insistence on their Sita-ness. Not until they were mortally wounded did they give up the charade. Rama could practically see the venom in the claws of the blood-drinkers, longing to shoot into Rama's veins—if only Rama got a little closer.

Finally, Rama released his arrow . . . but it lodged into a tree trunk, though he never missed a shot. Rama's hand trembled as he put a new arrow to his bow.

Lakshmana began grabbing arrows from Rama's quiver and never stopped, fervently whispering reassurances to Rama.

"It's a trick. . . . It's not her. . . . Don't let them get to you. . . . Don't let them see how much you care."

Rama was shaking. Each dying Sita was like seeing the worst come true. But he clung to Lakshmana's words and stayed by his brother's side. Lakshmana was the hero of that night.

It was possibly the longest night of Rama's life so far. By the end of it, when Lakshmana had killed the last impersonator, Rama's muscles were so tightly wound he couldn't speak. All he wanted was to get back to the ashram and see the real Sita with his own eyes.

But the battle was not over yet. From a distance, Rama saw two blood-drinkers charging toward them, their bodies changing in midair. A feeling of recognition ran through Rama. He knew one of them. Then the blood-drinker's original form was gone and in its place appeared a snarling leopard. The two beasts charged toward Rama, sure of their victory. Rama's roar rivaled the beasts' as he shot his arrow, pinning one of the shape-shifters to the ground. He left it there for Lakshmana, running in pursuit of the other leopard, the blood-drinker he had recognized. With Rama on his heels, the blood-drinker dropped his disguise and ran in his true form. Rama knew at once. He could never forget the first blood-drinker he had known: Marichi, Ayodhya's former prisoner. Two years earlier, when Rama was sixteen, he had been protecting Vishvamitra's fire ritual. In close range, Rama had shot Marichi with an arrow that shattered his chest and flung him up and away. Vishvamitra had said the demon was drowning in the ocean eight hundred miles away.

Rama's body was hot with fury as he pursued Marichi. The blood-drinker looked over his shoulder at Rama; his eyes were mad with terror. Rama tightened his grip around his sword and closed in on Marichi. His arms twitched and his hands flapped through the air.

Rama caught up to him and roared, "Turn around and fight, coward, so you can see my face one last time and remember that it was I who killed your mother and your brother!"

The callous jab was meant to enrage Marichi, and it did. He hissed as he turned around, lifting his sharp claws. His fangs were bared, but when he faced Rama, terror filled his eyes. He froze, his claws suspended in the air. He breathed heavily, staring at Rama with so much panic, Rama lowered his swords. What did Marichi see that made him so crazed with fear?

One of Marichi's claws swiped through the air halfheartedly. Rama lifted his sword again. Marichi choked and fell to the ground with a gasp. Rama pointed his sword at Marichi's throat. Was he surrendering?

"How did you survive?" Rama demanded.

Rama's arrow had hit Marichi with such force, he had been hurled beyond the clouds—a sure death for Marichi. Yet now, here he was—alive!

"Rama, Rama, Rama," Marichi started mumbling, staring all around him as if he was seeing thousands of Rama's surrounding him. He was convulsing like a rabid animal.

"How did you escape?" Rama demanded, digging the tip of his sword into the demon's neck.

"The ocean. I'm dying. I'm changing the ocean," Marichi whispered. "I'm dying. I'm dying. I'm changing."

With eyes bulging, the demon looked at Rama like he was living his worst nightmare. He clutched his chest and gasped for air.

"Rama, why do you hesitate?" Lakshmana was standing behind Rama. "Kill him."

"Look, it's Marichi! I was sure he was dead."

"I'm a fish, I'm a fish, I'm a fish," Marichi rambled on.

"Kill him, Rama." Lakshmana stepped closer. "What is wrong with him?"

Marichi was rubbing his head against the ground; tears ran in rivers from his eyes; his face was red and contorted, his flaming hair spreading out around his face like fire.

"I'm a dying fish!" Marichi cried, his arms limp on the ground.

"Wherever he fell, every bone in his body would have been smashed."

"I'm swimming, I'm swimming, I'm dying, I'm swimming."

"Wait, Rama. . . . I think he is answering your question."

They looked at each other. "The ocean," they said at once.

The pieces of Marichi's words melded and they saw the scene unfold. Rama's arrow had hurled Marichi farther than they had thought possible. Falling from the clouds into the ocean with a fatal arrow through his body, Marichi had turned himself into a fish, dropping into the water without harm. Despite the damage to his body, he had been able to swim to shore and survive.

Rama eased the tip of his sword from Marichi's neck. Marichi gasped loudly, as if Rama had swung his sword at him.

"Please, please, please," Marichi cried. "Spare me." He resumed chanting his supplication.

"How can I kill him when he is on the ground like this, helpless and pleading?"

"Sparing him makes no sense, brother. He is our natural enemy. He tried to kill us. The gods only know how many holy ones he has murdered."

Lakshmana pointed at a prominent disfiguration in the center of Marichi's chest. It looked like his whole breastplate had been crushed and reset, the scar tissue rippling out from the center. "That's where your arrow hit. Finish him now."

Rama prodded at the old wound with his sword.

As if Rama had pushed a button, Marichi snarled and flew up from the ground, taking several forms—a lion, a bull, a deer—before he landed on his feet as himself. Rama and Lakshmana lifted their weapons with lethal speed, but the terror-stricken Marichi was faster.

No sooner was he on his feet than he no longer had any. Morphing into a massive eagle, he swung up into the air, hitting Rama and Lakshmana with his wings. Rama swung his sword, and feathers and blood splattered on the brothers. Rama's vision was obscured by the smack of Marichi's wing, and then he was gone. Marichi had disappeared. The sky held nothing but moonlight.

Rama felt a chill ripple through his body and couldn't stop staring into the empty darkness of the night sky. Rama had a premonition that Marichi would cross his path again.

They returned to the ashram, and Rama went straight to his cottage to find Sita, unmindful of the sweat and dirt on his body. There she was, his beautiful princess, sleeping peacefully. For a long time, he sat there studying her features half concealed by night.

During the day that followed, Rama rarely left Sita's side. If he hadn't memorized her every feature already, he did that day. In daylight, the tricks of the drinkers were clear. Of course they could not have kidnapped Sita. If ever a monster tried that trick on Rama again, he would show no mercy.

CHAPTER 18

Sita and the Water

Even though I knew I was dreaming, that the nightmare was beginning, I could not wake myself up. It was my recurring dream, a compulsion my mind had not grown beyond: I stood by the barred gate alone with growing unease. How many times had I stood here, helpless? The swirling mist of golden light emanated from beneath the doors. The edges of the light shimmered with darkness, one fighting the other. Women moaned, sobbed, and sighed; they were trapped within and I was trapped without. When would the gatekeeper come and let me in? I didn't know why I had to gain entry, only that the distressed women depended on me. Their call was one of the strongest forces I had ever felt. Were they the ones bringing me back here time and time again?

I awoke with Rama's eyes intently on my face. His manner was relaxed; I guessed he had been sitting by my side for a while. Seeing him, the unease of my dream evaporated. Rama studied my face. His ardor was unmistakable. Something had happened during the night. I felt a twinge of concern flutter in my heart.

"Rama," I whispered, reaching up. When I touched his jaw, he placed his hand over mine, pressing my fingers to his face. "Usually I'm the one gazing at you in the morning light."

He did not smile in response to my light words. I felt the strong bones underneath his smooth skin and how he clenched his jaw together, the muscles playing under my fingers.

"What is it, my love?" I pushed myself up with my elbow. As my hair fell back behind me, the fragrance of flowers wafted up. I had forgotten to remove the blossoms before I fell asleep. I returned Rama's searching gaze, wondering again what had provoked this earnestness.

"I couldn't bear to lose you," Rama said. He pressed my hand, imprinting my fingers on his cheek. Rama had not said these words to me before. Why did he fear losing me now?

I sat up to face him. "Has something happened?"

"I have a weakness," he answered. "You."

I don't think I liked being seen as a weakness, and so I chose not to question him further. Instead I responded to his urgency by leaning toward him and resting my forehead against his chest. Sighing, I closed my eyes. Without looking, I knew he had closed his eyes too. We breathed together in silence, connected. I didn't have to tell him that he would never lose me. I was his beyond forever.

He pulled me into his lap and cradled me against his chest, holding me so tight I couldn't breathe. I didn't mind. I had been taking deep, languishing breaths all night while he had been out hunting blood-drinkers with his brother. Something out there had made him fear for me. Had the blood-drinkers tried to attack me while I was asleep?

I melted into his protective embrace. As we sat together like this, Rama murmured in my ear, words of love that he reserved for special moments. I savored his nearness, as the sun's soft morning rays lit up our dwelling. And then he took hold of my flowing hair and wrapped himself in its length, as if it was his protective cloth. I laughed. And the day asserted itself; it was time to pick the crushed flowers from my hair, to bathe in the waters of the river, to greet the new day.

Moving my face away a bit, I looked up at Rama. Did I need to say out loud any of the reassuring certainties that had passed between us silently?

Cloaked in my black hair, Rama looked like he was on his way to a secret mission, disguising himself. There was mirth in the corners of his lips and his eyes sparkled. The solemn moment had passed.

Even so, Rama walked very near me as we headed to the riverbank. The morning was quiet, birds chirping here and there. The forest dwellers never spoke in the mornings; as we walked to the river hand in hand, it seemed like there was only the two of us in this forest. Lakshmana, my secretive brother-in-law, was nowhere in sight. Sleeping, I thought.

Rama would not have agreed with me that Lakshmana kept secrets. An open book, he called his brother. It was true. He was given to rash outbursts that seemed to expose his mind completely. And yet . . . he had uttered my sister's name so few times, I felt sure he kept his most intimate feelings private. That was certainly fine, in my mind. It just left me feeling that I didn't quite know his heart.

"What are you thinking about?" Rama asked. We were standing at the river now.

"How rare it is for us, you and me, to be together alone."

"Lakshmana protects you more than you know."

I half smiled. Rama had heard Lakshmana's name in my omission. And why not? If I savored our alone time, it was to the exclusion of my loyal brother-in-law.

"I know. Lakshmana's selflessness is exemplary."

"Without him," Rama said, turning to me, "I could be dead. You . . . could be dead." He covered his eyes with one hand, shielding himself from a memory.

"What happened out there, Rama?"

"Nothing you need to worry about, my sweet wife. Just know that as you are my other half, Lakshmana is too."

I pondered this for a few moments. "Do you feel divided between us, like we are vying for your attention, for your love?" There was a small hitch in my voice. I had wondered about this many times.

"Sita," he said, pulling me to him. "I never feel divided when I'm with you. You make me whole. With you, I feel like a true man, strong and capable. Before you, I was only a boy."

"And I was a girl," I said while tugging him into the water, bow in hand and all.

Letting himself play along, he threw his weapons off with a carelessness I had never witnessed and plunged into the crisp water with me. Swimming in the river with Rama, I had the desire, that came to me at times, to stay forever in this moment. But time had never yielded to my fantasy and it did not this time either.

The forest came alive as the sun warmed it. A herd of deer lapped the water on the opposite bank. I swear I saw the orange flash of a tiger too. Perhaps it really was, because the deer had turned skittish and disappeared. The serene morning was stolen by the dominating sun. I pointed out an elephant to Rama. It kept plunging into the water, only to emerge and roll in the mud. Now she—for Rama told me it was the matron of the flock—was content on the bank, the drying mud on her cracking like a second skin.

Emerging from the water, we sat in the sun, our clothes drying. Rama wore only a bark cloth around his hips. It was dry in no time. His matted locks always took a longer time, often dripping hours after his bath.

My beloved faced the sun and closed his eyes in meditation. Unless something out of the ordinary startled him, he would sit like that, journeying inward, for close to an hour. I admired him for a few minutes, his straight back and his broad chest, the strength of his arms, the shimmering luminescence of his emerald skin. Wondering at his stillness and patience, I turned my eyes to the river. The sun sparkled on its moving surface like a million diamonds.

Using my finger, I traced outlines onto the water's surface, watching my creations create small ripples before the current took them away.

I recalled the moment when the Ganga had risen up, as one with the swirling waters and yet distinct. That's how I was in relation to the Earth, always one with it, yet my own person. In truth, Ganga's form had alerted me to how inseparable a being can be to its element. Ganga had been more water than human, more ethereal than embodied. Despite the resonance I felt, I knew I was different. I was embodied. I felt myself to be of the Earth, but I was not a manifestation of the Earth, as I knew my mother would be if ever I would see her with my human eyes.

"I am a human being," I traced in the water, as if writing an affirmation. "I am a daughter, a sister. A woman and a wife. A princess."

Using the surface of the water as a parchment, I continued to write on the ever-changing surface. I decided to write a letter to my sister, whom I often conversed with in my mind, as I otherwise would have in daily life.

My dear Urmila,

I wish you were here. I want to share the wonders of this life with you. I want you to lighten Lakshmana's heart. He needs you. He doesn't say it, but it's there in everything he doesn't say. If I had known what I know now, I would have insisted and begged for you to come with us. You could be happy here with Lakshmana, as I am with Rama. Lakshmana is not content the way we are.

Remember the very first time we met Rama and Lakshmana in the arena? Rama had shattered Shiva's bow and I garlanded him. You couldn't take your eyes off Lakshmana, though you didn't want to admit it to me. I think about that first meeting sometimes. I told you that I felt as though a shield around Lakshmana deflected my very glance. You asked, "Do you think he is jealous of you?" Only you would ask such a direct question. Which is why I miss you! I know that Lakshmana is not jealous of me. But . . . I still feel like I'm being deflected. Why, I do not understand.

There are dangers here, but Rama and Lakshmana hide them from me. They protect me. I'm almost like a child, kept in the dark. Even today, Rama would not tell me what terrors he faced, though I could see that he was shaken. My protectors keep me safe. They would have kept you safe too.

Your sister always,
Sita

I pushed the water in the direction it was already going, hastening my "letter" to its destination. Maybe my sister was sitting by the Sarayu right now. She would be surrounded by servants, guards, and all the attendants a princess like her would have. The fact that I did not see myself as a princess anymore made me smile; the idea that my water missive might reach my sister made me smile more. The forest had taught me how mystical the workings of the world truly were.

I glanced up at Rama, who had not stirred. How could anyone be so astonishing? I felt like I could see the world converge in him; he was a manifestation of the universe, the way Ganga was a manifestation of the river. With my eyes on him, my fingers dipped into the water again, and this time something surged up my fingertips, as if someone had left a message for *me* in the water!

I got so shocked I pulled my fingers out of the river. But that was silly, since I sat with legs half submerged. Surely a real message could find its way to me through my feet also. Slowly, I dipped my fingers into the water again, prepared to hear.

"Not all of us are free," I felt the pulsating current say. "We will never be free as long as we are ruled by darkness."

"What do you mean?" I whispered. "I bathe here every day. I've only felt an auspicious cleansing. Never this darkness you speak of." It was shocking to see the waters turn murky before my eyes.

"You are above it. For now. You don't feel it because it's so opposite to you. I'm by nature the holder of darkness, fathomless depths, and creatures you would certainly call monsters."

I understood then. I was not in communion with the river, but the father and the source: the ocean. Who else sheltered monstrous creatures in its deep? Who else had depths unknown to man?

I struggled to frame my words. "And yet . . . you . . . who say your nature resonates with the deepest darkness . . . you warn me of darkness that rules even you?"

"There is darkness and there is *darkness*," he said. "One darkness merely contains the absence of light. That is the darkness that I am. So deep into the Earth, the sun does not reach. But the darkness I cannot tolerate is the one whose sole purpose is to usurp the light, to extinguish it."

I felt like the daylight and sun could be swallowed in an instant by the force he referenced. I looked over at Rama for solace. He began to stir but did not open his eyes.

"Yes," the ocean confirmed.

The hold on my fingers felt more forceful.

"Why are you telling me this?" I demanded. I was afraid. And then softer, "What can I do, if anything?"

"Be who you are," he said. "That will be more than enough."

Then he was gone—my hand released and dropped into the river. The unexpectedness of it made my whole body follow, and I fell into the river, submerging completely. For one instant, I panicked, experiencing the darkness. But this was not the dangerous kind. I could

see the sunlight sparkling on the surface above me. This was just the river I bathed in daily. I came up at the surface and saw Rama standing on the shore with worried eyes.

"I'm fine," I said, concealing my burst of fear. The water had sent me a warning, telling me what Rama was concealing from me.

"You usually don't throw yourself in like that," my beloved observed.

"This is an unusual day, my love," I agreed.

"Was there a reason for your sudden desire to bathe again?" he asked, offering me a hand to help me up. "It looked like you fell in or someone pushed you." He looked puzzled. The concern from the morning was back in his eyes.

So he had seen me fall in, as if pulled or pushed by an invisible force. I hardly understood the ocean's words, the veiled warning, or his final words. So I said, "No, my love, it just happened."

After all, he had his secrets, things he did not or could not share with me. And I, who couldn't bring myself to reveal what I'd learned from the ocean, had mine.

Lakshmana Tested

After several months at Sharabhanga's ashram, the trio wandered farther into Dandaka. Though Lakshmana and his brother had worked tirelessly to kill blood-drinkers, Lakshmana braced himself for the unexpected. The last time they had roamed freely in the borderland they had gotten trapped in a Kinnara maze and then attacked by the giant blood-drinker Viradha.

Rather than feeling homeless yet again, Lakshmana felt invigorated by their departure from Sharabhanga's protected ashram. Without knowing it, he had been restless to move on. The three of them kept a steady pace. The brothers paused only intermittently to make sure that Sita was comfortable with their speed. At mid-morning they arrived at a large, crystal-clear lake. A very subtle melody drifted through the air, reminiscent of the Kinnaras love songs.

Lakshmana stood at the bank of the lake, looking around to locate the source of the song, which seemed to emanate from the middle of the sparkling waters. The sun danced on the surface of the lake; it was dazzling almost to the point of blindness. Lakshmana's throat was parched, for they had gone without water all morning. He bid his brother and Sita to drink first. He would not be taken in by the apparent serenity of the lake. Dandaka was a treacherous place. For all he knew, a man-eating creature could rise from the depths of the lake and attack them. Lakshmana would stand guard while the others drank and cleansed themselves.

Lakshmana shaded his eyes and peered across the lake and all around. He noticed that the quiet song made him mellow. He was not alarmed by this, reasoning that it had the same effect on beasts and blood-drinkers: He was safe.

Rama and Sita drank deeply from the lake and brought some for Lakshmana before submerging fully clothed in the refreshing water. The sun was hot enough that a few minutes on land would dry their clothes. When Sita emerged from the water with her abundant hair loose and her clothes clinging to her body, Lakshmana turned away. Rama came to his side, radiating coolness and sparkling like the river.

"Your turn," he said. "I will keep watch."

Rama strapped his weapons back on his body, and Lakshmana gratefully went into the lake. First he drank to his heart's content, and his throat and mind relaxed. Knowing that Rama was on guard, Lakshmana began to enjoy the melody. Grabbing large handfuls of the dirt at the river bottom, he scrubbed himself clean. When he ducked his head underwater, the song grew stronger, filling his ears completely. Had the others not heard it? He opened his eyes under the water. A large rush of air escaped in bubbles from his mouth. A beautiful nymph with a woman's face danced not far from him. She was not alone, and her friend was singing harmonious notes to the same song. *Apsaras!* Lakshmana thought, celestial maidens known for their allure.

When the Apsaras saw Lakshmana looking at them, they swam to his side and caught hold of his arms. Their long, silky fins wrapped around his legs. He protested loudly, but only bubbles emerged. The water nymphs encircled him and pulled him deeper under. Lakshmana struggled to no avail, and they sang the same sweet song. The two Apsaras who held him were like night and day; one had long black hair, and the other's was light, like the rays of the sun. It swirled around them, as enchanting as the tune they sang. Three more Apsaras swam toward them, singing and smiling at Lakshmana. Their skin shimmered in different tones and they were dangerously beautiful. Something stirred within Lakshmana and he kicked wildly with his legs. He was a warrior! He would not be captured by these water nymphs. The mellow tune formed into a warning. *Do not struggle.* He started to feel the lack of air. *Let us help you.* He saw stars. *Do not be afraid.* All went dark.

With his next breath, he gasped and was awake. He was still underwater, still in the hold of the singing damsels. Only now, he could breathe and understand the words of their song. They were actually speaking, and every word formed into the melodious song.

"He is not ready," the black-haired beauty was saying.

"He is," another sang back.

"He is too stubborn," the red-haired Apsara said.

"He is not," the golden one sang.

"He is not worthy," the first one said.

"He is," another insisted.

Lakshmana's gaze darted from one to the other, their faces so finely sculpted he had to admire them by turn. So long did this dispute go on that Lakshmana at last only heard, "He is. He is not. He is. He is not."

He didn't think he could get further enchanted, but he did. He floated effortlessly underwater, circled by the swimming and singing women. Not one of them was the same as the other; their skin tones shone of various stunning colors, the color of their hair in deep contrast to their skin. Lakshmana's heart beat in tempo to "He is, he is not, he is, he is not." Every time they said "he," they looked Lakshmana deep in the eye. Sea-green eyes. Night-sky eyes. Sky-blue eyes. They sang and they begged him to signal if he was or was not. Without his permission, they could not proceed. This he finally understood. He did not know what came next. But, oh yes, he did. "He did, he did not, he did, he did not."

A strange look came into their eyes, and all at once the five Apsaras undressed. They were not part aquatic at all, as Lakshmana had first assumed, but distinctly human and female. He had taken the swirling garments for parts of their bodies. Now only their long, long hair obscured their female beauty whenever the waters willed it. Their hues were golden, creamy, and dark. Their hair billowed around them in strong colors: black, brown, gold, and red. The more Lakshmana looked, the more the warning bells erupted in his heart. He had never seen any woman unclothed but Urmila. A deep stirring rose, from far beneath his loins. He didn't want to see this and clamped his eyes shut.

Look at me, one of them commanded.

She swam close to him, her soft hair wrapping around Lakshmana's head.

Lakshmana's alarm grew into panic. Why were they doing this?

We will not let you go until you look at us, she sang. *Look at me.*

Lakshmana opened his eyes and saw. The black-haired one was before him, moving her hair aside to display her naked beauty. The sight scorched Lakshmana, for he had never planned to look at anyone but Urmila in this state. He had sworn upon all he held holy to be chaste during this exile. The stirring that had started within rose with terrifying speed. It had but one moment in the light. A question: Could he really live fourteen years without a woman's company? It was followed by overwhelming shame. Tears would have run from his eyes, had he not been underwater. The Apsara before him was a flawless beauty, more beautiful than any human woman could be.

She swam even closer, her black hair shifting softly around her.

Her sea-green eyes were full of yearning. *Stay here with me*, she said. *With us. We will fulfill all your desires.*

Lakshmana's shame melted away. The song once again filled his mind.

Look at me, the golden-haired Apsara said, and each of them commanded Lakshmana thusly, each taking a turn to stand before him and enchant him. Each nymph took a turn commanding his gaze until she was satisfied that he had seen her the way a man looks at a woman he desires. But he didn't want to!

"You do. You do not. You do."

With all his power, he shouted, "I do not!"

His wordless cry was a dissonant chord in their song. Lakshmana sprang into action, kicking his legs, lunging for their garments, determined to cover their nakedness as if he was their father, they his daughters. He wanted no part in this! Why had he allowed himself to listen to their song? He kicked and screamed in soundless outbursts and squeezed his eyes shut.

He pleaded with them. *Let me go. I'm here to serve my brother. Rama needs me.*

Their song changed at once. *He is pure*, they sang. *He is strong.* The melody and the mood was a celebration.

Lakshmana dared to open his eyes, just a little, and he saw that their colorful garments were back on their bodies, and they swam around him jubilantly.

Pure and strong. Pure and strong.

The song was the sweetest Lakshmana had ever heard, and it was a heart song meant just for him. The question returned full force: Could he live for fourteen years without a woman's company? And the answer was pure and strong. Yes. He could.

Pure and strong. Pure and strong.

The same two that had caught hold of him, took his arms again, pulling him up from the depths. All the way up, the Apsaras swam around him, singing. This time Lakshmana felt clearheaded. The enchantment had lifted. He was himself. And also more than he had been before.

Pure and strong. Pure and strong.

As they got closer to the surface, Lakshmana began to gasp for air.

They continued singing softly into his ears until his head pushed above the surface.

Pure and strong. Pure and strong, they whispered.

Then he was released and he rose, water dripping from his matted hair. The lake sparkled brightly. Rama stood with feet firmly planted and his eyes swept over Lakshmana and continued beyond. Lakshmana's heart sang with joy when he saw his brother. But Rama's eyes had not paused on Lakshmana. Lakshmana stared at his brother and realized what this meant.

In reality, he had not been gone long. His absence had been as short as it took to dip one's head underwater and return. Rama, who was standing guard, had not seen him gone longer than that. Here, the playful melody was naught but a whisper in the wind. Not a ripple of water betrayed the presence of five playful water nymphs.

Lakshmana's gaze searched for Sita. She was sitting under a tree, with her eyes closed. She shone with an otherworldly beauty and her golden cloth billowed around her. Lakshmana did not avert his eyes this time, for he was not afraid to see her beauty now. He knew that he was pure and strong. His whole body was vibrating with this knowledge.

He clambered up onto the bank of the lake and simply sat there for several minutes. He was overwhelmed by the experience and what he had learned about himself. The Apsaras had been determined to destroy his chastity, but in so doing they had turned out to be his protectors instead. He did not know they had treated him as they did. But they had exposed his desires, and the desire to serve Rama and to be chaste had been stronger than anything else. If he had succumbed, would he have been trapped within the lake for all time?

Lakshmana stretched out and enjoyed the warm sun. He felt purged of something heavy, and when he stood up he felt the difference. His head was lighter, his sense of self more confident. The naked nymphs had presented him with the ultimate test. Now he didn't have to carry a secret shame with him for fourteen years. It was a wonderful affirmation, one of the few times Lakshmana felt transparently proud of himself.

He approached his brother and looked Rama in the eye. "Something wonderful happened," he said. "I was submerged under the water longer than you know."

"Oh?" Rama studied his brother and began to smile. "Yes, I see the wonder in your being."

"But we must leave this lake, for the melody you hear in the wind is powerful. I will tell you everything once we make camp this evening."

"Will I be allowed to hear?" Sita asked, walking toward them.

Her eyes were soft, and Lakshmana said, "Certainly."

But he didn't imagine he would ever feel bold enough to speak in detail with her regarding this particular experience. He sensed it was something only a man could truly understand. If Sita was listening, he would relay a harmless version and speak with his brother in detail at another time.

"I look forward to hearing your experience, brother," Rama said.

It was time to walk in search of food. The cloth around Lakshmana's hips had quickly dried and by now the heat lay on him again like a warm blanket. He strapped his weapons back on. Though it was cumbersome, Lakshmana liked their reassuring weight. The blood-drinkers constantly invented new tricks to trap them. The aquatic maidens could have enchanted Lakshmana for countless years. In Dandaka, one needed all the weapons one could get, even if one was strong and pure.

CHAPTER 20

The Monsoon

The summer's debilitating heat wilted plants and humans alike. The humidity warned Rama that the rainfall would soon begin. The monsoon would drench the land with ceaseless rain. The clouds gathered in the sky; Rama and Lakshmana stood together looking in the direction of the loud rumbles of the rain-filled clouds. The sun would rise and set, but the rain would never stop. Monsoon was approaching . . . but not yet.

Forewarned by Sharabhanga of the monsoon's misery, the travelers found a cave to live in. Using what skills they had acquired over the past months, they gathered food supplies and set up the cave for habitation.

For the next two months of the monsoon season, it rained and rained. It was impossible to go anywhere or do anything without becoming one with the elements—that is to say, wet through and through. Activity seemed to cease everywhere. Animals, beasts, and even blood-drinkers retreated to their holes, hiding from the rain so thick you couldn't see an arm's length ahead.

Every morning Rama and his companions took a bath simply by standing outside the cave and letting the rain shower down upon them. Despite the dampness and the feeling of never being quite dry, they found the monsoon was a time of cleansing and even hope. Once the land had soaked up what the clouds had offered, new life was on its way again. But like all the forest's creatures, Rama had to bide his time.

Holed up together with no other companions or pursuits, this was a time for stories and reminiscences. As Bharadvaja had observed at the beginning of the exile, each of them had their own version of the very same story. Comfortable enough in their cave, they took turns telling stories or recalling memories both old and new. Such intimacy had never been possible in Ayodhya, where numerous people were always in attendance at the many events and social gatherings, even during the monsoon. Rama's duties had never ceased, and Lakshmana had always been by his side. Rama did not like to compare this life to that life, for there were pleasures in both. Mostly, Rama preferred not to think of the life he'd left behind in Ayodhya, even though it marked his every word and action. If he wasn't the prince of Ayodhya, descendent of the sun-line, son to King Dasharatha, he was nobody.

Often they spoke of Ravana, whose name was heard much more in the jungle than in civilization.

"The last king of the Sun dynasty who saw Ravana in person was King Anaranya," Rama said. "He's the one who made the prophecy, or curse perhaps, that a son of the Sun dynasty would slay Ravana. No wonder then that he seems a distant threat to us, not even our great-grandfathers have seen him."

"And yet there was the incident, in your father's lifetime," Sita said. She had found the records in the royal library and had been incensed. "More than one hundred women were abducted from their homes. Ravana's work. It was the letter by one of Ayodhya's citizens that really chilled me. *My wife is dead*, he wrote. I think his name was Lochana. His wife was one of the many who was abducted. Just like that, he abandoned her. How could he swear before the fire to protect his wife and then dismiss her as dead?!"

"Perhaps she was dead," Lakshmana said, which is exactly what Rama had said when Sita had brought this episode to his intention.

"Perhaps she had been tortured," Sita countered. "Perhaps she had been violated, perhaps she had suffered unimaginable horrors. What she would need the most is her home and her husband's love!"

Now as then, Sita was unusually vocal, her anger crackling in her voice. The small cave could not peacefully contain her energy. Rama felt the waves of heat bouncing off the gray stone.

"That is sentimental," Lakshmana said, with his usual knack for speaking without censor.

Sita would not be stopped. "Did you know that Rani, our powerful little Rani, back home in Ayodhya, who knows how to do everything, was one of the victims? Her family shunned her, without even listening to her side of the story. She was only ten years old when this happened! You cannot maintain that it's sentimental! That she deserved this!"

She waited, looking at Lakshmana, in case he would continue his challenge.

"The laws are wrong," she said, a little softer.

Rama waited for the rest, but Sita fell silent. Rama was relieved that she did not repeat what she had said that night: that when she had read the record, she had been gripped by a dreadful foreboding. She had asked Rama what he would do, if she was abducted and returned. Rama had not been able to give her a clear answer. For he was a king's son first and foremost, and in this position, he could not follow his heart alone. Now he spoke up. "If it were my wife, I would do anything to win her back, to avenge this crime."

"You will rewrite the laws when you become king," Sita said with a smile.

Lakshmana disagreed. "Those laws were written by Manu, the first man! Father never changed a word in those laws, neither did Grandfather Aja, nor his father before him. The Sun dynasty has upheld Manu's laws since Ayodhya was built; it's inviolable. That's why I call this talk sentimental. Not because I don't feel for the victim. I do. But it's not grounded in actuality. It's not grounded in the laws."

"Then what's your solution?" Sita asked.

Lakshmana crossed his arms. "I'm Rama's servant. I follow his command. It's not for me to think of these matters."

The conversation tapered off, as night made it impossible to see one another. The next day would bring another opportunity to speak. They had weeks to go, hibernating in the cave.

To Rama's surprise, Sita was the freest with her speech. As the days went by, she revealed that she missed the company of other women. She spoke about how strange it had been at first to wake up and not wear her jewelry or ornate silk dresses. Rama and Lakshmana knew the feeling well. They too had been used to wearing many adornments.

"Without my crown and the other jewelry I've worn since my birth," Sita said, "I felt as if I was walking about unclothed."

"You still wear many jewels," Rama pointed out. "Queen of the jungle."

Her soft laugh echoed in the cave.

She played with one of her earrings, as she often did when full of thought. When they walked out of Ayodhya, Sita had removed all her large pieces of jewelry but had kept her family heirlooms. They were a second skin to her. Rama admired them on her now: golden anklets, bangles inlaid with gems on each wrist, shark-shaped earrings with emeralds in each ear, her marriage necklace with its light pink pearls, and, finally, the delicate hairpiece from her father. All in all, they were the basic ornaments every woman in Ayodhya wore. Sita's garment, the gift from Anasuya the wise, always shone golden and bright, illuminating the cave when it was at its darkest.

Sitting in their cave, feeling always damp and watching the rains shower down, they couldn't stop their thoughts and words from returning often to their family in Ayodhya. Sita spoke about her sister and two cousins who had married Rama's brothers. Although Rama noticed that they often came away saddened, they couldn't resist this topic. The distance from their family was so huge, speaking about them felt reassuring. It made them more real. Many years loomed before they would set eyes on any of their family again. Even then, they had no guarantees what would greet them when they returned.

"We thought Father would be alive," Lakshmana said. "Until Bharata came to us with the news, we expected Father to be the first person to greet us. Father was in excellent health. If he could wither away within days, how can we know for sure whom we will see when we return?"

Lakshmana's question got no answer from his two companions, nor did it need one.

"You know as well as I do, my brother," Rama said, "that we cannot know what the future holds. But we do know our future takes its form from the thoughts in our minds."

"But that's not true, Rama! Don't tell me this exile was born from your thoughts!"

Even though it was dark in the cave, Rama could see Lakshmana's impatient gestures.

"Be calm, my brother. Listen. You are right that destiny and the future she holds for us is as unpredictable as the slyest of blood-drinkers. Still, our life here and now is molded by the thoughts we carry about the future we seek."

"I'm lost . . . ," Lakshmana said, and dropped his chin to his chest. His wave of anger had passed.

"If you let yourself imagine that Urmila has left this world, then the pain of that thought will take root in your heart and that future has already happened, if only in your mind."

Rama felt Sita startle next to him. Perhaps he had spoken too bluntly about Urmila, who was like a silent person ever in their company. And Rama had used her name on purpose, for it was true what Sita observed, that Lakshmana rarely spoke of his missing wife.

"Am I causing myself pain," Lakshmana said, "by entertaining negative thoughts about our family?"

"Yes," Rama said, though what he most noticed was that Lakshmana himself did not use Urmila's name.

"But, Lakshmana," Sita said, "if I know my sister at all, she's counting every moment until you return."

"She will never forgive me," Lakshmana mumbled.

Sita's face was animated. She longed to speak of her sister. But Lakshmana turned away. He put his head on his knees and hid his face from them. Sita turned to Rama. The whites of her eyes shone bright in the dark. Silence descended in their cave. The rain drip-drip-dripped down at the entrance of the cave, like tears dropping from a cheek.

When the rain became a trickle and they could see the forest from the mouth of the cave again, they knew the next season had begun. What a feeling it was to walk out from the narrow confines of the cave and behold the landscape, fresh and clean. The mountains gleamed. The streams and waterfalls gurgled all around them. Although the land would not show its fertile blooms until the next spring, the Earth had absorbed the rich moisture. A feeling in the air told them anything was possible.

Sita and Ravana's Spirit

Now I will take you with me to the moment when I could no longer ignore who I truly am. Yes, I had begun my journey with the elements at the outset of our exile. Fire responded to my thoughts, more resonant than a close friend. But months later, despite my open heart, I still had only a tentative relationship with them. I was a novice in my self-awareness. Even the Earth, my proclaimed mother, was a stranger to me. I felt her presence whenever I turned to her, but I admit that my human way of thinking maintained its doubts, since it all took place in the abstract realm. I feared I was being simply overimaginative. I dismissed my experiences too easily, fearing insanity. I had never heard or known of anyone who could commune with nature. I told myself what I did was no different than what Rama did when he closed his eyes in mediation. And what was it that I did, really?

I had imaginary conversations with Earth's elements. That was all. See, that's how easy it is to discount your innermost truth. I often received whispers and messages from various elements. But I felt like a passive receptacle. That was about to change. It was time for me to step into my power. But I would have never done it unless I was pushed over the edge. Ironically, I have Ravana to thank for it. My greatest tormentor was also my emancipator. I deny him credit, however, for it was not Ravana's intention to empower me. Certainly not. I know now that he, despite his ten heads and near omniscience, had no idea what happened on this day, this pivotal moment in my self-discovery. Instead I learned so much about him, but more important, about myself.

After two months holed up in a cave together, we were grateful to walk freely in the vast forest. It did not take many days before we came upon the dwelling of another revered sage, by the name of Sutikshna. As we walked into Sutikshna's ashram, we were greeted warmly, and I believe he saw into my heart. He knew some of what was to come. My beloved and his brother were soon engrossed in conversation with Sutikshna, speaking about celestial missiles and their uses. Rama had a whole arsenal of them but was still learning their use and purpose. I was free to wander and explore the ashram.

As I came to the outskirts of the ashram, I noticed a hidden bower where an altar of worship was perched. I walked inside, lifting a few branches out of my way. Seeing the smooth, black stone, as large as a human head, in the center of the altar, I knew this temple was to Shiva. The altar was impeccable, freshly cleaned. Someone had placed flowers all around it, and I got the strong sense that Shiva was not just worshipped but adored in this corner. As I stood admiring this sight of worship, a flame sparked in one of the clay pots. My eyes darted to the fire. Then a twin flame appeared on the other side. I was quite certain I had not created those sparks. Twilight was upon us, and the intimate glow of the fire lulled me into a sense of safety. That's when I saw the creature standing directly behind the Shiva-linga, staring at me with eyes that haunt me to this day.

They were the eyes of a man driven to madness, deprived of every sensual pleasure, living only for the day when he might get a drop of satisfaction. How had I not seen him before? He was terribly emaciated, more skeleton than man. I felt the danger of his need and took several steps back, before I realized it was no man but a spirit made of nearly invisible particles. No wonder he looked so starved. He was trapped in a form that allowed him no fulfillment. And for that I was glad, for I sensed what he would do to me, or any woman, if he had the ability. The most visceral part of him was his eyes, burning flames in his sockets. I cannot say how long we stood there, assessing each other. Why did I not run away or scream for help?

Truly told, I was not afraid. Instead, I was angry . . . a slow rage building in my center that he dared stand so arrogantly, looking at me up and down, up and down. And so when he came toward me, I stood my ground, determined to stave him off. He was not a real man of flesh and blood. He could do nothing to me, I who was no ordinary woman but the daughter of the Earth.

As he came near to me, I knew my mistake. His bony hand snaked around my wrist, his touch icy. I could not pull my hand away. He was stronger than I was. Much stronger. My anger turned to horror and my cry for help came out as a small yelp. The next second his other hand was covering my mouth, stifling my scream. My entire body cringed as his insubstantial form made contact with mine.

Stop, stop, I cried in muffled terror, but no words escaped. He was trying to take total control of my body, to replace my spirit with his. That was his best hope for satisfying his disembodied need. I pushed against his energetic force, remaining firmly embodied, claiming my body as my own and shutting out his intrusion. So he stayed pressed against me, now in battle with my spirit as well as my body. I didn't know how long I had the power to shut him out.

Then the branches parted and a kindly sage came in. Just seeing him gave me strength. Relief washed over me. *Help me*, I struggled to say.

"I heard you cry out," he said. "Is everything all right?"

Could he not see that I was trapped by a spirit intent on molesting me? I could neither nod nor speak. The malignant spirit covered my mouth. But I looked at the sage with eyes full of the helplessness I felt.

"I see that you've found Ravana's altar," the sage said kindly. "We seldom come here, as it is haunted by his spirit, which he left behind. He is such an ardent worshipper of Shiva, you see, that he left behind a part of himself to keep the service going. Not a day has gone by without fresh flowers appearing and the fires being kindled."

The spirit of Ravana was satisfied by the praise, and so I knew the words were true. But what did I care for such knowledge when I was held captive by this evil? *Help me*, I called out to the sage. *Help me!*

The sage heard nothing. Saw nothing. After a few moments, he seemed satisfied that I was alone and safe. Without another word, he turned and walked out, as slowly and gently as he'd arrived. My eyes followed his movements, my hope for rescue disappearing. I felt my resistance slipping away, and Ravana's strength grew, feeding on my perceived weakness. The anger I'd felt in the depths of my belly returned. It was like reaching into the womb of the Earth and bringing with me her fire.

I shouted, "You are not a servant of Shiva!" No sound came out, but I knew he could hear me. "Let me go"—I squirmed to try and break his hold—"if you have any desire to survive."

He had already crossed beyond all propriety. His intrusion was unforgivable, and I could see what he planned to do with me if I let go of control. My anger at his intrusion became all-consuming. I felt the fire at my core flare up and overpower me.

Water rose in my eyes and a torrent of rain gathered above. The Earth trembled. The sky rumbled. Fire shot up around me like a shield. Power exploded from my center, and I cast the spirit out. He was pushed beyond the ring of fire, away from me. I was free.

But he did not give up. He was persistent, single-minded. The flames of the fire flickered across his hungry eyes. He moved around the fire, seeking entrance. I exhaled, and a strong gust of wind blasted him away, destroying him. But he reassembled within seconds, starting with his eyes—his body made of subtle particles. Not for a moment did his desire for me change course.

Dark clouds gathered. The thunder above was my voice, the bolts of lightning striking at my command. The dark storm clouds above me were a replica of the storm in my mind. His skull cracked into pieces, his eyes rolled in their sockets, but stubbornly he continued to re-form, moving around the ring of fire with his hunger. His persistence sealed his fate. Until then I might have been compelled to forgive. If he had surrendered, I might have allowed him to stay at his place of worship.

In my complete fury, I saw the possibility, for I had seen it before in my dreams: The fires at the core of the planet raged and pushed toward the surface, demanding more space to breathe. The Earth split apart and was no longer one. The ocean claimed the planet. Hungry waves swallowed the rich soil of the Earth, turning it into sea bottom. When the fires sighed in peace and the waves forgot to be hungry, the Earth had split into thousands of pieces, scattered across the ocean. All the while, I was the silent witness. Once the fire would reach that level of rage, it would not be stopped. But that time had not come. Not yet.

But the Earth did begin to tremble under my feet. She parted under Ravana's spirit, opening up a black cavern in the ground. He hovered in the air, and with all my power I flung him into the Earth. He was sucked down into the hole, which was deeper than thought and had no bottom. There, he ceased to be himself, absorbing into the particles of Earth, water, and fire that the planet was made of. In a sudden moment of compassion, I summoned the golden pot given to me by the Goddess Ganga. Quickly I sprinkled some of the holy water into the cavern, giving absolution to the tormented fragment of Ravana's mind.

The fire around me crackled. I watched the cavern close up, the Earth sealing back together. My fury was gone the moment he was. The ring of fire disappeared, but I stood within a perfectly drawn circle, the grass black and charred in a flawless circle around me. The skies cleared, nature grew peaceful. I became myself again.

Though not quite. I could never be the same Sita again. Now I had learned what I am capable of. Every thought and feeling I have is tied to the Earth. If I break, she will break. For the powers that I invoke are no powers at all, but as second nature to me, as breathing is to my human body. I just had not known it, and then I did.

As I stood in silence, regaining normal breathing, the final confirmation took place. One by one, the gods of the elements appeared before me. Agni, lord of fire. Vayu, lord of wind. Varuna, lord of water. Indra, lord of storms, and last of all, Bhumi, goddess of the Earth.

They swept forward, touching my feet, indicating that I was their queen. They appeared and disappeared so quickly, I had no time to make a response. I immediately understood that their urgency was fueled by fear; they were begging me for help, asking me to be their savior. It made no sense to me then; how could these divine, all-powerful beings be afraid of anything, when they could move heaven and Earth? They had powers no mortal could dream of. I didn't know then that even a goddess must wield her powers with great care or destroy the balance of the world. I also didn't know that someone had snatched away their decision-making abilities. That's why they swept in at my feet, longing for my intervention. I, who was the daughter of the Earth, who had the power to rule the elements, as she once had done. These divine beings longed to acknowledge a new master. Thus, they crowned me as their queen. They wanted their powers to be at my disposal.

My mother disappeared with the other gods, and the Earth quieted beneath my feet. The fire in my belly had died down. The crack where Ravana's spirit disappeared had seamlessly sealed itself. I looked at the Shiva-linga in front of me. The flowers had wilted and the two sparks of fire were extinguished. A new servant would have to worship here. One more worthy of his master. The spirit of Ravana was no more.

As fate would have it, Rama and Lakshmana, my protectors, came rushing in only then, when all was said and done. My beloved came to my side, alerted by the sudden upheaval of Earth and sky. Rama took in the clouds above us, the charred circle around me, and finally he looked at me. And what did he see? I think he saw me in all my glory, shining with power and victory, the queen of the elements. But later events would challenge this notion. Had Rama, who sees more than other humans, seen me truly? Or did he simply see this: Sita, his beloved, her golden Cloth of Essence billowing in the wind, a vision so beautiful it took his breath away and made him forget what he had come to investigate? I don't mind having that effect on him. He is my beloved too, after all.

At that time, I sank down on the Earth, my mortal frame shaken by the powers that had been channeled through me. I would never be the same Sita again. My understanding of myself had come to me slowly. Only after I became a fully grown woman, only after I went through hardships, only then could I stand to see myself truly, only then was my nature revealed to me. Now I understood that I had known it all along, that this truth of my nature was the very thing I had been resisting. My deepest fear was rooted in a fear of being myself. Imagine my relief when I discovered that there was nothing to fear. The truth of who I am and will always be is eternally true and inviolable. The veils that obscured my vision, they were the distortion, they were the shadows. They were the shields that protected me, before I was ready. My first friend was fire, and perhaps therefore, the intense devouring flames became the dearest to me, the element I feel closest to, even now. Fire is my very heart, just as the center of the Earth holds unimaginable heat.

When the phantom of the ten-headed enemy accosted me, I learned that I could invoke all the elements to protect me. The ring of fire stood around me like a shield. I did not have time then to register that I was supremely protected from harm, when any other human being would have been scorched.

All I could see was Ravana's hungry eyes, his phantom hands reaching for me. I felt the power in my own eyes, which held his gaze without fear. The stormy sensations were so great, I did not at once understand the magnitude of this experience. My companions, by now accustomed to the magic of the forest, did not question me. They accepted me. For this, I am ever grateful.

None of this would have been possible if I had been constrained by the palace walls. They are not only built by man but are a symptom of his thinking and his way of life. If either of my companions had voiced concern or opposed the phenomena that emerged from me, I would have been immediately curtailed. That had been the story of my life until the exile. I did not know it, but the biggest frailty of my human body had been my mind. A fine, sensitive instrument, but a mind nevertheless, which by nature is always balancing between reality and illusion, darkness and light, sanity and insanity. It was only in the fantastical setting of the forest, with all its existent magic, that I was able to bypass my own mind's constrictions. My community and my peers, which were now limited to two other human beings, no longer constricted my growth. The all-knowing sages who crossed our lives had the glow of the self-realized. They did not truly need us, and so we were not bound to them. Rama and Lakshmana became my everything. As we wandered deeper into the jungle, the three of us became inextricably bound to one another, as vital to one another's existence as breath and blood are to the body.

Ten Years Later . . .

CHAPTER 22

Ten Years

Rama and his companions had roamed the forest of Dandaka, learning every part of it. Now Rama did not lift his arrows against any of the forest creatures. Much like an elephant, he knew how to navigate the terrain without intruding on territory belonging to the lions and tigers, the most predatory of beasts. He had learned how to spot magic afoot, for in such areas the mind grew unhinged, and less sharp, a sure sign that the area was not governed by Earth's laws. He avoided such places and steered his companions clear; they did not engage with Kinnaras or Apsaras as they were seldom trustworthy.

Ten years had passed, and Rama was now a man of twenty-eight, a respectable age, when no Ayodhyan would dispute his authority if he had been king of that realm. But he wasn't. And he wasn't the same Rama who had left Koshala on the brink of his eighteenth birthday. In Ayodhya, he had taken the counsel of men. Here, he took counsel equally from Sita and his brother. In these exile years, Rama had grown into a wild and free man, the protector of the forest. And yet he had not grown, for he had not been

in the association of the civilized. He had not learned the lessons of Ayodhya or evolved into the refined person Ayodhya would have expected.

Rama's matted hair lay along his back and reached almost to his knees. Once, Lakshmana had gazed intently at him and then said, "Thirty gods, brother, you look like Father." Rama thought the same about Lakshmana, who had Father's complexion and colors, more so than Rama. Lakshmana's square jaw and straight nose were exactly like Father's, though he had his own mother's gentle eyes—that is, when he was not in a temper. Lakshmana had not changed much in that regard. Yet in Lakshmana's other changes, Rama saw his own, for Lakshmana was now adept at life in the jungle. He had developed a second sense; he knew when the season was about to change; he knew when blood-drinkers were near. Such skills had never been crucial in a life surrounded by guards and walls. Would he and his companions ever fit into Ayodhya again?

Rama wondered this especially about Sita. One year behind Rama in age, his princess had turned twenty-seven. By now, they would surely have had several children, had they followed the course initially set for them. Sita would be a queen and a mother. Instead, the couple lived the true lives of ascetics, from their diet of fruits and roots to their restraint of their senses. She wore her long hair free, which flowed like a river down her back, and she roamed about like a priestess, absorbed in her own magical realm, surrounded always by her friends, the animals. Sita had undeniably grown into a woman. She had always appeared intensely female to Rama, the only female he desired and looked upon the way a man does, the way Father had looked at Kaikeyi, his favorite wife. But when Sita grew into her womanhood, only then did Rama realize she had been only a girl when they first met. Rama saw the changes in her body. Despite their austere diet and small food portions, Sita's body filled out, growing more curvy and lush, her breasts growing rounder, her hips more pronounced. Mentally, she developed a daunting maturity, a wisewoman's way of being always two steps ahead, especially in regards to emotions and the inner workings of things. On several occasions, Rama had shared a new realization with Sita, only to find that Sita was already there with a fully formed thought, having known it before, having waited patiently for him to reach her level of understanding.

Would Rama have noticed this about her if they had been in Ayodhya, a place where men ruled? Kausalya, his revered mother, held great power. But then, she was less womanly than most women; she did not display her emotions in public, ever. She restrained her softness, her femininity, and for this she was respected. Because of this she was listened to, while Kaikeyi, a woman reveling in her beauty, had not gained much true power—except over Father's heart. What kind of woman was Sita, really? Rama had no one to compare her to here in the forest, save for the women in his memories, the queen mothers. He saw her affinity to nature: the way she would lay her cheek on the ground and whisper to the Earth. She could stay like this for a long time, engaged in conversation, as long as Rama did not pay direct attention to her. If he approached, she would stop at once and sit up; so he knew she did not wish to share this part of herself. Just as Rama would never bring forth his celestial missiles without due cause, Sita tolerated the rain and the cold, harsh winters like every other creature. She did not sway nature in her favor, though Rama suspected she had powers over the elements.

There was something daunting about Sita, something that had almost frightened Rama once or twice. She was innocent in the ways of the world, having lived as a wife for only a brief time before they were expelled to the forest . . . where they by necessity could not live as man and wife. And yet she was not innocent. Rama had never witnessed her ruthlessness, but he sensed it in her when, on the rare occasion, she grew angry. She was capable of destruction. If Sita were ever angered beyond forgiveness, her anger would affect the entire world. Aside from the unbreakable soul connection he had with Sita, he held her in great awe and esteem. Could Sita, a woman with unconventional attributes, ever rule the realm of man? Would she ever be respected and listened to, or would she be admired only for her beauty—as long as she kept quiet, demure in her role as Rama's wife?

Ten years had passed, and all three of them had grown so much, and yet they had not . . . like children bereft of guidance grow feral and self-sufficient but unkempt in the eyes of the world. Rama's longing for his home, for Ayodhya, had diminished over the years. Instead, he grew increasingly aware of how complex the transition to civilization would be. Rama heard rumors of a lone woman wandering the forests, and he wondered if it was Queen Chaya, Kaikeyi's long-lost exiled mother. He wondered if Kaikeyi's hair had grown long again, or if she kept it shorn. Knowing well the pressures a king's son was under, Rama wondered if Bharata was sleeping on the ground, as he had vowed. By now, many things could have changed in Ayodhya. Bharata's wife, Mandavi, could have borne a child; Bharata was not under a vow of celibacy.

Rama had word of Ayodhya through an unexpected alliance with the king of vultures, Jatayu, a friend of his departed father. The great vulture had spoken of a battle in the twilight realm, where a demon named Subahu had gotten too close to the emperor. Jatayu had come to the rescue. Rama knew that the scar across Father's upper lip was from this battle, so Jatayu was a firsthand witness in that battle. It had given Rama immense joy, hearing of his valiant father's prowess on the battlefield, where he had received his name, Dasharatha, meaning "Ten Chariots." The great vulture had recalled every detail vividly, and Rama and Lakshmana had listened with rapt attention for many hours. Rama, who was adept in the language of birds, had translated Jatayu's screams for his companions. They had been spellbound by the age-old tale.

Afterward, Jatayu swore to oversee Rama's safety and come to his aid should it ever be needed. He promised that he would be always within a call's reach, though he warned that his hearing was not what it once had been. He had spread his wings and beckoned the three of them to sit across his back. Riding on the giant vulture had been thrilling and transformative.

They had flown up through the clouds. As Jatayu had picked up speed, the wind had whipped against Rama's skin. The air that had been perfectly pleasant now stung with its chill. The moisture in the air had clung to them. With a bird's view of the forest, the land had ceased to be a place in need of protection and had instead turned into a green ocean, where all the creatures lived and fended for themselves. Even the ocean had sharks and other predators. Exterminating every last threat to the lives of the holy ones was not nature's way. Rama had felt this truth resonate in his heart as he beheld Dandaka beneath him. With the wind purifying him, Rama had felt released of his promise. He had given ten years of his life to it, and then he had been set free.

Beyond the reminiscences with Jatayu, Rama knew nothing with certainty about Ayodhya; they had not heard of the great city since the first year at Chitrakuta. Instead, the forest was full of its own news.

In fact, as the years went by, Rama's attention was absorbed in the happenings of the forest. Even in this remote realm, news traveled and things happened. From the holy ones, Rama learned that Marichi, Rama's enemy, had drastically had a change of heart. He had given up blood-drinking and was now holed up in a cave, on his path to true holiness, fearful of Rama's name. To the far south, the Vanara kingdom in Kishkinda, ruling all simian creatures, was in turmoil. Two brothers fought for the throne, and this news saddened Rama, for it reminded him too closely of his own fate. There were whispers about a large faction of blood-drinkers sent to infest Dandaka. Rumor had it that this was a battalion of actual warriors, not the common blood-drinker living underground who could come out at night only. Yet no one knew for certain if the rumors were true or where this army was stationed. Rama had met so many holy ones over the years; he had observed when Sharabhanga gave up his body at will, leaving this world for the three worlds above.

In their tenth year, the world began to close in on them again. Their routines and rhythms were disrupted more frequently, as if destiny wished to warn them of something to come. The first upheaval occurred when a great fire began to devour the forest. The distant smell of smoke preceded the appearance of the flames. Rama and his companions did not discover the devastation until the angry fire had mercilessly consumed large portions of Dandaka, and they saw a stampede of animals fleeing.

Sita sat perched on a low-hanging tree branch, her feet dangling playfully and her long braid swaying behind her. The bloodred flowers on the flame-of-the-forest tree were in full bloom. Sita's creamy skin was smooth as the full moon and her almond-shaped eyes sparkled like stars. Her thick eyelashes fluttered as her eyes began to sting slightly from the wafts of smoke. Lakshmana was resting, an arm tucked under his head. Rama stood leaning casually against the flame-of-the-forest, arms crossed, conversing with Sita. They were not yet alarmed by the burning smell, having grown accustomed to Dandaka's lively ways. But when elephants trumpeted in the distance, Sita's feet stopped dangling.

"Should we investigate?" she asked.

Lakshmana was the one who usually climbed trees to report on their surroundings. He was flat on the ground, however, his arm now thrown over his eyes. Rama did not want to disturb him. Clouds of thick black smoke began wafting toward them through the treetops. Rama coughed, and Sita covered her nose with her golden cloth. Lakshmana still did not move, and Rama worried that his brother was growing drowsy from the smoke.

He went to his brother. "Lakshmana, wake up."

Unwillingly, Lakshmana opened his bloodshot eyes. "Elephants," he said.

The honking had grown louder, and the Earth rumbled, a sure sign a stampede of animals heading their way.

Sita slid off the branch. "It's a forest fire," she said. "The biggest one we've ever seen."

Actually they had never seen one; they had only seen the barren and charred ground where the fire had raged. Lakshmana began coughing, and Rama felt sweat running down his brow. Heat engulfed them. Branches fell and the forest was being trampled.

"Go, go, go!" Rama shouted above the deafening noise. "The tree!"

The three of them clambered up, seeking its highest branch. The herd of elephants ran below, other smaller animals streaking by much faster. The roar of fire was near. Once the elephants had passed, Rama slid down the tree trunk and made sure Sita landed on her feet. It was time to run. And they did, Sita's hand in Rama's.

But one cannot outrun fire. Within minutes they were surrounded from all sides, Rama's skin melting in the heat. The fire rose around them. Trees were devoured in seconds, the flames rising from the treetops, toward the clouds. Rama could see nothing but all-devouring orange and red billows.

"This way," Sita said, taking the lead and pulling Rama's hand.

Rama saw no way through the flames. He reached for a celestial missile, when a cooling sensation settled on his skin. Sita's hand turned to ice in his, but her grip was firm.

"Lakshmana!" Rama shouted.

"He is safe," Sita said. Her voice was directly in his ear, though she was facing ahead.

No longer burning, Rama saw the colors sparkling in the fire, the life in every flame, the energy so strong, no life on Earth could withstand its powers. He followed Sita. She walked without difficulty through the heat.

As they stepped out from the fire, the fresh air greeted Rama. He took a deep breath. The icy sensation lifted. Heat wafted once more toward Rama's back. The fire was raging behind him. Quickly he moved away, reaching for Sita's and Lakshmana's hands. Together they rapidly departed from the fire, which did not pursue them. The fire was contained, much like in a fire pit.

The three of them kept walking, leaving the forest fire behind. Not one hair on their body had been burned by the flames that had licked their skin. Rama's breaths grew calm. They had escaped the destructive heat alive. Rama's eyes were on Sita, but she only looked directly ahead, a pleased smile on her pink lips.

Rama was reminded of the incident at Sutikshna's ashram, where Sita had stood at the center of a storm and a ring of fire. She had destroyed a spirit of the demon Ravana, she said, before she sank into his arms, energies spent. Sometimes when Rama beheld Sita, he saw energies swirling around her, the vortex of great power. With every passing day, Rama knew that Sita was not an ordinary woman, not an ordinary princess. Months would go by and she would appear to be only his sweet wife, a delicate woman who cried when others were hurt. But on days like this, when they walked through fire without being burned, Rama knew Sita was more than any human mind could fathom. Coming closer to the end of their exile,

Rama wondered how she would be contained once again within the palace walls and strict etiquette of Ayodhya.

A change was near. Rama could feel it. Something was afoot in Dandaka. It was time to leave before destiny wrapped her tendrils around them. Rama could already feel the world grow narrow around him, but he was determined to find a way out, just as he had walked through the fire without being burned.

Sharpen Your Claws

Lakshmana was no longer a youth but a man. He knew this because he had given up hope; the question *Has Urmila forgiven me?* had long since been replaced by *Has she forgotten me?* He understood now why grown men went days without smiling, why they had no desire to play. After ten years without his wife, Lakshmana was used to a life without her; surely Urmila too was now comfortable without him. Lakshmana's heart was like his right hand, a useful instrument hardened with calluses and scars in order to better do its work. He needed a certain strength to endure the loneliness that came upon him, especially at times when Sita and Rama gazed at each other in that private way. Though a man of twenty-eight years, Lakshmana was a mystery to himself; it was easier that way. And therefore he kept Sita at a distance, the way one worships a venerable person from afar. She had grown only more beautiful, like a wildflower left to bloom. She had that double-edged female nature, which made her appear at times completely helpless and dependent; at other times she walked her own way, needing no one, fierce with self-will. Who would ever understand the ways of women? Above this, Sita did things that were pure magic to Lakshmana, as when recently, a feeling of ice had settled upon their skin when a forest fire had threatened to devour them. Still, Sita was all heart, all woman, and Lakshmana was uncomfortable with her probing questions. He did not need to discuss Urmila or his feelings, least of all with his wife's sister. All he needed to feel strong was the knowledge that he was his brother's most loyal servant.

Therefore, Lakshmana knew that Rama was ready for a change. For ten years, they had exterminated blood-drinkers. Now the crisis in Dandaka had passed. The blood-drinkers had dwindled in numbers, and despite rumors of a large army set to invade, there had been no evidence of this. Rama felt it was time for the three of them to withdraw from forest affairs. Rama hoped the sage Agastya would direct them to a safe haven, like Bharadvaja had done ten years earlier. Following Rama's lead, the three wanderers went in search of the holy Agastya.

Even after regularly interacting with seers, Lakshmana had not grown used to their perceptive powers, and this held true when they met Agastya, whose wisdom spanned ages of human existence. Unlike his brethren, Agastya did not hesitate to use his magic on the blood-drinkers. Naturally, the man-eaters had stayed away, knowing he meant a sure death for them. As they got closer to Agastya's forest, the Earth felt soft and full under Laksh-mana's feet. The foliage was shiny and green. A tremendous protective energy pervaded the entire place, making it as comforting as a mother's embrace. Rama was eager, leading them with ready movements; he had waited a long time to meet the great seer he had heard so much about.

Lakshmana, who had been impressed by Sharabhanga's ashram so many years ago, saw Agastya's ashram spread out like a city. There were fire pits everywhere, roaring and flicker-ing with the wind, while sages chanted hymns and poured ladles of ghee into the flames. Mantras pervaded the air. The energy was so high, Lakshmana felt the hairs on his body stand on end.

Agastya was a compact bundle of energy, short of stature and brimming with vitality despite being older than Jatayu, the ancient vulture king. His abundant beard and matted hair was shining black with strips of stark white. Though he did not smile once, Agastya's happiness was evident. He embraced Rama for several minutes and profusely praised Sita for the sacrifice she had made, taking on Rama's exile as her own. He made no attempt to engage with Lakshmana.

Agastya's intense eyes were often dimmed by a faraway look; he was seeing the past and the future. He directed them to Panchavati, a place he enigmatically promised would have *everything* they sought. He then gifted Rama a golden bow, which was indestructible and one of a kind. With it came an inexhaustible quiver. Lakshmana surreptitiously pulled out one of the shafts to examine it, his eye trained on the empty place where the arrow had been. Sure enough, once the arrow was out of the quiver, another appeared in its place. It was astounding.

"The time has come," Agastya told Rama. "That is all I can say, and even then I may have said too much."

Though they had all longed to linger in Agastya's protected forest, the sage had made it clear that only those who were on the path to salvation were allowed to live in his forest.

Right before they departed, Agastya caught hold of Lakshmana's arm, addressing him directly for the first time. In a whisper so only he could hear, Agastya said, "You think he needs you now, loyal brother that you are. He will need you even more yet. The roles you play now will be reversed. Fortify your heart." With that, he let Lakshmana go.

After several days, and with some help from the spirits of the forest, they arrived at Panchavati, which was all Agastya had promised. A waterfall sparkled with millions of little rainbows, blossoming fruit trees promising sweet fruits, and foliage as glossy and strong as those in Agastya's forest. With speed and dexterity, Lakshmana built them a cottage. Within hours it stood sturdy and inviting, with clay walls, long bamboo crossbeams, and a thatched roof—as real of a home as one would hope for in the forest.

When Rama saw it, he said, "What would I do without you, Lakshmana? I have no way to repay you but with my affection."

Saying this, he embraced Lakshmana to his heart. Lakshmana felt Rama's love flow into his body, and his being was fortified. If in the future their roles were reversed—whatever that meant—Lakshmana had observed his brother long enough. He would always follow Rama's example.

As they settled into their home in Panchavati, their life grew peaceful. The seasons came and went. Winter visited them three times, and the cottage Lakshmana had built was ample protection from the seasons. The cold winds would slowly start blowing. A thin layer of frost would cover the Earth. The water they bathed in became painfully frigid, and Lakshmana would long to feel the sun's warmth on his skin. Even summer seemed idyllic compared to winter's harsh demands. And yet, it was Rama's favorite season. Lakshmana could still not fathom why. They stayed close to their fire, wrapped in buckskins, roasting pumpkins and drinking hot water boiled with ginger. The return to Ayodhya was creeping closer, but they hardly spoke of it. In truth, Lakshmana could not imagine the return. He had truly renounced it. When the time came, would he be able to tear the walls down and reveal his heart to the ones he had left behind?

To tame his restlessness, Lakshmana roamed the forests around Panchavati. He enjoyed imagining himself one of the animals. He took handfuls of mud and smeared it across his chest and arms to lighten his human scent. For fun, he imitated birdcalls, and he climbed trees with troops of monkeys.

On this day, he began a conversation with a murder of crows that began to follow him, flying from tree to tree. In his schooling days, Lakshmana was taught the language of the five-clawed beasts. His twin, Shatrugna, had found it most amusing when Lakshmana was the first to master the language of crows. Even that had been incredibly difficult, and

Lakshmana didn't remember much; it could have served him well here in the forest. Rama, as always, had mastered it. Lakshmana still remembered Sita's triumphant look when Rama shooed a tiger from their path rather than kill it. It was easy to screech like a crow; it didn't require much finesse, for which Lakshmana was happy. Even though Lakshmana couldn't understand what the birds were cawing, it entertained him to closely mimic what he heard and hear the responses.

Despite Panchavati's heavenly beauty, Lakshmana sensed danger lurking. Agastya's words were clear in his mind, and then there was the inexhaustible quiver and golden bow, quite a significant gift. Because Lakshmana had ventured out by himself, he had packed his quiver with arrows. He also had his sword and knife with him. He'd left the shield, chain mail, finger guards, and armlets at the hermitage. The protective armor slowed him down, and it was daytime, anyway. Blood-drinkers rarely came out in the daylight, and so far they had not seen a single one of that kind here.

Suddenly, Lakshmana's bird followers began screeching to one another. Lakshmana heard the warning. Instinctively, he sought refuge in a tree. There, he crouched on a branch, searching with his eyes and ears. Although he couldn't see, he could hear that two large beasts were approaching. By the pattern of their movement, they were engaged in some kind of game, slowing down and speeding up at intervals. Lakshmana's blood started pumping faster, his adrenaline rising along with the animals' approach. He wasn't afraid, but there was a level of danger involved in the unknown. Even Sita had been unable to tame five-clawed animals. Lakshmana heard the beasts approach and froze into stillness.

Two magnificent leopards were engaged in a mating game. The female leopard slowed down and looked over at her mate, her tail hitting the ground lazily, but the moment the male leopard came closer, she flew through the air, away from him. It was a beautiful dance. Their almost golden yellow, shiny pelts glimmered in the sun, which shone through the leaves and hit them from different angles. Lakshmana guessed that the chase had been going on for some time, only because both beasts were slowing. They were getting close to the culmination of their chase and would begin to run with each other soon. Lakshmana was shocked by what he saw next.

The female leopard stopped running. She sat on her haunches, waiting for her mate. Her yellow eyes looked steadily at the great leopard approaching her. Lakshmana shifted his eyes to the male and noticed that his ears were flattened down, as if he was sensing danger. The closer he got to his mate, the stranger the great cat behaved. His pelt twitched as if his body was convulsing. With his ears flattened, he gave in to his instinct and shrank away from the waiting female leopard. When the leopard shrank back, the female cat pounced on him as if she'd been waiting for that moment. She sank her sharp teeth into his neck and thrashed her head about violently. They rolled around on the ground together, the male leopard beating his tail against the ground while trying to shake her off . . . but to no avail. Blood seeped out of his neck, painting his yellow pelt pink. She did not let go, and finally he went limp in her jaw.

Lakshmana's mind reeled. Why would a female leopard attack her mate so violently? This was not natural. Any abnormal behavior in the forest animals was a sure sign of something foul afoot. Before Lakshmana could think further, the answer appeared before his eyes.

The female leopard changed form, and Lakshmana gaped at a blood-drinker who was by all signs a female. In all their years uprooting and killing the demon clan, he and his brother had never encountered a female of this kind. It was easy to think of them as monsters without kin, but here was a woman, implying untold tales of mothers, sisters, and wives. However, this female in front of him invited little sympathy.

The hideous blood-drinker spit the leopard out of her mouth, her face smeared with blood, and blood dripping down her fangs. While she had been a magnificent leopard, she was anything but beautiful in her natural body. Lakshmana noted her obvious disdain for her own appearance. Why should she, when she could take any form she pleased at a moment's notice? Her copper-colored hair was a matted mess of dirt and blood. Her skin was jagged, like the tough, scaly membrane of a crocodile. Her stomach had large flabby folds hanging down over her thighs. She didn't bother wiping her mouth clean. She sat next to the carcass and absentmindedly stroked its pelt. She looked lost, as though she were considering what to do next.

Lakshmana held still. He could kill her. But she was a woman, and he was not sure what his duty was. Vishvamitra had instructed Rama, long ago, to kill Tataka, the giant demoness. *A monster is an abomination and has no gender*, Vishvamitra had said.

Still, Lakshmana hesitated. Just then, the blood-drinker did the last thing that Lakshmana expected: She burst into tears. She sobbed loudly, thinking there was no one to hear or see her. She hugged the dead leopard to her chest, saying, "I'm sorry, I'm sorry."

She looked up, tears streaming down her pockmarked cheeks. "I still miss you," she said. "I will always miss you. Don't think for a moment that I will ever forgive my brother for killing you."

Then her face twisted with anger and she flung the dead leopard away.

Disgust and empathy rose in Lakshmana. In her display of sorrow, she had turned from a blood-drinker to a woman. Lakshmana had never seen a blood-drinker act remotely human.

He was so drawn in by her emotions that he had forgotten to remain still. He didn't notice when she stiffened. She lifted her nose into the air and sniffed. She inhaled deeply, then turned her head and looked straight at Lakshmana, who was hidden behind the leaves. She had caught his scent. Lakshmana fought the urge to shrink back, but slowly closed his eyes instead. Taking a very slow breath, Lakshmana stilled his breath and his entire body. He had smeared himself with dirt to mask his scent, but his exertions had made him sweat. He tightened his grip around his bow, knowing exactly where his arrows were and how to reach them.

Lakshmana opened one eye, peeking at her. She sniffed the air a few more times and finally wiped her mouth with the back of her hand. Looking several times in his direction, she began to wander off into the forest, her fiery hair hanging limp in dirty clumps. Lakshmana did not move. He knew how tricky these blood-drinkers were; she had at least suspected his presence. For a long time he stayed where he was, his senses alert. She did not return.

Coming down from his hiding place, Lakshmana stretched his limbs and walked over to the dead beast. It had not listened to its instinct. Lakshmana admired the leopard's beauty, even though it was dead and a victim of a blood-drinker's brutality. As the foremost predator in the forest, the leopard had not been prepared for this attack. Lakshmana considered whether to skin it and take its pelt. But it was spring now; they didn't need the pelt, however beautiful it was. The return to Ayodhya was a constant thought in Lakshmana's mind; he reasoned that they would not want to carry anything extra on their long walk home. Lakshmana decided to leave the animal where it was. The messy affair of skinning the large beast might attract *her* back.

When Lakshmana arrived back in Panchavati, Rama and Sita were swimming in the nearby river, which was brimming with lotuses. A few years ago, Lakshmana would have felt compelled to stand guard if Rama was swimming and didn't have his weapons handy, but now it was different. They were not half as vigilant or fearful as they used to be. There was nothing in this forest that they were afraid of anymore, not even a bloodthirsty female who killed leopards for fun.

As soon as his brother was done bathing, Lakshmana shared what he had witnessed; Sita and Rama reacted much like Lakshmana had. They sat together on the ground, talking, being amused and horrified.

Lakshmana was in the middle of describing the female when she sauntered into their presence. Standing at the edge of their hermitage, she stared at them.

Lakshmana's skin crawled and his heart thudded. She had followed his scent after all!

The blood-drinker walked toward them with easy steps, approaching as if she knew them. Lakshmana stood up, his hands on his bow and arrows. Her cheeks were caked with dry blood, and Lakshmana found her even more appalling now that she stood in Rama's presence. She, in turn, did not take her eyes off Rama, ogling him as if he was one of the thirty gods. Her eyes flickered only briefly toward Sita and Lakshmana. She had not come to drink their blood, at least not yet. Instead, she was looking at Rama and batting her eyelids. It was the most grotesque sight.

"Who are you, most beautiful human man?" she asked Rama.

Her voice and modulation were refined, and she addressed them in the common language of the people. She was not as uncouth as she appeared.

Rama raised his eyebrows lightly and answered politely, "I am Prince Rama of Ayodhya, son of Emperor Dasharatha."

"A prince!" She looked delighted, as if the word in itself was a treat. "By your impressive physique and handsome face, I knew you were no ordinary man. Why are you dressed like an ascetic with matted hair? Why are you here in this forest? I have never seen a warrior like you here before."

Rama patiently answered her questions, though she was gulping him up with hungry eyes. Lakshmana observed her closely. She was long past her youthful years, and her pointed fangs were hard to ignore. With clumps of leaves and dirt in her unkempt hair, she looked deranged. And yet she was courting Rama; it was clear in every movement of her body. Lakshmana did not know how to respond, and neither did Rama, by the looks of it. Rama pressed his lips together, trying to hide his growing mirth.

"Now tell us who you are," Rama said with a broad smile.

Sita half hid behind Rama's back; she did not like this exchange.

"I am Shurpanakha, the sister of Ravana, the ruler of the worlds."

Ravana's sister? Could it be true? Lakshmana looked at Rama in astonishment. Could this half-mad creature be sister to the most powerful being in the universe? It seemed unlikely. Though Ravana's name was heard often in these parts, Lakshmana still thought of him as a legend. Her claim to be Ravana's blood relation had to be a sign of madness. Her name had not escaped his notice: Shurpanakha, or "Sharp Nails." Her nails were long claws with sharp, pointy tips.

"I am powerful in my own right," Shurpanakha said, putting her hands on her hips. "I live as I choose, under no man's rule. For countless years I've roamed this jungle, enjoying the company of whomever I pick. But never in all my years have I seen anyone like you, Prince Rama, with your broad shoulders, muscular arms, and beautiful eyes. Your skin glows in the most unusual way. Your smile is so pleasing, so attractive. Everything about you, your skin, your smell, your magnetic energy, all this makes you irresistible to me. Even without having seen you wield your weapons, I feel certain you are a true hero. My heart is overflowing with desire for you. Come with me, handsome prince, and I will fulfill all your desires. We can roam these forests together, like a true king and queen. I can assume any form you wish."

She twirled slowly to show herself. Rama looked at Lakshmana. Lakshmana shrugged his shoulders minutely. He could not fathom what Shurpanakha thought her appeal was. Yet she was certainly serious about her proposal. She glanced sideways at Rama, coyly tilting her head. She completely ignored Sita, as if the princess was not there behind Rama.

"That is a very generous offer," Rama responded with a smile that contained a much bigger suppressed laugh. "But I have to say no. I am already married. Sita is the queen of my heart."

Shurpanakha squinted at Sita, looking her up and down several times.

"Leave that pathetic woman aside," she said, dismissing Sita with a wave of her sharp nails. "She is nothing compared to me. She looks like she will snap in half any second. Her face is so pale, I can tell she must be very bland. She is ugly and worthless."

Rama threw his head back and laughed, showing his teeth. Never in all their years had they heard Sita described in such a way. Even Sita smiled, peeking from behind Rama's back.

"By insulting her," he said, the broad smile still on his face, "you insult me. The fact is that I have made a vow to love only Sita. I have foresworn my right to accept more than one wife. This will be so, even if Sita is taken to the land of Yama before me. She is the love of my life. I cannot accept another consort."

Shurpanakha gave Sita a nasty look. A shiver ran down Lakshmana's spine.

"Unlike me, though," Rama said, "my brother is alone. Perhaps you find him suitable."

What are you doing, Rama? Lakshmana thought. But contagious laughter bubbled up in his stomach. They had been killing blood-drinkers without a second's apprehension, shooting them on sight. Now here they were, not only talking to one but egging her on, entertaining her romantic proposal. Shurpanakha's eyes settled on Lakshmana. Her gaze appraised him shrewdly. He felt completely unclothed. Lakshmana gulped.

"Yes," she said, batting her eyelids again. "I don't see any unshapely woman clinging to you, Lakshmana. I could make do with you."

She waddled over to Lakshmana, her hips swaying in an exaggerated fashion. Lakshmana tried to hide his revulsion as she approached him. All he could think about was the blood dripping from her fangs hours earlier. But Rama's eyes were still dancing with mirth, and Shurpanakha was determined. If she was set on being a fool, so be it.

"Most beautiful one," Lakshmana said, continuing the jest, "I'm a slave to my brother, while you are royalty, the sister of Ravana. You deserve more. You cannot be the wife of a slave."

Shurpanakha returned to Rama, her lips pouting. "Rama, give up that pathetic woman hiding behind your back. Abandon your lofty morals and follow your heart!" She held one hand to her heart; the other she offered to Rama and wiggled her sharp nails.

"Lakshmana is being too modest," Rama said. "Look at his strong arms and broad chest. He is my right-hand man. Without him I would never have survived in the forest. Truly, he is more worthy than I am. Don't let his words dissuade you."

She seemed so taken with desire she did not realize the game they were playing. By praising each other, Rama and Lakshmana sent Shurpanakha back and forth between them. Rejected a third time by Lakshmana, Shurpanakha narrowed her eyes, darting them back and forth before she went silent. Lakshmana saw a flash of the desperation she had displayed after killing the leopard.

"I see now what you are doing," she said, her chest beginning to heave. "Why? You toy with me as if my offer is a joke. I am the woman of your dreams, for I can take whichever form you wish. Look at me!"

And she looked down at herself and startled. A full-body horripilation. Horror spread across her face as she looked down at her claws. She turned her hands about, staring at them with disbelief. "My own skin," she muttered. "But I conjured my Apsara form, the image of Rambha."

The air shimmered around her. Her skin flushed. Her cheeks puffed out. But nothing happened. Her voice came out in a hiss. "Who is doing this? Is it you? You? You?"

She pointed to each of them in turn. "I don't know what magic you are doing to stop my magic, but I am the most skilled *kama-rupini* among my people. I am the most attractive woman you will ever know, for I can even take her form!" Her arm was stretched, one digit singling out Sita.

Lakshmana did not even look at his brother. His mirth was gone. They should never have toyed with this blood-drinker.

"If it wasn't for that slut," Shurpanakha seethed, "you would not be rejecting me like this. Men fall at my feet, pleading for my company. That hideous creature stands between me and what I want. If she wasn't here, you would have come to me. I will eat her, limb by limb, gorging on her flesh. I will suck her bones dry!"

Claws raised, Shurpanakha hissed and hurled herself toward Sita. She would murder Sita like she had the leopard. Rama crouched, ready to tackle Shurpanakha with his bare hands. He was unarmed, his bow out of reach—leaning against their cottage. He pushed Sita fully behind his back, shielding her with his body. He called out urgently to Lakshmana, never taking his eyes off the enraged demoness. Lakshmana ran forward, unsheathing his sword.

Shurpanakha changed course and attacked from another angle. Lakshmana was behind her, his sword raised. Shurpanakha snapped her fangs in the air at him. She could take all three of them down. Lakshmana grabbed her hair and yanked her away. Sita never faltered; she glowed like the sun.

Shurpanakha howled. "I will kill that slut!"

Lakshmana's anger rose hot like fire in his entire body. She moved her head frantically, trying to sink her teeth into Lakshmana's neck. Her sharp claws scratched Lakshmana's arms, drawing blood. He swung his sword at her but did not run her through with it. With three swift strokes, he cut off her nose and ears. Blood gushed from the wounds, and Shurpanakha collapsed to the ground, howling and covering her face.

Her horrific scream raised the hairs on Lakshmana's neck. Panting with anger, Lakshmana faced the she-demon with his sword still upraised, forcing himself to look at her mutilated face. He couldn't bring himself to kill her.

Shurpanakha screamed so loud, the blood vessels in her eyes popped. She started crawling away on all fours as fast as she could. Reaching the woods, she got onto her feet and began to run, all the while howling at the top of her lungs.

Rama pressed Sita's left ear against his chest, covering the other with his hand. He stood perfectly still, apparently calm, but Lakshmana saw his eyes. Shurpanakha's scream pierced them to the core of their beings. Something terrible was about to occur. There was no going back now. They had to face what was coming.

CHAPTER 24

The Massacre

Shurpanakha's blood-curdling shrieks had only just subsided in the distance. The sound of other blood-drinkers approaching began almost instantly, like figments of Shurpanakha's vengeful imagination. Only these blood-drinkers were real and intent on vengeance. Lakshmana hadn't even had time to replay the event in his mind, searching for ways he might have averted the attack on Sita. The princess was locked in Rama's embrace and smiling bravely. Rama's eyes were wild. Shurpanakha's desire to rip Sita's limbs apart and suck her bones dry had been too vivid. The sudden danger had sent jolts of fire through Lakshmana's system. What made Lakshmana so livid was that the she-demon had not only dared to attack Sita but she had actually gotten close to her goal. Did Shurpanakha think they would simply stand by and watch while she devoured their princess? Had she seriously thought this would turn them in her favor?

The tip of Lakshmana's sword was wet with droplets of Shurpanakha's blood. The gashes from her nails on his arms throbbed. Now Shurpanakha had summoned others to punish them. She would not give up. Whoever was coming for them didn't bother with stealth; instead, they announced their approach with every pounding footstep.

"A group of at least ten," Rama said. "Sita, stand behind me. We have no time to hide you away."

Sita leaned into Rama's back. From a frontal view, she would be almost hidden from sight, her billowing dress the only giveaway. Lakshmana stepped close to Rama. Just as they huddled together, shoulder to shoulder with Sita hidden behind them, the blood-drinkers came into full view. Lakshmana gulped, glad that Sita could not see. Shurpanakha seemed like a cute, tiny doll compared to the approaching monstrosities. They were twice the size of Rama and had sinewy muscles and war-ravaged bodies. They had flaming red hair, like Shurpanakha did, and bronze skin. Crisscrosses of scars had remade their faces completely. They had missing eyes, half a nose, and no ears. Lakshmana could not imagine what their true features had been.

They were fourteen in number, and spread themselves out in an even arc in front of the brothers. Seeing Rama and Lakshmana armed and waiting for them, they bared their fangs in grotesque smiles. They smirked and gestured at one another as if to say, *Why did all of us come?* One of them grunted loudly in disapproval. The fourteen demons towered above the brothers, guffawing, snorting, and pointing at one another: *You go!* None of them wanted to waste their energy on these tiny, short-lived humans before them. Lakshmana was aware of how steady his own breaths had become, and Rama was breathing calmer still.

Rama looked steadily at the loud-mouthed gang but whispered through his teeth, "Move away from me. Keep Sita hidden behind you."

Lakshmana immediately did as he was told, stepping backward with his eyes firmly focused on the demons of the night. He kept Sita behind him as he stepped away from the oncoming threat. Sita stepped back with him, though he could feel her straining against his arm, wanting to see Rama, where he stood. For her safety, Lakshmana held her back. Those monsters should not get a glimpse of Sita. Who knew what Shurpanakha might have said, or if she had specifically instructed them to capture Sita? Sita had, after all, been the catalyst for Shurpanakha's blood thirst. Rama did not wait for them to launch their attack.

In one swift move, Rama grabbed a handful of arrows from his quiver, exactly fourteen. He lay them flat across his angled bow and pulled it into an arc, the feathered backs catching against the string. None of the blood-drinkers had launched a single weapon into the air. One of the demons raised his arm in sudden alarm, the spiked club in his hand swinging up, but Rama was several seconds ahead. Sweeping his bow through the air deftly from left to right, Rama released all his missiles. The fourteen arrows shot straight into fourteen hearts. The blood-drinkers grunted one after the other, as the arrows burst into their blood-pumping organs. Their heavy bodies thudded to the ground, their faces frozen in surprise. Rama dropped his bow and looked back at Lakshmana with a grin. That had been too easy.

"Lesson number one: Never underestimate your enemy," he said.

Lakshmana stepped away from Sita, releasing her from his protective stance. Rama examined each body, an arrow on his bow just in case. They had all been dispatched to the land of Yama. Lakshmana put his hands around the iron club, testing its weight. All the muscles in his arms labored to lift it into the air. He swung it around his head, but the force of it pulled him with it. This was not a weapon he could use. He let go of the club, letting it fly through the air. It plummeted to the Earth with a loud thud. That would have smashed a human body beyond recognition. Thank the gods that the blood-drinkers had not learned lesson number one. What would Lakshmana have done with Sita behind him if that spiky cudgel had flown through the air?

Just then a shriek hit their ears. There was no mistaking the voice.

"Shurpanakha!" Lakshmana hissed, twisting toward the screech.

And there she was, a few paces away. Lakshmana's hand tightened around his bloody sword. Shurpanakha snarled at them, all civility in her mannerisms lost. She clawed her own face, drawing blood. She spat at them, cursing in the language of the blood-drinkers. Though they didn't understand her words, her threat was clear. Before they could move, she threw herself into the forest, howling loudly.

"There must be a clan of them nearby," Rama said, his face turning dark. "These monsters appeared so swiftly. She is running for reinforcements as we speak. The wise Agastya has sent us straight into the arms of the enemy! Scorned by us, Shurpanakha thirsts for revenge."

Lakshmana shuddered.

Rama put an arm around Sita. "You will be safe, my princess. I promise."

"She could have killed Sita," Lakshmana said. "Mutilating her was a fit punishment. What else could I have done?"

The other course of action was clear. Lakshmana could have ended Shurpanakha's life. Without hesitation, Rama had dispatched her brethren.

"It was a mistake to joke with her," Rama said. "One should never engage with base creatures."

"I should have killed her when I had the chance!" Lakshmana said darkly, an arrow now on his bow, aiming at Shurpanakha's retreating howl.

"But you did not, my brother. You followed your instincts. Thanks to her, perhaps we will get to destroy these blood-drinkers once and for all. Maybe this was what Agastya wanted."

Rama pointed to the dead. "Leave the bodies here. Soon there will be many more. Do you hear the jackals howling in the distance? This, I'm sure, is only the beginning of a much bigger battle."

The sky had turned a murky red color, though twilight was hours away. Crows were screeching, and the animals around them were skittish and nervous. The forest was making it clear that it agreed with Rama's forecast.

"Remember the cave?" Rama asked. "If Shurpanakha returns with more demons like these, we will have to keep Sita from sight."

"How many could there be? Have we not killed thousands of them already during these thirteen years? I was hoping we had exterminated the majority of them."

"Yes, but these were different. They were seasoned fighters, not merely thirsty for blood.

When have we seen a group as large as fourteen working together? Until now, we've encountered them roaming alone or in pairs. Now the wasps have been awakened. There is going to be a swarm of them soon."

The omens that Rama had pointed out only became more pronounced. The dull red clouds grew crimson, and bloodlike rain began pouring from the sky; jackals howled, and all the smaller animals of the forest disappeared in panic. The three of them looked up at the sky as the clouds rumbled in warning. As the skies went silent, another rumbling began, and the animals that had fled now returned, fleeing in another direction . . . away from the new threat. A frightened antelope with long horns ran past them, heedless of their presence, followed by a group of hyenas. They had never seen such oppressive omens before. Something dark and dangerous was about to happen.

"Lakshmana, we can't wait any longer," Rama said urgently. "Take Sita at once and go to the caves. Don't come out until it's over."

"But—"

"This is my command, Lakshmana! I will handle this. I cannot think clearly with Sita by my side. If I know Sita is safe, that will be the biggest service you can do for me. Please take her and go now. And I mean now!"

Rama didn't have to add that he was the stronger warrior of the two. Lakshmana knew that.

Yet Sita clung to Rama's side. "Let me stay with you."

"No," Rama said grimly. "As long as I know you are safe, Sita, I will face this evil gladly. Let Lakshmana guard you. Go now."

"Rama," Sita pleaded, and stood her ground.

Rama looked down at her, half smiling to reassure her.

Lakshmana saw that his attention was elsewhere. Perhaps Sita hadn't seen that look before, but Lakshmana had. Rama was about to be ruthless.

Lakshmana took hold of Sita's hand and began pulling her away with him. Sita shivered and hurried her steps behind Lakshmana. She was scared of the enemy, yet more frightened to see Rama facing them all alone. There was nothing meaningful she could say now, no words of love or support.

Rama was already in another consciousness, preparing his mind for the battle he felt coming. As they left, Rama was strapping on all his weapons, including the chain mail he had rarely used, and the armlets and finger guards. The finger guards fitted around his signet ring on his left hand. He had no helmet here, but that could not be helped now. He picked up the inexhaustible quiver and placed within it the special arrow that Indra, lord of storms, had given him. That was the last Sita and Lakshmana could see of Rama before the trees obscured their view. Lakshmana could feel the rumble in the Earth, like a small earthquake.

"Hurry!" he said urgently, breaking into a sprint and pulling Sita with him.

He wanted to get her into the cave before any of the blood-drinkers would be near enough to smell them, let alone see or hear them. Shurpanakha was bent on revenge, and Lakshmana was certain that Sita figured prominently in the she-demon's plan. He found the

tree they had marked and located the cave up ahead, completely obscured by a thick net of vines. The opening was so small they would have to crawl inside. Lakshmana prayed that no predators had taken up residence in the cave since they last checked it. He grabbed a handful of pebbles at the cave's entrance and chucked them through the black hole. The pebbles echoed as they landed on the inside of the cave, followed by stillness. The cave was empty.

"Sita, go in first."

As she crawled in, he lifted the quiver off his back, not wanting the arrows to spill when he went on all fours to get through the narrow opening. Once inside, the cave was large, and Lakshmana made his way to the rear, leaning his torso against the wall, feeling the uneven rock surface dig into his back. He tried to relax. He didn't want to be there in this cave, like a prisoner. He wanted to be out with Rama. He knew what a large army felt like under his feet, the way the Earth seemed to undulate to distribute the weight. The more he had listened and felt the vibrations in the Earth, the more certain Lakshmana became of the magnitude of danger approaching them. Not a hive of wasps but a giant army of blood-drinkers. He estimated no less than ten thousand pairs of feet trampling the ground. Lakshmana wanted more than anything to be there fighting alongside his brother, but Rama's order was clear. Keep Sita safe. So Lakshmana tried to relax, calm his breathing, and stay as far away from the opening of the cave and the muffled sounds they could hear. He wished Sita would do the same. She huddled, instead, by the opening of the cave, listening to every sound, searching for Rama's voice. He couldn't see her eyes, but he imagined they were darting restlessly. She kept startling at the sound of sudden noises.

"If you hear that he is in danger, will you go?" she asked.

"Of course," Lakshmana said. "But I know that won't happen."

He hoped his words were true. "No one is a match for Rama."

He didn't tell her that Rama was about to single-handedly face an army of at least ten thousand or that he was nervous too. Even if she wouldn't guess the exact number, Sita could hear the muted screams and calls. It was no minor attack. Rama had never faced anything like this before, whether in the forest or in the battles of Ayodhya. Sita twisted her shawl in her hands, and when it was wound all around her fingers and arms, she started with her long braid.

"Sita, why don't you move away from the opening?" Lakshmana said. "Close your ears to the sounds of the battle. There is nothing you can do. There is nothing I can do. Rama knows what he is doing."

"Rama is out there alone. If he needs us, we must be ready."

"He won't need us," Lakshmana retorted, and as he said this, he knew it was true.

He trusted Rama's unparalleled skill. Rama was the son of Dasharatha, a warrior whom the gods had called upon. In the massive battle between the gods and the demons, their father had fought so ferociously that his chariot appeared to be not one but ten. Lakshmana was confident Rama would find a way.

They heard a loud twang, the sound of Rama's bow. Sita turned toward Lakshmana. He could not see her face through the darkness, but he anticipated her question.

"Rama is proclaiming that he is ready," Lakshmana said.

The sound a bow made without an arrow was slightly different. Rama was both testing the string of the bow and warning the enemy that his weapon was ready. Lakshmana sat back, determined to stay in the rear of the cave. Sita persisted in listening to every sound; Lakshmana prayed she would not do anything rash. Despite what he'd told her, his ears also were trained on every single sound from outside the cave. There was, of course, the possibility that someone would be searching for them and find their hiding place. There was no use pretending his mind wasn't on the battle. Neither of them moved. Both minds were focused on only one thing: Rama.

Hearing his brother and his beloved retreat, Rama stood with both his feet firmly planted on the ground, feeling a surge of power fill his entire being. He was ready for this fight. The golden bow in his hand came alive, and the sharp arrows transformed into messengers of Yama, the lord of death. He tightened the string of his bow. He was grateful that his celestial bow was not made of wood, like his other bows. He marveled at the way the hardy frame yielded to him, allowing him to pull it into a perfect arch, the string holding it into place. It was flexible yet indestructible. Even a slight pull on the string promised to shoot an arrow quite some distance. Rama bared his teeth in something like a smile and pulled the bow and string as far apart as was physically possible, his strong right and left arms pulling against each other. As he released the string from his fingertips, his fierce grin widened. The twang was deafening and continued to ripple out until the string stopped vibrating.

All this Rama did with full focus. He would not let a single one of the monsters escape today. However, in another part of his mind, all he could see was Sita. Her large eyes full of different emotions. Love. Laughter. Innocence. And most recently: terror. He wanted to destroy every reason for her to be afraid. He had to keep an eye on Shurpanakha.

He had seen that the thwarted she-demon was all the more determined to get to Sita. The demoness was, after all, convinced that the only thing standing between her and a love affair was Sita. When she saw that Sita was not with Rama, would she realize that Sita had been hidden? Would she try to seek out Sita while Rama was fighting?

The image of Shurpanakha's fangs and her supernatural speed flashed through Rama's mind. And because it was the vision he least wished to see, his mind produced it, clear and detailed: Sita's smooth, white neck, her black hair hanging in loose waves around her, Shurpanakha's sharp fangs buried in Sita's tender flesh, Sita's rose-red blood running down her flawless throat, as she hung limp in Shurpanakha's arms. The scene was as vivid as if it had actually happened.

Rama let out a rip-roaring scream, dispelling the image from his mind. He raised his bow to the sky in salute. He could barely contain the energy that was rushing through his body, begging him to fight, fight, fight!

He knelt on the ground, pushing his palm into the Earth, feeling the tremors coming in waves. He silently gauged the size of the oncoming army, although he already knew it was shockingly large. Ten thousand, he thought. . . . No. More. He held still, resisting the fire burning his body from the inside. . . . Fourteen thousand. He pulled his hand out, taking some dirt and smearing it across his forehead for good luck. "May your power be mine!"

It was both Sita and the Earth itself he invoked, both goddesses of the Earth.

In Ayodhya's battles, he had quelled armies twice the size of this. Of course, that had been with an army of his own and with Lakshmana by his side. He didn't think about this.

Instead, he stood and looked around, bringing to mind the shape of the surrounding terrain. Soon, he thought, responding to the impulse, the fire raging and swelling each moment within him. He would need this impulse, since it was pushing him to do what no man attached to his own life would reasonably do: run headfirst into an army, the army he knew outnumbered him grotesquely.

Before he did that, however, he needed to think. If there was a plan to be made, he needed to make it now. In the distance, the elephants trumpeted. Rama knew every single animal would be fleeing from the army. Herds of them would be running in the opposite direction. There would be stampedes across Dandaka, demolishing the forest's landscape. A plan began to form itself in his mind. He also noticed that the blazing sun was close to setting. The murky rain clouds had disappeared.

Rama gave in to the rush of anger and began to sprint. He ran away from the army, alongside the rush of tigers, deer, and screeching birds. United against a fiercer evil, the natural enemies ran together like friends. How well Rama knew each tree, each boulder, and each rock. He knew exactly which one would support his weight, which one he could rely on to leap from, without it cutting into his feet. And there was the long line of banyan trees, with their strong aerial roots. He landed from his leap, catching the roots midair, twining his free hand into them momentarily and swinging farther. He had practiced this. It pleased Sita to see him fly through the air like a Gandharva, the male counterpart to the celestial Apsaras. He wouldn't think of her now. The sound of the army grew minutely louder; they too were moving swiftly, matching his urgent speed. Faster, he thought, running away from them. He needed to run faster. He flew from tree to tree in pursuit of his idea.

Soon he found what he was looking for. The wild elephants were moving restlessly about but had not yet begun to run like the smaller animals. Any moment, surely the matriarch would give her signal and the herd would take off in a stampede, crushing everything in their wake. There were more than one hundred elephants in this herd. Rama thought of his father's army, one of the four divisions entirely comprised of elephants that heeded the command of their mahouts.

Rama swung himself onto the closest elephant, gracefully landing on its back. The great animal shuddered, its leathery skin twitching, but returned to swinging its trunk and shifting its body from leg to leg. Rama needed to find the leader of the herd. She would be somewhere near the middle of the circle. Rama's eyes scanned the gray moving mass of elephants and found her. Her large trunk nuzzled the baby elephants, calming them. She moved in a circle around them, her long, sharp tusks swaying in agitation. The other elephants trumpeted every few seconds, calling out their distress. The rumble of the approaching army must have sounded deafening to them as they absorbed it through the spongy pads of their feet. Rama took a deep breath and resumed his run, leaping from elephant to elephant, until he reached the majestic matriarch. He landed on her, sinking down onto her neck, straddling her. She bellowed loudly, and the others followed her, lifting their trunks high into the air. Rama begged her to aid him in the destruction of the blood-drinkers.

"Run with me!" he pleaded.

With his arms and legs he directed her toward the oncoming threat, the opposite direction she would naturally go. She swayed her trunk back and forth wildly and continued her agitated trot around the inner circle. Rama waited until she turned full circle and was facing the blood-drinkers head on. Rama leaned forward across her head. He took out his knife, leaving it sheathed. Like a mahout, he found the soft spot by her ear. Digging the blunt edge into her thick skin, he applied strong, clear pressure and called out: "Now! *Run! Charge!*"

She reared onto her hind legs, trumpeting loudly. As soon as her front legs hit the ground, she was running. The herd arranged itself in lanes behind her, matching her fast pace. The calves were flanked by their larger family members on all sides. Joining Rama's cause, they were running directly toward the enemy. Despite their huge bodies, the panicked herd covered the span of landscape faster than Rama had.

It seemed like only seconds had passed before they encountered the rush of demons. The blood-drinkers appeared in great explosions, like red-hot lava taking over the forest. The sight of the ugly mass of thousands of armed blood-drinkers infuriated the agitated herd. The matriarch bellowed, charging forward.

Hundreds of blood-drinkers were trampled by the crazed elephant herd, which plowed a line right through the entire army. Taking advantage of the confusion the elephants created, Rama jumped up from his straddle. He turned around and ran across the elephants' backs, retreating as far as a mile to the rear.

For a moment, he heard Shurpanakha's voice above the clang of weapons. It was unmistakable in its shrillness: "I want their blood!" she chanted over and over again.

Among her own kind, Rama had expected her to revert to their demonic language—the growling words she had hissed at them earlier in the day. She was Ravana's sister, he reminded himself. He believed it now. Shurpanakha was at the top of the hierarchy of the demons. However incompatible Shurpanakha's behavior and appearance was with this fact, she was a princess, as was Sita. This was hard to reconcile. To say that Sita and Shurpanakha were complete opposites was not even close to describing the gap between them.

Rama hurled himself off the final elephant, rolling into a ball on the grass and running into the trees. He couldn't deny the power that Shurpanakha displayed there. She had been ridiculed, rejected, and finally mutilated. She meant to inflict the same pain on them a hundred times over. Now she had mobilized an army of fourteen thousand to seek her revenge. She was no ordinary demoness. He had to keep an eye on her and never let her out of sight.

With this in mind, Rama climbed a tree, the rough bark ripping into his skin. For a brief moment, he rested, wiping the sweat from his brow and eyelids, feeling the sting in his eyes. He had to announce himself and herd Shurpanakha and her minions away from Panchavati and away from the secret cave.

What better way to announce himself than through his arrows? He grinned to himself. This was not the way among royalty and in a battle among equals. There, you were bound to verbally announce your identity and declare your intentions. It was the etiquette for warriors to launch verbal missiles at one another before the real fight began. Lakshmana was excellent at this, inventive in his insults. Rama planted his feet firmly on the thick branch and put an arrow to his bow for the first time. This was not a battle among equals. Already, they had violated every code by attacking in such an outnumbered way.

Within one second alone, Rama shot several arrows. The arrows flew across the distance easily. Five blood-drinkers fell to the ground shrieking, blood squirting out of their wounds. Rama continued with five arrows per second, an unhurried and comfortable pace, his arrows precise. Before they understood that they were under attack, Rama had sent more than eighty of them to the land of Yama. They began to look around frantically, trying to locate the source of the deadly missiles.

Rama began leaping from tree to tree. He paused on each tree for a few seconds, firing twenty to thirty arrows. He saw the bloodlust in the blood-drinkers' eyes and felt the same pulsing in his own veins. A feral feeling rose within him; he was no longer Prince Rama but a hunter focused on the kill. Until that moment he had aimed at their vital organs, their hearts and stomachs. Quick deaths. With a menacing growl, he shot one of them in the eyes, one arrow in each socket, seeing how the mortally wounded blood-drinker, without sight, began swinging his axe on his own kind.

He would enlist them in his battle, the panther-Rama thought with pleasure. He was not himself anymore, but another being altogether. Everything was blood and death, and the more he could accomplish, the more elated he felt. He leapt into another tree, feeling the tree vibrate from the impact. Now he shot arrows that wouldn't kill but only enrage. Like puppets in his hands, the blood-drinkers began to slaughter one another. The death cries became louder and more frequent.

"He is in that tree!" he heard someone shriek. The relentless Shurpanakha, directing her soldiers.

He renewed his determination to keep his eye on her. He knew they listened to her, for Rama saw an avalanche of weapons hurled in his direction. A big iron bludgeon with iron spikes lodged into the tree, breaking it in half. Rama roared and jumped away as the tree crumpled under his feet. A giant boulder swooped past him.

"I want his blood! I want his blood!" Shurpanakha shrieked.

How had Rama been stationed so close to this massive army without knowing it? Rama felt a chill run through his body as he thought of how close to danger they had been, living next to an active volcano. The lava erupting from a volcano would not have looked very different from the mass of monsters pouring incessantly toward him. They were fully intent on Rama's every move and ready to die to get closer to him. There was no reason for Rama to

hide any longer. Now the fight would really begin. If they only knew how elated he felt that they were coming toward him, running into the embrace of death.

Giving up his subterfuge in the tree, Rama ran toward them, roaring as loud as was humanly possible. "I am Rama, prince of Ayodhya!"

Was he reminding himself or them?

The swelling sea of hideous blood-drinkers came to a halt for a split second, seeing their opponent clearly for the first time. Then they answered his shout and came running toward him, this one lonesome warrior they meant to devour in one gulp. Each one of them wanted to be the one to rip off the human's head, to drink his warm blood, to leave a little drop for Shurpanakha so she too might avenge herself.

But none of them managed to come close to Rama. No matter what route they took or what weapons they hurled at him. Rama fired arrows at such speed that the blood-drinkers were dead before they could know what hit them. They were thrown back against the ones behind them, smashing one another down. Had these hideous creatures once been children? With doting mothers? They were hideous, with limbs stuck into the wrong places, arms protruding from their heads, eyes in strange places. Not a single one of Rama's arrows missed its mark. They struck with such force that one arrow went through nine bodies, until it stuck into its final target.

The deadly arrows that rained on them made the multitude go wild; their weapons flailed blindly, falling indiscriminately on one another; thick, dark blood spurted into the air along with pieces of flesh ripped from their bodies. Mad with the pain of the arrows, those who survived began to kill one another. In their crazed desire to reach the human, they trampled one another, a stampede of blood-drinkers. In their hurry to swing their axes, clubs, and swords down on Rama, they gouged out their own eyes and severed their own limbs. They howled like rabid hyenas. Still, because they so outnumbered Rama, the living ones climbed over the dead. They closed in on Rama slowly. Like angry wasps, they began to swarm around Rama and surround him from all sides.

Trickles of blood flowed from Rama's left forearm, the skin raw from his relentless bowstring. Rama saw their attempt to come at him from every direction. An avalanche of spiked clubs rained toward him. Rama invoked Bala and Atibala, the sister-shields, just in time. They surrounded him with their brilliance; nevertheless, Rama felt the impact of the demons' missiles, denting his bones. His skin was torn all over his body, blood flowing freely.

Rama roared. Keeping his left foot firmly on the Earth, he placed the right behind it, digging his toes into the soil. Using this as his anchor, he swiveled on his grounded foot, releasing a volley of arrows in a perfect circle around him. Not for a split second did he interrupt the movements of his upper body, his right arm reaching for his arrow, placing it on the string, pulling the string to his ear, and releasing his hold on the golden missives of death. From the outside, he appeared to be a golden ball spitting arrows from every side. A double-bladed axe managed to penetrate Rama's shield of arrows, skimming along Rama's right forearm and drawing blood before it smashed into the ground behind him. Rama did not even glance at this first real wound. He felt the sister-shields imbue him with energy, the wound healing as he kept moving. Instead of grabbing one arrow at a time, he grabbed as many as could fit into his fist. He placed them easily on his bow, shooting a hundred arrows in a second. With Indra's inexhaustible quiver, he didn't have to restrain himself or ration the arrows.

Even though they were dying in huge numbers, the demons managed to keep up a steady stream of profanities and threats. From the few words that Rama actually understood, it was clear they desecrated Rama's heritage, insulted his wife, mother, sisters, and brothers.

After Rama heard their boastful threats, his chivalry was ignited. This was not so different from fighting warriors of his own kind! He could rise to the verbal challenge.

"I am the son of Dasharatha!" he thundered. "A direct descendant from the sun god! The power of the sun runs in my veins! My father moved so quickly, there appeared to be ten of him, not one. Witness how my arrows mirror my father's chariot. I will kill ten of you with one arrow."

Rama continued like this, calling out to every valiant warrior in his dynasty—Anaranya, Bhagiratha, Ikshvaku—naming their deeds, their victories, and matching his own arrows to their feats. His arrows cracked down on his enemies like lightning from the sky.

Then, the sun's setting rays reflected off a sword in the enemy lines, blinding Rama for a split second. He missed his mark, his arrow swallowed up in the mass of blood-drinkers, hitting someone else, somewhere. The blinding light gave him another idea. Had he not proclaimed himself from the Sun dynasty?! They were from the shadows and he from the light.

Invigorated by his new idea, Rama ran away again, this time toward the setting sun. Where was that mountain that the sun set behind? Rama listened for the waterfall, shutting out the growls, grunts, and cries of his prey. They were slow to notice that he was not in front of them anymore, although a handful of them were in pursuit. To make sure they indeed did follow him, Rama turned his bow around, shooting backward at them, as he sprinted forward.

The mountain peak swelled up ahead of him, the forceful waterfall obliterating other sounds. The sun was right above the peak, perched at its tip. Rama ran through the shallow pond, the water splashing against his hot skin. How would he get up there without leaving his back completely bare and vulnerable? He would need both his hands to wrestle his way up the steep slope. As he considered his options, he noticed that the blood-drinkers cowered from the sun's rays, as if the sun burned them. His pursuers squinted against the sharp light. When Rama thought of it, the demons had chosen to fight under trees, staying in the shadows as much as possible. They were not called night-stalkers for nothing! He threw himself at the mountain, feeling its familiar shape mold against his arms and chest. His bow rested impatiently across his chest, the taut string cutting into his skin. Like a limber mountain cat, he made his way up the steep incline, the muscles in his calves and upper arms engaged. He felt the mist from the waterfall cling to him. He moved quickly, before his hands would get too slippery. Behind him, the crazed blood-drinkers hurled insults.

He reached the top of the waterfall faster than he thought and stood upright, looking down at his enemy. Even though he was in clear view, the huge sun globe behind him swallowed him up, obscuring him from their sight. The blazing sun warmed his back, and he paused to assess the damage, reveling in their blindness and the clarity of his own sight.

There was a trail of bodies—or more like piles—as far as the eye could see. The forest was painted red with fresh, oozing blood. Hundreds of trees were uprooted. It looked like a merciless tornado had demolished all in its wake. And there was Shurpanakha, clawing her face again, distraught that Rama wasn't already dead. As Rama watched, she turned away and ran in the direction of Panchavati. Would she leave the battle scene to seek out Lakshmana and Sita?

Without thinking about why, Rama shot arrows in her direction but not at her body. As an arrow flew past her ear and through the tree behind her, she jumped away, hissing. The wound where her nose had been started bleeding again. His arrows forced her away from Panchavati. The sun would soon disappear behind the mountain. He had only a few more minutes of protection by the sun. The sun set Rama ablaze, its rays extensions of his own being. The arrows Rama fired off now blazed like flames of fire, scorching the demons who embraced darkness.

The blood-drinkers were increasingly wary of Rama's deadly arrows and unable to see him or pursue him. They turned their backs on the bloodbath and started running away. Rama had no mercy, shooting them down as they deserted. They were not noble warriors deserving of an honorable death!

Hundreds of others had succumbed to their blood craving, falling to the ground to drink the fountains of red liquid that gushed out of their dead kin. Crazed from the smell of blood, they gnawed at the limbs of the dead bodies that were piling up high as mountains.

The sun set behind the mountain, yet daylight would be Rama's ally for some time more. Having narrowed down the enemy from thousands to hundreds, Rama flung himself off the mountain, landing on the closest pile of bodies. Jumping on them, from one pile of corpses to another, he pursued the fleeing demons. Rama knew how much havoc just one of the blood-drinkers was capable of. He would not let a single one of them live. Not only bodies, but weapons were scattered everywhere, making the escape more difficult for those who were still alive. All threats and bravado were gone. The leftover demons whined in fear as they struggled to escape death.

Rama put an arrow to his bow, but the blood-drinker he aimed at tripped over a body, impaling himself on a gigantic truncheon. Smeared in the blood of his enemy, Rama looked like the formidable Parashuram, who had relentlessly killed twenty-one generations of warriors with his axe. Now Rama had killed fourteen thousand demons. Rama paused, an arrow perched on his bow. There was no one left to aim it at.

Panting and victorious, Rama raised his bow to the sky, looking at the heavens. Only then did he notice that he had an audience. The sky was full of celestial beings who had come to behold Rama's feat of prowess. A loud cheer erupted from the sky. Dusk was brightened by these heavenly beings, who sparkled like stars. With Rama's signal of victory, they showered down flowers on him, singing with delight in their heavenly voices. Rama recognized

Jatayu, the giant vulture, among his supporters. With satisfaction, Rama noted that he had not needed to invoke his celestial weapons, nor the help of his father's old friend.

Still, the fight was not quite won.

Three chariots drawn by mules with demons' faces charged into the clearing. All the other night-stalkers had been fighting on foot. The three night-stalkers standing in the chariot were certainly of a different caliber, one of them with three large heads on his massive shoulders.

Shurpanakha ran out from the shadows, toward the approaching chariots. "Khara, my brother!" she cried. "Look what Rama has done. I trusted you prematurely, you who boasts of your prowess in battle!"

"Quiet!" Khara retorted angrily. "Have I not promised that you will drink Rama's blood and his brother's too? Dushana alone will take care of this now. Do not doubt us."

Rama waited for their interaction to conclude. Taking deep breaths, he calmed his racing heart. He felt like Yama himself, waiting for the demons to stretch out their necks so he might place his noose around them. He straightened his right arm and felt the slight throbbing from the repetitive motion of laying the arrow on the bow.

The first chariot came forward, and the demon standing in it cried out, "I am Dushana, son of—"

Rama didn't wait for Dushana to proclaim his identity, as expected of one fighting from a chariot. With one arrow, Rama beheaded Dushana. Dushana's body remained standing and his chariot continued several paces before his body collapsed and the chariot came to a halt. The demon-faced mules brayed unpleasantly.

The two remaining blood-drinkers, Khara and the three-headed one, began arguing loudly about who would be the one to kill Rama. Both were confident that they could do what the army of fourteen thousand could not. Dushana's half-dead head did not warn them of what their fate might be. The three-headed one's name was predictably Trishira, meaning "Three Heads." This he proclaimed to Rama, once he had convinced Khara that he would be the one to kill the human.

"No one has ever lived to speak of his victory over me! Prepare yourself to die!" he bellowed, his three heads speaking in unison.

Rama bowed slightly but didn't dignify Trishira's challenge with a verbal threat of his own. Instead, he fired six arrows from his bow, killing the five demon-faced mules and splitting Trishira's chariot in half. The three-headed demon was forced to face Rama on foot. The main benefit of having three heads, as far as Rama could see, was that Trishira could speak three times as many empty threats. He said so to the demon, leaning on his bow nonchalantly. Trishira became enraged, snarling like a possessed witch. He picked up huge boulders and hurled them at Rama. The prince easily dodged the boulders, shooting them away as if they were playing a sport.

"*I will kill you!*" Trishira howled with all his three mouths.

It was true that he was very fast. None of Rama's arrows had so far pierced him in any fatal area. Trishira had at least twenty arrows in his arms and legs but was still on his feet.

Rama's eyes narrowed, searching for Trishira's weak spot. He fired at Trishira's throat, and one of his heads flew off, but a new one popped up.

Following his instinct, Rama aimed at all of Trishira's heads. When the three arrows pierced Trishira's three skulls at once, the arrogant demon finally dropped to the ground, dead. Shurpanakha shrieked. Rama considered shooting an arrow into her mouth, silencing her perpetual noises, but didn't. There was no time; Khara was coming toward him.

"I've been watching you, prince of Ayodhya. All this time, I've been watching you. Impressive, but not impressive enough to stay alive in battle against me."

"Are empty threats a family trait?" Rama shot back.

Khara snarled and jumped out of his chariot, his bow in hand. Before Rama could blink, Khara's arrow severed the string on Rama's bow. Rama inhaled sharply. Then grinned.

"More than empty threats, then," he acknowledged.

Khara's second arrow flew directly at Rama's skull. Rama whipped his face away. The deadly arrow grazed across his forehead, ripping a thin line of skin off. Blood trickled into Rama's eyes. He barely noticed. Now there was an actual fight in the making!

Rama sized up Khara with new respect.

While Khara's third arrow was on its way, Rama had time to rip his extra bow from his back. The string was not as taut as he would've liked, but there was no time to restring it, no time for even a split second's delay. The third arrow pierced Rama's shoulder. His jaw clenched as he ripped out the arrow.

Smiling a charming smile, as if befriending the furious Khara, Rama doubled his own pace. Now he severed Khara's bowstring, rendering the weapon useless, and shot his armor off, leaving his chest exposed. Khara looked stunned at Rama's precision.

Like Trishira, he reverted to using boulders and trees as weapons, but unlike Trishira, he didn't simply hurl them at Rama. He used them as a shield to swing Rama's arrows away. He ran toward Rama with mad determination. Rama's arrows made cracks in Khara's boulder, but the massive rock remained in one piece. Khara hid behind it, hoping to get close enough to Rama to sink his deadly fangs into Rama's flesh, or claw Rama with his venomous nails. Only when one of Rama's arrows nailed Khara's foot to the ground did the demon stop with a howl, hurling the boulder at Rama. The boulder grazed Rama's other shoulder, knocking him onto his back. Pain shot through Rama's entire arm, but the bones were intact.

Khara freed his foot from the ground, and Rama was on his feet again. For a second, the two warriors, demon and prince, faced each other. Rama was dimly aware of Shurpanakha's exultant face. Then, twilight hit.

Khara, the last man standing, visibly swelled in size, getting a surge of energy from the approaching darkness.

And from the sky, intervening for the first time, the celestial beings began to goad Rama: "Kill him! Don't wait! His powers will double once night falls! Do not play with him any longer!"

Although Khara was a fierce opponent, Rama was playing, because he enjoyed the fight. He was prepared to fight for many more hours. Leaping from one pile of bodies to another,

Rama forced Khara to pursue him. Khara, who was intoxicated and empowered by the smell of his own blood, renewed his fight against Rama. And then it seemed that *he* was playing with Rama. The darkness settling in around them filled up the demon, empowering him like the sun had empowered Rama. Khara was now so close to Rama, he clawed at Rama's arms and face. Blood trickled from Rama's forehead, into his eyes. Impatiently, Rama held his matted locks against the wound, soaking up the flow of blood.

Khara laughed maniacally. "I can already taste your blood in the air! Shurpanakha and I will gorge on your flesh and then we will hunt down your weakling brother who, like a coward, made you fight alone. We will save the best for last. Your darling wife, that whore you call a princess, the woman Shurpanakha has so mouth-wateringly described to us."

All Rama's playfulness disappeared in an instant. His body felt cold instead of hot with anger. He reached for Indra's golden arrow.

One arrow was all it would ever take, and that one arrow found its way to Khara's throat, ripping his head off, his laughter still emanating from his throat. Khara's body remained upright, his arms lifted. The headless body took two tentative steps toward Rama, the arms clawing the air. Trembling with anger, Rama closed the distance between himself and the walking body. With one kick, he sent the body flying. Rama landed on his feet, looking from Khara's body to its head. Would the two pieces crawl toward each other and find each other again? Would another head sprout from his body?

No. The demon was dead. The battle was finally over.

Two hours had passed since he had sent Sita and Lakshmana to the cave. The sun had finally set, and victory was his. Even Shurpanakha seemed defeated. She was silent, her jaw hanging open, her clawlike hands hanging limply to the ground.

Rivers of blood flowed around Rama's feet, painting them red. Hyenas and vultures were already greedily drinking blood and gulping up the feast of bodies. The smell of blood permeated the air and, soon enough, the flesh-eating animals of the forest would have a real feast. There was enough here to last them a lifetime.

Rama turned away from the piles of bodies, the morbid sight of entrails, and the malodorous bodily fluids running in rivulets. He wiped the blood and grime off his own brow. His whole body was dripping with sweat. He was covered in wounds, despite the sister-shields that were buzzing with energy to heal his body.

Then Rama noticed the strangest thing. If he kept his gaze on the Earth, the massacre was horrible. Putrid death in all its ugliness. It was the only aspect of war and fighting that left Rama despondent. He never liked to view the battle scene once it was over. It wasn't the sight of dead bodies everywhere, but that all these animated, vibrant bodies now were reduced to mere matter. Where there once had been life, there was nothing. No sentience. Nothing. And he had been the cause of this destruction, this obliteration of life.

But as he raised his gaze, his spirit was raised with it. Above the battlefield hovered thousands of glowing sparks. The celestial beings? No. They had disappeared. These sparks were smaller, like distant stars, yet so close that Rama imagined he could leap up and catch one in his hand. Rama stood still and absorbed the sight, his mind making sense of it all.

Immediately a memory appeared. The death of Viradha. They had stood at the blood-drinker's grave, and a glowing, shimmering light had arisen from the ground. The vicious violence in the air had disappeared. They had been had transformed, seeing the beauty and serenity of the soul set free.

This was not so different. Thousands of souls floated above him, serene and full of life. *Did I really do this?* Rama wondered. *Did I set all these souls free?* In response to his question, the sparks glowed brighter and moved closer, shimmering around Rama, caressing his skin. Rama stood still, in complete wonder. He was surrounded by their love, their forgiveness, their happiness, their boundless bliss.

He closed his eyes and felt a tear trickle down his creek. The beings were redeemed, and so was he. Yet there was one soul Rama had forgotten. One soul who was all but free. Rama opened his eyes and saw her. She was hovering at a safe distance, poised to transform into something else in an instant, if Rama so much as pointed a finger at her. She did not want freedom. She did not see any of that. All she knew was that Rama's blood, trickling from his wounds, was driving her mad. She plunged her face into the blood of her brethren, gulping it down, her eyes never for a moment leaving Rama. Very slowly, she got up, her eyes locked on him, her chin dripping with dark-red blood. She touched the place on her face where her nose had been, feeling the leveled surface, the slits caked with blood. Her eyes were full of such hatred, Rama could not look away. This time she did not shriek or howl. But her silence let Rama know that this was not the end. She had not given up and she never would. And then she was gone.

Fourteen thousand souls shimmered above Rama, flying up and away, disappearing, quick as a dream. Then Rama stood alone in the night, as if the battle had been in a nightmare and he was now waking up. Somewhere far away, he heard a voice calling his name.

CHAPTER 25

Sita and the Sky

Sitting at the mouth of the cave, I kept my senses on full alert. I felt every foot-step Rama took on the Earth, measuring his strength and well-being through the pressure of the imprints he made. I could have helped him. The dilemma of who I truly was presented itself to me with full force when I was least interested in consid-ering it. Why had I not shared my nature with Rama? I thought he understood me, but he had sent me to safety. This told me he did not trust my abilities. Perhaps he would have sent me away regardless, I reasoned, rather than trusting something as unpredictable as nature's assault. But I sat there, prepared to brew up thunder and rain, earthquakes and forest fires, to protect Rama as he faced an army of monsters. And yet, as I observed the battle through the vibrations of the wind, the pressure on the Earth, and the fire burning in Rama's soul, I knew he did not need my help. I began to relax, though I stayed at the mouth of the cave. The darkness and close quarters struck me as too intimate with Lakshmana there. He does not have a small energy field. I could feel his presence keenly even as he sat quiet at the back of the cave.

I thought about Shurpanakha, wondering where she was. I thought I heard her scream, she who stood in the center of all this, the catalyst of everything that was to come. I thought about her mutilation—but before that, the feelings she had provoked in me. At first, compassion. Though her flirtatious act was full of confidence, the loneliness seeped from her pores. But when I saw she was serious about taking Rama from me, my goodwill evaporated. My womanly possessiveness took over. Rama was *mine*. I have never doubted Rama's vow to love only me, yet the awakening of my claim to him was unstoppable. The feeling fascinated me, for I had never felt it before. No one had, after all, ever openly dared question my exclusive right to Rama. My closest rival is Lakshmana, whose brotherly love I can never begrudge. Jealousy felt to me like I was shrinking in my place and Shurpanakha growing. The voice of jealousy began to whisper that perhaps Rama had always fancied running off with a shape-shifting blood-drinker. I quietly laughed at that thought. It was too preposterous. But the voice continued whispering, and I got the sense that sooner or later it would find the right chord to pluck. The goddess who invented jealousy certainly knew what she was doing.

The moment that Lakshmana raised his sword and cut off her nose and ears remains fixed in my mind. It happened so quickly, I could not have intervened even if I'd wanted to. Did I want to stop it? Or did I feel she got what she deserved when Lakshmana intercepted her trajectory toward me? Her scream of horror and humiliation rings in my ears to this day. I cannot, no matter what the crime is, stand to see anyone tortured.

What would I then have done with Shurpanakha, who certainly had flown into a rage that was beyond reasoning? Certainly she would have sunk her claws into me and devoured me on the spot. There is no doubt about that. I can speak dispassionately about it now—the relationship between the two of us being deeper. I would have sent her into the Earth, where she would have been both imprisoned and cleansed. Only then would I have looked into her eyes to reach her soul. But Shurpanakha's fate was not in my hands then. Had it been, the entire story would have unraveled so differently . . . and so I cannot say either that Lakshmana's swift decision was wrong. That is how most stories are, after all. In everything good, the seed of bad exists; in everything bad, the promise of goodness to come vibrates.

In the cave, I heard Lakshmana stir and sigh. For a brief moment I considered sharing my thoughts with him. But I knew it would not blossom into a two-way conversation. So I focused on listening to Rama's presence out there. When I heard the final twang of Rama's bow, I counted the seconds and waited. When enough seconds, in my estimation, had gone by, I crouched and began to crawl out.

My left hand tugged me back. I looked down and saw it wrapped in golden silk. I quickly unknotted the end of my garment, which I had been working around my fingers. Fastening the silken cloth around my waist, I crawled out of the cave.

Coming up behind me, Lakshmana protested, but I was already halfway out. I ignored Lakshmana's admonition to wait. I needed to get out of the black cave and find my way to Rama. Lakshmana muttered to himself. He clearly thought I was taking advantage of his protection, risking both of our lives by going against Rama's orders.

"It's so quiet now," I pointed out as I straightened up, standing again under the sky.

I didn't add what I knew, that the Earth was sighing in relief that it was over and was drinking the blood that flowed from the dead. The dark of night had set in. I was barely aware of any difference between the darkness here and the one in the cave. My eyes had adjusted, and I could see the bark on the trees and the roots that protruded from the Earth.

"Rama told us to wait here until his signal," Lakshmana said in a firm tone.

His brother was his king. He would follow his brother's order if it meant sitting in that cave the rest of our lives. I, on the other hand, could not bear to sit there for another moment. All I could feel in Lakshmana's presence was his veiled heart, the way I was shut out from it. He never, ever allowed me to see his true feelings, and this made me uneasy around him, as if a secret stood between us. After ten years together, the silence between us had only grown. I trusted Lakshmana with my life, but not with my heart. In barring me from his, we had lost the opportunity to be actual friends. Although my heart was not closed to Lakshmana, it found no sustenance in our connection. The flower of love between us was there only because we both loved Rama. I had no idea what Lakshmana's thoughts were regarding our relationship. How could I? He was determined not to share his true feelings or thoughts with me. That's why we could not coexist without Rama. He was our fort, the one who knew us both. Without Rama, Lakshmana and I were like two creatures in a vast ocean, living in the same environment but as disconnected as two sea anemones.

I breathed in the pleasing night air. It felt so freeing to be out of the cave. With my ears alert to any sound of Rama, I began to move in the direction I thought he would be in.

"Where are you going?" Lakshmana asked.

He still appeared incredulous that I dared disobey Rama's orders. But I did not think of it that way. Rama wasn't my king but my heart. I needed to see him.

"I need to make sure that he has been victorious," I said as I kept walking.

"And if he isn't?" Lakshmana demanded behind me. "What would you do?"

I turned to Lakshmana, looking into his face, seeing only the night's shadows. He wanted me to acknowledge that I was merely a helpless woman in need of constant protection. He wanted me to stay in the cave with him until Rama returned to us. If I was the Sita I had been ten years earlier, I would have cowered and agreed.

And so I have great compassion for women who are surrounded by men who wish them to remain helpless. Every person, man or woman, will harken to the limits that are placed upon them. Eventually the bold will break free, as I did.

For it required great courage for me to believe that I was not an ordinary woman but a goddess with unimaginable power. What could I say to Lakshmana?

I wanted to send a shower of rain upon his head, rumble the Earth under his feet, send him flying back to Ayodhya into my sister's arms, but . . . I saw in the firm set of his jaw that he would never attribute any such phenomenon to me. When Ravana's spirit had accosted me and nature rose to my aid, my protectors had not even suspected that I had conjured any of the outbursts, even though I was at the center of it. Not until I did something drastic, like walk into a fire willingly, would Lakshmana know me for what I was.

Therefore I chose the most rational course a woman can take. I appealed to his intelligence. "It's over, Lakshmana," I reasoned. "Listen to the forest. . . . It's returning to its harmonious state. The horrific battle sounds have quieted down. Rama's bow has been silent for a while now. We need to find him, to make sure he does not lie wounded, unable to come to us."

He moved rigidly behind me and didn't overtake me to lead the way, as he usually would have. *This will be on you*, he seemed to say. *So be it.*

After being held up in the cave for hours, I looked at the sky: expansive and never-ending. It was dark but bright with stars. The very sky seemed to reach into me and unfurl all my tight muscles and nerves. Just those few hours confined had curbed my nature. I would not thrive when restricted or imprisoned.

"And you never can be," the sky assured me, speaking in that way I had grown accustomed to. It came from deep within me, yet as clear and distinct as a real voice. "Your nature is like mine, spacious, expansive. Come dance on the stars."

Closing my eyes, I felt my oneness with the limitless space. Its darkness was my hair and the stars were the delicate white jasmine buds I sprinkled in my locks. The Earth, the moon, the stars, were all contained within me.

From this expansive state, I looked down upon Rama, seeing him surrounded by bright sparks, the dancing souls freed from their embodied existence, liberated by Rama's touch. I saw Shurpanakha rushing with the speed of light to another creature like her, someone unknown to me, whom she called Marichi. She spoke urgently to him, pointing him in our direction. I saw my father sitting alone in the garden of Mithila, by my favorite lotus pond. I saw Kaikeyi galloping on a horse, her hair flying behind her. I saw Rama's mother at her altar, praying for our return. I saw two armies marching at each other, fighting over a border only they could see; they would never accept that the Earth could not belong to them. And I saw Shurpanakha fly across the southernmost ocean to a golden island. There she spoke to someone hidden from my view. The sky had no access; the air was entirely different in that place. I was rebuffed so sharply from the golden island I was flung from the sky and back into my body.

I tripped over a root in my path, stubbing my toe and stumbling forward. Lakshmana hurried to my side, but I caught myself on a branch. My spirit might be as expansive as the sky, but down here on Earth I was limited to the human form of a woman. The irony of it struck me on several levels, for the word for woman is *stri*, which means expansive. I marveled at everything I had seen, everything I now knew. The strangest discovery was this: There was a place on Earth where the elements did not have dominion, a place so alien, even the sky could not enter.

To test my strength, I kept my hand on the tree and reached into the sky. Again I became one with it, wrapping around the Earth, seeing everything there was to see, knowing everything there was to know. But because my heart was still Sita's, I actively sought my sister, whom the sky had not found. Aided now by the wind, I scanned all of Ayodhya, seeing Bharata in a simple dwelling outside the city walls, supine on the floor, his body lean, his eyes haunted. I sent a purifying wind through his quarters, lifting his spirits, and then sought onward. All this took less than a second, for Lakshmana had not yet become restless by my side, where I stood as Sita. My awareness of Lakshmana brought me closer to Urmila, for the two were interlocked in my mind. I saw her then, submerged under the water in the river Sarayu, holding her breath so long, I was afraid she had drowned. I reached into my powers of the Earth and pushed against the bottom of the river, ejecting her gently from the water onto the riverbank. I didn't know if I had saved her or startled her; her utter surprise was all I managed to see, and then I was back in my body as Sita again.

The wind blew through my hair, and Lakshmana looked at me with a worried expression, as though he feared I would faint. Never mind that I had not fainted once during the exile.

Without meaning to, I blurted out, "Urmila dwindles without you!"

He turned away so fast I could glimpse nothing on his face. So that's where it stood between us—a giant, insurmountable wall. At least I felt certain that both of us had written "Rama, Rama, Rama" on each of our sides. I called for Rama then, and let my feet lead me toward the spot where the sky had seen him. As I looked up into the vast expanse, the night above us started shimmering, creating waves of light as the souls left this world for the next.

I have powers that I was only beginning to understand then, but I do not have *that* power, to release a soul from the bondage of birth and death. For death does not guarantee liberation. It means another birth, another body. I know this as clearly as I know that the Earth is surrounded by the omniscience of the sky. Neither I nor the sky can break the bondage of a soul. But Rama can, and therefore even his violence is a blessing.

CHAPTER 26

The Thirteenth Year

The sound of Sita's voice in the distance woke Rama from his trance. He did not want her to see this. He was covered in blood. The ground was muddy with it, as the Earth drank the frothy liquid. He didn't even want to glance across the ocean of dead bodies again. He couldn't imagine what this would look like in Sita's eyes. Why had Sita and Lakshmana left their hiding place? Hadn't he strictly told them to wait until he called them?

Rama turned around and retraced his steps toward the waterfall. Here there was little change. Victory or defeat, the water cascaded ferociously. Without bothering to take his weapons off, Rama stepped under the waterfall. It pounded onto his head and shoulders, kneading into his flesh, ripping into his wounds. Bala and Atibala had protected him and healed him from life-threatening injuries, but his mortal frame was still bruised and bleeding. He made sure all traces of battle were washed off. The deepest of his gashes continued to produce fresh blood. This was the best he could do. He couldn't let Sita come near this site of the massacre.

Refreshed, he began to sprint toward Sita's anxious voice. His brother's voice was conspicuously absent next to Sita's call, but Rama knew Lakshmana was at her side. *Lakshmana knows I was victorious*, Rama thought with satisfaction. Lakshmana would never let Sita out of his sight.

Rama continued sprinting easily. There was no danger now in the forest. Even the most predatory animal was in hiding; the others were dead. A few paces from Panchavati, but miles from the massacre, Rama saw the reason for his existence: Sita.

It was like seeing her for the first time. *My princess. My beloved. My life.*

He couldn't take his eyes from her. Lakshmana was right there too, he knew, but Sita was all he could see: her shining eyes swelling with passion, serene and pristine, innocent and pure.

Sita threw her arms around Rama so fiercely, he winced. Sita dropped her arms at once, but not before Rama's blood was smeared across her arms and chest. Several of his wounds reopened, fresh blood seeping out. They looked into each other's eyes intently.

"You are alive!" she cried, tears streaming down her cheeks.

Lakshmana kept a purposeful distance. It was the lovers' moment to reunite.

"I told you to stay in the cave until I returned," Rama said, but the admonition was halfhearted. He broke his eyes away from Sita to look at Lakshmana briefly.

"I couldn't stop her from leaving the cave," Lakshmana explained sheepishly. "And it had been silent for at least ten minutes. I heard your bow twang until the end, so I knew you were victorious. I thought it would be safe."

Rama locked eyes with Lakshmana. Yes, it was safe now. There would be no more fights in Panchavati. Rama reached out for Sita. She settled herself gingerly under his arm. Lakshmana wrapped Rama's other arm around his shoulder.

"I'm fine," Rama protested. Hadn't he just been sprinting vigorously toward them?

"We are just so happy to see you again," Lakshmana murmured, but didn't release Rama's hand.

Sita was quiet, staying as close to Rama as was humanly possible, her cheek pressed into his heart. Her salty tears stung the scratches on Rama's chest. Rama's arm was tightly wrapped around her waist, his other arm secured around Lakshmana's shoulder. Huddled together like this, the trio started walking slowly toward their home in Panchavati.

"How are your arms, Lakshmana?" Rama asked, looking for the scratches from Shurpanakha's venomous nails.

He would have to tell Lakshmana that Shurpanakha had been the only survivor of the massacre. That he had hesitated, just as Lakshmana had, when it came to the deadly shot, allowing the she-demon to escape.

"You are wounded from head to toe from a ferocious battle," Lakshmana exclaimed, "and you ask me about these trivial scratches!"

He held out his right arm for Rama to see how puny the four lines across his forearm were. But even in the dark, Rama could see they were red and inflamed, turning a dark shade around the serrated edges of Lakshmana's skin.

"You will need to take care of that soon, Lakshmana. Looks like the poison from her nails is doing its best to take your arm off."

"Looks like you'll have two sick patients on your hands, Sita," Lakshmana said.

Though Lakshmana said it jokingly, Sita of course responded seriously.

"We have turmeric root. Saffron stalks, cloves, mint leaves. I will need fresh aloe to reduce swelling. . . ."

"Tomorrow," Rama said.

He was growing heavier in Lakshmana's arms, leaning into his brother. The surge of power from the battle was gone. Rama began to feel his arms aching, the cut on his forehead, and the blood seeping from his larger wounds. A wave of fatigue hit him. He could not take another step.

"Almost there," Lakshmana coaxed.

He could carry Rama if need be. He would have to sling his brother over his shoulder. Sita did her best to prop up Rama on her side, wrapping his arm across her slender shoulders. When they stepped over the threshold and into their cottage, Rama slumped into their arms, becoming a dead weight. His eyes were closed, his body limp.

They maneuvered his substantial form onto the black pelts on the ground. He collapsed onto their sleeping place, lying on his back with his arms and legs splayed. He was as still and unresponsive as a corpse. Yet he was aware that Sita pressed her hand against his heart. The strong pulse calmed her. Together, Lakshmana and Sita removed Rama's chain mail and the rest of his armor.

Moving quietly in the dark, Sita found several chunks of turmeric root and, with two rocks serving as mortar and pestle, she crushed the orange root into a pulp. She gathered the pulp in her hands and applied it to every part of Rama's wounded body. She packed the turmeric compactly into the deepest wounds, covering them completely. The antiseptic root would stop the bleeding, clean the wounds, and quicken his healing.

She then covered Lakshmana's forearms in the paste too.

Soon, the two of them collapsed by Rama's side, escaping into the world of dreams, where Rama was waiting.

The next morning, Sita's affection was boundless. She fluttered around Rama like a butterfly around a flower. He sat up and stretched his bruised arms. There was nothing unbearably painful anywhere. The turmeric paste was dry and caked across his wounds, yellow streaks across purple bruises on his green skin.

"I'm a rainbow," he said.

"Don't move," Sita cautioned.

She had several mixtures of medicinal herbs prepared. She applied fragrant sandalwood pulp to cool his arms. The goo from the aloe plant went onto any swelling bruises. Finally, she made him drink water boiled with saffron to reduce fever and inflammation. Rama was amused and let Sita nurse him. Even when Rama was smeared with all sorts of herbs and there was nothing more to do, Sita didn't leave his side, even for a moment.

The sun reached its midpoint in the sky, and Rama felt the glory of the victory take hold of him. He had cleaned up the jungle once and for all. The forest was a safe place once again!

"Sita, look at the sun blazing in the sky. Panchavati is safe. The enemy is vanquished. I must thank Agastya after all and bow to his ancient wisdom. Our thirteenth year is coming to completion. I feel as though I have finally accomplished what I was meant to do in this forest, and you are by my side, my princess. Let's celebrate!"

Before Sita could protest, Rama bounded up, pulling her with him. Sita's face lit up when she saw his festive mood. He didn't give her time to consider what he was about to do. If he let her concern for his healing get the upper hand, she might confine him to bed rest. Rama had accomplished something superhuman, and the cells in his entire body pulsated with this knowledge.

"Don't wait up for us, my brother," he called to Lakshmana as they hurried past him. "Like Kinnaras, Sita and I will roam the forest like Gandharvas and Apsaras. They will be astounded by our joy today! Our happiness in being free and alive!"

Lakshmana watched the two lovers take off. Now the day belonged to Sita, the true recipient of Rama's wellspring of eternal love.

Sita and Rama ran with the breeze, for the joy of it.

"Today I'm faster than you," Sita teased.

The wind changed direction and there was a rotten smell in the air. Smoothly, Rama turned Sita away from those stinking dead bodies. They were already polluting the air as they decomposed. He hadn't fought far away enough from Panchavati! For a moment, Rama considered what that scene would look like today, the odor unbearable at the site itself. The blazing sun would cook the putrid meat.

Sita's laughing voice brought him back, the scene of the massacre gone.

"Can't we go on the magical path?" Sita wondered aloud.

She meant the route they usually took that began with the cluster of vines that allowed Rama to catch hold of her and swing them high up into the air. This led them to the majestic waterfall that had millions of tiny rainbows reflecting off the mist. They could bathe in the cool water and watch the sun's marvelous rays color the water golden. The sprays from the gushing fall would transform from water to diamonds dropping from the sky.

"I'm sorry, my princess. It doesn't exist any longer."

Of course, the waterfall stood intact, with its abundance of rainbows reflecting off it, but the water in the pool was pink with blood, with piles of hideous corpses scattered around it. That terrain had been completely demolished. It would take years for the forest to recover. Deftly, Rama guided Sita elsewhere, exploring the opposite side of Panchavati.

Now the forest was their friend, the animals their playmates. With the entire battalion of blood-drinkers destroyed, they were at complete peace. Flocks of birds sang songs above them and a gentle breeze flowed through the trees; the feeling of danger was a distant memory. All that mattered today was Sita. All that mattered was Rama.

With no worries in the world, Rama picked berries from a bush, feeding Sita and himself.

"Look, Rama." Sita held out her palm to show the red juice of the berry that had burst open in her hand.

It was a deep maroon color, similar to the henna the women of Ayodhya used when painting decorative patterns on their hands and feet.

"Let me see," Rama said, picking a berry and looking at it.

He held her hand in his and used the berry to trace a pattern on her palm. When the berry ran out of juice, he picked another one and continued. Becoming absorbed in the beautiful patterns, they sat down together, knee to knee.

When her hand was brimming with swirls, dots, and patterns, Rama picked up her other hand and began filling it up too. Every so often, Rama held still, tightening his grip on her hand, and just listened. It was by now instinctual, a habit he could not stop. Slowing down his other senses, his hearing sharpened and scanned the area around them, anticipating any change in the soundscape. Rama heard a flock of parrots bantering loudly; a few boars grunted, their tusks and snouts nuzzling into the ground. Feeling assured, he returned his attention to Sita's hands.

"I didn't know you were so good at this," Sita said with awe, studying her right hand, admiring it from different angles.

"Didn't you know that I'm good at everything I do?"

Sita raised her eyebrows in mock surprise. "Oh, and I thought that humility was your foremost quality!"

Rama looked up at her and carelessly squashed a berry against the palm of her hand.

Simultaneously, he popped one into his mouth. Both berries burst open, splattering their maroon liquid on her hand and his lips. But when Sita looked down from Rama's red lips onto her hand, the red liquid seemed to have fallen into all the right places. The elaborate design looked, if possible, more stunning.

She sighed. "I will not want to wash my hands for days. Look at this." She held up her hands side by side. "It's astonishing; a work of art."

Together, they admired Rama's handiwork. Rama half smiled at first, but the more he looked at the swirls of red, they took on the shape of something else he'd recently seen, rivulets of blood that he had extracted with great precision. Without thinking, he took the remaining berries and dropped them into Sita's open palms and pressed his large callused hand around her delicate hands.

"Rama—no!" she protested.

The juice from the berries seeped through her fingers onto Rama's. Sita was dismayed and opened her palms to see the designs gone. Both of their hands were stained various shades of red and pink.

"The decorations that you drew on my palms," Sita finally said, "reminded me of the palaces in Ayodhya. But now, this abundance of red on our hands reminds me of the forest."

"I don't understand," Rama said.

She could not be thinking of the massacre, as he was, but she too was seeing something more than red swirls of berry juice on their hands.

"The palace is beautiful, organized, and decorated in a precise and intricate manner. Like the patterns you made on my hands. Everything in the palace follows these structures and expectations of beauty. Flowers and trees are planted in well-planned rows and patterns. The forest, on the other hand, is wild and unpredictable in its beauty, kind of like our palms right now."

She opened Rama's palms and held her own next to them. There was no pattern, nothing expected in the way the shades of red varied, from deep maroon to light pink, interacting with Rama's green skin in one way and Sita's cream skin in another.

"I see what you mean," Rama said. And then: "Didn't I tell you I'm amazing at everything I do?"

"Oh! You're hopeless!" Sita exclaimed, pushing his hands away.

"Hopelessly in love, my princess."

Rama reached out for her hands again and pulled her into his arms. They were not the only ones celebrating. The whole forest seemed to be buzzing with new life. Bees hummed around fragrant flowers. A wealth of butterflies fluttered about. Elephants trumpeted in the distance. Flocks of birds flew high and low.

A beautiful sunset tinted the forest orange and pink. Sita and Rama sauntered into the enchanted night without a destination, guided only by the rays of the rising moon. Sita's hair came loose and draped around her body like the night sky around the moon. With every step she took, her hair danced around her in soft, swirly motions. Absentmindedly, she plucked a flower and secured it behind her ear.

By the time they came to the bank of the river, to a place they had not been before, the full moon was glowing in the cloudless sky. In their hearts, ancient memories stirred, but they could not have been put into words.

Rama freed himself from his weapons and took Sita's hand. Together, they swam in the river, like so many times before. But this night was enchanted. The moon's rays reflected on the ripples of water as far as Rama could see. The water was golden, and aside from a lone deer lapping water, the two of them were alone. Underwater, Sita's golden cloth swirled around her, like shimmering fins.

When Rama came up for air, he saw several elephants approaching the river. Rama recognized the old matriarch, and dove down to the bottom of the river, grabbing handfuls of mud. Carefully, he approached the elephants on the shore, holding up the mud toward the matriarch. She swung her trunk back and forth and eyed Rama. Finally, she nuzzled his chin, her trunk going around his neck. He rubbed the mud into her tough skin. She kneeled and allowed Sita to climb on top of her; with bronze eyes, she beheld Rama steadily as they scrubbed her ears and trunk. When she was covered in mud, Rama did not hesitate but gently pulled her trunk, guiding her into the water. Like a queen, Sita remained on the elephant's back. The matriarch sprayed them both with water, and they splashed her back, cleaning the mud. Sita laughed often, and Rama's heart throbbed with joy. After some time, the elephant blessed them, touching her trunk to the top of their heads. She ambled off with her flock.

Like dolphins, Sita and Rama sported in the water, swimming and singing to each other, throwing crystals of water at each other. When Sita emerged from the water, the droplets of water on her body made her sparkle in the moonlight. Small rivers ran down her back and legs from the locks of her hair. The rays from the distant moon outlined every part of her: her strong shoulders, slender waist, and ample curves. Rama was surrounded by a soft glow that emanated from his own body. Sita put her hand on her heart, and she stood in front of Rama, gazing up at him.

Sita's large lotus-shaped eyes were dark with immense depth and power. Putting his lips to her ear, he whispered an ancient hymn, and Sita sank to the ground with her eyes closed. And though they remained an arm's distance apart, the words of love eternal seeped into their very pores. She was not Sita in those moments, nor was he Rama, but the eternal lover and beloved. Their union went beyond body, beyond words, beyond anything imaginable in the human realm.

The few animals that happened to be there would see only two glowing people sitting, gazing at each other silently, intently. The ancient ode to love flowed between them:

> *You are the center of my universe. Everything revolves around you. Without you, I cannot go on. My body may breathe, my eyes may see, but breathing and seeing will be a burden, every breath a duty, for you are the breath of my body, the reason for my sight. Having once set eyes on you, there is nothing more for me to see. Given a choice between any heavenly delight, I would choose to be in your company. Given a choice to hear any celestial music, I would choose to hear the sound of your laughter. You are the center of my universe, the soul of my being. Without you, I cannot go on.*

It was neither Rama serenading Sita, nor Sita declaring her love to Rama. The words flowed between them, and the poem caressed the air around them, flowing from Sita to Rama, Rama to Sita. Sita Rama. Sita Rama.

The glistening water itself seemed to listen and swell with emotion, whirlpools appearing out of nowhere. The flowers exuded honey, and the tree branches intertwined with one another.

Hand in hand, Sita and Rama strolled through the night, the silence between them thick with love. The air around them vibrated with energy, and the two of them glowed like the moon. At the same time, their love was like the sun spreading its light far and wide.

Never had any lovers been as happy and content as they were with each other.

Lakshmana Breaks

The days passed by quickly; Lakshmana could hardly believe that the thirteenth year was coming to its end. The exile would soon be over. It was also hard to believe that Dandaka was free from the menacing blood-drinkers. Lakshmana had seen the decomposing bodies for himself while inspecting the area. Scattered across Janasthan, the carcasses were crawling with maggots, and scavengers of all kinds were cleaning up the horror. Lakshmana commended Rama's foresight in leading the inimical forces away from Panchavati. Living too close to the site of battle would have been impossible; the stench had been unbearable.

There had been no sign of Shurpanakha or anyone else from her clan, and the forest and its animals had returned to a peaceful state. Lakshmana hoped it would stay like that for all time. Springtime was all around them as they greeted their final year in exile, just weeks after the dreadful yet glorious battle.

Lakshmana was carefully twining rope for bowstrings when a glimmer of gold caught his eyes. He looked up to see a most stunning and beautiful creature: a golden deer. It was the daintiest deer Lakshmana had ever seen, with large dark eyes. Its hide was shimmering with shades of gold and it was covered in glowing flecks, all the colors of the rainbow. The golden deer seemed to blend in perfectly with the spring ambience, like another blossoming bud. Waving its little fluffy golden tail, the deer emanated innocence. This naturally made Lakshmana suspicious at once. Quickly getting over his initial astonishment, Lakshmana grew certain that no animal of the forest could look like that. That was a shape-shifter for sure. Which meant it was a blood-drinker. Not even those innocent lotus eyes could fool him.

To confirm his suspicion, Lakshmana looked around and noted that all the other animals were gone. Sensing the trickery, all the other animals kept their distance from this golden intruder. The more he looked at it, Lakshmana was actually surprised that a blood-drinker would take such an obviously unreal form. He decided to ignore it and went back to twisting new bowstrings for himself and Rama. These promised to be strong and long-lasting.

But soon he noticed that Sita was playing with the golden charmer. He should have expected this. She loved deer above all other animals. He set his work aside for a moment, wondering if he should warn her. He noticed that Rama was watching too, in amusement, a golden princess and a golden deer, creating their own dance of distance and closeness. Whenever the princess got too close, the golden deer jumped away nervously. Once, when Sita was perfectly still and patient, the creature came up and licked her on the nose with its small pink tongue. Sita clapped her hands together in joy. It was clear that she was completely enamored of the deer and couldn't see past its charming appearance.

Lakshmana stood up, deciding to share his suspicion with Rama, but Sita called to Rama first.

"Rama," she said breathlessly, "do you see this little deer? Have you ever seen anything as charming as this? It kissed me on the nose!"

"I saw that," Rama said, smiling.

Lakshmana gagged silently. Kissed by a stinking blood-drinker!

"Rama, I have never seen anything like this. I could bring him back home with us. He will fit so perfectly into the palace." Sita's eyes shone bright.

Rama seemed pulled into Sita's enthusiasm. "You should definitely bring one of your pet deer back home with us."

"Sita," Lakshmana said, walking up to them. "You must give up your attachment to that creature."

"Why?" Sita asked.

"It's a demon in disguise."

"No!"

"Look how all your other friends avoid it."

As they looked over, the golden deer was innocently nuzzling the grass a few feet away from two other deer. The blood-drinker had anticipated their scrutiny; it was playing its game well. Lakshmana only felt surer, but Sita was less convinced.

"It is far too perfect to be a natural occurrence," Lakshmana said.

Rama asked, "Even if it is a blood-drinker in disguise, Lakshmana, how could it harm us?"

"Better to shoot it here and now," Lakshmana advised.

"No, no, no!" Sita interjected, her large eyes widening.

She pulled Rama's arm, looking at him imploringly.

Rama regarded Lakshmana severely and said, "Sita has not asked anything of me or you in thirteen years. She has made no requests until now."

Lakshmana cast his eyes down. It would turn on them and sink its fangs into Sita's neck. He was sure of it. How could he convince them?

"Let us catch it, then, and examine it," Lakshmana suggested.

When they scrutinized it closer, both Rama and Sita would see it for what it was. Lakshmana joined Rama and Sita as they surrounded the golden deer, aiming to trap it. Sometimes it let them get so close that they could run their fingers against its shimmering hide. Sita cooed at it, speaking sweat endearments, but always the creature skipped out of their reach. Lakshmana could have sworn he caught one of its hooves, but either it slipped out or shrank in his hand. He couldn't tell.

"It's getting frightened of us," Sita said. "I'm afraid it might run away and never return."

Now only two golden ears and a small nose peeked from behind a bush.

"It's going to disappear," Sita said. There was a catch in her throat.

Lakshmana recalled Mila and Lali, and the many other deer Sita had loved over the years. A chill gripped his heart. If this trick was aimed at Sita, it had been tailored to aim at her weak spot.

"Let me go catch it," Lakshmana said, eager to end the game.

"No," Rama said, "I want to do this for Sita. In all our years in the forest, she has not asked me for anything."

He looked at Sita fondly. "I won't be long."

As he spoke, Rama picked up his quiver and bow. Rama touched his fingers to Sita's cheek for a moment and then turned to Lakshmana.

"Don't let Sita out of your sight for a moment. I'm leaving her in your protection. In case it is as you suspect, be extra vigilant. We know how deceptive and manipulative these creatures can be. Stay with her at any cost."

"I understand, my brother. I will keep her safe. I promise."

How many times had he safeguarded Sita? This time would be no different.

As Rama headed out, Lakshmana walked next to him, saying quietly, "Rama, mark my words. If it proves hard to catch, shoot it. If it really is a deer, at least Sita can have its hide."

Rama nodded; he half heard. As if the golden deer had understood their every word, it stood at the edge of the clearing, waiting for Rama. As soon as Rama was within arm's reach, it bounded off—a streak of gold and a shimmer of colors. Sita sighed, completely charmed.

The golden fawn was gone, and Rama disappeared after it.

Half an hour passed, and Lakshmana began to pace back and forth. What was taking Rama so long? Sita sat still.

When more than an hour had passed, she asked, "Should we be worried?"

Lakshmana laughed. "We should never worry about Rama."

"I mean it, Lakshmana. He said it wouldn't take long. You are pacing. The deer was small, easy for Rama to catch. I didn't expect it to take this long."

Lakshmana stopped pacing and sat down. He wasn't worried, but he felt edgy. "Things are not what they appear to be in the forest, Sita. Remember that."

Sita turned away. Though she knew the demons could be vicious, she didn't want to believe that the enchanting deer was a hoax.

"There are also plenty of magical and mystical things here," she reminded him. "Things we had never imagined and never knew to be real."

Lakshmana couldn't argue with that. Still, he knew this was different. The golden deer was a blood-drinker in disguise, and he had an uncanny feeling they were playing along to its plan all too perfectly. Why didn't Rama simply kill it and end the game? He had to be chasing it with the hope of bringing it back alive.

Suddenly, the forest shook with a piercing scream: "Sita! Sita! Sita!"

Sita looked up at once, alarmed. "Rama's voice."

"No, it wasn't," Lakshmana replied firmly, dismissing the replica of Rama's voice as false.

He had seen something like this coming from a mile away. He wasn't sure what the blood-drinker wanted. Perhaps there was no plan. They were up to their usual tricks; that was clear. Lakshmana knew Rama would appear any moment, laughing, telling them another crazy blood-drinker story.

As Rama's voice echoed through the trees, Lakshmana became more determined to stay calm. He would not be pulled in by the blood-drinker's scheme. But Lakshmana had not anticipated Sita's reaction.

"But it *is*!" Sita stood up, hands trembling. "It is Rama's voice. He is calling for me."

"It sounded like Rama, but just think clearly for a moment. When has Rama ever needed to call out for help? He is invincible. Believe me. This confirms that there is trickery afoot in the forest. They are playing games with us. We cannot play along."

Sita was breathing in short, shallow gasps, tears spilling over her eyes.

Then, another call: "Lakshmana!"

The desperation in Rama's voice made Lakshmana's skin tighten with goose bumps.

"Lakshmana!" Sita echoed, turning to him. "He is calling for you! Go to him!"

"Sita," he said again, "it simply is not Rama's real voice. It's a trick."

"Please. Please. Please," Sita choked out between panicked breaths. "He might already be . . ." She couldn't say the word. Stricken, she covered her face, unwilling to imagine the worst.

"Sita, don't worry like this, please," Lakshmana said. "There is nothing out there that can touch Rama."

He didn't attempt to convince her again, it was so clear to him. But the more resistant Lakshmana became, the fiercer Sita's reaction. While Lakshmana felt he was demonstrating how completely he trusted Rama's ability, Sita did not at all understand his complacence. And he did not understand her panic. Did she not have more faith in Rama?

Sita turned her eyes on Lakshmana with a look he could not decipher, but he did not like it. She started backing away and then turned and ran. She darted out from their ashram, tracing Rama's steps. Her intention was clear. If Lakshmana wouldn't go to Rama's aid, she would.

Lakshmana caught up with her easily, blocking her path.

Her eyes smoldered with anger, tears shooting out like missiles.

"What are you doing?" Lakshmana demanded, truly bewildered. What did she hope to do by running out into the forest alone, unprotected, without even a knife or weapon in her hand?

"Get out of my way," Sita replied through clenched teeth, while she tried to dodge Lakshmana and get around him. Her movements were urgent.

Lakshmana was not prepared for her hostility. His mind reeled.

He tried to reason with her again. "Sita, I felt the hair on my neck rise too when I first heard the plea for help. It was a very good imitation of Rama's voice. But I know they can do that. They are expert at these mind tricks. You must steel yourself. Take shelter in your trust for Rama."

She didn't hear him. She struggled against Lakshmana, trying to push him out of her way.

"Let me go!" she cried. "I must go to him."

"Sita, calm yourself, please."

"How can I be calm when Rama is in danger?" she demanded, looking up at Lakshmana, with red eyes. "How can you be so calm? Rama is calling for our help!"

"Because I know it's a trick, Sita!" Lakshmana cried. After taking a deep breath, he continued. "Rama told me to stay here with you. He told me to guard you and not leave you for a moment. You heard him, Sita. Those are Rama's orders. Please trust me."

Sita cried into her hands. Her whole body shook.

Lakshmana had never ever seen Sita like this. Of course, Rama had never apparently been in danger like this before. He had never called for help before—all the more proof to Lakshmana that it was all false. Still, he didn't know how to soothe or convince Sita.

"Come," he said, "let's go back. Rama will come soon."

He gently held her arm to lead her home. Sita looked down at his hand and then snarled at it, as if she was a lioness and his hand a snake.

"Don't touch me! Don't you dare touch me." A terrible look was in her eyes.

Lakshmana dropped his hand and backed away from her.

"You are the worst of our enemies," Sita said. "All these years, I took you for a loyal friend and brother. I didn't mind your secrets. Now I see what a snake you are! You left Urmila willingly because you never loved her. You have waited for this day to come. You have waited for this moment so that you can claim me for yourself!"

Lakshmana felt like a hot iron rod had impaled his heart. The burning heat spread in his chest like venom. Her words were so false, but Lakshmana could hardly defend himself. For the first time, Lakshmana felt a deep compassion for Bharata, who had also been wrongfully accused and judged.

"The reason you never say my sister's name is because you do not love her!" Sita continued. "You do not love her and yearn for her, the way Rama does for me. You have waited for this moment to get me to yourself. Why else have you followed us so persistently? Why else do you never cry out my sister's name in your sleep? Why else do you never let me out of your sight, while hiding your heart from Rama and me?"

Despite the burning in his heart, Lakshmana tried to reason with Sita, but she was explosive; her accusations only grew worse. Her eyes were red, hot tears ran down her face, drenching her upper garment. It was impossible to look at her. Her beautiful face was unrecognizable. He could not bear it for another second.

Even when he covered his ears and closed his eyes, he could still feel her words ripping him apart. Staying now would be an admission. It would give credence to her words. He had to find Rama. That was the only solution. With his mind made up, Lakshmana felt some relief from Sita's relentless accusations. He pushed away Rama's order.

Without defending himself and without words of farewell, Lakshmana did what every man would do faced with an irrational woman: He turned and ran. He couldn't help but look back again and again, to make sure that she stayed where he left her. He saw her sink down on the ground, her arms covering her face.

CHAPTER 28

Sita and the Enemy

I suspected the unthinkable even before I heard Rama cry my name. You see, the very pulse of the Earth slowed, my heartbeat with it. My mind turned sluggish, as though I was trying to breathe through water. I was systematically being cut off from the connection to Earth's elements that had become intrinsic to my being. That was the beginning of the slow torture that would take me and re-form me, only to throw me back into the pits of the Earth. It was when I felt them separate from me that I came to know they had always been part of me, even during the early years when I had not acknowledged it. I felt their absence as clearly as the cold vacuum one feels when a loved one's physical touch is gone. I didn't under-stand what was happening. I reasoned that they were taking rest, tired of holding me up, exerted by sustaining our connection. That is what I told myself, though I had never experienced anything but deep resonance with them. I began to feel so drained of life, I reached out to each one of them in turn, seeking the life-giving fire, wind, water, sky, and Earth. I went to the fire first, tapping into the heat at my core, which connected me to the greater fire at the core of the Earth. The flames flickered feebly, struggling as much as I was, to just stay alive.

I gasped for air, and I could feel the wind forcefully moving into my nostrils and lungs, filling me with air. "I'm sorry," the wind whispered. I understood that it was not its choice. It was struggling to hold on to me with the same desperation I was feeling.

I didn't even try to find the water; I was dry like a desert. Instead, I flung myself up into the expanse, ready to embrace the entire Earth planet. But I went nowhere. I understood then exactly how any human would feel, trying to do magic and failing, like an utter fool for having believed it possible in the first place. My failure cruelly told me there was no such thing as sky omniscience.

I looked at Lakshmana, wondering how he had the strength to pace about. I could barely lift my arms. Whatever was happening to me was not affecting him. In my last attempt, I bowed to the Earth, pressing my forehead to her sacred soil. I felt her respond for a brief moment, a kiss on my brow, and then she too was gone. Even before I heard the scream, I suspected that Rama was no more.

The air filled with Rama's scream turned my veins to ice.

Rama was dying. That explained it all. The whole world was retreating, changing, dying, as Rama was dying. Desperately, I flung my spirit into the sky, again and again. Then I would see where Rama was; I would know beyond certainty what was happening. Only, I fell to the ground, a heavy body bereft of its use.

I turned to Lakshmana. My only hope. He could go to Rama's aid. He could reverse this terrible stagnation that weighed down every part of me. But Lakshmana refused. He refused to move. He refused to let me go. He physically restrained me, and when I saw his hands on my arm, holding me back like I was an obstinate girl and nothing more, the fire in my belly raged.

The feelings that overtook me were a thousand times stronger than when the ghost had accosted me. The Earth would have cracked into a million pieces. I could hardly breathe, I was so angry. Part of me waited for nature to respond, enacting and embodying my deepest feelings. But the Earth and sky were empty. I was alone in my heart. I was a helpless woman now, at the mercy of this man before me who laughed at my tears. And why did he laugh? More than ever, Lakshmana was an utter stranger, his every word and action shocking me. Why did he not go to Rama's aid? Why did he not show *any* concern?

I felt an intrusive energy wrap itself around me. I draped the Cloth of Essence like a screen, trying to hide from the feeling that I was being preyed upon, that someone was devouring me with their eyes. I felt sick, with no way to protect myself from the onslaught of lust that circled me . . . suffocated me. "You are mine now," the tendrils of energy told me. They were closing in from all sides. A male's energy. A male's desire for me. More powerful, more intrusive, more aggressive than any I had ever experienced.

The only man I could see here was Lakshmana, the one who had held his heart secret from me all these years. I looked at him but couldn't believe the truth that was unfolding in my heart. It couldn't be. I had never felt Lakshmana look at me that way. I had never felt uncomfortable with his touch. But today I did. Today I felt ill in his presence. His eyes held secrets that I shuddered to discover.

Now I have a deep empathy for every person who is overcome by illusion, because that is what happened to me. Something dark moved within me, something so hidden, I had not known it lurked within me. It swiftly attached itself to everything I knew and wondered about Lakshmana, and drew them all together, forming a whole that I had never before seen. It formed a conclusive answer to all the questions I'd had about him, and the most pressing question of all: Why did he refuse to go to Rama's aid?

As the suspicion gained force within me, the hungry eyes continued to grate on me. It was like being surrounded by ten of Ravana's ghost.

My implicit trust in Lakshmana vanished, and impressions from the past rose in my mind—Lakshmana gripping my hand, Lakshmana turning his eyes away when I emerged from the river half clothed, Lakshmana telling me to come closer into the cave with him— moments that had seemed innocent now took on another color in my consciousness.

"You are the worst kind of enemy," I told Lakshmana, so angry my voice quavered. "All these years, I took you for a friend and loyal brother. I didn't mind your secrets, thinking them harmless. Now I see what a snake you are!"

The tears that shot from my eyes burned my skin.

I beat my chest with a violence I never knew I possessed.

I lost touch with reality. I was prepared to kill myself. Truly told, I can no longer recall all the words I said, the threats I made. I was so far beyond reasoning that I can hardly access the memory past this point. Lakshmana was utterly unable to defend himself or remain calm in the face of my volcanic, all-encompassing rage. If anyone had told me I was capable of becoming more volatile than Lakshmana, I would have laughed. But now he could not match me. For he became angry too. My unfair words got under his skin; his face turned red, his eyes bloodshot. He could not stand my presence for another moment. He grabbed his bow and ran.

When he left, I thought I would breathe easier, the crawling eyes on my skin gone. But they weren't. I still could not breathe. The whole world was falling apart without Rama.

I couldn't stand on my feet any longer. The burden I was carrying made my heart a heavy mountain, crushing me from the inside. I crumbled to the Earth. I felt like I was burning within, and yet I was painfully cold. I was completely empty yet full to the brim. My breath came to me in small bursts. I listened for the sounds in the forest, for another call by Rama.

All I could hear was the rustling sound of leaves in the treetops. They chattered like a man's teeth in the chill of winter. Something cold and menacing was sweeping through the forest. The warmth of the Earth rose up around me like a protective shield. So I sat, lifeless, receptive to the messages carried by the wind.

I felt a dull ache in my stomach, a growing dread . . . as if I were a deer walking know-ingly into a trap. The wind caressed my cheeks, carrying away my tears. "No matter where he takes you, I will follow," the wind promised. The words made no sense. They hit me with their portentous warning. And then I remembered that there was a place on this Earth, a golden island, where even the sky could not enter.

My eyes darted back and forth. Was someone there, watching me with lecherous eyes? I felt the distinct need to cover myself, to hide from someone's invasive stare.

"Bring my beloved to me," I whispered to the wind. "Find him in the halls of death and bring him here. Find him alive! He must return to me at once!"

I felt stronger after I spoke these words, conveying my decision to believe that Rama was alive and well. He would come to my rescue, if I needed to be rescued. Truly, I couldn't believe Rama was dead. He was so alive in my heart. I just didn't know what to make of my deadened senses, the silence of everything that used to be alive around me.

"You can go anywhere within a split second," I told the wind. "Fly, as only you can do, and bid him to come at once. I fear that the enemy is near."

I thought of the golden deer I had sent my beloved to catch. The thought of it was alluring, as if it was imbued with a spell to pull me to it. I had heard the name of Rama flutter in the deer's heart, along with a tremendous amount of fear. But its heart was pure. It glowed like his glossy fur. I was still enthralled, enchanted. Lakshmana's words rose in my mind: *It's a trick.*

I prayed he was wrong. I prayed that Rama would return with the golden deer tethered to his hand. We would be reunited. The final year of the exile would be upon us, and then we would return to Ayodhya. I willed all this to be, whispering fervently to the wind. It gathered in force, brewing like a hurricane around me. For a moment I felt I might lift up from the Earth, as if the wind would carry me away. Abruptly, it stopped and was replaced by a stillness so complete I felt sure my next breath would return to me empty of air.

The breath I took was laborious, the air so thin I couldn't fill my lungs. When I beseeched the wind, I got no response. The treetops were quiet, the leaves limp. It reminded me of the moments before the massacre, when the forest and all

its animals had gone into hiding, anticipating the forceful intrusion of fourteen thousand blood-drinkers.

My breaths came rapidly now, in quick bursts. It was the only way possible to breathe in the dead air. Despite the wind's promise, it was not there with me. I did not dare to think my thoughts through to their conclusive endings. I dared not face what was ahead.

For a moment, I ceased to be Sita and melted into the Earth to rest in my mother's embrace. I could have stayed there forever. When I heard the call of an unknown voice, she withdrew from me with gentle hands, a mother disengaging herself from her child's cling-ing arms. I was alone. But no. . . . There was that voice again, demanding my attention. I was called back to the present moment, to this place where Rama was not.

I got up and saw a forest dweller, clad in bark cloth and smeared with ashes, calling to me. He was a worshipper of Shiva, the lord of destruction.

I couldn't neglect the guest at our door. Wiping my tears resolutely, I automatically picked up a jug of water. The traveler would be thirsty. It was not his fault that he had come upon us in this crisis. It was my duty to greet him.

I pushed away the feelings that vibrated within me, piercing sounds of the highest octave.

I bravely stepped toward our guest. When I had come this far, unfailing in my duties, I would not turn back. I couldn't say what made me say this to myself. He was only an innocent sage, travel-weary and in need of a few moments' respite, nothing else. But as I answered the ascetic's persistent call, with the jug of water on my hip, I whispered a few final words to the wind, my messenger: "Be my witness. Tell Rama everything you see. Send him back to me. Let him ride by your side and come to mine."

With every step, I felt I was entering a place where I would never be heard or seen again.

The unbearable sensation of being suffocated slowly grew stronger. But with my senses dull and my mind on Rama, I did not study the visitor. I served him water and greeted him as best as I could, though I looked over my shoulders every few seconds, hoping to glimpse my protectors. More than ever, I felt helpless. The sage asked me many strange questions about myself, but I did not become suspicious until he began speaking of my body.

"What is a princess with such round, perfectly shaped breasts doing with a pathetic human prince, banished from his own kingdom?"

"Who are you?" I asked then, stepping away and looking at him properly for the first time.

"Whoever you want me to be, enchanting one."

I took another step backward. I swept my golden cloth across my chest. "You should leave at once. My husband is returning at any moment."

"Is he?"

The sage laughed, now staring openly at every part of my form.

I couldn't recall being looked at in this way since the contest for my hand, when men like the king of Kashi molested me with their eyes.

"Stop this at once!" I commanded in a strong voice. "This does not befit your station. You are a renunciant. And I am a married woman, a princess, the beloved of Rama."

"If he loves you so very much, where is he now? Why has he left you alone and defenseless?"

I thought of Lakshmana and couldn't answer. I had sent away my final protector, accusing him of desiring me. I was facing someone whose desire was so overpowering, my skin crawled. I felt the threat from him clearly, as though he would pounce on me that very minute.

"Do not be afraid," he said. "I have come here to woo you."

I couldn't believe my ears. Every word he said was nonsense. "Who are you?" I demanded. "Why are you speaking to me this way?"

"I am the one you will come to love more than any other person," he said.

Slowly, he began to change form. I stared at him, mesmerized despite myself. I had never seen a being shape-shift before. Too late, I realized this fraudulent sage was drawing my energy into his transformation. The vision before me started taking on Rama's features, claiming Rama's form as his. Quickly, I closed my faculties, slashing my hand sharply through the air. The shape-shifting stopped. Still, the man before me was exceedingly handsome, looking very much like he could be one of Rama's relatives.

Terror had not yet taken hold of me. I crossed my arms over my chest and glared at him. Did he think I would be impressed by this new form? I could see his sharp eye for detail and love of finesse in the form he had taken. Besides Rama, I have never seen a man so physically perfect. An illusion, of course, but a well-crafted one. From then onward, I was careful to avoid his eyes. In them I saw something that frightened me beyond all else: genuine yearning.

Only then did I know. Lakshmana had been right. It was a trap. And I had sent us into it.

"I can become anyone you wish," he said. "This is but one of the many forms I can assume. I have become so enchanted by you, I have forgotten every other woman. I will make you my queen."

"What of *my* desire?" I said coldly. "If you truly wanted to honor me, if you cared for my desires at all, you would leave this place at once."

I looked over my shoulder, unable to stop my eyes from seeking my protectors.

"Your precious Rama will not come," he said. "He is dead."

"No!"

"You heard his death cry. Isn't that why you sent your brother-in-law to his side?"

"You were spying on us? What is the purpose of all this?"

"To win your heart, fair maiden. No other reason."

He took a step toward me. "I am Ravana, the lord of the universe, the controller of the elements. Yama, the lord of death, bows at my feet, and no one is more powerful than I. And yet, I wish to lay my heart at your feet. So powerful is the magic that you wield, goddess."

"And yet you come in stealth, a true coward! You did not even dare to face Rama, my valiant faultless husband!"

He shrugged, unmoved by my indignation. "When you have lived as long as I, you will understand. Stealth becomes more enjoyable than open warfare. Humans are so tragically willing to die. It's grown very tiresome."

"If you despise humans so much, why are you here, laying your heart at a human woman's feet?"

He licked his lips. "Let's not pretend that you are a human woman, Sita. I don't know what you are exactly, but I know you are not human."

Tears clouded my eyes. I felt less than human, utterly powerless, as every woman Ravana abducted must have felt.

"Please stop this game," I said, my voice turning soft. No success would come from challenging his power. Perhaps he had a heart of his own that I could reach. "The moment I set eyes on Rama, I belonged to him completely. Nothing can change that. Whatever desire you think you have for me is misdirected, bound to be hopeless. Guard your heart against this demon of desire. It will lead you not to success but to destruction. My heart can never be yours."

"Let me be the judge of that. I have changed the minds of the most stubborn women."

I felt a huge wave of energy press against me. Later I understood this as the power of his ten minds working together, attempting to gain entrance into my soul. I straightened my back and exhaled, pushing away his energy. It was not easy, but not so difficult either. I could see the shock in his eyes, and then the glimmer of pleasure.

"I have met a worthy woman—finally," he said. He offered me his hand. "Come now, Sita. There really is no choice here."

I grew angry. "You speak of winning my heart and robbing me of choice all in the same breath, you foul coward! You stealer of virtue! I am repulsed by you and this so-called handsome form that you stole from my very imagination."

"Clever girl," he said. "But we are running out of time. You must come with me now."

"Please, please, please," I cried, my only recourse this pathetic plea. "You will only destroy yourself if you follow through with this. Leave me here. Leave."

"Never. Now that I have seen you, I will never give up. You will be mine."

Seeing how little his disguise impressed me, he changed tactics. He grew before my eyes, sprouted heads and arms, and became the real flesh-and-blood king of the blood-drinkers. The famed scars of Vishnu were thick red streaks across his chest and neck. And yet he had lived. Truly, no one was more powerful than him. I could see all the elements trembling at the edge of his effulgence, for yes, he was radiant, as potent as the smokeless fires at the time of dissolution. My connection to the Earth was nothing compared to his powers. He was connected to the universe. His energy pervaded the cosmos. His desires and whims were the timeline all souls were subject to.

Worse, I was bound to him too. I had dreamed all my life of standing at enormous black gates, unable to gain entrance. The gatekeeper was this ten-headed monster, none other than my archenemy. I had seen him once before, in a vision from within the Earth, safe in my mother's embrace. I had stood at the gates, watching them grow small and distant. When the gates were a small speck on the horizon, the form containing the gates grew visible. With every one of his ten heads and twenty eyes, he had looked at me, only for a split second, for he was busy scanning the entire universe. I thought he had forgotten me, Bhumi's little daughter, just as I had forgotten him. But here he stood. We were destined to battle. Horror rippled through me like waves of nausea.

My abject horror must have been visible, for his temper flared and he abandoned all illusions of courtesy. My body reacted by itself, moving away from his hungry arms, and then I was running and screaming ear-splitting warnings. Branches whipped my face, arms, and legs. A monstrous laugh echoed behind me. I thought of Rani, abducted at ten years of age, and all the other nameless women this monster had pursued, as he was doing to me now. His laugh was the only sound in the universe—and it permeated my cells and my nightmares for years to come.

All his heads are laughing, I managed to think, and then his arms encircled me. I could not tolerate his touch. It was anathema to me, and I fled, though my body was captive. As I fell into black unconsciousness, I saw a gentle light. Emerald-green light embraced me. Rama was with me. I felt safe and continued falling until the light embraced me completely and the darkness could touch me no longer. There I rested, in the gentle light of all-knowingness, where time didn't matter and I was forever united with my beloved. But even in that faraway place I felt the tremors of my body, the desperate way it was calling out again and again. The same name, again and again.

Rama. Rama. And just like that, I was wide-awake, feeling the terror crashing through my body as I called out to Rama. Like the waves of the ocean, I flowed back and forth between my place of all-knowingness and the terror of my mortal situation. One moment I was terrorized by the twenty clawed hands that held me in an iron grip as we flew across the incongruous blue sky. Nightmares were not meant to take place with the sun as a witness.

I felt the bond tying me to Rama, but I had heard his last cry. I did not know if he was alive or dead. Salty tears streamed down my face, plentiful as the ocean, bottomless and dark. I did not want to live anymore in my body. I could not stand the way Ravana was looking at me as we flew away from all I held precious.

The many-headed one coveted me only because of this form I had. I had never meant to be more beautiful than any other woman. But when my soul took its form, it molded itself around my natural essence, so that in this world I knew I was more goddess than human. But now, because of this body of flesh and blood, I was torn from my beloved, unable to be in his presence because I was bound to the mortal frame.

Thinking this, I felt enraged at this intruder who dared covet me and separate me from Rama. Now when I called for Rama it was not to soothe my soul, but to call him to me, to instill fear into the monstrous heart that was beating too close to mine.

"Rama, save me! Come to my aid! Lakshmana, forgive me for pushing you away!"

What if they truly are dead? I wondered. Another shiver ran through me and I felt the golden light beckon me. But the ten-headed monster laughed at my words.

"You are mine now," he said.

The words echoed ten times, snarling from his fanged mouths, echoing a hundred times in my ears because they frightened me. I could not deny that his voice was beautiful. I felt his mind probe against mine. Endlessly, he sought entry into my soul. This is how he possessed all other women. He claimed their very essence for himself. It was part of his immortality, the core of his power. I could see he was baffled to find my resistance. The elements protected me. The wind wrapped around me. The fire blazed in warning. The sky covered my mind like a shield. Even if I was severed from them, I was still their queen, though he, the usurper, thought himself the king.

White clouds wet my cheeks as the monster plunged farther away from my home in Panchavati. The sun's rays mocked me with their brightness. The silken cloth that covered me shone golden in the sun, like one of its rays. But I was so cold. The monster's arms burned like ice. His hands held me lightly, but I could feel the bruises growing under my skin. I no longer knew where I was; looking down, I could see the green sea of the forest, undulating beneath me. My home for the past thirteen years. If I had made any friends in this time, surely they would bear witness to my distress.

"Wind, sky, clouds, trees, and all my friends on Earth, if you can hear me, come to my rescue. Bring word to Rama. Please, please, tell him where I am!"

"Rama is dead," the ten heads said. "You will never see him again."

I flung myself from his grasp, falling into the deadly unknown. Falling through clouds and surrendering to gravity. Death would be my savior. But the lecherous monster easily caught me and held me firm. His hands closed around my wrists like manacles.

"Rama will never forgive you!" I cried. "Even though he is the most benevolent, he will never forgive you for laying your hands on me!"

"No one is more powerful than I," he boasted.

I covered my face with my hands, though they trembled violently and only made my hair fly around my face. Even my own hair seemed ominous, slithering around me like poisonous snakes. Why had I asked for the golden deer? Why had I sent Rama out of my sight? I was finally the one to blame for my predicament.

This is all my fault. All my fault. All my fault.

Even so, I could not stop from crying out Rama's name.

He did not come, but someone else did. Someone heard my cry and was coming to the rescue: Jatayu, king of the vultures.

He was as large as I recalled, giving me hope for the first time.

"Jatayu!" I called out. "Fly at once to Rama and tell him all you see. Tell him not to sleep or eat until he kills this monster holding me captive!"

I could see in my mind's eye, Rama's arrows destroying Ravana's heart. This would all be over soon. But Jatayu did not heed my words. He attacked the blood-drinker king, swooping and ripping huge gashes into Ravana's back. Ravana roared, drawing his sword. The giant vulture flew all around us, clawing at Ravana with his talons and smacking the coward's heads with his wings. With each stroke, feathers rained on us, and Jatayu closed in, pecking at Ravana's eyes.

I twisted about, struggling fiercely against Ravana's hold.

"Jatayu, fly away!" I cried again. "Find Rama. Go now before it's too late!"

My words were drowned out by a horrible cry as the ancient vulture lost a wing.

"Let him go," I begged Ravana. "Just take me and leave."

I did not want to see this faithful friend butchered in his attempt to save me.

Neither bird nor blood-drinker heeded my words but attacked each other violently. Jatayu circled around us, airborne still with only one wing. But the powerful bird had only two claws and one beak, while the demon had twenty arms and sharp claws on every appendage. Still, Jatayu was in his element there in the sky, and we were at a complete standstill, hovering in the sky like an arrested meteor. No matter how vigorously Ravana slashed, he could not inflict another fatal wound on my half-winged, brave friend.

I said a fervent prayer for Jatayu, all else forgotten for the moment. He had come to my rescue, and he was my only hope. A hope that was already bleeding to death. Blood poured from the wound of his missing wing. I stopped struggling. The second I felt the monster's hold loosen ever so slightly, I wrenched myself free again, falling into the sky toward the Earth. Ravana's hands clawed the air to catch me, but Jatayu's relentless attack made him less quick than before. I continued falling, the air pressing against me, a comforting embrace. I was free. For this split second, I was free.

The spirits of the forest rose to cushion my fall, and I felt triumphant.

I will escape; the gods are with me.

The moment my feet hit the ground, I said a prayer for Jatayu and began to run. Ravana had been flying south; I ran the opposite way, quicker than I had ever been. I clutched my golden sari in one hand and flew among the trees. My heart pounded in my ears, and I could hear Jatayu's screams behind me. One of my anklets got stuck on a bush; I wrenched my foot away, some of the golden bells scattering. Suddenly everything slowed down around me, as if time was stopping; the nightmare began again. No matter how fervently I ran, I seemed to be going nowhere, and whatever direction I turned, the ten-headed coward stood there waiting for me to run into his arms.

"Rama! Jatayu! Lakshmana!"

I called their names in vain. The monster snatched me up into his blood-stained arms and we were airborne again, leaving behind the mutilated, half-dead body of the brave bird who would never fly again.

As my last hope of rescue disappeared, I began to lose consciousness. But Jatayu's self-less sacrifice fueled me. I *had* to do something.

Straining against Ravana's arms, I tore my jewels from my body, ripping off whatever I could reach and flinging it to the Earth. I hoped this would create a trail for my beloved to follow. It was so desperate and futile, the monster did not even try to stop me. He seemed amused and watched me keenly as I flung down each precious ornament, what I prayed was a golden trail. Blood trickled from my earlobe after I sacrificed my earring. I shed every adornment I wore, jewels I had worn day and night, like a second skin. Nothing mattered now. Monkeys howled in the distance. The Earth disappeared beneath me, replaced by an endless body of water. I was lost to the world.

Rama's Madness

When Rama had pursued the golden fawn for well over an hour, he fit an arrow to his bow. The deer could be captured no other way. The golden creature fell to the ground, pierced by Rama's arrow, and called out, "Sita! Sita! Sita!"

With chills of horror, Rama realized it was his own voice coming out of the little fawn's mouth. Rama quickly calculated that he was many miles away from Panchavati, but the voice crying Sita's name was so loud that Rama's ears were ringing. The golden deer was not crying out for his own benefit—of this, Rama was chillingly certain.

As soon as Rama heard "Sita!" being called from the blood-drinker's mouth, he knew instantly this had been all about her in the first place. She was the golden deer being meticulously captured. Already, Rama saw the pieces of the puzzle falling together, orchestrated by some unknown evil hand, and he, Rama, had fallen into the trap.

The deceptively endearing fawn was still thrashing about, struggling for breath. Filled with dread, Rama fired another arrow into its heart. With its last breath, the golden fawn called out, "Lakshmana!"

Lakshmana's name reverberated through the forest and in Rama's ears. The golden fawn morphed into a blood-drinker, and one Rama instantly recognized: Marichi! This was the only blood-drinker who had escaped death, dodging Rama's missiles twice before. Rama turned away from the blood-drinker who had crossed him for the third and final time.

Rama refused to believe that the game was over and began to run, backtracking his long trek away from Sita. He concentrated on calling to Lakshmana in his mind: *Stay! Whatever you do, Lakshmana, stay by her side!*

"I'm coming!" he roared as loudly as he could, his voice not carrying half as far as Marichi's deceptive scream.

With the fearful conviction burning in his mind, Rama ran heedlessly, unmindful of the branches and twigs whipping his arms and legs. Jumping from a rock, swinging from a branch, he flew, feeling his bow slamming into his back with every sprint. All this he felt but did not feel. The branches ahead to dodge, the slope he might slide to gain time—all this he saw but didn't see.

Rama knew and had always known that Sita was his weak link. There in the forest, she was his only vulnerability. That's why Lakshmana was invaluable. Together they were strong and Sita was always safe. Knowing Sita to be the chink in his armor, he had treasured her, watched over her, gone overboard in his measures to protect her. It was always the foremost thought in his mind. They had *never* left her alone, ever. He prayed fervently that that day was no different. Lakshmana would keep Sita safe.

"Sita, I'm on my way!" he called again, straining to make his voice as loud as possible.

Rama felt increasingly sure that Marichi had not been alone. Why call Sita's name? Why lure Rama so far away? Rama hoped he was wrong but couldn't stop his thoughts. All he could pray for was that Lakshmana would stay with her. *He would never go against my order.* Rama felt confident of this. He trusted Lakshmana completely. Yet, why were birds and beasts approaching him, crying out their warnings? Rama ran faster, hurling himself through the forest, his heart thudding loudly.

"Tell them I'm on my way," Rama begged of the animals that were running with him. The birds above him flew away, soaring faster than Rama could run.

Then Rama's heart stopped; his eyes widened. Lakshmana was running toward him. He was not where he was supposed to be. Rama decided not to slow down or stop to speak to Lakshmana. Lakshmana's face showed relief, but his neck was red, as if he had recently been angry. Rama's disbelief was great. Now, of all times, Lakshmana had disobeyed him!

Without stopping, Rama ran past his shamefaced brother. He refused to hear a single word Lakshmana had to say. He would consider forgiving him only once he saw that Sita was safe. Lakshmana turned around to catch up with Rama's breakneck speed.

"I told you not to leave her under any circumstances, Lakshmana!" he cried when his brother caught up to him. "You have broken my trust!"

Lakshmana was silent, knowing it was true. Rama had no time to spend on this anger. Gathering it to him as fuel, he begged the wind to make him fly, and so he nearly did, like an airborne leopard.

As soon as he was near Panchavati, Rama began calling her name. He ran into the clearing that was their home and saw his worst fear confirmed. Sita was nowhere.

"She was right here when I left!" Lakshmana cried, pointing at a spot on the ground.

Rama ignored Lakshmana and sprinted into the cottage. Empty. Was she hiding? Maybe she was down by the river? Maybe she was picking fruits?

"Lakshmana, run down to the river and see if she is there!"

Rama ran to all of Sita's favorite spots, calling her name, louder and louder. Seeing a glimpse of yellow, the color of Sita's garment, Rama turned around. "Sita, is that you?"

But it was a vine with yellow flowers in bloom. Turning the full force of his power and charm on the forest, Rama asked every tree, plant, and animal that he saw, "Where is Sita? Have you seen Sita? Tell me!"

The forest did nothing to help him, nothing to soothe him. It was dead silent. Sita's name echoed through the forest, but there were no clues. The animals that had surrounded Rama, crying out their warnings, were absent now, as if afraid of something there. Did they fear whoever had taken Sita? Or did they feel dead within as Rama did, bereft of her?

Feeling every last sliver of hope vanish, Rama slackened his pace. Suddenly he heard something that awakened his heart again, only to fill it with an unbearable pain: Sita's plea for help! "Rama! Come to my rescue!"

It reached his ears, a dim echo of what it must have been.

The spirits of the forest had all fled in fear, but one or two solitary wisps of light had lingered. Through them, Rama heard Sita's voice. Sita had believed he would appear any moment and save her. Her call for Rama echoed in the fibers of every plant and tree, like a soft, desperate whisper. Rama could hear it now.

He followed the whispers and saw something on the ground: crushed flowers. They had been in Sita's hair, and now the blossoms lay scattered on the ground, evidence that Sita had been taken away forcefully.

Rama stared at the flowers in horror and began to scream, *"Sita! Sita! Sita!"*

He had left everything behind and had been content with Sita by his side. Why was she taken from him now?

Rama felt hot rage against destiny, against the world, against every single being who had conspired to make this happen. This anger filled him, pushing away every trace of sorrow. Sita disappeared. Lakshmana disappeared. Everything disappeared but this all-consuming rage, red-hot and coursing through his body.

Rama could feel all the energies hovering around him, as if caressing him, communicating with him. With a single thought he could pull them all close to him. Already it was so. A hush in the air, a stillness, only Lakshmana's eyes moving in alarm. Rama could gather the wind, the rays of the sun, and the gravity of the Earth to him. Lakshmana's ears popped and he felt like his insides were squeezed, all the elements closing in around Rama, eagerly.

Lakshmana was not yet aware that this was Rama's doing, standing there suddenly lethally calm, with bloodshot eyes completely still. Yet when one of Rama's knees hit the ground, causing a rumble that shook Lakshmana's balance, he looked at his brother with

new eyes. An arrow was on Rama's bow, his string dangerously pulled to shoot the arrow straight up into the sky. Then Lakshmana knew. His brother meant to destroy everything. How he was going to do it Lakshmana did not know, as so many things Rama did were unfathomable to him, but there was no time for thought, and neither was there a doubt in Lakshmana's mind that Rama would succeed.

Rama felt the energies of the universe gather around his arrow. He would bring them into his bosom, only to violently dispel them with his arrow, scatter them in different directions. They would collide in confusion, worse than a volcanic explosion; the Earth would fall out of orbit and smash into another planet, and all this would be over. Sita would be his again, by his side, her ancient soul tightly bound to his, so that even now he felt her pulling on him, tearing him apart from within to be by her side . . . but where she was on this little planet, separate from him, this, Rama did not know. With the Earth smashed, every living being would find another destination. Their souls would know where to go. Destruction, Rama knew, was simply another beginning, and Sita's soul and his soul would find each other and be united again. This terrible distance he could not bear. All this knowledge flooded through Rama's veins, as he stretched the string on his bow, readying to propel his arrow with maximum velocity. He was only dimly aware of someone shouting at him, running toward him. As his thumb and index finger were about to separate and let go of their tight grip on the fatal arrow, that someone smashed into Rama, crushing the bow and the arrow between them with all his might. Rama didn't struggle, but neither did he loosen his grip on his bow. He simply stared at Lakshmana, uncomprehending. Possibly he didn't know Lakshmana in those moments. Why had he been stopped?

The Search Begins

Lakshmana's arms were burning with heat, encircling his brother, immobilizing Rama's resistant arms. They stood still, breathing heavily and feeling each other's heart thudding in unison. What Lakshmana knew and didn't know simultaneously was that a premature ending to the world would cause a havoc of its own. The Earth itself would reassemble and function again, yet disoriented souls released too soon from their mortal frames would not know where to go. Their half-executed lives and complex interpersonal exchanges would have to continue. Ending it now would only cause an intermittent delay. Rama would be back and so would Lakshmana. In another form, in another way, only Lakshmana wasn't certain he would find his way back to Rama. He meant to stay by Rama's side as long as he could. All these subterranean thoughts appeared to Lakshmana only in the form of a deeply felt conviction that he must stop Rama. Just as Rama felt destroyed by Sita's absence, so too Lakshmana was overcome with fear of losing Rama, losing his place by his brother's side.

Lakshmana could see the glaring questions in Rama's eyes. Yet what most astonished Lakshmana was that he had the power to keep his brother's arms clamped down. Maybe Rama's resolve was weak! Lakshmana could imagine no other reason. No words passed between them, and the seconds ticked away. The energies that Rama had summoned with his mind were already growing placid, shimmering in the air, lingering, yet already dispersing. The arrow was no more than an arrow. Although powerful, it no longer had the power to alter the course of the Earth.

Rama began to relax in his brother's arms. The bow and arrow went limp in his arms and fell out of his hands. Then the unexpected happened. Rama began to cry, immense sobs that ran through his whole body in bursts.

"Sita!" he cried out at the top of his lungs, the way one mourns the dead in the private place of one's own home.

Rama's body trembled, and he was crying helplessly in his brother's arms; Lakshmana's arms were a support now, holding him steady. Lakshmana's tears flowed too, seeing Rama like this. After a few minutes, Lakshmana's mind began racing ahead, seeking what they must do next.

"Rama, we must make a plan," Lakshmana said, releasing his brother just a little. "We must pool together our resourceful minds and decide how to move forward. We have to think strategically. All this you know, my brother. All this I've learned from you. Yet . . . yet . . ."

Lakshmana could speak no further, for Rama was not listening, not hearing. He just stood there. Unable to bear his brother's vacant eyes, Lakshmana ran into the cottage and retrieved all their weapons: the golden-sheathed swords, the shields, the small knifes, the inexhaustible quiver. Weighed down by the load of his and Rama's weapons, Lakshmana returned to see Rama standing tall, head cocked, as if listening to something.

Lakshmana was flooded with relief. *Now he will tell me what to do. Now we will devise a plan to find Sita.* Rama had never failed before, ever.

But Rama was not himself. Lakshmana had to help Rama strap on his many weapons, as if Rama had forgotten their purpose or use. As Lakshmana strapped on Rama's quiver, he saw the old scroll that Rama had received from Vasishta. Certainty exploded in his heart as he ripped the scroll out. Surely the wise Vasishta had anticipated this. Surely he had left a message for them, some direction, anything. This must have been the very purpose of the scroll. With unsteady hands Lakshmana unrolled it, examing it from all sides. It was empty! Damn them all! He ripped the parchment into pieces and threw it on the ground. They had been abandoned at the most critical juncture. No one cared! Rama had not registered any of this; he didn't even look at the destroyed scroll which he had so carefully preserved for thirteen years.

Half blind with terror and feeling the full responsibility on him, Lakshmana pulled at Rama's arm, then grabbed his hand and started herding his brother along, senselessly and aimlessly plunging into the jungle. For all his desire for strategic planning, what he really wanted was to get away from this place where Sita so clearly was not. It didn't matter where they were going, for there was no clue in what direction Sita might have been taken.

As they searched through the forest, their voices became hoarse from calling her name.

When Lakshmana, who called more often, lost his voice altogether, they continued in silence. Like someone who has lost his hold on reality, Rama was not fully present. It was a great shock to see him so disoriented. Lakshmana felt like he was dragging about and directing a drunken man. Rama constantly heard the beckoning of some distant sound that made him tear at his heart and clutch his chest as if in terrible pain. He cried frequently.

Rama had indeed lost all sense of time and place. He was a man without purpose. If he couldn't simply end the world and return Sita to her rightful place by his side, then what? The world seemed so large, and Rama was already seeing how impossible it was to find Sita ever again. There were beyond millions of hiding places in the forest alone. It was hopeless. Impossible.

In their lifetime together, Lakshmana had seen his brother cry only a handful of times. And there was nothing Lakshmana could do to soothe him. At such times they simply had to stop wherever they were doing and wait for Rama's flood of emotions to stop.

"This is all my fault," Rama said repeatedly.

Lakshmana tried to reason with Rama, taking the blame onto himself.

"I was the one who left her unprotected," Lakshmana insisted. "It's my fault!"

But Rama's initial anger was gone; he did not accept Lakshmana's remorse. Sita was his responsibility, and it was ultimately his fault that this had happened.

The only times Rama's mind came into focus was when danger loomed. At such times, his heart stilled and his mind became as sharp as a blade. Lakshmana experienced this when finally they stumbled upon their first clue.

"Is that blood?"

Lakshmana jumped at the sound of Rama's voice. His brother hadn't said a word in hours. He looked in the direction Rama was pointing, but before he could say anything, Rama sprinted into action. Grabbing an arrow and placing it on his bow, Rama ran past Lakshmana.

"Look, Lakshmana! There has been a fight here. There is blood everywhere and black and brown feathers are scattered on the ground."

"This can't be Sita's blood, my brother," Lakshmana said, infusing his voice with certainty. "Look at it. It's thick and dark red, exactly like a blood-drinker's."

Rama seemed to agree. Without waiting for Lakshmana, Rama was off, following a trail of blood and feathers. A huge mass lay on the ground, breathing laboriously.

Pulling his arrow to his ear, Rama shouted, "If you wish to live, declare yourself!"

The next moment, Rama put his bow aside and fell to the ground next to the creature. "Jatayu, my friend! How did this happen to you, king of the vultures?"

Jatayu, the sixty-thousand-year-old celestial vulture, had also been their father's friend and the king of his kind. The last time they had seen Jatayu, he had promised to keep an eye on them.

Lakshmana was filled with premonition. He knelt next to Rama and the dying vulture. Above their heads, a large wake of vultures swooped around in circles, squawking in agitation. Jatayu, their king, no longer had wings, and the great bird's lifeblood flowed out where

his missing limbs had been. Rama and Lakshmana continued to kneel in the pool of blood growing around Jatayu. The dying vulture was crowing softly.

"What is he saying?" Lakshmana asked, unable to contain his urgency. He couldn't understand the way Rama could.

"He is saying sorry."

"For what?"

"He couldn't save her!" Tears rolled down Rama's face.

"He saw Sita! He tried to save her?"

"Jatayu," Rama said urgently, "who stole Sita from me? Who did this to you, my loyal friend?"

She begged me to find you and Lakshmana. Seeing her in the hands of that monster, I couldn't turn away. I had to fight.

"Who was it, Jatayu?" Rama's eyes were red with anger. "Who?"

It was the king himself, the overlord of the blood-drinkers. Ravana.

"Ravana," Rama said, shock rippling across his face.

They had never seen Ravana for themselves, let alone imagined that the ten-headed demon king had crafted such an elaborate scheme to carry away Sita. Was this Shurpanakha's revenge, then?

The great bird heaved a big sigh as if to continue but remained silent. With the last of his breaths, he motioned toward the south. Jatayu's beak fell open and his eyes closed. Rama and Lakshmana grew still. Jatayu was gone. That great being had died for them.

"Jatayu died to save Sita," Rama finally said. "We must honor him like we would one in our own family."

The brothers built a funeral pyre and heaved Jatayu's body onto it. As the fire consumed the vulture's body, Rama and Lakshmana walked around the blazing flames three times, praying for the freedom of Jatayu's soul. After that, they had to leave. They had received their first affirmation that Sita had indeed been abducted, and there was no time to waste.

As they left, the vultures up above swooped down and huddled close to the blazing pyre to bid farewell to their dead king.

"We head south," Rama commanded.

Rama's purposeful step did not last long. Lakshmana saw it coming and didn't skip a beat, stepping ahead of Rama. Lakshmana led the way, urging Rama to continue when he looked lost. The forest was unusually quiet. Whatever had happened had shocked the symbiosis of nature herself. Sita was gone, and with her, the spirits of the forest had fled in fear.

Never had Lakshmana been without Rama's guiding hand. Lakshmana struggled to keep going, like a drowning man gasping for air, almost giving up and surrendering to the soothing darkness just below. But no! They must keep going. At all costs, they must keep going. Only this, Lakshmana believed, would dissuade Rama from again bringing out that fatal arrow and annihilating them all once and for all.

The brothers were bruised for weeks with the perfect mark of a bow and arrow poised to shoot imprinted on their chests. It was a constant reminder for Lakshmana. He had held

Rama so tightly, using all his strength, knowing this was life or death, that a split second mattered, and he had almost been too late. Yet they were too late. Sita was nowhere.

They had been searching for weeks, always heading south, yet needing to scour the surrounding areas as well. After burying Jatayu, there were no further clues, not a whisper of Sita's whereabouts. The fact that Ravana had stolen her away made it all more ominous; the brothers only knew frightful stories of Ravana's bloodlust and had no inkling where Ravana might have taken Sita. When their search for Sita was at its darkest, Lakshmana's fear of that cosmic arrow surfaced.

Yet an even darker fear gripped him at times: that he had been wrong to stop Rama. Because now his brother had gone mad. Something had snapped in Rama's mind; he was no longer someone Lakshmana recognized. Rama woke in the night, calling to Sita; he murmured her name constantly while sleeping. During the day, he sat quiet, vacantly staring into the distance. He noticed nothing. Said nothing. He ate only when Lakshmana brought him food, and even then Lakshmana had to insist on every bite.

"It has been two weeks and three days now since she disappeared," Rama said, throwing down his morsel of fruit.

"We are going to find her," Lakshmana insisted, for what seemed like the millionth time.

"You don't know that for certain."

"Yes, I do! We cannot think anything else for a moment!"

Rama looked at his brother, darkness in his eyes.

"I'm a cursed man," he said. "Like a criminal, I was sent into exile. Now my princess, my life, has been abducted. I have no way of knowing whether she is still alive."

"Regardless, we will find Ravana and avenge her!" Lakshmana insisted. "This is not a hopeless quest! Jatayu saw her alive. We also know that they went south."

"Jatayu's words were unclear."

"But I saw the motion of his beak pointing us south."

Rama stood, and shouted out loud, *"Where are you, Ravana, king of cowards?"*

His call echoed throughout the empty forest, and Rama sank into the ground and back into his silent desperation.

Perhaps it was not the answer they hoped for, but destiny sent them something: a little deer very much like Sita's pet fawn. Lakshmana couldn't look at the deer without remembering that fatal golden one. This one stood perfectly still, waiting for them to see the flash of gold on its head. With a small jolt, Lakshmana recognized what it was: a small golden bell, a piece of an anklet.

"Look, Rama," Lakshmana said, directing Rama's attention to the deer.

Rama spotted the golden bell, and a spark of life animated his face. Careful not to make a quick move in his excitement, he held out his hand to the deer. The deer shyly approached Rama, nuzzling his hand. Carefully, Rama picked up the dainty bell resting between the deer's ears. It was most definitely a bell from Sita's anklet.

"This means we are going in the right direction," Lakshmana decided.

Rama was staring at the golden bell as if it was Sita herself, and then pressed it to his eyes. The bell tinkled gently.

"Time to keep moving?" Rama ventured, responding to the soft chime.

Lakshmana arose, pulling Rama with him. The fawn scampered off. Rama yanked a thin vine off a nearby tree and threaded it through the loop on the golden bell. He hung the makeshift necklace around his neck, next to his heart.

How are we going to find you, Sita? Lakshmana pleaded, his own version of an apology. The foul parting between them still scorched him. Lakshmana's remorse at what he'd inadvertently done was heavy on him. Yet he was determined to keep Rama going at all costs. This is what the ancient Agastya had warned him about. He was his brother's keeper, and they were surviving and searching, but Lakshmana needed Rama to think clearly, to come up with a plan. How on Earth would they find Sita when the wilderness stretched out around them for thousands upon thousands of miles in all directions?

Only Rama could find a way.

Acknowledgments

A HEARTFELT THANK YOU

Anna Johansson, my mother, whose dedication to her art has ignited and supported my own. I feel so lucky to be able to collaborate and work with my mamma. I would never have had the resolve to do this work without her.

My husband, Visvambhar Sheth, for always wholeheartedly supporting me and helping me to reach my potential in all areas of life, for being an attentive and affectionate father, and for reading everything I write.

Mirabai Lee Harrington, the fairy godmother of this work, for overseeing the growth of the trilogy as a whole and pushing me gently and confidently to a totally new horizon of thinking and creativity, and specifically for asking pointed questions about Sita and her powers.

The readers of my first draft back in 2010: Sara Halvorson Saha and Helen Simpson (Vegavati Devi Dasi) for taking the time to read the manuscript and give me detailed feedback.

The readers of *Shadows of the Sun Dynasty* (2016) and *Son of the Solar Dynasty* (2012) who have taken the time to speak to me personally and share their appreciation.

Carol Tewksbury (Ragatmika Devi Dasi) for initial proofreading.

Beth Mansbridge for one round of copyediting.

Jai Uttal for loving the Ramayana and telling the story with so much heart.

Our publisher, Raoul Goff, and the Mandala team that worked on all aspects of the book: Tessa Murphy, Rachel Anderson (in-house production editor), Joanne Farness (proofreader), Andrea Monagle (copyeditor), Pandita Geary (marketing and outreach). With special thanks to Courtney Andersson, for being such a stellar point-person and keeping the project moving steadily forward with cheer and diligence.

Mayapriya Long for her very competent design work, and Raghu Cornsbruck, who created the initial layout and look of the series.

Julia Cameron for her groundbreaking work, *The Artist's Way*, which dramatically and drastically changed my attitude and approach to my own creativity.

Dr. Clarissa Pinkola Estes for writing *Women who Run with Wolves* which really transformed my understanding of archetypes, fairy tales, and the need to dig out the bones of a story.

References: *Sita: An Illustrated Retelling of the Ramayana* by Devdutt Pattanaik, *In Search of Sita: Revisiting Mythology* edited by Malashri Lal and Namita Gokhale, *Many Ramayanas: The Diversity of a Narrative Tradition in South Asia* and *Questioning Ramayanas: A South Asian Tradition* edited by Paula Richman, *Sita Sings the Blues* (film) by Nina Paley. *Ramayana: Divine Loophole* by Sanjay Patel. *Sita's Ramayana* by Samhita Arni and Moyna Chitrakar. Orson Scott Card's work, including his Biblical retellings, and Rukmini Devi Arundale's Bharata Natyam dance dramas on the Ramayana that so beautifully bring to life so many vital scenes of the immortal tale.

Special thanks to Robert P. Goldman for agreeing to write the foreword. This work is blessed by his stamp of approval.

In memory of Bimala Faust Finnin, whose unpublished rendition of the Princess Rukmini story awakened me to new possibilities in storytelling.

Characters and Terms

Agastya – one of most well-known and powerful holy ones; directs Rama to Panchavati and gifts him a celestial golden bow and arrow

Agni – lord of fire

Ahalya – the stone-woman, Gautama's beloved wife; a mind-born daughter of Brahma

Aja – Dasharatha's father; king of Ayodhya before him

Ananta-Sesha – thousand-headed serpent on whom Vishnu rests

Anaranya – king of the Sun dynasty more than twenty-five generations before Rama; killed by Ravana in a famous battle

Anasuya – a rare female ascetic who gifts Sita the celestial golden cloth, which becomes Sita's signature dress for the duration of the exile

Apsara – celestial nymphs, known for their beauty, singing, and dancing, often associated with bodies of water and with devious plots to seduce holy ones from their ascetic paths

Asamanja – the only son of the Sun dynasty who disgraced his line; known for drowning his playmates in the river Sarayu

Ashram – a secluded dwelling or hermitage in the forest

Ashvapati – "Lord of Horses," king of Kekaya, father of Kaikeyi and Yuddhajit

Atibala – one of the sentient mantra-weapons Rama receives from

Vishvamitra, healer of wounds, sister to
Bala

Atri – a sage and a mind-born child of
Brahma, one of the authors of the holy
scriptures; husband of Anasuya

Ayodhya – the indestructible capital city of
Earth; Rama's birth-place and rightful
kingdom

Ayodhyan – citizen of Ayodhya, "the
indestructible"

Bala – one of the sentient mantra-weapons
Rama receives from Vishvamitra,
reliever of fatigue, sister to Atibala

Bhagiratha – Rama's ancestor who brought
down the sacred Ganga from the
heavens

Bharadvaja – an all-seeing sage who
directs the trio to Chitrakuta, their first
dwelling

Bharata – Rama's half-brother, second in
line to the throne; Kaikeyi's son

Bhumi – the goddess of Earth, considered
to be Sita's real mother

Bilva – a tree whose leaves are used in
worship and for decoration

Brahma – father of the universe, the
creator of all, and granter of boons

Chakra – Vishnu's legendary discus, one
of the weapons Rama receives from
Vishvamitra

Chaya – "Shadow," the exiled queen,
mother of Yuddhajit and Kaikeyi

Chitrakuta – the mountain-peak where the
trio create their first home

Dandaka – an uncivilized jungle
considered a borderland full of
supernatural creatures

Dashamukha – "Ten Heads," one of
Ravana's original names

Dasharatha – emperor of the Earth,
Rama's father; known for his great
skill in battle, hence his name "Ten
Chariots"

Devahuti – mother of Anasuya

Dushana – a blood-drinker and a general
posted in Dandaka

Ganga – the holy river, as well as the
Goddess of the river herself

Gautama – one of the *sapta-rishis*, or seven
sages, recognized as supremely exalted;
author of several ancient hymns found
in the Rig and Sama Vedas

Guha – king of the Nishadas, Rama's
friend; king of the Nishada forest tribe

Indra – lord of Heaven

Indrajit – "Conqueror of Indra," Ravana's
son and heir to Lanka

Indumati – Dasharatha's mother, queen of
Ayodhya

Janaka – king of Mithila; Sita's adoptive
father who found Sita in a furrow

Janasthana – a region in the Dandaka
forest

Jatayu – the king of the vultures, a loyal
friend to King Dasharatha and later
Rama and Sita

Kaikeyi – third and favorite wife of King
Dasharatha; queen 3; mother of Bharata

Kajal – a black-colored cosmetic used
around the eyes and sometimes on
forehead

Kama-Rupini – one who is able to take any
form at wish; a shape-changer

Kamadeva – cupid, god of love

Kardama Muni – father of Anasuya

Kashi – king of Kashi, one of the most
persistently aggressive kings under
Dasharatha's rule, slain by Rama in his
first battle as prince in command

Kausalya – first wife of King Dasharatha;
queen 1; mother of Rama

Kaushika – Vishvamitra's original name before transforming into a sage

Kekaya – Kaikeyi's birth kingdom

Khara – a powerful blood-drinker; one of Ravana's relatives and a most trusted general, posted in Janasthana, near Panchavati

Khus – vetiver, Rama's favorite fragrance

Kinnaras – half-human, half-animal celestial creatures known for their mischievous pranks and their single-minded focus on romance

Koshala – the land surrounding Ayodhya

Kuvera – treasurer to the gods, Ravana's half-brother

Lakshmana – Rama's closest friend and half-brother; Shatrugna's twin brother; son of King Dasharatha and queen 2, Sumitra

Lakshmi – the goddess of wealth and prosperity, Vishnu's eternal consort

Lanka – the golden island appropriated by Ravana from his older brother Kuvera

Mandavi – wife of Bharata, Sita's cousin, Kushadvaja's daughter

Manthara – "The Hunchback," Kaikeyi's hunchbacked confidante

Manu – the First Man, who built Ayodhya and fathered mankind

Marichi – Ayodhya's blood-drinker prisoner; son of Tataka; successfully takes the form of a golden deer to allure Sita

Menaka – a celestial damsel and dancer in Indra's court

Mithila – the capital city of Janaka's kingdom, and Sita's birthplace

Nishadas – the forest tribe loyal to Ayodhya, ruled by Guha

Panchavati – "Five Grooves," the final dwelling place of their exile

Parashuram – the notorious warrior hater

Rama / Rama Chandra – firstborn son of King Dasharatha; son of Kausalya, queen 1; next in line to the throne and wed to Sita

Rambha – a celestial damsel, one of the famous four

Rasatala – the hellish planet below Earth where the blood-drinkers were cursed to live

Ravana – "Loud Wailing" or "The One who makes the Universe Wail"; king of the blood-drinkers

Rishyashringa – son of Vibhandaka, mysteriously conceived by a deer

Romapada – king of Anga, close friend of King Dasharatha

Rudraksha – spiky beads worn by holy ones for auspiciousness

Sagara – Rama's ancestor, father of Asamanja

Sarayu – the river running alongside Ayodhya

Sharabhanga – a disciple of Agastya; a holy one who extracts a promise from Rama that he will slay the blood-drinkers in Dandaka; informs Rama that Ravana was on the path to becoming a holy one before he went astray

Shatrugna – Lakshmana's twin brother; Bharata's constant companion; son of King Dasharatha and queen 2, Sumitra

Shiva – lord of dissolution, who dances vigorously as the world comes to its end

Shrutakirti – Shatrugna's wife, Sita's cousin, Kushadvaja's daughter

Shurpanakha – "Sharp Nails," Ravana's sister; a skilled kama-rupini; rejected and mutilated by Rama and Lakshmana; the catalyst for the abduction of Sita

Sita – "Furrow," Rama's wife who appeared from the Earth, adopted by King Janaka as his own, also known as Janaki

Subahu – the impersonator who sets Marichi free; son of Tataka, brother of Marichi, killed by Rama and Lakshmana while they protected Vishvamitra's fire ritual

Sumantra – one of King Dasharatha's eight ministers and a loyal friend

Sumitra – princess of Maghada, second wife of Dasharatha; mother of twins, Lakshmana and Shatrugna

Sunayana – King Janaka's wife, mother of Urmila and Sita's adoptive mother

Surya – lord of the sun

Sutikshna – a sage in whose ashram Sita encounters Ravana's spirit

Tataka – the first blood-drinker Rama kills; a female monster

Trishira – an arrogant three-headed demon, slain in the massacre at Panchavati

Tulsi – the holy basil plant, an essential component in the temple's rituals

Urmila – Sita's sister, daughter of Janaka and Sunayana; wife of Lakshmana

Urvasi – a celestial damsel in Indra's court; often considered one of the four primary ones, along with Rambha, Menaka, and Tilottama

Varuna – the ocean god

Vasishta – the royal priest; preceptor of the Sun dynasty through countless generations, and one of the nine mind-born children of Brahma, the creator

Vayu – lord of the wind

Vedas – the sacred ancient text, divided into four divisions: Rig, Sama, Yajur, and Atharva

Vedavati – incarnation of the goddess Lakshmi, who cursed Ravana when he accosted her

Vibhandaka – ascetic, grandson of Brahma, father of Rishyashringa

Videha – the province of King Janaka

Viradha – the first blood-drinker the trio encounters in the forest, who successfully snatches up Sita, if only for a few moments; has a boon from Brahma granting him immunity from all weapons

Vishnu – the maintainer of the universe, present in every molecule of creation

Vishvamitra – Rama's mentor, formerly King Kaushika, exalted from warrior to sage

Yama – lord of death

Yuddhajit – prince of Kekaya, brother to Kaikeyi

Artist's Note

I never imagined that it would be a lifetime project to make Vrinda's and my books. But here I am, committed to make illustrations for all three volumes with the best art I can do. Stumbling, doubting, falling along the way? Oh yes. I still have doubts if I will be able to make the remaining pieces for the third book. I still pull my hair and want to quit when a painting does not do what I want it to do. Yet I am still wholly and totally intrigued by the creative process of trying to fill each chapter with at least one nice illustration. People sometimes think that it is easy to just sit by a drawing table or easel and put out nice work. This is as far from the truth as it can be; at least for me. For me, it is not an easy process. It is rather the contrary. Creating the art consumes my life. It is both a pain and a blessing, and sleepless nights are not unusual. But I love it and I feel blessed that I can share my art with others in this trilogy. It means the world to me. Although my daughter Vrinda is not directly involved in my creative process, I owe this project to her. The outreach efforts are her work; if not for her there would be no Kirkus review, no Sita's Fire website and no Facebook page. There would not be a trilogy to share. Thank you, my dear daughter. This project has gone beyond my dreams.

Perhaps my greatest 'breakthrough' in doing the artwork for the second volume is that I accepted wholeheartedly the luminiscent emerald hue of Lord Rama. In the first volume, I stubbornly maintained that only humanoid beings are depicted in green.

I have two people to thank for this change in my thinking. One of them is Stephanie Pui-Mun Law. In her watercolor book *Myths and Magic* she clearly shows how interesting and attractive it can be to portray skin colors in different hues. She is also one of my favorite contemporary watercolor artists. Her paintings are fluid, mystical, expressive and very beautiful. My second thanks then, goes to Gaura Vani Buchwald. His opinion in this matter made a deep impression on my mind because I see him as a serious spiritual seeker with a non-judgmental and open mind.

As I mainly use the Internet nowadays to gather information and inspiration, I often stumble upon many amazing, dedicated, and skilled artists. For instance, I used the digital artwork of Claudia McKinney as an inspiration for the picture on page 61 in the chapter "Sita and the Fire." McKinney is a true visionary and a talented book cover designer. I am also grateful to Ganga Sheth, who has taken time to do some modeling for me. She is slender and elegant, and it has been a pleasure to use her as a model for Sita.

Perhaps one of my greatest rewards in doing this work is when my little granddaughter Naimi looks through the book and turns to me and asks "Did you do this one Grandma?"

My hope is that I can be a part of the change we need in this world—even with such an odd contribution as to create artwork based on ancient Indian classics. My life truly rests on infinite grace. I would not be able to make any pieces of art were it not for the grace and kindess of Srila A. C. Bhaktivedanta Swami Prabhupada. His teachings changed and transformed my life forever. I am humbled and grateful to the core of my being.

Illustration Index

ILLUSTRATION INDEX

A Tender Moment
page 246

Panic
page 276

Sita Rama
page 250

Rama's Anger
page 279

Monkeys
page 254

Rama's Sorrow
page 284

The Golden Deer
page 259

Crowned Crane
in Flight
page 295

Mouse
page 262

Bharata and the
People of Ayodhya
page 296

Sita and the Enemy
page 267

Book One

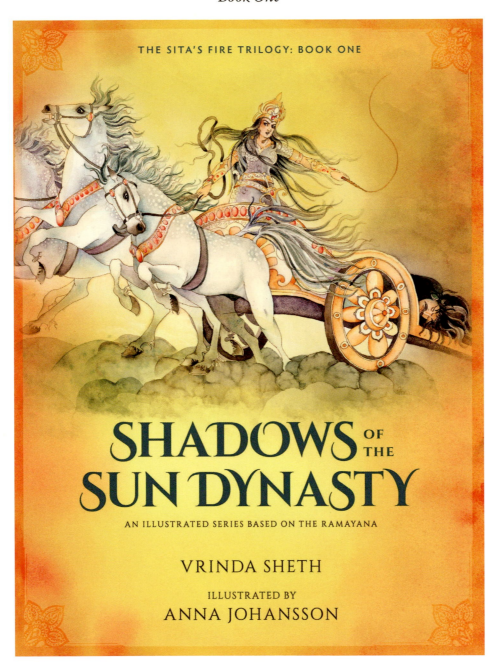

THE SITA'S FIRE TRILOGY: BOOK ONE

SHADOWS OF THE SUN DYNASTY

AN ILLUSTRATED SERIES BASED ON THE RAMAYANA

VRINDA SHETH

ILLUSTRATED BY

ANNA JOHANSSON

Available now from Mandala Publishing and at all major retailers.

Look for Book Three

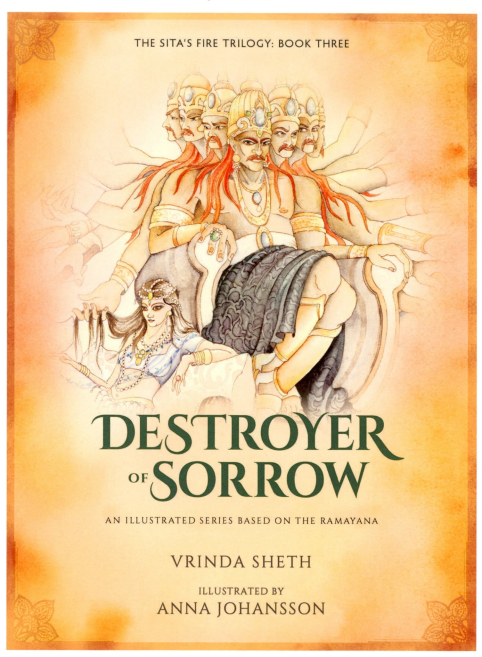

THE SITA'S FIRE TRILOGY: BOOK THREE

DESTROYER OF SORROW

AN ILLUSTRATED SERIES BASED ON THE RAMAYANA

VRINDA SHETH

ILLUSTRATED BY
ANNA JOHANSSON

Available Summer 2018